IN THE CASTEL SANT'ANGELO,
A VENGEFUL WOMAN
AWAITED HER SON'S RETURN . . .
AND THE RING SHE CHERISHED.

In the halls of the papal palace, there was the crunch of steel as the hinges of the door gave way. Anthony's soldiers burst through, the press of men crowding into the breach.

Anthony made his way down the length of the room. Blood dripped from his bare sword.

"Pope John!" he shouted. "By the command of my mother, Senatrix Marozia, and the people of Rome, I order you to renounce the Holy Chair of Saint Peter."

The pontiff drew himself up to his full height. "You are a traitor," he cried defiantly, "and the son of a traitor. The church's power is vested in me by God alone. It shall not be taken away by mortal man or woman. I demand your obedience to the Office of Saint Peter and to the Holy Roman Empire."

The pope raised his hand, holding out the signet ring.

Anthony strode forward. His soldiers glanced at one another with wondering, fearful eyes. For a moment, it seemed the young man would fall to his knees and kiss the ring. Then, two paces in front of the pope, he leaned over and spat on it.

The pope snatched back his hand as if he had been stung, and a groan went up from the men around the room. After that came laughter, at first hesitant, then hearty and joyous.

"Baronio, Flavius!" Anthony's voice rang out. "Bind his hands. Take him to the Castel Sant'Angelo. My mother awaits us."

POPE JOAN

E.L. HASTINGS

POPE JOAN

Miles Standish Press

Published by
Miles Standish Press, Inc.
353 West Lancaster Avenue
Wayne, Pennsylvania 19087

Dell ® TM 681510, Dell Publishing Co., Inc.

Printed in the United States of America
First printing—May 1984
ISBN: 0-440-06891-6

To DKM

Acknowledgments

For their extraordinary encouragement, support and patience, I would like to thank Peter Tobey, Susan Tobey, Alida Becker and Ernie Tremblay.

Prologue

Martigny, Province of France, A.D. *932*

I bring her food every day. Some days, as on this one, she is very calm, almost pleading. She looks at me with enormous madness-drugged eyes as if to say, What have I done, Lena? Why am I being kept this way?

I wish to answer her, but I cannot. Nor can I be lulled into false security, for at any moment she may attack me, her own sister, or any of the other nuns who serve her.

Marozia is dangerous. I know this and I wish it were not so. I wish that the spirit of God and Jesus Christ would return to her soul and make her whole again, but she was never a woman of strong faith. There is no reason why she should turn to God now.

Looking at her as she takes her food and animallike, plunges her hands into the bowl of gruel, I remember everything. I am forced to remember.

After all, we are sisters and once we were children together. I remember her at the villa outside Tusculum, her bare feet flying as she ran down the hillside, hair streaming behind her, so young, so alive. We played touch-and-run in my father's vineyard. We traded garnet stones we picked up from the cliffs. We called them jewels and matched them with kingdoms. All of the Byzantine Empire could be traded for Tuscany in those stones, traded on a

warm summer's afternoon with the *ponentino* blowing in
from the sea, bringing its scent of mulberry and thyme.

How could one not love such a sister?—and yet as
close as we were, we had opposite destinies. She was
beautiful; I was not, and that made all the difference. Even
in our youngest days, before she or I had the semblance of
a woman's shape, the shepherd boys paid more attention to
her. What was it that attracted them so? Those dark,
impassioned eyes or that wild black hair? Whether crossing the fields or going into town with the carriers to fetch
mead, whether watching the mosiac craftsman or praying
in church—no matter where we were, boys noticed her—
then men.

Beauty can be a force that drives men to distraction
and exalts a woman's spirit. But women are not all equally
desired. The devil in man demands satiation of his lusts.
Every man fancies himself discriminating, a connoisseur
of beauty. Men would always gaze at Marozia and shun
me. Despite even the thickest layer of woolen cloaks they
could see her slim, strong body, her narrow hips, her firm,
round breasts. Her every touch, her every movement
made them desire her more.

I grew up clumsy or flawed, who can say which? I
am told I have a pleasing face. May God find it so. I
prayed for beauty when the shepherd boys ignored me and
turned to Marozia. I prayed and I was jealous, fiercely
jealous, but prayer purged me. Saint Gregory has said,
"Every living thing was created by God." His words were
a comfort to me. I could not be Marozia, but I could take
up God's work.

Marozia was never unkind to me. She never reminded
me of my plainness. I think she loved me the more for it
because I could not rival her. I have served her, as I have
tried to serve all God's creatures, and I serve her still.

She is scratching now at the walls of her cell, crying out for more food. I must go to her.

Oh, dear God, look at the remnants of her beauty. Look at what sin has wrought. Dear God, forgive her— and forgive your servant Lena as well.

BOOK I

Chapter 1

Rome, A.D. *904*

It was four days after the spring equinox by Julius Caesar's calendar when Marozia went out in the night to meet Pope Sergius.

Our family, the Theophylacts, lived in a simple palace on the Aventine. We had few furnishings. The house was a sprawling, drab affair of plain brick and mortar, dating from pre-Byzantine times. Rooms and hallways rambled off in every direction from the central atrium with its dry fountains and unadorned ambulatory. Niches that had once held images of pagan gods were now vacant, and the once-bright frescoes of men at war and at games had long since faded. Here and there the empty places had been filled with plaster statues of Saint Augustine, Saint Columban or the Virgin Mary, but no attention had been given to the paintings or gilding, and the votive candles were lit only when church dignitaries came to visit.

For a house belonging to noble Romans it was barely adequate. The servants and slaves had separate quarters in the stables. The cistern near San Camerino was always full, so we had sufficient water, and the roof, thank God, did not leak.

The house was everything my father wished it to be.

He had his guards, his slaves, his family. What did he want with grand furnishings and splendid wealth?

My mother, Theodora, was always dissatisfied. Always. He was a senator, she reminded him. He deserved more, and so did Theodora, for she too came from a good family, that of the historian Eusebius. She had learned Latin from him, but she would inherit no wealth; it was all invested in his scriptorium and his researches.

Father it was, I felt certain, who had made the arrangements with Pope Sergius. Some drunken night Sergius had confessed man to man that he desired Marozia, and Gaius Theophylact responded by graciously offering his daughter to the pope. She was a virgin and at fourteen not yet betrothed, and my father was anxious to please the pope.

Gaius Theophylact would value the bond with Sergius. This I knew. Though not greedy, my father had his ambitions, his own sense of mission.

It was not a father's duty to lead his daughter to the bedchamber, chaste or not. No, that was left up to our mother. I heard her arguing with Father, but there was no use in her objecting; he was adamant. In the end Marozia was dressed and ready. Theodora had held out for wedding finery: sheer linen chainse under a richly embroidered chamarre that hung straight from shoulder to ankle, ungirt; new chausses and slippers; and a fine surcoat over all. She was washed and perfumed and a bronze and coral crucifix was placed around her neck. How Marozia longed for gold!

The slave Tasha and I tried to console her. Poor Marozia, she trembled like a leaf. There was so little time to prepare her, and the pope was renowned for his brutal demands. What could I say? The words intended for a wedding night were not appropriate for this occasion.

Perhaps Tasha knew best. The quiet pagan woman with her worlds of knowledge gave Morazia a salve. "Use this, signorina," she said softly. "It will soothe and . . .

and perhaps—'' She could not finish. She too sobbed. Our tears mingled as we three huddled together in the last moments before Marozia left us.

She went out into a strange new world and began a new life. Though I would see her often, she would never really return to me.

Rome was a stinking city. The streets were fetid with garbage. It was horrible at night, when dim figures lurked in the shadows and drunkards and beggars crawled from the doorways of the *insulae*, those wretched, ruined tenements whose chambers were filled with sin and poverty.

Theodora and Marozia were carried together in a double palanquin, a closed curtained chair borne by four slaves. Six guards from the House of Theophylact protected their flanks, a seventh in front bearing a torch. Like all the Theophylact men, the guards were badly equipped. Their swords were rusty and dented and they were badly trained. As they proceeded through the streets they talked among themselves. Now running ahead, now falling behind, they were rude and disorderly.

Inside the palanquin Marozia heard none of their noise, only the heavy thud of her heart. ''Why do you connive at this?'' she demanded of her mother.

''It is none of my doing,'' was Theodora's curt reply.

''Whose, then?''

''Your father's, of course.''

''But surely, Mother, I thought he would want me a virgin, to be married—''

''To be married to whom?'' Theodora sneered. ''Is there any man in Rome more powerful than the one you will meet tonight?''

''No man in the world.''

''Then be satisfied with your lot.'' There was small comfort in Theodora's voice. She seemed petulant, angry, as if the affair were all Marozia's fault. When my sister asked for advice—how she should lie in bed, how she could ease the pain and please the man—Theodora's replies were short and harsh. Every woman must learn for herself. It was painful, of course, especially when a man was rude and brutal, as Sergius was reputed to be. But a woman's purpose was to give pleasure, and if men found pleasure by using her roughly, so be it.

"But what if he harms me, Mother? I have heard—"

Marozia's voice was so shrill that one of the guards put his head through the curtain to see what was going on. Theodora slapped his face and drove him away.

"Move ahead. Move on, you stupid, lazy blackguards." She shut the curtain again and turned back to Marozia. "The pope knows of your beauty. He has seen you and he desires you. It is only a quick pain, and then the man's pleasure is done." Marozia leaned away as if she would be sick, but Theodora pulled her close to croon in her ear, "Perhaps he will be kind and gentle." She laughed a bitter laugh. "Who knows? You may find love. Who knows *where* you may find love?"

Ahead of them there was a scream and the torch wavered. "Magyars, Magyars!" a voice cried out. Then came the clatter of sword against sword.

The fearful slaves lost their grip on the palanquin and it fell to the street, almost overturning on the uneven cobblestones. Marozia and Theodora were thrown against each other. When they clambered out of the palanquin they saw around them a circle of glistening bearded faces.

The Magyars were the terror of Rome, Hungarian brigands who climbed up from the banks of the Tiber under cover of night to rape, pillage and plunder. No one could keep them out of the city; they moved too silently, too furtively. They always struck quickly and cruelly, then retreated to their hiding places.

The Theophylact family guards could fight well, and so they did. Their leader, Phoenicus, threw himself at the attackers with his blunted sword, catching one of them on the side of the head. He knocked another to the pavement and stood astride him, slashing and cutting. It proved his undoing, for another Magyar awaited, one who carried a longsword. With both hands he drove it through Phoenicus' heart.

Marozia was splattered with blood. She slipped and fell as she lurched away from him, and her outstretched hand clasped the crushed head of Phoenicus' first victim. Then something snatched at her from above, dragging her to her feet, and she found herself staring into the horrible garlic-smelling maw of a Magyar.

A Theophylact guard rushed to plunge a sword into the side of the filthy warrior. The Magyar fell, vomiting blood, and Marozia dragged herself away.

Shouts now came from the nearby buildings and Romans rushed into the street and surrounded the Magyars. The bandits turned to flee, but they were stopped on every side. The Magyars were hated, despised. They fell at the hands of the mob and were trampled and disemboweled.

Marozia struggled to her feet as her mother's voice sounded in her ears. Her tunic was torn, her gown bathed in blood. She stared down at herself while Theodora held her arm.

"Slaves, slaves," Theodora called. "To the chair, at once."

The Theophylact carriers appeared cowed and confused, but Theodora kept a whip in the palanquin for just such an occasion. She struck at one set of shoulders, then another, until she and her daughter were inside again and the chair was lifted. All around them the victorious Romans preyed like jackals on the corpses of the Magyars, first plundering them and then for vengeance cutting them open and strewing the roadway with their viscera.

"Move on," shouted Theodora, "move on."

The guards cleared the people from their path and the slaves proceeded, though slipping on the gore beneath their feet. Marozia's bloodstained clothing clung to her in the chill night air. A moan escaped her as she huddled back against the cushions.

"Silence, daughter," Theodora ordered. Then, viciously, "You carry a knife. You should have used it on that barbarian. Shame on you to cower so."

Marozia turned away. In silence, rocking and rocking, the chair moved on. Up it went past the Colosseum to Imperial Hill and from there to the palace of Saint John Lateran. Pope Sergius III would not be kept waiting, even by the Magyars.

Sergius was a man both hated and praised. He was tall, his body thick and muscular beneath his robes, and he had curly reddish hair. He looked wild and untamed, like a barbarian, but in truth his heritage was Tuscan. His father was Benedict, King of Tuscany, and his family had risen to become leaders in Roman affairs.

Like his father, Sergius was a man of the sword, a warrior, but he had long held the position of cardinal in the church.

He played a leading role in the Synod Horrenda, the trial of Pope Formosus. For that he and his Tuscan followers were excommunicated and expelled from the city. For seven years he bided his time, making war in the provinces and gradually increasing his sphere of influence.

Rival cardinals who were not killed in battle were felled by poison instead. Popes Leo and Christophorus found themselves thrown into prison and were murdered in their cells. It was Sergius' hand that did the deed—with joy, some said. When the Curia, all men of his choosing, offered him Saint Peter's Chair, he accepted with all due humility.

Now, though, his sins were forgiven and forgotten. He wore a magnificent papal tiara and a long white bliaud, an ankle-length tunic trimmed with regal Byzantine gold braid. He had begun to rebuild many portions of the Lateran palace and basilica, which had fallen to ruin under the reign of previous popes. On Imperial Hill he held court like a Byzantine emperor, giving great feasts that all the bishops and deacons of the Papal States attended.

Marozia was not fit to appear before Sergius with her tunic ripped, her hands covered with blood. Hunched with shame, she followed her mother into the lighted foyer of the Lateran palace, where drunken prelates wandered to and fro. She heard their whispers: "It's Marozia . . . Marozia . . . begrimed. A virgin? Look—what has happened?" And so it went until a howl from Theodora and a slap of her hand silenced the nearest of them.

"Curs, she *is* a virgin. We met Magyars—Magyars, here in the heart of Rome. While you cowards feast and parley, women cannot safely traverse the streets. Wretches, call a slave. I want dressers, a white tunic—and hurry. The pope awaits my daughter."

Shouting and commanding, Theodora cowed them with the sheer force of her presence. A tearful Marozia was led away to be bathed and changed while the clergy in the hallway made lewd remarks about her beauty.

Nor was Theodora ignored by these lusting admirers. She was scarcely past thirty, having borne me when she was fourteen years of age and Marozia when sixteen. They say that a woman of thirty is at her lustful prime—and shows it with hungering lips, shining eyes and a full body.

They also say that drunken men could scarcely tell the difference between this mother and her daughter. They admired the proud carriage, the delicate features, the luxuriant, shimmering black hair. Men awakening at night with the devil's dreams would scream aloud in passion for Theodora and Marozia together, so alike was their allure.

When Marozia emerged from her bath all freshly gowned in white linen, she was transformed. A hush came over the papal banquet hall when she entered, for she was radiantly beautiful, regal in her bearing. She was, after all, a Theophaylact, a noble creature, no peasant from the provinces.

Between the long tables she swept, stopping at the high dais where Sergius awaited. Silently she bowed at his feet.

He roared with laughter. "Come, Marozia. Come, my sweet. Give me a kiss." She had never kissed a man. At this she blushed scarlet, trembling, for laughter ran through the room and the concubines stood and shrieked at her.

She went forward; she had no choice. After all, His Holiness had spoken. When she was within arm's reach, he embraced her and pulled her toward him to plant his lips squarely on hers.

The scent of retsina, the pitch-flavored Greek wine he favored, almost made her choke. Suddenly tears were streaming from her eyes, tears of humiliation and rage. She did not know what he would do next. Would he strip her and take her here—here in the papal banquet hall—like some barbarian seizing a sacrificial virgin? How would this man behave toward her?

Worst of all—worse than the wine-flavored breath, the dark, flame-impassioned eyes, worse than the touch of his teeth and the flick of his tongue against hers—was the screaming in her ears, the derisive howls of the concubines who encircled the hall. It was as if she had already become one of them, as if she were being dragged down by this man's unyielding arms into a bottomless pit of filth, infamy and sorrow.

She hurled herself away from him, tearing free of his grasp with a strength she had not known she possessed. Hair unbound and flowing, her coif on the floor, one sandal slipping from her foot in her haste, she fled the pope as she had fled the Magyars, for they were one and the same to her.

Theodora was poised by the doors. She caught her daughter by the arms and shook her so hard her teeth rattled.

"Fool," she whispered, "do you wish to anger him? Do you know what he can do to you—to all of us? Child, do not resist. Do *not*."

Gradually under Theodora's hissed commands Marozia quieted. The shouts and merriment in the banquet hall seemed the roaring of a waterfall that flowed over her, seizing her, carrying her along to an unspeakable destiny.

She could not escape. She could see that now. In the foyer beyond her mother stood a crowd of leering men. Behind her were the cardinals and bishops and their concubines. Out on the streets of Rome lurked the Magyars.

No, there was nowhere to turn—and the pope's voice was calling her to come away with him.

In the bedchamber he became a different man and she a different woman. So it always is.

The room itself was such as Marozia had never seen before. There was nothing the pope asked for that he did not receive, and he did not hesitate to ask. His chamber was furnished with the finest tapestries, the richest mosaics, the most ornate Byzantine workings in gold and silver. The bed must have been imported from Constantinople,

Alexandria or perhaps even the Sudan, where the caliphs made a habit of frolicking. It was enormous. Silk sheets woven with hunting scenes covered its vast surface.

So dazzled was Marozia that for a moment she forgot her fear. Her gaze was drawn to an intricate fresco, then to a gilded cross finely worked with topazes and emeralds. The chamber was filled with the smell of incense and myrrh. Candles flickered, lighting the portraits of the saints. It was a scene of extraordinary richness and beauty.

Amused, Sergius followed her with his eyes. Marozia could not remain distracted for long. His presence was a demand, evil insistence she could not deny.

At last she turned to him. "What would you have of me?"

"You like my taste in furnishings?" he asked as if he had not heard her.

"I have never seen such splendor."

"Then why do you not take pleasure in it?"

She hesitated, then summoned her courage. "It was not of my will that I came tonight. I was sent unconsenting."

"You were sent because I wanted you," he replied, still staring at her. "You are lovelier by far than any of the things in this room."

She avoided his eyes. "And so you would buy me as you have bought them," she reproached him in a low voice.

Sergius smiled. "There is no price for you, as there is no price for what you see about you. Everything is a gift—to God."

He had meant to compliment her, but his words had the opposite effect. "Why did my father agree to this?" she said sharply.

He shrugged. "There should be peace between the pope of Rome and the senators of Rome, don't you agree?"

"A peace that is sealed with a virgin's body?"

Sergius' face clouded. "Enough," he snapped. "I have answered too many questions."

And with that he seized her with his enormous hands and just as before, planted his lips on hers.

This time there were no banqueters to look on, to shout and deride and make merry over Marozia's misery. It was only she, she alone, trapped in the bedchamber with this large-limbed, powerful man. He could do as he wished with her.

Tearing herself away, she fell to her knees, seizing the hem of his robe. "Please, please, Your Holiness, I beg you. I am a virgin. I beg you. In spite of what my father Gaius may have said, I am not worthy. I am unpracticed. I know nothing of love, nothing."

Sergius did not bother to reply. Instead he jerked her to her feet and slapped her hard across the cheek, so quickly that she felt nothing, was only stunned. She stood silently before him, allowing his rough hands to rip at her clothing.

Its hasp broken, the bronze crucifix flew away and clattered to the floor. The noise broke the spell and Marozia, sobbing, lunged to retrieve it. The pope caught at the hem of her shift and flung her backward, tearing the fabric from her body.

Now she was naked before a man. She felt the cold breath of the night, saw the candles flickering and the eyes of the saints upon her. The gold glittered in the shadows and Sergius came closer, ever closer. . . . Marozia whimpered and edged away, clutching the sheet from the bed to hide her nakedness. He tore that away too. He wanted to see her.

Finally she let him. He gazed so long that finally she could stand it no longer. "What?" she whispered. "What?" She hated to hear her voice tremble. "Evil man, let me go!"

"Never."

His undressing was all swift motion: the tiara set

aside, the rich bliaud pulled over his head and dropped, the velvet kirtle tossed away. Now he too was naked. He had curly hair like fleece all over his chest and shoulders.

Marozia huddled in the corner of the enormous bed, her back against the cold marble wall. There was no escape. He attacked viciously, pulled her toward him and under his body, his hungering mouth biting at her neck. She tried to push him away; her fingernails dug into the flesh of his shoulders, but her resistance seemed only to excite him further.

She thought of the salve hidden in her kirtle—the salve Tasha had given her to ease her first lovemaking—and she almost wanted to laugh aloud. What love was there in this?

And then suddenly she knew what she must do. She must let him have her. Let it be over soon, she prayed. She spread her thighs apart and the great mass of his body settled on her like a gigantic animal, crushing her breasts, her belly, her groin. He was there, huge, enormous, hard, pounding at her.

Let it be over. Let it be over. . . .

And then he was thrusting, his back arched like a bull's as he poured his juices into her. She felt the terrible penetration, the ravishment, as the sword of his body cut into hers. In agony she bit down on the lips that were pressed against hers.

With a bellow he pulled away, the essence still flowing from him, and hurled her aside. Like a caterpillar touched in its center she curled up, weeping while he cursed her.

Then he shouted for a slave and a woman servant—to clear his clothes and to apply balm to his bleeding lip. All the while Marozia huddled sobbing, her chilled body becoming one with the cold marble wall.

When the woman had applied the unguent to his lip, Sergius directed her to see to Marozia and remove the silken sheets from the bed. Plain cambric would do for her, he snarled.

But at least the woman was gentle. After Pope Sergius left, she sat with Marozia as she cried herself to sleep.

We came to her the next morning, Tasha and I, bringing her fresh garments and perfume and the needle-work that gave her pleasure. She had just eaten a fine meal of glazed ham and apples, pheasant eggs with fines herbes and a drink of sweet lime and cherries.

She could not leave the palace; the guards blocked her way. The pain had vanished, though, and the servants had been kind to her.

"How was he? A gentle lover?"

Tasha meant to be teasing, but Marozia's eyes flashed fire. "Give me a knife," she swore, "and I will kill him." I moved to comfort her, but she drew away. "Don't touch me, sister. There is nothing you can do."

My heart ached for her. "You must pray," I said, foolishly, for even I knew that prayer would be insufficient.

"There is nothing to pray for but his death."

"Hush, Marozia, you must not." I could feel the black knot of terror in my soul. How did she dare oppose him? What power he wielded, this man who possessed the Crown of Saint Peter!

Marozia remembered only her pain. "Lena," she said piteously, "he has abused me."

I could think of nothing but platitudes. "It is the hard lot of women," I muttered. "Is it not so, Tasha?"

"Yes, signorina," Tasha agreed, but she quickly changed the subject. She signaled to the house slaves who had brought Marozia's trunk, and they came forward. At once my sister sank to her knees and began going through her familiar things, the bliauds, mantles and undergarments she had worn since she was a girl. A terrible nostalgia overcame her at the sight of these possessions, as if they belonged to a person now dead. She wept openly over them.

"Marozia, you mustn't." I held her in my arms, but there was no consoling her. All morning Tasha and I stayed with her, trying to comfort her and make her forget, but it was to no avail. I would have grown angry, but she seemed pitiful and helpless. Yes, and dangerous, for I feared she would actually put her hatred into action, seizing some instrument of destruction to end her suffering.

As for Sergius, he had gone boar hunting that morning and did not return until the sun was nearly down. I am told he was jubilant that day, full of high spirits. Seven boars were killed, and he rode far into the *campagna*, exhausting those who accompanied him. Perhaps he had gone on the hunt for some other purpose than to brag of his new concubine and show his prowess, for during the chase he suddenly turned on one of the clergy, Cardinal Tantus from Turin, and accused him of treachery. The cardinal, aghast, protested his innocence, but the pope's henchmen surrounded him at once, deprived him of his arms and lashed him to a horse.

That night Cardinal Tantus was tried in the Curia, found guilty and sentenced. The torturers applied hot brands to his hands and feet, and a white-hot bronze helmet was set upon his scalp. All this took place in the Lateran prison. The screams of the dying man accompanied Marozia's second night as the pope's paramour—and lingered in her mind long afterward.

Chapter 2

Marozia's misery continued unabated. For long hours she sat in the sewing room with pious nuns who were working on tapestries and embroideries that depicted the saints and their miracles. These shrouds and vestments would cover the holy relics. Marozia was fond of embroidery, and her fingers flew as she stitched the multicolored thread into patterns of birds, butterflies and animals of the forest. She had learned the technique from an old Gypsy woman, Soeur Felice, who sometimes camped near the family's vacation villa in Tusculum.

For Marozia the twisting of the thin strands, the steady labor in the silent room seemed to provide comfort, but she would sometimes burst into tears and drop her work and rush away.

The pope did nothing to soothe her. At night she lay in his bed and submitted to his wishes, but her passivity angered him.

"Do you feel nothing?" he demanded. "Does nothing stir you, even when I touch you there or there?"

"I do not know what you mean," she replied.

Finally he could endure her sullen patience no more.

"Be God and the spirits damned," he roared at her, "you walk about like a dead woman. This is not what I wanted. I saw a young girl, beautiful, ripe and alluring, and now I take to bed a corpse."

"I am sorry I do not please you."

"You say you are sorry, but you do nothing. You care nothing for pleasure."

"I do what I must."

He slapped her forehand and backhand, hurling her this way and that, and left her sobbing on the bed.

"Do something with her," he roared at one of the women-in-waiting. "Teach her lovemaking, wench; otherwise she goes."

He shook his fist at Marozia. "Do you hear me, maid? I will return you to the House of Theophylact. You may tell your mother and father I found you unfit. All Rome will know the truth, and may the greater shame be attached to your name." He left the room in a towering rage.

All the next day, while her fingers worked at the needle and the nuns stole curious sidelong glances at her, Marozia considered. That night she was prepared for him.

"What have you to say?" he demanded, entering the bedchamber.

"I want my freedom."

He glowered at her. "You are free to go about the palace as you wish. My men and women are ready to serve you. You feast at night, bathe by day in the papal chambers. A thousand women would go down on their knees for a tenth of what you have."

Her jaw was firm. She had decided. Like a tigress she faced him, her eyes burning. "Let me come and go as I wish—else you may defame me, drag my name and my body and my family through the mire, cast me out, but never have what you wish."

Then she dropped her robe and stood before him. Whatever objections he might have made were silenced. Marozia was beautiful, but on that night her fury and her determination made her radiant. She was a coiled viper, ready to strike, a passionate animal in the firm, lovely flesh of a woman.

Sergius' tongue touched his lips. He could not take his eyes from her.

"God's wounds," he whispered, "you shall have all you wish."

She was true to her word. She gave herself to him completely. When he plunged into her, she threw her arms and legs around him to hold him in a passionate embrace. Sucking air through her teeth, she hissed and cried and panted as he thrust into her. His demands seemed to stir in her some dark, unmentionable anger that could be expressed only by the fury of her passion.

In the morning Marozia left the palace early and went to the House of Theophylact on the Aventine. I was astonished to see her, since there had been no messenger to announce her arrival. For this occasion she wore a magnificent long powder-blue tunic edged in gold. There was a *couvre-chef* over her beautiful black hair and her neck was wrapped around with a wimple.

The guards themselves brought her in a large palanquin lined with purple velvet. When I appeared at the doorway, she dismissed them and they hurried off with the chair.

We embraced tightly. As I looked at her face, which glowed with a new kind of radiance, I saw new fierceness too. The face and the lines of her body had not changed, but somehow she appeared wiser and more mature.

"Are Mother and Father here?" she asked.

"Yes, and old Eusebius."

Marozia smiled. Our learned grandfather had taught us writing and Latin when were were younger, and we both felt very close to him.

"Have you broken your fast?" she asked.

"Not yet."

"Then we will do so together." She seemed delighted at the prospect, but as we passed through the grey hallways toward the atrium, her face fell as if with disappointment. She touched my sleeve.

"Oh, Lena, how plain and dingy it seems. Can't you do something to brighten this old house?"

"Hush, Marozia," I said gently. "You know how hard-pressed Father is. It is a constant source of dispute between Mother and him. You mustn't mention it."

Marozia fell silent, but I could almost read her mind. Already she had become accustomed to a different way of life. Her clothes, her gestures, the scent of rosewater that wafted from her body, all were the appurtenances of a fine rich lady. Now that she had returned to the House of Theophylact, its very drabness was a shock to her. After all, if she must be sold . . .

Her gloom fled when our father came into the dining chamber. As was his custom in the morning, he wore a light green linen tabard over his tunic. His auburn hair was trimmed short across the front and back in the Roman style. The lines in his face gave him a haggard look, making him seem more than his forty years. A slim, alert man with quick gestures, he had a distinctive way of expressing his annoyance, a deep frown that furrowed his forehead and a glance sideways, as if seeking an escape. He gave that look now, apparently annoyed that this strange woman should intrude on his breakfast hour.

Then he recognized her.

In a moment she was on bended knee before him. He leaned forward and kissed her on the forehead. He seemed calm, and yet I knew he could scarcely contain his joy.

Our mother came in later, but her greeting was cooler. She seemed perturbed by Marozia's finery, and when she kissed her daughter's forehead, her touch was lighter than the stroke of a feather.

Marozia seemed not to notice. Already she was chattering away, describing the grandeur of the palace and the ambitious plans of the pope as if they were somehow her own.

Sergius had set workmen to repair the damage done during the last earthquake, just after the trial of Formosus. In another two or three years, Marozia declared, the Lateran palace would be as plush and fine as it had been during the reign of Constantine. Gaius listened with a kind of bemused wonder, but Theodora's look of harsh skepticism only deepened at her daughter's words.

There was an interruption as our grandfather came in. White-haired and round-faced, Eusebius was dressed in the plain brown surcoat and hood of a monk. The top of his head was shaved smooth in the style of a clergyman's tonsure, and his shoulders were stooped from long hours poring over his manuscripts. At the sight of Marozia his grey eyes lit up with pleasure. He touched her as if she were some fine and precious thing.

With a clatter of crockery and a rattle of wooden bowls Tasha and the Maria, the cook, brought in the morning breakfast, a thick gruel laced with honey and accompanied by hard rye biscuits, dried figs and dates. Two amphorae of warm wine were set in the center of the table.

As Marozia dipped into the gruel with her plain wooden spoon, a trace of a grimace flickered across her face. She hid it quickly, but I understood. Our humble way of life was no longer acceptable to her.

Then I glanced at our mother and I knew that she too had seen Marozia's expression. Theodora showed, if only for a moment, a look of such envy and concentrated hatred as I have never seen before or since.

*   *   *

As in many family conversations, much was left unspoken in the rapid-flowing talk. An undercurrent of tension pervaded the room, something only a family member could have perceived. Now and then one of us would cast a sly, curious look at Marozia as if to say, How do you see us now? Has your life been changed?

To all appearances only Rome concerned Gaius, and before long he launched into a familiar theme. "We are captives," he declared, thumping the table, "a city under siege. Saracens to the south and east of us—through the hills of the Sabine almost to L'Aquilo. To the north the Franks and Lombards—and still we must fear the Magyars. Bah! Those scum. They should have been blotted from the landscape ages ago."

"Few pilgrims can make their way from the north," I observed. "Many have wounds. Their dead are strewn across the roadways." I shuddered. It was customary for a pilgrim to cut off the finger of a dead companion so the deceased might touch the sacred relic he would never see in life.

"This is the darkest age of Rome," Grandfather said gloomily. Already he had drunk too much wine and his tonsure gleamed with perspiration.

"Nonsense," Theodora briskly put in. "You dream of a past that never was, Father. When Rome ruled the world barbarians and slaves were held under the yoke of pagan masters. At least now we are Christians and the Word is spreading."

Gaius nodded his agreement. "Even the Lombards may be assimilated one day soon."

"Never." Grandfather's face turned beet-red. "Never so long as I live." He leaned forward. "We are Romans, pure Roman stock. Forget that, Gaius, and you lose everything."

Father seemed angry. "Well, what then?" he demanded. "Would you deny the existence of the Lombards? At the snap of a finger would you eliminate Berengar, who calls himself King of Italy even without the pope's donation? And what of the upstart Alberic? Already in six months' time he has taken seven cities."

"Who is this Alberic, Father?" For the first time Marozia raised her voicé.

"A young, brutal and fearless Lombard," Gaius said grimly. "Only a fortnight ago he laid siege to Spoleto and took the city by stealth. He clove the tongue and took out the eyes of Duke Arnulf, the pope's appointed ruler. The poor man was blinded and driven through the streets as an example to all Spoletans."

"Arnulf is a fool," muttered Theodora.

Gaius looked up. "So he may be, wife, but an upstart Lombard who captures seven cities in a matter of two seasons is a force to be reckoned with."

"What would you do, then?" Eusebius was still agitated. "Bow to the Franks? They'll be next, they and the Magyars. Will you hand them the keys and let them rule Rome?"

"Not at all," retorted Gaius. "I would subjugate them, not by force, but through political means. You yourself know that it's possible." A trace of sarcasm crept into Father's voice. "Berengar—even Alberic—must bow to the hand of the pope. Once he subjugates them, they must pledge their troops to his crusade."

"Crusade?"

"Against the infidels on our very shores, Eusebius, those Saracen heathen who pound at our gates and kill our brothers."

Father paused and there was a deathly silence at the table. We all remembered Father's brother Paul, and just then we felt his presence strongly. Three years previously

Father and Paul, as close as any two men alive, had embarked on a campaign against the Saracen stronghold at Fraxinetum. A fierce battle ensued and Paul was captured. Gaius Theophylact met with Caliph Husayn to ransom his brother and a price was agreed upon. The transaction was to be made at dawn the next day.

By the appointed hour the Saracens had fled across the river and into the mountains. As the sun rose only one figure remained in the Saracen encampment, a Roman tied naked to a cross. His feet had been severed and laid on the ground before him. Blood dripped from his mutilated limbs, soaking into the dry earth.

Paul was still alive when Gaius got to him, and it was his brother's knife that put an end to my uncle's torment.

The crockery had been cleared. One amphora of wine was finished, the other half empty. Tiberon, Father's gaunt old retainer, shuffled into the room to announce the names of those who waited in the atrium.

In the manner of an old Roman patrician Father asked Tiberon to tell him the family background of each applicant for his attention. On meeting each of them he would astonish them with his knowledge of their personal lives, congratulate them on recent births and offer condolences for a death in the family. It was etiquette almost forgotten in the world of Christian Rome, but Father observed it faithfully. Eusebius, a half smile on his lips, listened with approval.

Only Theodora seemed dissatisfied. Stirring restlessly while Tiberon droned on, she finally burst out, "Why do you waste your time with them?"

Gaius looked at her in astonishment. Her face was flushed and she trembled with suppressed rage. "These nobles, these merchants and churchmen," she said, "they come to you for favors."

He stiffened slightly. "Of course. As a senator and *princeps* of Rome, I have certain obligations."

"Obligations," she snorted. "Obligations with no rewards. These men collect their tithes and taxes, they fill their coffers, and then they come to you asking for yet another grant of impunity so they can trade with pagans and non-Romans or reap exorbitant fees from their grain sales to the militia. And all the while you sit about pondering the fate of Rome."

Gaius glared at her. "That's enough."

Theodora was not to be silenced. "Look at this chainse, Gaius Theophylact." She tugged at the edge of her undertunic. "Threadbare, and not a scrap of gold or linen that can be spared for me." She glanced at Marozia and once again there was no mistaking her jealousy. "It is long past time we moved from this dreary Aventine to the Via Lata. You know how much better they live near the Church of the Apostles, all these applicants who bow and kiss your hand for favors. No plain crockery for them."

"I have more important things to concern myself with," retorted Gaius.

Theodora snorted again. "Yes, everything you do is for the greater glory of Rome, but do you really think your allies have such goals?" She paused. Then, seeing that her words had had no effect, she suddenly stood up and strode away. She turned in the doorway. "Well, dear Gaius, if you cannot think selfishly for yourself, you might at least consider your wife."

Eusebius and Gaius glanced edgily at each other after Theodora had gone, then burst into laughter.

"She always had a temper, that girl," commented Eusebius.

"I only hope her daughter learns a different grace," Gaius added almost apologetically. I could tell the confrontation had made him nervous. He beckoned. "Marozia, come here, my dear."

She shot him a resentful glance but came to him and sat on his knee. He smoothed her hair. "Is she not beautiful?" he asked our grandfather.

Marozia lowered her eyes. It might have been taken as a sign of bashfulness, but I knew better. Her temper could burn white-hot when she was toyed with in this way.

"She is," said Eusebius, but he agreed almost reluctantly, as if he did not want to be part of this easy admiration. Then, to change the subject, "What does Phidias want of you?" Phidias was one of the solicitors whom Tiberon had announced.

Father shrugged easily. "Oh, a matter of some papal and Roman property where he wishes to establish a bronzeworkers' guild. Since the allotment is conjoined, he must have the approval of both the Senate and the pope." Caught up in his thoughts of politics, Gaius no longer paid any attention to the slim, beautiful girl on his knee. But with his hand he unconsciously stroked her hair.

"Will approval be given?" Eusebius studiously kept his eyes and mind off the pair before him.

"Undoubtedly," Gaius replied with a laugh. "I will certainly give my approval, and needless to say, the pope is now beholden to me. He will go along with—"

Before he could finish, Marozia wrenched herself away with a small, sharp cry of outrage and then a gasping sob. It happened so quickly that I was stunned. For a moment I could not move or think. Then it dawned on me what he had said.

At the same moment my father seemed to understand. "My God," he muttered, getting to his feet. "I did not think . . . I did not mean. . . ."

But it was too late. Marozia had fled the room.

"It seems I have angered almost my entire family,"

my father said weakly—but even he, I think, did not appreciate the full gravity of his error.

I pleaded with Marozia to make her peace with Father that very day, but she would have none of it. Calling for Tasha, she donned an old surcoat. Then almost begrudgingly she asked me to accompany them. She would not say where she was going or what her errand was.

It soom became clear, however. We descended from the Aventine past the chapel of Santa Prisca and came around the Circo Massimo on the Via Ostensis, where she turned her steps toward the Forum and its market.

The place was full of noise and confusion, with street peddlers and peasants pushing their carts, beggars crying aloud and hungry children howling. Street musicians banged their tambourines and set up a squawk with their krummhorns, while leeches and pagan apothecaries bellowed boasts of their remedies and quick medicines.

From the gutters that emptied into the loathsome Cloaca Maxima came the stench of human waste. It mingled with the scent of wet, untanned leather and burning green wood, the sulphurous reek of the limekilns. The air was almost impossible to breathe.

Rushing ahead so furiously that Tasha and I were hard put to keep up with her, Marozia seemed oblivious to all.

Not everyone was oblivious of her, though. Even in her plain surcoat she made a striking figure. Men gaped as she passed and women paused, suddenly cautious and whispering, tugging at their children's hands to draw them aside and bid them take notice.

In the Rome of our day rumor was a fleet and powerful messenger. Borne on the lips of slaves, handservants and—I blush to confess—even nuns pledged to vows of silence, news spread like wildfire. Calumny and truth were reported alike, fact mingled with myth. This dollop of truth only gave the stories more power, so that a kind of heady expectation caught the imagination of the people. What was breathed in the Lateran palace was whispered throughout Rome until finally every man, woman and child knew of the scandals and intrigues that were afoot.

So it was when they saw Marozia. "The pope's mistress," they murmured. "Beautiful, is she not? Look at her." Peddlers turned at her approach, whispering to one another. Even the loudest and surliest peasant was dumbstruck.

I saw their faces, and following Marozia, felt something glow in my veins. I was only the plain sister dressed in the ugly brown cassock of a nun. It was she they wanted to touch, to speak to and admire, she who carried the radiance of fame and scandal.

Still, I felt it; I shared it. The power streamed out and embraced me. I knew the true meaning, the very feeling of reflected glory.

I was ashamed of my pride. I tried to ignore those awed passing strangers, to avert my head and be humble, yet my heart pounded faster. I could hardly still the rush of envy and longing that was in my soul. Oh, to have what she had!

Already she was careless with her power. As we came onto the Piazza Venezia at the foot of the Palatine, the terminus of the Via Lata, where lies the very heart and center of Rome, she turned in to the richest guildhalls. In these arcades, where the master craftsmen displayed their wares, she lingered, choosing here a filigreed brooch, there a fine jeweled ring. In the weavers' hall she selected length upon length of the richest, most brilliant-colored satin woven with strands of silver and gold. At the cobblers' guild the men stood back in amazement as she went from stall to stall, selecting satin slippers with mink-lined soles, delicate sandals with pearl ties for dancing, gold-rimmed shoes for the day of the Sacrament.

She was a whirlwind, a fury, lightly touching the goods, flickering toward the merchants and craftsmen a look of veiled seductive longing that made them wince with the pain of their own desire.

She paid for nothing. "To the Lateran." She would murmur it very low, with only a tiny wave of the hand, so all the merchants had to bow and scrape and keep close attendance to get her orders.

They never missed once, though. "At once, signorina."

Nor did she forget me. Now and then she would turn and ask, "Will you not have this? What of this fine shawl, Lena? It would become you so well."

To humor her I would display whatever she thrust at me, turning this way and that. She laughed. It delighted her, I could see, to find this vanity in me. But in the end I always refused her gifts, and the smile would leave her lips, as if I had disappointed her.

Only one episode marred the pleasure of that afternoon. We had entered the Basilica of Santa Maria in Cosmedin, a church much frequented by senators and noble families. As was their custom, they met in the back of the nave, exchanging private goods and services along with news of imperial Rome.

For Marozia it was the last visiting place of the day. I think she went there for a reason—to show off her finery, to prove to them all how high she had risen. If this was her hope, then her entrance was everything she might have wished. The hubbub in the cathedral faded away to silence as their exchanges ceased and they stood uncomfortably, wondering how to approach her, what to say. Jealousy could immediately be seen in the other women's eyes.

Marozia seemed to revel in their discomfiture. She went from group to group with regal gentility, holding out

her hand in greeting. If any thought her a harlot, none
dared speak it.

During these formalities I noticed a strange cloaked
figure who hung back at the far end of the sacristy. He
seemed anxious and hesitant, and when I glimpsed his face
I received a shock, for he was painfully thin and wasted.

Finally as we were just about to depart he mustered
his courage and came toward us. As he was a stranger,
Tasha stepped forward to intervene, but something about
him caught Marozia's eye and she put her hand on the
slave's shoulder.

"Hold, Tasha, I will speak to him."

"If you please, signorina."

"What is your petition, signor?"

He bowed very low. He had a rasping, brittle voice
that was very hard to hear. "Please, honored Theophylact,
it has to do with the Bishop of Ravenna. I thought, as you
have some influence with the pope—"

"Are you being insolent, knave?"

"Please." His thin voice cracked. "I wish no
disrespect, but something must be done for the people of
Ravenna."

"How so?"

"Bishop John is a cruel taskmaster, signorina. He has
bled the peasants dry, taxed them until they have little or
nothing. There has been sickness—"

"So I have heard, though I did not know the cause."

"The cause is Bishop John." Even in his weakness
the man's tone was ugly and threatening. "He starves the
people. They weaken and die and he blames it on disease.
I tell you, signorina, he drives them into the fields and
slaughters them in ditches. The land is filled with their
graves, masses of them all together. My own family—"
He choked, unable to go on.

"I understand," Marozia replied. She looked around

as if distracted, then said, "Here, take this," and slipped a gold ring from her finger.

The man gave her a wounded look. "I did not come for alms."

"I understand why you came," she replied harshly, thrusting the ring into his hand, "but you must feed yourself nonetheless." She turned away. One might think she had already put the matter out of mind, but I caught a glimpse of her face and it told me otherwise. The man's suffering had deeply affected her.

"I beg you, honored signorina." The torturous croaking of the man's voice sounded again he stepped toward her.

Marozia halted. "I have heard your plea. I will do what I can, but I am only a woman." She said it as if it were a thing to be detested.

"Oh, signorina, I thank you, I thank you." He fell to his knees.

She looked down at the gaunt figure with a kind of despair, "I will pray for the souls of your family," she murmured before turning away for good.

Chapter 3

When Sergius heard that robes, brooches, jewels and trinkets had been ordered at his expense, he was furious. Had Marozia chosen only one or two items, the transgression might have been overlooked, but everything she ordered had been done in pairs or dozens. All afternoon merchants, guildsmen and slaves delivered a stream of goods to the palace door.

"Send them back, whore," he roared at her. "I am not buying a harlot's wardrobe."

She took out her old gown, the one she had been wearing when she was first brought to him, and shook it in his face. The surcoat was brown with the bloodstains of the Magyars. "What? Would you have me wear this through the streets of Rome? You would only shame your own name, Sergius." Then she smiled. "Everyone knows I am the pope's mistress."

That silenced him, but she could see he was still angry. His baleful grey eyes, so pale they seemed whitewashed, sometimes frightened her. And now, through the heat of her defiance, she sensed the depth of his rage. Something had to be done. She had gone too far.

"I am preparing for my bath, Your Holiness." She fluttered her eyelashes at him as she lowered her head seductively. "Will you accompany me?"

His heavy-lidded eyes surveyed her. Abruptly he

laughed aloud. "Yes. Tell the servants. Have the alcove made ready."

The Laterani family had built the original palace in pagan times, when the pleasure of bathing was freely enjoyed. Originally, a library, music room and gymnasium had adjoined the enormous bathing room in imitation of the famed baths of Caracalla. And like the Caracallan, the Lateran had a circular *calidarium* where the steam vapors could be taken.

In his renovation of the Lateran Sergius implemented the repair of the aqueduct and the restoration of the bath. It was now among the most splendid rooms in the palace; nobles, clergy and concubines were free to spend hours of pleasure there. The few chaste priests and nuns refused to speak of the place, but all knew what occurred in that steam-filled room. All knew of the alcoves where men and women retired in a farcical semblance of humility and modesty to indulge in licentious play.

It was to this bath that Marozia brought Pope Sergius. As was the custom, she wore a small apron across her midriff and he a suspensory that covered his groin, but these small vestments were doffed when they entered the common chamber.

As water flowed over the red-hot brazier, it filled the room with steam. Servants tossed herbs and fragrances onto the coals and the air turned heady with the smell of spices. Dim shapes emerged from the water, and recognizing His Holiness, bowed to him or kissed his fingers. From the curtained alcoves came chortling female voices.

Pope Sergius stretched prone on silk cushions laid by the side of the pool. A servant brought oils and Marozia poured them onto his back and massaged them into his skin with her hands. The warm room, the steam, the sensuous fragrances, the ecstatic murmurs of men and women in pleasure—all combined to produce a kind of abandonment that Marozia had never felt before. Steadily, rhythmically she pressed and kneaded Sergius' back with her oil-slick hands. She observed the tensing of his buttocks as the hazy light from the single overhead embrasure caught and gleamed on the curly bronze hair that nestled between his thighs.

When they finally glided together into the heated water, Marozia was almost delirious. She leaned against Sergius and groped for his genitals beneath the water. He entered her, pulling her close, crushing her breasts against him.

Later he carried her to an alcove, laid her on a bed and drew the curtain. There she ministered to him, taking him in her mouth and sucking the juices of his body. At the same moment he gave her pleasure she had never known before by touching her with his tongue.

This is much the way I have imagined such baths, these dens of carnality and sin, and nothing that Marozia told me was surprising. I still could not comprehend how she derived pleasure from a man who had so misused her. Truly the human flesh is an animal that does not obey the cautions of the soul.

It was Marozia's way, however, never to give anything without demanding something at least equal in return. Now that she could come and go, buying what she wished, living in a way that suited a pope's mistress, she yearned to see the source of his power. When she again turned bad-natured and resentful and withheld her favors, Sergius finally was compelled to ask what troubled her.

"I wish to attend the Curia."

He looked at her with great surprise. "That's impossible. Only papal matters are discussed at the Curia. Laymen are not allowed—"

"I will only witness," Marozia insisted. "I will not speak."

He abruptly dismissed her. "You are an arrogant whore to dare make such a request of me."

She was silent then, but as time passed her resentment grew. She wanted to know everything that was happening. Being so close to power, hating the man who possessed it, she had indeed grown in arrogance. To Marozia, swayed by what she saw around her, no aspiration, no dream was beyond reach.

As the days grew warmer Marozia deserted the silent nuns and her needlework to stroll through the Lateran gardens.

In his refurbishing of the palace Sergius had not neglected horticulture. Monks from the Order of Saint Benedict, skilled in cultivation and pruning, carefully oversaw the planting of fruit trees, flowering plants, scented herbs and spices. The pathways were lined with Corsican mint; crushed underfoot, its delicate flavor wafted into the air. Grape vines hung from the cornice stones of the garden walls and tall asters swayed as the gardeners brushed by.

Marozia had recently become friendly with Sister Teresa of Tivoli, a young woman with handsome dark Etruscan features. Pope Sergius had issued a dispensation that released Teresa from her vow of silence, and in the afternoons they often strolled through the garden, talking quietly and occasionally sharing confidences.

One day in late June they were seated in a bower near the cardinals' residence when a group of clergymen emerged, talking hotly. They stood some distance away, waving their arms as they disputed an issue of clerical domain. Marozia could tell from their dress that they were all high officials, cardinals, bishops or archdeacons.

One figure in particular attracted her eye. He was a tall, hawklike man, angular and handsome. There was something in his arrogant handsomeness that almost sug-

gested a bird of prey. Unlike his peers, he was richly
clothed in bejeweled and gold-trimmed robes with Byzantine designs. Now and then he boldly glanced toward the
women seated in the bower.

"Who is he?" Marozia finally demanded of Teresa.

Disdain showed in her quiet features. "Bishop John
of Ravenna."

At once the memory of the gaunt man she had met at
Santa Maria in Cosmedin returned to Marozia. She gazed
at the bishop with new interest. His eye caught hers for an
instant. Then he resumed his conversation, turning his
back on her.

Marozia flushed with anger. "What do you know of
him?" she asked Teresa.

"He is said to be ambitious and greedy."

"The same could be said of many."

"His rise in the world has been rapid, signorina."

"Where is he from?"

"He was born in Castel Tossignano near Imola, but
his career began in Bologna. There he was consecrated
deacon by Bishop Peter."

"And then?"

Teresa turned her head away as if a passing bird had
suddenly caught her attention. "This same Peter was mysteriously drowned."

"Did John have a part in it?"

At Marozia's frankness Teresa looked anguished. The
nun was speaking treason and knew it. "You can judge for
yourself," she replied in a lowered voice.

"How did he come to Ravenna?"

"His friends in the diocese continued to support him."

"But I thought that Archbishop Kailo—"

"Yes," interrupted Teresa, "Kailo was a strong archbishop and well liked. Unfortunately, he fell ill not long
after John paid a visit to Ravenna."

"Kailo died of some disease?"

Teresa's expression did not change. "A disease that resembled hemlock poisoning—or so I am told." She prepared to leave the garden. "The heat has become unpleasant. Should we not move back indoors?"

Marozia did not stir. Her eyes glittered. "No, you go on. I wish to speak to that man."

"Marozia!"

"Don't worry. Nothing you have said will cross my lips."

Teresa's face darkened. "A sister of our order was accused of betraying our deacon. She prayed for forgiveness, but our deacon took a lance of barbed steel—"

"Say no more," Marozia cut in. "I have promised."

After Teresa left Marozia remained in the garden, as did Bishop John. When the last of the clergy had drifted off, he turned to her and approached with outstretched hands.

Marozia did not rise to greet him, so Bishop John had to bow to kiss her fingers. As he did so she had the sudden unpleasant vision of a falcon swooping in for the kill. She was acutely aware of being alone with him in the bower. This close he seemed even taller than he had from a distance. The rich details of his ornamented gown glittered in the sunlight, and the aroma of frankincense drifted toward her.

"Signorina, if I may introduce myself? I am Bishop John of Revenna, formerly of Tuscany." Though he had been disputing with the other cardinals in Latin, he addressed Marozia in the Italian patois. His speech had a slight Tuscan accent.

"You are already known to me, Bishop John." She inclined her head slightly and withdrew her hand.

A smile crossed his lean features. "And you to me, signorina. If I may say so, you are a picture of grace seated in this lovely garden." He paused. When she did not reply, he added, "The House of Theophylact is a most noble family."

"I am glad you regard us so."

"You bear your mother's beauty."

"You know my mother, then?" Marozia tried to conceal her surprise.

"She takes an interest in the affairs of Rome—as do I, of course."

"Do you visit Rome often?"

"Alas, I am forced to. Our pope, as you know"—he paused, his eyes taunting—"is an ambitious man, a man who does not countenance disloyalty. One might say he feels most comfortable when the deacons and bishops of his benefices are all around him, where he can keep watch over them."

To her surprise Marozia found these remarks about Sergius offensive. "I know he has frequent meetings of the Curia," she said stiffly, "but surely that is what is best for the Papal States."

John seemed amused at her ready defense. "But my dear Marozia, the Papal States are such a narrow span of empire, scarcely from here to Ravenna and back. Even on the Via Tiberina it is scarcely safe to travel. One must be constantly on the alert for Magyars, Saracens and Frankish bandits."

"What do you propose, then?"

He shrugged. "A broader empire, if you please. Rather more along the lines of the Byzantine."

"But that is heresy," she said, astonished. "Ravenna has long since thrown off the yoke of Eastern Orthodoxy." She rose, her face flushed. "No Roman, no Italian, no

Christian would once again subjugate himself to the rule of Constantinople.''

If the fury of her response surprised him, he gave no sign. His brows rose only slightly. "Marozia, calm yourself. I would not embrace Byzantine rule, of that you may be assured. I willingly and honestly honor this pope and feast at his table.'' He smirked. "But I wish the peninsula to be safe again, and that can be accomplished only with imperial power.''

She sank onto the bench. "You have high aspirations, Bishop John.''

"Not for myself; it is for the good of all. I think only of the people.''

"So I have heard.'' At this he flinched, so she hastened to add, "Perhaps the people of Ravenna deserve your attention first of all.''

"Alas, it is so.'' His tone was easy, but he stirred as if the turn of conversation made him nervous. "But what am I to do? You see how I must spend my days in the Curia. Everything in Ravenna is entrusted to my deacons.''

Marozia withdrew a linen handkerchief from her pocket. "I have heard there has been much sickness in that city.''

"Some, yes. But there is sickness everywhere.''

"Sickness and suffering.'' Marozia daintily touched her lips, then lowered her handkerchief. "They say the people are taxed and tithed into poverty and starvation, then driven into ditches to die.''

At her words a spell seemed to come over the garden. A light breeze moved the fronds of a fern that clung near the top of the wall, but all else was frozen. Marozia became acutely aware of the man who stood close to her.

Bishop John's breathing turned fast and sharp. "Someone has been speaking lies.'' He took a step backward. There were beads of sweat on his pale brow. And then almost to himself he murmured, "Yes, she is much like her mother."

As the call of a yellow warbler broke the stillness, Bishop John seemed to recover his composure.

"I'm afraid I must go now," he said, smiling. "The Curia . . ." He gestured toward the palace, but his eyes remained fixed on Marozia. "It has been a pleasure meeting you, my dear. Sergius has admirable taste."

Then, as if further delay might seduce his spirit, he bowed, kissed her hand and hurried away through the garden gate to the courtyard beyond.

Despite her victory Marozia was left feeling breathless and out of sorts. She had made an enemy, of that she was certain, but it was more than John's animosity that disturbed her. Almost from the moment of greeting, he had expressed a certain contempt. In his easy manner with her, in his unthinking flattery, in his every word and gesture there was a kind of knowingness that she had never felt with a stranger, least of all a male stranger.

The ideas of empire he had expressed to her—why had he made her privy to such thoughts? Did he believe she had some influence with Sergius?

Perhaps, but she saw clearly that the Bishop of Ravenna was deeply self-serving. It would not benefit him to have his own views of government carried to the pope through a female emissary. No, he was speaking to Marozia as a Theophylact, one of that noble Roman family, who might wield power.

Marozia raised her head and looked about her. She was alone in the garden. Beyond loomed the massive, flat wall and paired spires of the Lateran basilica with the octagonal baptistery outlined against its flank, a symbol of papal power, rebuilt by Sergius for all to see.

Suddenly it struck her what was oddest about the conversation that had just transpired. John had spoken of

Theodora, of Marozia, of Sergius, but in all his words there had been no mention of Gaius Theophylact.

Of course I had not been mentioned either, but then there was no reason why my name should be raised. After all, I had voluntarily withdrawn from the world's affairs, and I clung now to shreds of gossip and rumor and private confidences, stored like clothing in a secret trunk. I did not expect to share in the power, influence or passions of the Theophylacts. Instead I hoped in some small way to do God's work.

I was then in training to take my vows at the Convent of Saint Peter's within the Leonine walls. The basilica, which every pilgrim knows, stands on the hill where Saint Peter was put to death, and his remains are stored in the crypt beneath the altar—all, that is, but his head, which resides with some other holy relics in the vestorium chamber in the Lateran.

The basilica was reconstructed during the time of Leo IV. Someday, God willing, Saint Peter's will be a grand edifice, but now it is only a small chapel built of brick with a floor of Aventine marble. Sixty years before my time the Muslim infidels swarmed over it, stealing its gold and silver reliquaries.

But now with the building of the walls we have gathered God's gifts again. The gold altar is a work of glory. It stands above the crypt with an opening just beneath. Our holy deacon allows the pilgrims to come there and lower their vestments so their clothing may be blessed by contact with the sacred relics.

As with every true nun in Rome, I held it my duty to serve the pilgrims and aid them in their devotions. Thanks to the beneficence of our popes, we have many hostelries fot such visitors. Diaconiae, they are called. There we provide care for the sick, lodging for the homeless, food and spiritual guidance for travelers.

Many of these pilgrims have journeyed hundreds of miles in the cause of Christ, and they arrive footsore and weary. I shudder to recall the decrepitude and misery I have witnessed. Of course many die on the way, and there are those who, having come to Rome, will never leave again. Racked with the beggar's cough, subject to fainting spells, bearing the boils and pustules of the suffering, they struggle from site to site along the Holy Way until at last they drop and are heard of no more. Theirs is a sacred journey, so they praise God, knowing that He is good and that their suffering will end. And each of them, no matter how poor, has preserved some gold or gem that is donated to the good of God, whereby the church prospers.

For my own part, I found it a simple life. With the aid of my grandfather Eusebius I excelled in the study of Latin. It was easy for me, and I must confess I sometimes strayed from the Gospels to read the accounts of the pagan Caesars. Now and then, for Eusebius was free in his teaching of such matters, I would delve into the writings of the Sabine poets, whom I found sinful but delicious. My dreams for days afterward would be plagued with gods, nymphs and satyrs, and I sometimes awoke in a sweat of passion with the devil's fork piercing my soul. Still, I partook of the Sacrament and I did penance, may God forgive me.

In time I came to know all the churches and their relics throughout Rome: Santa Maria Maggiore, which shelters the manger of Christ; the refurbished Santo Clemente and Santi Apostoli; and San Marco, Hadrian's own church, close to his family palace. Through the holy crypts at Santo Prassede, Santi Quattro Coronati and Santo Stefano degli Abissini I led the faithful pilgrims—and finally to San Silvestro in Capite, which houses the relics of Pope

Sylvester and the sarcophagus of that noble Roman lady, Aurea Petronilla.

Despite the state of the kingdom these churches grow rich in furnishings; new buildings and baptisteries are added to them as well as pagan houses, made over in the Christian design. All about the city workmen labor to sheathe the walls in marble, install silver chandeliers and create splendid mosaics of the apostles in patterns of glazed tesserae.

Saint Peter rules over all. Neither the church nor the saints' relics can give ample idea of his spiritual power, but it was felt all around me. The power of the church lies in Saint Peter's hands, through his blessed representative the pope. The lands are his, and the riches and the people, and the papal kingdom is the realm of Saint Peter's estate.

I can say these things without pride, for I saw hundreds—more, thousands—transformed by Saint Peter's power. The noble and the weak, the humble and the blessed, all come to the basilica to touch the relics that lie at the heart of his sacred domain.

In my role as a nun of Saint Peter's I held special privileges. I could wander among rich and poor, young and old alike. I heard many things. I was privy to politics, gossip, the matters of church and Rome.

My position gave me both the status of a spiritual confessor and the unwanted burdens of a woman of the world, for I often heard things I did not want to hear, carried burdens I did not want to bear. Even to Marozia, had she asked, I might have told things she did not know.

For instance, that day when Bishop John spoke to her in the garden, I already knew that our mother Theodora was his mistress.

Chapter 4

Three months after her deflowering my sister Marozia missed her monthly bleeding. She told no one. Even Sergius was in the dark. At the appropriate time she lied to him, telling him to stay away because it was her woman's time.

He paid hardly any notice. Rivalries in the Curia were brewing. The Franks threatened to cross the Alps again, and the Lombard Berengar was fighting against them. In the south three more cities, including that held by the Bishop of Gaeta, had given in to the Saracens. Sergius constantly feared disloyalty and new invasions.

Marozia was in turmoil. She tongue-lashed her women-in-waiting and flew into tantrums at the slightest provocation. I begged her to tell me what was wrong, but she said nothing.

Tasha visited her one morning and noticed a horrible smell about Marozia. Afraid to let the servants see she was sick, Marozia had gone to a dark corner of the public jakes. There, silent and miserable, she had vomited.

Each day she prayed the bleeding would begin again. Each day she hated more the man who had done this to her. She wanted to murder him, but she was maddened by his preoccupations, his indifference. Even after she told him her woman's time was over, he did not attempt to make love to her. Her vanity was offended. She was enraged.

"Am I no longer a woman to you?" she shrieked at him one morning. "How is it you no longer desire me?"

He gazed at her in open-mouthed amazement, then reached out for her. "Come, come, my sweet Marozia."

She approached, spat in his face and flung herself away. He would have beaten her, but he had learned better. Instead he stormed out, ordering the guards to keep her in her room.

Her howls and screams could be heard up and down the halls of the Lateran palace. Finally Sergius had to give up on even that punishment; no one, including him, could stand the noise.

"You promised me my freedom," she reminded him sullenly when next he appeared.

"You have your freedom," he replied harshly. "What more do you wish?"

The question threw her into another frenzy. She raged at him, reminding him of every injustice and mistreatment she could think of. Denunciations, recriminations and foul expletives poured from her lips. She told him everything— everything, that is, but that she carried his child.

At last he shrugged and departed to the banquet hall, where he drank, feasted and bedded a concubine. Marozia sobbed until dawn.

A week later, when the pope declared that he would attend the annual Corso del Palio in Siena, Marozia insisted on going with him. At first he resisted, but Marozia was determined. For three nights she plied him with her kisses. He sensed her new voluptuousness, her increasing hunger, but it seemed to him only that her body had become riper and firmer through love. He did not guess that her raven-ous caresses had a purpose. She truly felt her whole life was over, finished. She wanted to indulge in some final pleasure before she was destroyed by the fetus within her.

Sergius sensed none of this. All he knew was the nights of unparalleled, violent passion.

"Oh, please, may I go? Please, Your Holiness," she begged, lying on his chest, curling his hair with her delicate fingers.

And when at last he said "Yes," she clung to him even more desperately, responding to his thrusts with delighted cries of soaring ecstasy.

The cavalcade to Siena was a colorful array of cross-emblazoned knights, high-stepping chargers and splendid high carts with fluttering banners. It was a journey of eight days along the Via Cassia. Each night the pope's entourage rested in a *domus* or monastery in a loyal benefice. All around the countryside anxious monks and vassals plundered storehouses, fields and stockyards to provide a feast for the pope and his train.

The mead tasted here of savory, there of cloves or cinnamon, depending on the preferences of the region. Meats and fish were gilded with powdered egg yolk, saffron and flour mixed with gold leaf. Courses of quail, partridge, roast swan and heron with carp were delivered before the pope, followed by beef pies, eel pies, fish aspic, meat galantines with lamprey, roast kid, venison and peacocks with cabbage. None dared leave the table before midnight, when a dessert of cheese and junkets, French beans, pickled ox tongue and sugared cherries was brought on.

To Marozia it was a time of heady excitement. Never had she traveled so far from Rome. The speed of the horses over the old imperial road, the days of hard, relentless travel past fields, mountains and lakes in a landscape painted green with new grass and dappled with wildflowers —all this mingled with the danger of bandits, the heat and hunger and thirst to give her a mounting sense of expectation.

With each day's end there was the welcome of a cool hospice, country girls in scarlet gowns with white sleeves waiting to greet her, the refreshment of a bath in spring water warmed by the sun and the bustle and flurry as trunks were unpacked and fresh damasks spread on the hostel beds.

In every domus she was treated with honor. She sat at the high table, and none dared shun her or whisper behind her back. All the petty gossip and bickering of Rome were left behind for the simple awe and obedience of the country folk. She felt released from a cage, as if she could fly free like a great swan across the campagna.

Marozia could see that Sergius too was pleased. At each domus he held court before the feasting. In quick succession deacons and bishops, priests and abbots, nuns and priors as well as laymen appeared before him. He rapidly passed judgment, offering dispensation to legitimize children and annul marriages, ordering excommunication or death for such major offenders as heretics and traitors.

His judgments were swift and sure. Where Lombard law contradicted papal edict, he overrode the foreign court. Before the night's entertainment began he enforced the punishments he had decreed. Floggings and executions were carried out before his eyes. He insisted that a man condemned as a heretic be burned immediately, that a convicted turncoat for the Magyars have his eyes and tongue cut out in the abbey courtyard. Only when the last screams of the suffering had faded would Sergius turn away and summon his followers to the banquet hall.

Word soon spread that papal law was transcendent. As the lively procession with its fluttering banners and gay colors made its way into the provinces, it became a triumphant march to the greatest festival of all, the race for the Palio in Siena.

*   *   *

It was in Siena that Marozia first met the Lombard upstart Alberic—and another whose name I almost fear to mention, a man called Gallimanfry.

In the confusion of the two-day celebration before the race, Marozia's head filled with new sights and sounds. Surrounded by so many strangers, she was in a constant state of awe and fear, as if at any moment she might lose her grip and topple into nervous derangement.

On the morning of the race, the calends of July, all the confusion seemed swept aside. The day was cool and clear. Following the dictates of tradition, the Palio, a magnificent black and gold fringed banner, was blessed in the archbishop's church at morning's first light. In each of the *contrade*, the local wards of Siena, the riders and their horses were blessed at the altars of their churches.

Each following a fluttering banner bearing the symbol of his contrada—Unicorn, She-wolf, Snail, Dragon and Tortoise among them—the riders took their positions on the narrow cobbled road that surrounded the Piazza del Campo. Pages, horsemen, drummers and trumpeters paraded past, all preceded by the standard-bearers, who tossed and twirled their heavy silk banners. While the crowd cheered and applauded the procession moved about the piazza until the cart with the Palio finally appeared, drawn by white oxen decked in gold and black trappings.

It was then that Marozia saw him, a tall, broad-shouldered man with a lion rampant on his tunic, his blond head crowned by a finely worked brass headpiece. She had no need to ask his name. Through the crowd ran murmurs: "Alberic the Lombard, Berengar's general." People stood aside as he passed.

His horse was a high-strung black *barbero* with a strong neck, finely proportioned head and flaring nostrils. Unlike the other riders, whose heavy saddles were trimmed with gaudy ornaments and giltwork, Alberic had only a light leather saddle with high stirrups. All but Alberic carried a long, vicious *nerbo*, the oxhide whip favored by the local jockeys.

The pope and the Archbishop of Siena were seated on a high purple dais at the edge of the piazza. Marozia stood on a lower platform near Sergius' left hand. As Alberic passed by and bowed for the papal blessing, his gaze drifted to her and lingered.

Marozia caught her breath. His youthfulness startled her; he could not have been more than twenty years of age, but it was his beauty that caught and held her attention.

His eyes were a steady, limpid blue. With his fair complexion and blond hair he seemed alarmingly innocent and vulnerable. The smile that traced its way across his lips held boyish innocence.

His obligatory respects to the pope, archbishop and cardinals were almost insolently casual. As his restless mount stirred under him, eyes rolled back, hooves pawing the cobblestones, he allowed his appraising gaze to return to Marozia as though she were a fine gem that he had come to judge.

Curious without knowing why, Marozia returned his gaze. His smile broadened as swiftly as a gull's wing touches the water and a slight inclination of the head acknowledged her regard.

She felt her face flush. She wanted to turn away but could not. In the sudden entrancement of the moment, with the heat and noise of the crowd swelling around her, she felt faint. Then all at once, so swiftly she hardly saw it happen, the Lombard touched his heels to his mount and was gone.

Marozia's heart was pounding. She wanted to burst from this crowd, to hurl aside the howling, waving mob of Sienese who surrounded her. Almost in panic she turned from side to side, but the servants were oblivious, talking among themselves, pointing to their favorites, who were gathering at the starting post.

At the same time Marozia became uneasily aware of the presence behind her. Dressed in purple splendor, the seated pope had turned silent as a rock.

Fearfully Marozia glanced up at him. His eyes were upon her, boring into her, and his face had assumed cruel indifference.

She met his eyes and suddenly the faintness was gone. She felt joyful, radiant. For the first time in her life she was certain of her beauty, and she let it play on him like torchlight shining in a darkened cave, jubilant as she tortured him.

At the trumpets' fanfare the horses sprang from the starting post. The race began in pandemonium: clattering hooves, flailing nerbos. The riders lashed out at their mounts, at each other, at everything in sight. Then the uproar resolved itself into thunder as the horses gathered speed and the babel of the crowd rose to a shriek. En masse the citizens of Siena pressed forward, swayed and pulled back to the edge of the piazza. A small child was left stranded. His father lunged to retrieve him, caught the boy in his arms and rolled out of the way just in time as the first wave of contestants pounded past.

Two riders held a clear lead: Alberic on his black barbero and a small jockey wearing a She-wolf blazon and riding a sleek grey colt. As they rounded the far curve, hooves clattering on the cobblestones, the grey lost its footing for just a moment. Hearing the crowd groan, Alberic glanced over his shoulder.

The other jockey pulled his mount's head around and it recovered, but he had lost three strides. The pack was gaining on him. Cursing with fury, the She-wolf jockey dug his heels into the mount's flank, lashing out with his nerbo. Coming out of the curve the young horse sprang forward.

Alberic took no more backward looks. Poised over his small saddle, knees pressed forward at his horse's withers, head bent low, he rode with easy grace. He and his horse seemed one, their attention fixed on a distant goal. Confident and relaxed, they might have been running in an open field, far from the howling confusion of the race.

But the She-wolf jockey was once again within reach. The crowd gasped as he lunged forward. His nerbo snaked out, the needle-sharp tip as deadly as an arrow, lashing at the hindquarters of Alberic's black stallion.

Alberic's horse reared its head. The magnificent stride faltered, narrowing the gap between the two riders. Alberic seemed unconcerned. He put strong, soothing pressure on the reins, regaining control, leading the stallion back on course.

Coming into the next turn the two riders were dangerously close. The noise of the crowd was a wave now, a torrent that swept over them, roaring over even the racket of the hooves. Again the nerbo shot out, and this time its vicious tail lashed at Alberic himself. The stroke drew a shower of blood.

Alberic had no whip. He was defenseless. His black stallion's stride had changed; his own easy determination had fled. Now two horses and two riders were locked in deadly combat.

They were neck and neck, with the She-wolf jockey on the inside. His relentless lashing was giving him the lead. In a saner moment he might have tossed his whip aside, pressed his advantage and finished the course, but he was furious, frenzied, determined to destroy his rival, and so the lash flicked out again and again.

Few in the crowd could describe what happened next. Only those who were closest saw it, and even to them the motion was a blur, the work of an instant, then over. Alberic's hand lifted from the reins to catch the nerbo in midflight. Without changing stride, without even glancing at the other rider, he gave a short, sharp tug.

There was no warning. Caught unawares, the other jockey could neither brace himself nor release his grip on the oxhide whip. A brief glimpse of his face as he fell showed terror and astonishment. A sigh went up from the crowd: the murmur of awe and regret that was often heard at an execution.

The rider was down. His horse tumbled over once, hooves flailing in the air, and lunged, struggling for purchase on the cobblestones. Then, with a lurch and a shower of pebbles the riderless colt was up again and racing off toward his goal.

The jockey screamed as he rolled to his feet, then staggered and fell. He looked up aghast at the horses charging toward him. He was much too far from safety. Like a man pleading with the forces of nature he seemed to beg them for mercy. In a final, furious gesture of despair, his hand clutched the fallen nerbo and lashed out with it.

The riders did not swerve. In a single wave they bore down on him, their horses' hooves thudding against his broken body as he was crushed against the cobblestones.

Marozia watched the race, her hands trembling. She was unaware of the handkerchief she had torn to shreds, of the crowd around her, of their shouts mingling with the clattering of hooves.

When Alberic won the race the crowd went even wilder, but the Lombard paid no heed to their cries. Instead, reining in his stallion, he returned to pass in front of the papal stand.

Marozia sensed motion behind her and looked up. Pope Sergius was flushed, whether with anger or excitement she could not tell. It was Sergius' duty to bless the winning horse and rider, but to the astonishment of the crowd, Alberic rode on past, ignoring the pope and his retinue.

He trotted directly to the fallen man, then swiftly dismounted and leaned over the crumpled body. A moment later he rose and crossed himself.

The rider from the She-wolf contrada was dead, the nerbo still clenched tightly in his hand.

Chapter 5

That night Alberic sat in the place of honor at the high table on the right hand of the pope and opposite the Archbishop of Siena. The banner of the Palio was behind him, its gold threads gleaming. At the beginning of the banquet a prayer was offered to the Madonna di Provenzano, in whose honor the race had been held. There were toasts to the fallen rider and to each of the contrade as their banners were raised.

Slaves with pitch torches were posted around the room. The black stallion, its mane and tail bedecked with flowers, shiny ribbons and gilt bands, was led into the hall and paraded among the feasters. They led the stallion up onto the middle table, where he stood with nostrils flaring and eyes rolled back—stamping, proud and magnificent—until Alberic ordered the grooms to take him away.

Only then did the feasting begin. Sienese maidens in red and white bliauds brought platters of roast pork, wild fowl and pasties. As the plain pies were cut open, live blackbirds with long ribbons on their beaks and claws burst free and rose to the ceiling. Conjurers performed the beheading of John the Baptist, then restored their victim to life. On a platform stage a Gyspy troupe presented *The Temptations of the Maiden* and *Lucifer's Punishment*, eating fire and breathing smoke at the appropriate moments.

Marozia was hardly aware of these entertainments, nor of the sumptuous feast. She had little appetite. As the courses came and were cleared away she picked at her food, while all around her others gorged themselves. Sergius ignored her and no toast was offered to her beauty. As for Alberic, he did not even glance in her direction. Consumed with his victory, his face flushed from wine, he behaved like a brilliant orator in the midst of a crowd of awed sycophants. The men around him appeared spellbound. His wit was magnified by their admiration until every word that fell from his lips was greeted by shouts of laughter, shakings of the head and exclamations over his brilliance.

Marozia felt vaguely disgusted. It was all a man's game, she reflected. Alberic had won the race. For this the company praised and applauded him, but tomorrow they would no doubt feel different.

Nevertheless Marozia made note of the Lombard's followers, especially a man they called Lambert. He had a strong, studious look with darting eyes and a serious smile. He seemed hardly more than a youth, but when she asked one of her maids, she heard that he was a captain, Alberic's right-hand man, and had aided in the capture of Spoleto. They said that Berengar, now king of the Lombards, intended to make him a duke.

On this occasion the Lombards, Tuscans, Sienese and Romans mingled freely, their differences forgotten in triumphant celebration of the Virgin's holiday. It was a testament to the Virgin, Marozia reflected cynically, that she could so harmonize these differing factions and races. Marozia knew too that the harmony was calculated. Pope Sergius had traveled to Siena on business, and this banquet feast was a large part of his reason for coming, yet another symbol of the consolidation of his power. Before the evening was done all would kiss his hand and receive his blessing.

Only one of Alberic's followers hung back from the others. This was a man whom Marozia could not help noticing for both his extraordinary appearance and his incredible appetite. A short, dark figure with long hair and a ragged beard, he had a nose that looked as if it had been hammered and twisted on a dozen anvils. He moved with a strange sideways bandy-legged scuttle that made forward motion seem foreign to him.

Darting about the room, he continually harassed the performers, revealing the conjurers' tricks, interrupting the actors' speeches with his own slurred soliloquies and setting the musicians on edge by banging away on a stolen tambourine.

The Sienese women in their Tuscan costumes seemed to hold a special attraction for him. Every now and then a shrill feminine scream would announce that he had buried his head in a pillowy breast or probed an unwilling set of thighs. Laughing uproariously, the banqueters hurled puddings at him, but he continued his antics, oblivious and cheerful. From table to table he scuttled, here seizing a flagon, there a fistful of brandied sweetmeats.

Now and then, however, he drifted near Alberic and whispered something in the Lombard's ear, pointing at one or the other of the revelers. And each time Alberic seemed to listen attentively, as if this strange little man had something important to say. It was obvious that some bond deeper than trust bound these two, the high, powerful Lombard and the clown.

During one such conference Marozia suddenly became aware of Alberic's eyes upon her. Again that look passed between them. She snatched her eyes away.

Why had he looked at her that way? What was it that his look said to her? It was only stupid flattery, she told herself angrily. He was toying with her. Everyone knew she was the pope's concubine.

Marozia glanced toward Sergius. He appeared more at ease now, and well he might. He had won, had made of her a wanton, a whore. All men saw her as a fallen woman, nothing more.

She retired early without making apologies.

When her surprised handmaidens appeared reluctant to leave the festivities, she disgustedly ordered them to remain. They could not conceal their glee. Undoubtedly they would find among that howling mob men to lie with this night, she thought as she left the noisy hall.

During this visit to Siena Marozia had taken her own chamber in the abbess' house. The halls were empty, since all the nuns were at the feast, but the door to her room was guarded by two of the archbishop's soldiers. They eyed her lasciviously as she passed.

Still feeling wretched and abused, Marozia undressed and slipped into her nightgown. A single taper burned on the mantel above the hearth. She was just about to extinguish it when she heard a sudden racket in the hall. A moment later there was a loud knock at the door.

Marozia started and looked about her, recalling the guards' lewd glances. On a wild, abandoned night such as this, with men deep in their cups, none could be trusted.

She bent to her traveling trunk, raised the lid and took out a razor-sharp stiletto. She tucked the knife in her waistband and threw a cloak over her shoulders. The hilt of the knife was concealed beneath the garment's folds.

As the knock was repeated, she heard someone coughing, then muttering and curses. A blow was struck. The sound was reassuring. Perhaps they were merely street brawlers who could easily be driven away.

"Who calls at this time of night?" she demanded.

"Please, signorina, there is a man here asking to see you."

"Tell him to go away."

The muttering was repeated. It was followed by more coughing, then low, growling curses. Marozia heard more blows.

"Please, signorina." The guard was breathing heavily, as if the wind had been knocked out of him. "He says he must see you. He will not go."

Marozia slammed back the bar and unlatched the door. Two guards stood in the hall, struggling to hold a dark, squirming figure.

A pair of black eyes looked up into hers. A broad smile lit up the bearded face, revealing chipped front teeth. Marozia's hand flew to her throat as the grinning figure ceased fighting the guards and stood still, staring at her with sickly pleasure. It was the man she had seen whispering in Alberic's ear.

"What does he want?" Marozia addressed the guards.

"He wishes to speak to you."

"HRRRRRGGGH."

"What was that sound?"

"Speech," replied one of the guards.

"No," said the other, "he was clearing his throat."

"What is he doing now?" Marozia asked.

"Scratching himself."

"Perhaps searching for lice."

"No, he's not searching. He's scratching."

Marozia eyed him. "Is this a creature of God?"

"I am, signorina." The man ceased scratching and crossed himself.

To her astonishment Marozia found herself smiling at him. "Then you *are* capable of speech."

"More," he barked. "Capable, signorina, of long threads of thought. I thrive on speech. It is my home and nesting place, the place to which I return when all other refuges cast me out. The weft and warp of words are the blanket wherein I warm myself, cheer myself, transmit my sentient—'' He belched.

An odor of wine reeking with garlic wafted toward Marozia. She stepped back, covering her nose.

"In that case you are no doubt capable of telling me what you want."

"I was capable, signorina. Capable, nay, even composed and prepared, up to the moment that this door opened and a radiant beauty like the rising sun—"

"Shall we take him away, signorina?" The guard appeared ready to pounce on the man.

"No, leave him." Marozia studied her visitor. "There is something in there, if he can only get it out. "

"Just what I fear"—the man drunkenly raised one finger—"that it will all pour out at once in a rampant deluge. Which is to say, I am ill. Not well. Having feasted."

"I know you have feasted. You are drunk. Now what is your name and what brings you here?"

"My name." He paused to think. "Gallimanfry." He paused again. "What brings me: service to my liege, Alberic."

"I'll hear no more," Marozia said suddenly. She turned to push the door closed, but as quick as light Gallimanfry moved forward and jammed his foot into the crack. Alarmed, Marozia touched the hilt of her stiletto. The guards reached for him.

"Get away," Gallimanfry barked over his shoulder. Astonished into obedience by his tone, they stepped back.

His voice fell to a murmur. "Now, signorina, this and only this: your loveliness—remarked upon, cherished. By him, Alberic. You understand? Forbidden, circumstances being what they are. I mention only one name: Sergius. The circumstances." He seemed to lose his train of thought, hiccupped, then recovered. "Finally," and he reached into his trousers as Marozia's grip on the knife tightened, "this." In his hand, hidden from the guards' sight, was a curious black ring.

"Here."

Without reflecting Marozia lifted the ring from Gallimanfry's outstretched palm. It was almost weightless in her hand, so light it hardly seemed to exist. With the tips of her fingers she felt the twisted strands of horsehair, bound tight in a circlet.

"Done." Gallimanfry grinned victoriously and removed his foot from the doorway. "Gratified. My lord's will done." He got loud again for the guards' benefit. "As for me, I have seen a lovely woman in her chemise. My night is made, by God's grace."

"No, come back. You cannot—"

It was too late. Already he was gone away down the hall, careening from wall to wall as he sang at the top of his lungs.

> *"The maids of Siena,*
> *They bring me such joy,*
> *All baubles and bangles*
> *For Gallimanfroy.*
> *With bosoms like mountains*
> *And maidenhair fine,*
> *The maids of Siena*
> *Are mine, only mine."*

Bewildered, for it had all happened in an instant, the guards lingered in the doorway. Then they bowed their apologies and turned away.

Already Marozia had forgotten them, forgotten even the crazed figure who now staggered to the door of the abbey. She had forgotten all but the ring she held and the hands that had twisted tight and bound the fine horsehair.

Chapter 6

In Rome, in the meantime, Theodora took advantage of the pope's absence to make herself a member of the Senate of Rome. Had Sergius been there, the free election would never have occurred. He hated my mother—and she him—for reasons I was to understand only later. And though the Roman Senate pretended to act independently of the Curia, everyone knew that the approval of the church was essential in all matters of importance.

Within the Senate itself Theodora faced furious opposition from Marcellus and the other members of the patrician party, those rich, old Roman families whose homes surrounded the Via Lata. A jealous assembly of aristocrats with a bitter and vain nostalgia for the lost glory of Rome, Marcellus and his followers opposed Theodora's election with all the oratorical power at their command. They claimed, quite rightly, that there had never been a woman senator—senatrix, they called it—in all the history of Rome. They even went so far as to chide their fellow Romans with having become effeminate.

But these were feeble arguments against considerable political might, for my noble father, Gaius Theophylact, was chief consul of the Romans, the man responsible for the jurisdiction and administration of the city. No higher position could be held by a layman.

Gaius Theophylact had been duly elected by popular

vote and the inauguration ratified by the pope just three days after Marozia went to the Lateran. So Theophylact's position was secure, as was apparent to all.

Only the disapproval of the populace could have put an end to Theodora's ambitions. The people held no grudge against her. She had never flaunted jewels and riches—ironic to favor her for that—and she was respected both as the daughter of Eusebius the scribe and as the wife of Gaius Theophylact. Also, she was beautiful. Her bearing and loveliness brought honor to the city.

Perhaps a change had come over our Roman citizens. Through pagan and Christian times they had watched the men who ruled Rome. They had seen empires rise and fall, witnessed graft, war, deceit and machination. Perhaps there is in each of us something that wants a gentle but firm hand to guide the way. Rome was beginning to prosper under Gaius Theophylact, and the presence of his wife in the Senate might add just that much more strength to the city's future.

Finally, I too may have played some small part in my mother's success. Though I accomplished no brilliant works and held no high office, I was assiduous in my duties and sincere in my enterprises. I was known to be a Theophylact, and people praised my works, though God forgive me, I had many sins to confess. And so perhaps the citizens felt kindly toward our family and wished us well. Still, whatever the forces around her, it was Theodora herself who looked out for her future.

The day after the pope left Rome she induced my father to present her name for election in the Senate. It took two days of fierce oratory to overcome the opposition of Marcellus and his patricians, but finally on the fourth day the senatrix was elected by a narrow margin. On the fifth her name was presented to the populace, by whom she was acclaimed. Thus by the time Sergius, Marozia and their party reached Siena, Theodora had already given her first speech and accepted the inauguration.

In the absence of the pope it was the duty of the Bishop of Ravenna, as the secondary archdeacon of the Papal States, to guide the Curia. The power to ratify city patricians lay just within the power of that church body.

And so on the seventh day Bishop John of Ravenna duly ratified the civil election of Senatrix Theodora, an irreversible decision of the clerical court.

Only a Lateran messenger could present the official news to the pope, and understandably, no one was overanxious to order out an emissary. It was not until the papal party arrived in Viterbo, still three days' journey from Rome, that Pope Sergius heard about Theodora's induction as a member of the Senate. He turned cold with rage and ordered the messenger to be put in chains.

The party was quartered in a small domus near the abbey hospital, and all night long the wailing voices of the sick and dying could be heard. Sergius came to Marozia that night to take her violently, to vent his rage in the sexual act. She had known him like this before, but this time she fought back. She pummeled him and kicked his shins with bare heels.

Her anger seemed only to excite him further and he thrust into her until she cried out like the fevered patients in the nearby hospital. When he was done she huddled in the corner of the bed, weeping.

His fury spent, he seemed sullen and ashamed. He did not try to comfort her—it would have been no use—but he lingered by her side, talking on into the night.

After a while he seemed unaware of her. He rambled in a dry, rasping voice, and finally even Marozia's misery could not blot out his words. Still hunched among the bedclothes, she listened as he confessed, sitting there thick-set and naked with his hands on his knees, staring into the distant light of memory.

His life was a catalog of intrigue, battle, lust and vengeance. Why he chose to remember and recount it all now she could not say; she hated him for it.

He said he had an understanding with God in all things but one—the posthumous trial of Formosus. In that, he knew, he had erred, and his initial punishment was swift. The day after the trial an earthquake shook the Lateran until the walls crumbled. Yet it was not enough; God punished him to this day. Demon shapes recurred in his dreams and even now he cried out in the night when they came to him.

He recounted every detail of the ugly and infamous Synod Horrenda. Its purpose—his purpose—was to obliterate the honor of the late Pope Formosus. There had been political reasons, justifiable in Sergius' view.

At his behest the prelates disinterred the corpse and placed it on the papal chair in the Synod House. Yes, the corpse—Sergius shuddered. They placed Formosus on the chair dressed in his papal robes and tried him.

They harangued and insulted him for his past misdeeds. Laughing at and deriding the corpse, they asked Formosus to speak in his own behalf. There were no eyes in the sockets, but the cadaver seemed to stare at them. It was staring at Sergius still, accusing him.

Judgment was delivered and Formosus condemned. Three fingers of his right hand, the fingers of papal blessing, were severed. It was Sergius' hand that grasped the dried flesh, his knife that dismembered the corpse.

Marozia pulled the damask blanket tightly around her. The room was still. A moth fluttered around the taper.

After all the pope had said there was one question still unanswered.

"Sergius," Marozia asked, "Why should my mother hate you?"

He looked up, calm now, and pulled a bliaud over his body. "A woman scorned is a snake in the grass."

Marozia caught her breath. She did not dare ask—but she must. "Did—did she come to you?"

"To me? Yes." He did not look at her.

"And you—"

"I turned her away. I did not want Theodora. I wanted her daughter."

Marozia's hands clenched. She trembled, feeling consumed, suffocating. If only he would strike her now, kick her, spit on her or revile her—anything, so she might hate him again. Instead she must see his abashed face, filled with regret and disillusion and . . . Dare she think it?

No. No, it was not possible. Such a man would not be capable of love, but only of greed, lust, violent ambition.

"She made me another offer," Sergius went on in a low voice. "A price." He looked up. "She is greedy, your mother. I am afraid your father's simplicity cannot satisfy her. So much as she asked, I myself would be content to enjoy. It was only a small part of the pope's riches, true—but I refused. I did not wish to pay for you."

"You have called me a whore."

"Never in earnest."

Marozia felt her heart jump to her throat. She did not want this to be happening. Where his brutality could not touch her, softness overwhelmed her, sent her spinning. Here he was, a man, a thing of flesh and bone and sinew, who loved her. This was the man who sat in Saint Peter's Chair, but he was flesh; he was of earth.

Perhaps the hatred was her fault after all. Perhaps

there could be love between them if she would only allow it.

The memory of Alberic's eyes flickered, but he was hazy, dim, already a dream. That arrogant, boyish smile—what was that to the pain and power she could see in this man, who had spent all the hours of the night with tales of his ambition, triumph, suffering and remorse?

"Sergius," she said softly, "I am with child."

He blinked. She prayed that he would hold her, touch the womb that sheltered the infant.

Instead he laughed. "Oh, very well, very well." The dry, rasping voice cut her to the heart. He turned and strode the chamber door. Before he went out he said, "Remind me, Marozia, when we get to Rome. We will see to it."

Then he was gone.

Chapter 7

The day after her return from Siena Marozia paid a visit to the House of Theophylact. At that time I did not know of her new distress, but I noted a special pressure in her embrace.

"Marozia," I asked, "what is it?"

She shook her head and pulled away. "No, Lena, not now. I will tell you in time."

With Tasha she held closer conversation, and I felt something akin to jealousy as the two of them retreated to Marozia's old bedchamber. Once or twice I passed by as if by accident, and glancing in, saw their heads bowed close together, hands touching, heard their voices held low. I felt a certain pang that Marozia could confide in a servant but not in me.

Tasha was a Saracen, captured when she was ten and brought home by our father as a household slave. When she came, I was only two years old and Marozia was just born. Tasha was lovely in those early days, with jet-black skin, and long-lashed dark eyes—tall and slim, very strong. She quickly learned our language, though with an accent and an occasional Saracen word.

She converted to Christianity, of course, for to have a heathen in the household would have theatened us with excommunication, but though she attended church and spoke her Paternoster, the ways of Islam still clung. Five times a day she retreated from our presence. No one followed her or asked where she went, but we all knew. And when Marozia and I were children, we used to watch from our hiding place as she spread out her rug in a secluded room and bowed to the southeast. We used to laugh at her behind her back, but I think we were a bit in awe as well.

Then, too, there were the jinn. She finally told us about them—visiting spirits. Once it was her father, killed in battle, then her mother, who warned her to veil herself and obey Mohammed. Once she saw her ancient Sicilian grandmother, who brewed potions and visited Tasha in her sleep. After these tales Marozia and I would lie awake whispering and giggling, but we were fearful, too. The jinn seemed very close, and well we knew what a heathen spirit could do to Christian souls.

In later years, as I began studying to take my vows, I tried to lead Tasha away from her faith. I do not think she understood or appreciated my concern for her. In fact, she began to avoid me. She could not be weaned from her devotions. At set times throughout the day, as if some distant voice called, she retreated to that private room and bowed to Mecca, murmuring strange Arabic prayers.

So her closeness to Marozia was doubly painful for me. The woman we had once shared—who had dressed us, washed us, healed our scrapes and listened to our worries—now seemed to belong only to my sister. For all my good intentions I had driven her away.

Their conference could not last long, however. Marozia was obliged to appear at the table to offer her congratulations to our mother for being elected to the Senate. Marozia's praise was sincere and Theodora fairly glowed. They were more cordial with one another than I had seen them in many months.

It was only when Marozia began to speak of Siena—of the feasting and celebration that took place along the way, of the sights and sounds of that glorious event—that I saw the old jealousy and hunger return to Theodora's eyes. There was much our mother wanted, many riches still beyond her grasp. Even then I wondered what means she might use to obtain them.

As for my father, he was in rare form. Jovial and boasting as if the Theophylacts now ruled the world, he argued heatedly about the state of the empire.

Marozia's pregnancy was not noticeable—or if it was, no one commented on it. I think, though, that my father noted a certain pensiveness in her. He insisted that she stay the whole day through and bend an ear to the applicants in the atrium.

Now that Theodora was a senatrix, the number of petitioners had more than doubled, for the Theophylacts now exercised power far out of proportion to their modest holdings. It was indeed a time of influence for our family, and I think we all gloried in the sense of purpose. In the hands of the Theophylacts, it seemed, Rome would grow and prosper.

Nonetheless, there was one subject that seemed to cause Marozia some concern; I could not help noticing her anxiety when the subject came up. It was Marcellus, leader of the patrician party, who first raised the name of Alberic. Marcellus was not a frequent visitor to our house, having often warred with Father on the floor of the Senate, but I think he realized that both Theophylacts would have to be appeased if he was to make his voice heard.

He was a tall, bald man—some might have said statuesque—but he had gone pigeon-toed at an early age and his gait was hardly graceful. As a figure of some importance he affected the imperial style, a toga with a purple border. Everywhere he traveled he was accompanied by his sharp-nosed private secretary, a twisted little chancellor who carried sheaves of manuscript and could never find anything.

The effect was ridiculous. Awkward and pompous, his ferretlike chancellor scurrying behind him, Marcellus seemed always on the edge of some important decision. When he opened his mouth, however, out came long, rambling overtures with no fire and little substance.

On this particular day my father took some glee in being brusque with the patrician, urging him to come to his point. Finally after a long preamble Marcellus began to scratch at the source of his discomfort.

"My brother-in-law Lambruschini has some holdings at Spoleto. Rather valuable holdings, in fact."

Gaius nodded solemnly, but there was a twinkle in his eye. "I'm sorry to hear it. Undoubtedly he depended heavily on the protection of Duke Arnulf."

Marcellus flushed. "Indeed he did, Gaius. And you needn't laugh—"

"I am not laughing, Senator," Gaius replied, striving to control his twitching lips. "It is a hard thing indeed to lose a dukedom, especially to one so young as Alberic. And a Lombard, too."

"That cursed Alberic!"

Gaius clucked. "I am told the young Lombard seized the city by stealth in the middle of the night."

"So he did, though the walls were soundly guarded."

"Not soundly enough, it seems."

Marcellus drew himself up to his full height. "Gaius, I insist! A man like Arnulf, honest and above all loyal to Rome, loses his dukedom overnight—to an upstart, one of Berengar's sworn men. How can you make a joke of it?"

"Come, come, Marcellus; you mistake me. The situation is serious, that I grant you. And what of your brother-in-law?"

Marcellus assumed an aggrieved look. "Tertian," he barked at his secretary, "the cartulary."

At his master's command Tertian shuffled frantically through the papers, scattering them. Finally he produced the necessary parchment. With flushed face and watering eyes he handed it over.

"See here," said Marcellus. "The court, convent and abbey of Lambruschini, all handed over to Alberic by this command."

"Yes, yes, I see"—Gaius did not even glance at the document—"but what's to be done? Why doesn't Lambruschini take an oath of fealty and leave it at that?"

"Fealty . . . to *Alberic*?" Toes together and heels lifting, Marcellus assumed a pose of offended dignity. "My dear Gaius, that man is no Roman. He's scarcely a Christian. He's naught but another of that barbarous tribe that threatens to sweep over us."

Gaius' smile never wavered. "Perhaps you are being too harsh. I have heard him well spoken of, and he is gaining influence."

"Influence, indeed," Marcellus snorted. "He is brash, Gaius, brash. They say he had the gall to appear at the Palio in Siena in front of the pope himself."

Gaius glanced at Marozia, who all along had been standing nearby. "Is this so, Marozia?"

She lowered her eyes almost as if she did not wish to answer. Then she boldly looked up at him. "Yes, Father, he was there. Alberic won the Palio."

"You see, Gaius?" Marcellus burst out. "You see the danger. That upstart, that dirty Lombard! Today Lambruschini, my own brother-in-law, must kiss his hand. Tomorrow it may be you or me or . . . ." And again he was off, bemoaning the decadence of Rome, the intermingling of blood, the lack of patriotism. My father listened, bemused, now and then nodding, shaking his head or clucking his tongue. But I no longer listened to Marcellus, for I had seen an amazing change come over Marozia at the mention of Alberic's name. She was all flushed nervousness, as though trapped and wishing to escape.

There was color in her cheeks, an angry, sharp glint in her eye. She bowed, retreating—though Marcellus was too deeply immersed in his harangue to notice—and crossed to the window. I saw her looking out and almost went to her, but she seemed strangely preoccupied. From her cloak she had taken a small round object—a ring, very dull and black. This she turned over and over in her fingers, not even looking at it, as if the texture and shape of it were familiar but foreign. Then suddenly, impatiently she tucked the ring into her cloak and left the room without a word.

That evening before she returned to the Lateran palace, Marozia asked Father's permission to take Tasha with her. Marozia said she was lonely in the great palace and needed companionship. Reluctantly, for he had never quite approved of our closeness to the Saracen, Father granted her request. It was from Tasha that I later heard an account of the extraordinary events that followed.

It happened on the ides of July, the evening Pope Sergius III met the High Curia in the secret council chamber of the Lateran palace. Marozia was in her bedchamber with Tasha. It was late and she was making her final preparations for retiring.

A man appeared at the door, apparently an ordinary apothecary in a long muslin gown, but he was not the pope's usual apothecary. He seemed rather to come from the streets. His breath reeked of onions and wine. He was a rapacious-looking figure with beady black eyes, loose lips and flared nostrils. Two of the Lateran guards stood behind him.

"What brings you?" Marozia demanded.

"His Holiness sent me," replied the man.

"Come back tomorrow." Marozia signaled Tasha to shut the door, but a guard stepped in the way.

"What is the meaning of this?"

The guard, a hand on his sword, kept his eyes downcast while the apothecary came forward with an unctuous smile. "Please, signorina, the pope insists. I am skilled in matters that pertain to . . . ah . . . your condition."

She looked from one to the other of the guards. "Is this the truth?"

One of them nodded apologetically. "The pope has given us orders."

Marozia hesitated. "Very well, then. He may come in. Guards, you are dismissed."

"Thank you." The apothecary stepped inside and closed the door behind him. "They have been told to wait until we have consulted." He glanced at Tasha. "Perhaps you would like to dismiss your servant."

Marozia shook her head. "No. She stays. Now, what do you want?"

The apothecary seemed unhurried. "Please, signorina, His Holiness informed me that you would be most reasonable."

"His Holiness does not speak for me."

If the apothecary was shocked, he hid it with a smile. "He speaks for all of us, I am sure, in the sight of God."

Marozia shot him an angry glare. "He does *not* speak for me. Now please, sir, state your errand and I shall be pleased to consider your services, *if* I should have need of them."

The smile vanished. The apothecary's eyes hardened. "Perhaps there has been some mistake then. The pope informed me that you knew of my coming. He said—"

"He told me nothing of this." She stopped short. Unbidden, Sergius' words on the road from Siena echoed.

A flush crept across her face. "I fear, sir, if your skill is what I believe it to be, that you have wasted your time."

"No, no." The man came closer. "You do not appreciate my abilities. You are fearful, as are most women. I assure you the matter is painless, soon over. You will feel nothing. But a day in bed and you will be healed, a maiden again."

"Vile creature!" She struck him hard across the face. "You call yourself a man of healing?"

His expression turned ugly. "You will be sorry for this. The pope does not brook opposition in these matters."

"I have no doubt of that," she spat at him. "And how long has Sergius retained you, may I ask? How many young women have you rescued with your skills from the infamous mothering of bastards?" She grasped the front of his gown to push him away, but instead he seized her wrist.

His grip was like a vise. His hot oniony breath was in her face. "I have never failed," he whispered, "never. It can be done gently or by force, whichever you prefer, but I would not dare tell His Holiness that the deed has not been done, for then I should certainly die."

Marozia paled. "Let go of me, sir."

"You agree to submit gently?" he demanded. "It will go easier with you."

"I agree to nothing."

A sinister smile warped his face. "Then I must summon the guards. They have orders—"

"They will obey *me*," she cried.

"Not in this case. Believe me, signorina, I do not wish to call them."

"Send for Sergius." Marozia's voice grew hysterical. "I will speak to him myself. You have misunderstood."

He gave a harsh laugh and released her. "I never

misunderstand, signorina. When the pope calls on me, it is
for one purpose and one purpose only—''

He did not finish, for the stiletto appeared from
Marozia's kirtle, streaking toward his throat. He saw it
coming and twisted as he hurled her aside. The knife
clattered to the floor, but not before it had grazed his
cheek, leaving a single stringlike gash.

"Enough. I lose patience." He hit her once, then
again, harder. Dizzied by the blows, she wavered, almost
losing consciousness. "Relent," he snarled, shaking her,
"relent, bitch, or I swear by God's blood I shall—''

Tasha leapt forward. She grabbed his neck and tightened
her grip. The apothecary choked out a strangled gasp; then
his eyes widened, bulged. Suddenly with the desperate
twitching of a drowning man he loosed his grip on Marozia.

She sank to the floor, shaking all over. Dazed images
swam before her eyes: the apothecary clawing at his neck,
at the powerful black hands that clenched his throat.

A last feeble cry escaped him. Her body tensed, her
glistening features contracted with the effort of the struggle,
Tasha bent to her work.

Marozia's vision cleared. There were the dark eyes
concentrated in fury, the hard tendons on the black squeez-
ing hands. The abortionist thrashed the air with helpless
blows and kicks.

"Tasha, no, no! Let him—''

Marozia heard a sharp crack. The apothecary sagged,
then crumpled and fell from Tasha's hands.

The Saracen stepped back. As if coming awake at
last, she stared at Marozia. "Oh, Allah, what have I done?''

Marozia rose to her knees, her eyes on the limp
figure. She made the sign of the cross over him. Then she
looked up. "You have saved my life, Tasha, and my
child's." She hesitated. "You have done nothing. The
deed was mine—all mine.''

A trickle of blood flowed from the corner of the apothecary's mouth. His staring eyes still bulged. Lifting her stiletto from the floor, Marozia smiled before she slashed his throat. "There, you see? It was my doing."

Tasha said nothing. Instead she turned to the wall and buried her face in her hands.

Marozia took a new grip on the knife hilt. She paused, frowning. Then with no change of expression she leaned over the corpse and commenced a gruesome task.

More than one hundred years before, the Frankish emperor Charlemagne met in the secret council chamber with Pope Leo III and his followers. There they ordained the agreement between emperor and pope that laid the foundation for the Holy Roman Empire.

Though the years had their influence on that transaction and the papacy changed hands many times, the room lost none of its splendor. Dominated by an imperial throne encrusted with sapphires, diamonds and rubies, the chamber was lined with gilt tapestries embroidered with shimmering silk and threads of silver.

The cardinals and bishops who attended the ides meetings were seated on carved Byzantine chairs with ivory-inlaid hunting scenes on the pedestals and fine camlet cushions on the seats.

For all its richness and grandeur the chamber was intimate. Servants spoke in hushed voices as they offered wine, marchpane and sherbet to the assemblage. Scribes and chancellors swiftly moved among them, sandals hissing against the stone, painfully conscious of each crinkling of parchment.

It was time to account for tithes, and the High Curia had worked late into the night. Among those in the room were the pope, Bishop John of Ravenna, Peter of Tuscany, the Archbishop of Siena and cardinals from the duchies under papal control.

Hearing a commotion in the hall, all turned their heads. Pope Sergius, who had been listening to the tally of Ravenna's holdings, raised his hand for silence. The scribe ceased speaking.

A guard appeared at the door, his face creased with concern. "Your Holiness, I beg pardon. Signorina Marozia is here."

Sergius flushed. "Send her away."

"Your Holiness, I regret she refuses—"

"Send her away," the pope roared.

It was too late. Pushing past the guards, Marozia appeared in the doorway of the council chamber. She wore a white bliaud. Her braided hair was pinned under a coif, emphasizing the graceful curve of her pale neck. Statuesque and calm, she seemed at once pallid and radiant, as if a noble ghost of beauty had been warmed with the breath of life.

"Your Holiness," she called, "I beg an audience."

She stepped forward so that all could see what she held in her hand, a square ornamented teak box no larger than the span of her fingers. Bishops and cardinals moved back, eyeing her with amazement, as if a beautiful witch had unexpectedly appeared among them to work a charm.

"Who summoned you?" Sergius demanded angrily.

"No one, Your Holiness. I came of my own accord."

"We are undertaking church business. I will speak with you on the morrow."

A smile played on Marozia's mouth. "This too is church business," she replied, "since it is a matter that concerns you."

Sergius had turned quite red but the others were curious now, some hiding smiles. "Very well," he said at last, "I will meet with you aside." He surveyed the assembled prelates. "My lords, I ask your indulgence. This will only take a moment."

With ironic bows the members of the Curia took their cue. Servants were called and in a moment the chamber was filled with conversation.

With that strange half smile still on her lips, Marozia came to Sergius. He stepped down from his chair, his face showing the depth of his displeasure. "Harlot," he muttered, "you will be punished for this," and then, "Did my man not visit you?"

Marozia nodded. "He did, my liege."

"He must have been gentle, since you are up and about."

"In his own way he was gentle."

Sergius studied her with growing unease. His eyes rested with curiosity on the box in her hand. "Still, you should be abed."

"I wanted to bring you a gift, my liege." With a veiled look Marozia indicated the box. One delicate forefinger stroked the carving on its edge. "I thought it most urgent."

"What is this, then?" Sergius glanced around to ascertain that no one was looking. To all appearances the others were deeply engaged in their own business.

"It is my answer to your request, Your Holiness."

He seemed taken aback. "I—I have requested nothing of you."

Marozia shook her head. "On the contrary, you asked a great deal." She held out the box to him.

Reluctantly he took it and raised the lid. A look of disgust swept over his features. Then he slammed it shut. Holding the box awkwardly in both hands as if not certain whether to hurl it away or bury it, he delivered to Marozia a glare containing the full weight of his fury and contempt.

"I did not ask you to bring me the fetus," he said with undisguised venom.

She shook her head. "That is no fetus, my liege. That is the heart of your abortionist."

The High Curia was soon dismissed, though many matters of the secret council were still undecided.

A few hours later the guards who had waited outside Marozia's door delivered the apothecary's body to the churchyard of Santa Agata de Caballis, where for forty ducats he was given Christian burial. With the remaining money from Marozia the guards fled into the hills.

The next day Marozia sent word to the pope that she would be joining her family at their summer villa in Tusculum and would remain there until autumn.

Chapter 8

Rome is insufferable in summer. The noise, the choking smells, the oppressive crowds, all seem intensified in the heat. By noon the pavement is hot enough to singe the feet and the stink of people and rotting vegetables is enough to drive a sane person to madness.

All those who can do so flee the city to the surrounding campagna, and our family was no exception. We were fortunate enough to have a villa at Tusculum in the Etruscan hills. By mid-July preparations to move the entire household from the Aventine to this country estate were under way.

Tusculum was an enchanted place, a little walled village nestled in the hills. The town was tiny, with a motley garrison, and if it should ever be besieged, I don't know what the villagers would do. There was no need to worry, though. These were poor, simple people with few possessions, not likely to be tempting prey. Even the town's archdeacon had only one item of any worth, a crystal chalice that was brought out once a year for Easter.

As for our villa, it was well outside the walls along a country lane that wound up the mountain to Saint Martila's lair, a minor sacred site still visited by pilgrims. The villa was built in the traditional manner, with an ample atrium full of flowers. This garden was surrounded by spacious low-ceilinged rooms and broad porticoes facing east and south. The peasants on our land harvested grain and grapes and kept milk cows and pigs. Of course, every household had a kitchen garden as well.

Many of my happiest memories are associated with Tusculum. There as young girls Marozia and I awoke to the sound of birds and the smell of baking bread, and we were free to wander through the fields and ride the ponies that my father kept in his stalls. It was a quiet life and very peaceful.

I do not mean to imply that we were isolated. Even at Tusculum business with Rome continued almost as usual, with visitors frequently making the day's ride along the Appian Way to visit the family and consult with my father. When visitors arrived there was always much feasting and celebration, with wandering minstrels or mummers called in to abet the proceedings with their songs and entertainment.

As I grew older I participated more in these feast times, especially after I took my vows. I had an obligation as hostess in my father's house whenever my mother was absent. I also took a lively interest in the talk of the wealthy and powerful personages who came to pay their respects.

True, I felt torn by my duties to Saint Peter's and to the pilgrims in Rome, whom I could not very well attend from Tusculum. However, the danger of yellow fever was always present in the city during the summer months, and it was perilous to mingle with the populace in the pestilential damp heat by the banks of the Tiber. Had I sickened and died, I could not have performed God's work even in the winter, and so I consoled myself with the refreshment that the country brought to my soul. I had my reward; I felt stronger in spirit, ready to return to my tasks at the season's end.

*   *   *

In the litter on the way to Tusculum Marozia told me she was pregnant. I said nothing, though I feared the consequences of her rashness. Many of the clergy would be threatened by a papal heir. I knew there would be danger to Marozia and to the unborn child if the pope wished to claim this infant as his own. I knew, too, the fear that must be in Marozia's heart, for giving birth is terribly hard and frightening.

When we arrived at Tusculum, we fast fell into the routine of daily life. We rose early and bathed in the spring-fed pool, splashing and laughing. I saw then how Marozia was rounder and fuller in the belly and breasts. It looked odd on one so young, for she was still only fourteen, to see these signs of motherhood. She asked me not to tease her, but I did anyway until she grew angry.

I think she feared that after the birth she would turn fat and ugly like the peasant women in the village. They sat in their doorways, suckling their infants and looking like grandmothers. I reminded her that our mother had given birth twice and had not lost her looks.

Of course, Theodora could have told Marozia far more about all this than I, but our mother wasn't at Tusculum that summer. She had gone to Tivoli, ostensibly to enjoy the social life of the patricians who frequented the gardens there. Secretly, I believe, her purpose was to meet Bishop John and indulge in her amour.

If Father knew anything of this he gave no sign. The villa at Tusculum was run just as usual. Maria saw to the cooking and feast preparations, Tiberon supervised the house servants and Marozia and I behaved like schoolgirls. Only Tasha seemed unhappy and I paid little notice, not knowing of her crime. I assumed she was subject to despondency and decided to let her be. And perhaps too I was sinfully grateful that Marozia now paid more attention to me than to the slave.

* * *

Inevitably Father noticed Marozia's condition, and as the days passed he regarded her with increasing concern. I thought it fearfully unjust for her to withhold her confidence from him, especially when he must discover her sooner or later, but nothing I said or did could make her speak to him forthrightly.

In the end it was he who broached the subject.

"Yes, Sergius is aware of my condition," she replied.

"And what does he say?"

"He does not wish me to have the child."

Gaius nodded. "Then of course you will comply with his wishes."

"I will not," Marozia said steadily. "I have already made that clear."

Gaius looked at her in astonishment. "My dear daughter, you know, this is not fitting. If you should have a bastard whom the pope refuses to recognize as his own—"

"I am sorry, Father," she interrupted. "I will have this child. If, God willling, I live through the lying-in, there is nothing in heaven or on earth that can prevent me from holding this infant in my arms."

"But Marozia—" Gaius was aghast. "What then? Don't you realize the danger? A natural heir to the pope in our family!"

A mocking tone came into Marozia's voice.

"Isn't that what you wished?"

He flinched. "No, no, not at all. I only wished—"

"To see that your position as princeps was secure."

"Nothing of the kind," Gaius replied impatiently. "Sergius looked on you with favor. You should be flattered—"

"I am not flattered," she snapped. "The pope is a brute."

He evaded her hostile eyes. "Nonetheless, he has his wishes."

"And none dare to deny them?"

He drew in his breath. "Your bitterness is unbecoming, given the favor you have been shown."

"Unbecoming, yes." She let out a short, bitter laugh. "Perhaps experience has made me ugly."

"Marozia, please."

She fell silent and turned away as if to go. After a hesitation he stopped her.

"One moment. I must consult with the pope. Since you refuse to prevent the birth, he may see fit to arrange a marriage for you."

Marozia shook her head. "That may be, Father, but I think I have had enough of arrangements between men. When the time comes, I shall marry whom I wish."

"No!" Enraged, Gaius resorted to his habit of stroking his head, rubbing in a circular motion as if to grind down the heat of his anger. "No, daughter, you will not marry whom you wish. You will marry suitably."

"And who might be that?"

Gaius considered this. "Petronius," he replied shortly, "the son of Marcellus."

At first Marozia said nothing, regarding her father with a look between pity and loathing. "Petronius," she said at last. "Feeble, pompous and above all a patrician. With such an alliance, your reign would be assured indeed, would it not, Father?"

He glared at her. "No, you misunderstand. I am only thinking of your future. And he *is* suitable."

"Perhaps," she replied witheringly, "but I am afraid I am not suitable for him."

Without another word Marozia turned and left the room.

*   *   *

She recounted this conversation to me nearly half a month later. It was a day in mid-August; we were making our way at Marozia's behest up the dusty hillside path toward Saint Martila's shrine.

We were both dressed in pilgrim garb, cowl, simple tunic fastened with a tattered rope, thong sandals. I think Marozia regarded this costume as something of a prank. She had cut herself a willow staff, which she leaned on heavily, mocking the foot-weary believers who passed along the path. I was hard put to prevent her from talking to these strangers, especially a group of Celtic monks with their odd tonsures, the hair long in back with a half circle from ear to ear across their shaven pates. They were sincere and pious. Marozia, on the other hand, was merely a Roman lady on a day's outing, and I feared her ways would offend them.

We had visited Saint Martila many times as young girls. What possessed my sister to want to return there that morning, I do not know. It was a whim.

Once we were on our way her enthusiasm infected me. I might truly have believed we were pilgrims had I not from time to time caught a glimpse of her shining face beneath the cowl and seen the skip in her step as we made our way up the road.

"Petronius might not be so bad," I suggested when Marozia told me what had transpired between Father and her.

"Lena, you dunce." She sighed in amazement at my innocence. "Petronius reminds me of the eunuchs they keep on the Via Lata—very sweet, very polite and quite useless."

I was put out. "I fear you have grown selfish, Marozia, to oppose Father this way."

She lifted her willow stick and planted it firmly in the dust. "You trust and obey Father," she replied in an undertone, "and I'm sure he deserves your respect. He has made the right choices for you. But for me?" She looked away, hiding behind the cowl. "For me I am not so sure."

"But Marozia, you cannot rule your own fortune. You must accept—"

"Must I?" Her sharpness startled me. "I am not so sure. You forget, Lena, that I have been sleeping with the man who wears Saint Peter's Crown."

"I have not forgotten."

She continued as if she had not heard me. "There is nothing he does that could not be done as well by a woman—except rape. In that," she spat, "he is a beast."

I could not help glancing over my shoulder to be sure no one had heard her.

"Never fear," Marozia laughed. "We're only pilgrims, remember? No one would suspect us of heresy." Then her mood brightened. "But look, Lena, see how far we have come." She stood poised at the edge of the winding roadway, peering down at the hillside and the valley.

It was indeed a beautiful sight, magical Etruria with its green, rolling hills, its fields and villas and vineyards. From where we stood, we could just see our own villa, its dark shadow cast in sharp relief against the landscape. There on the eastern slope, warmed by the morning's rays of sunlight, the whole earth seemed alive with color and beauty. In Tusculum a bell rang out, echoing over the valley.

We continued, stopping only once to bathe our faces in a clear stream. Near the peak the breeze from the sea announced itself, first in the sighing trees, then touching our skin with warm pressure.

There was a tiny chapel at Saint Martila's lair, which huddled on a rocky crag that faced north. Martila had lived ten years in a small cave behind the chapel wall. He never left the hillside, but ate the moss that grew on the rocks and picked at carrion left by the crows. His prayers for a vision were rewarded at sunrise one Easter morning, when a great stag appeared to him leaping over the rocks. Between the ten prongs of its antlers there burned a shining cross.

In the chapel the antlers with gilt cross between were carved in stone above the altar. The skull and loincloth of the saint rested in the crypt below, and before the altar lay the offerings and votive candles left by his devotees.

As children we used to visit the shallow cave behind the chapel wall. It was damp, frightful and mysterious, with little niches carved by the saint's fingernails, where he kept his relics. Though long vanished from the earth, the sacred hermit would appear to us as we touched the walls and sat in the hollows left by his body. His voice was soothing, his words kind, but his living presence was strange to us. Sometimes I would swoon and Marozia would have to carry me into the sunlight.

On this day, however, we avoided the cave and knelt by the altar. Other pilgrims were present, but they were silent and no one disturbed us. I thought perhaps Marozia's worship was a mockery, as our short pilgrimage had been, but she rose abruptly and crossed herself, and I saw that there were tears in her eyes.

On our return we passed through Tusculum. It was market day and the streets were bustling. We still wore the garb of pilgrims and by now we were genuinely dusty and tired. Hence, the merchants ignored us. Only the purveyors of relics approached, offering us articles from Alexandria and Jerusalem.

We turned away from these false relics. We were hungry for sustenance, not mementos, so we purchased half a ducat's worth of plain black bread.

I saw the baker glance with astonishment at Marozia's

fair features as he handed her the loaf, but he said nothing. Although I urged her to leave before we were recognized, she insisted on lingering. Much to my dismay her steps led toward the lower part of the town, the dingy grey houses with sagging, moldy thatch where the pagans were known to live.

The very air of that district seemed vile. As we passed the shuttered houses, I caught a gleaming eye taking note of our passing. I was truly alarmed and tugged at Marozia's sleeve, but she seemed preoccupied with her surroundings, pausing in the bleak, litter-strewn square to stare at the dilapidated hovels.

It was then that I saw him. How long he had been following us or where he had come from I do not know. One instant the street was empty and the next he was there, skittering from a doorway, sidling toward us with a crablike gait. With straggly hair, unkempt beard and a twisted nose he appeared nothing short of bizarre. Even so, there was something oddly attractive about the little man, and the flash of his crack-toothed smile was almost alluring.

With purposeful movements he approached Marozia and bowed to her as if they were old friends. I saw her hand clutch the staff more tightly, but she made no move to back away.

After bowing he withdrew a short distance, keeping a wary eye on the hand with which she clenched the staff.

"I hardly recognized you, signorina," he began in a croaking voice. "To muffle such beauty under horse rags, however pious, is a shame. By zooks, God pulls a funny cowl over the best of us." He glanced at me curiously. "You note I wear no cowl, since I have nothing to hide. God must look at me as I am, and I Him, more's the misfortune. Why should I wear a cowl, since then I would be cowled by Him, and He would be a mere herder leading his cowl to pasture?"

"Come, Marozia, let's away," I urged. "This is blasphemy." He turned an eye on me again. I must confess, a quiver ran through my soul. Never have I seen such a debased individual, and so arrogant besides. But his smile was strangely winning.

"And this must be your sister Lena. I have heard of her piety but not her loveliness. To be wasted on a nun!"

Extraordinary as it may seem, I could detect no sarcasm in his voice. As he gazed on me, I blushed and turned away.

"A shy one. And you, Marozia—you made my night, but by the morning I was unmade. Hair tousled, shirt undone. Or was that my master? So faithful I am, I hardly know. One of us wept, tore his hair, rent his shirt—it must have been he, for mine is still intact, and this is the only one I own. Threw himself, I say, into despair. And why? Because a fair woman does not have the kindliness, the gentleness, the manners to return a small message with a token of her favor."

This conversation was all strange to me, but Marozia seemed to understand. "Why have you come here?" she asked.

"Why? To bring good news, of course. My master creates good news. It precedes him like a beam of light and follows like a wave of goodness."

"How did you find us?"

"Why, visiting your father, of course. Nepi has fallen to Alberic, thank God. The benefice is reclaimed from the Saracens and rests in Christian hands. That's the good news. The better is that Alberic's heart has not changed." He winked. "The danger is that Alberic will ring Rome as he would ring a lady's finger. The problem is that Rome may fall to his winning before the lady falls to his wooing."

Marozia paled. "I trust you said nothing of this to my father."

The little man winked again. "Gaius Theophylact is a broad-minded Roman. He should be kept informed."

Marozia gasped and clutched her staff for support, but the man only shrugged.

"There is information and information," he said placidly. "An army may be in formation, as is my liege's, and that is the good news I bring to Theophylact. But lovers in formation, that is a more subtle and intimate form. And there I had nothing to report to the Senator."

Marozia stared at him, a flush creeping across her cheeks. "Get out of my sight," she commanded.

He looked aggrieved. "Then there is nothing I can say to Alberic? Nothing at all?"

Marozia hesitated and I saw her touch her pocket. Then I remembered the ring I had seen in Rome. Suddenly I understood.

I must have made some gesture, for Marozia looked at me, her eyes full of pleading. "Lena, you must say nothing."

"Marozia," I burst out, "Alberic? A Lombard?"

I was instantly sorry I'd said anything, for my disapproval seemed to touch a chord.

"And what of it?" she demanded. Angrily she turned back to the man. From her loose sleeve she took the remaining chunk of our bread and tossed it to him.

Startled, he lifted his hands to catch it, missed and juggled it on his fingertips before it fell to the dust.

Marozia laughed. "There, Gallimanfry. Deliver that with my compliments. Mind you give Alberic the crust only, for that's what he's worth to me."

Grinning, Gallimanfry tucked the bread under his arm. "A steep temptation, signorina. This is one loaf that has had a fine nesting. I shall be tempted to gnaw—nay, devour and ravish—it. But I shall refrain. Such is my deference to my master.''

"I do not wish to see you again—nor your master." Marozia flashed a look in my direction as if to say, There, I have dismissed him forever.

But Gallimanfry seemed imperturbable. "Gladly. I and my loaf, we go. Farewell, Marozia. Good day to you, Lena, whose temperament I would know better. You seem milder than your sister, but there may be heat withal." He swiftly retreated up the street.

After he went I heard a shutter slam, then another and another. I looked around at those grim pagan houses and felt a cold hand clutch at my heart.

"Marozia . . ."

She sighed. "Come along, and quickly. I want these rags off me. I need a bath. Oh, how could he? How could he?"

She repeated this to herself as we made our way out of the walled town toward the safety of the Theophylact villa.

In the days that followed I tried several times to speak to her about Alberic, for I could see that the encounter with his servant preyed on her mind. She anticipated my disapproval and dismissed the entire subject. "Don't be ridiculous," she said curtly. "He is nothing but a tribesman, a barbarian."

However, I could see that her thoughts tormented her and made her restless. And my father, unconscious of this private battle of hers, did not make things easier. The news of Alberic's added victories had impressed Gaius, and he seemed hungry for further information. He took to questioning every messenger, clergyman and senator who came to visit to discover the latest news about the Lombard.

I too was haunted, but by that strange messenger we

had encountered on the streets of Tusculum. I would often think of his dark glittering eyes and hear again that voice. *I had heard of her piety but not her loveliness*.

From the lips of such a man came the first compliment I had ever been paid.

Chapter 9

In the hills of Tivoli the summer ponentino blew gently, lifting the leaves of the olive trees with a gentle sighing. On the grounds of Hadrian's ancient villa stood numerous buildings, reproductions of the grand temples and dwellings the emperor had seen in his travels. Here were reconstructions of the Lyceum, the Academy, the Prytaneum and the Stoa Poecile, all copied from their original Greek counterparts. There was a replica of the Egyptian sanctuary of Canopus, with a canal cut through solid rock. Swimming pools and domed libraries dotted the estate.

Strolling through the gardens, pausing now and then to gaze at the splendid vistas, were two figures. The man, tall and lean, strode with proud intensity that betrayed itself even at a distance. He was dressed in the Byzantine manner, with a glowing yellow surcoat that came below the knees. At his side in a flowing *cyclas* that seemed to take wing on the summer breeze walked a slim, dark woman with coal-black hair and dark brown eyes.

They lingered by a marble fountain, watching a pair of swans drift on the pool. Their voices could just be heard above the splashing water.

"You seem dissatisfied," she murmured.

"I do not wish to leave you." There was irony in his voice, but his hawklike, piercing eyes were serious.

"Must you, then?"

"Yes. There are matters to attend to in Ravenna. There is an abbess there, one Engemunde, who is causing unrest among the people. She speaks against high taxes."

"Surely you can have her dispatched to a distant abbey—Saint Catherine's in the Wilderness, for instance."

He shook his head. "She has followers. They must not be aroused."

The woman turned to him with a sultry, seductive look. She laid her hand on the chest of his magnificent robe.

"There is something else that troubles you."

"Something else, yes," he replied vaguely, gazing over her head at the swans.

"Ambition." Her voice was almost mocking. "Ambition, dear Bishop; it is a yoke you wear like a sash of office."

"Is it so obvious, then?"

She laughed. "Indeed yes, though perhaps only to those who love you."

"A small number, I am afraid." His features twisted sourly.

"Tell me what is on your mind."

He paused. "Can you not guess?"

"Cherished desires must be spoken." Her voice was low.

"You know, then. I would be pope."

"I have guessed as much. It would suit me as well, dear John. The present pope is no one I love overmuch."

"Nor I."

She smiled. "Perhaps together we can accomplish what cannot be put into words."

"Surely you know there is a decree against the Bishop of Ravenna becoming Bishop of Rome," he replied. "Poor Formosus was tried for just such a crime."

Theodora waved her hand impatiently. "Trumped-up

charges, and the tribunal was a mockery of justice. We need not fear that such a farce will be repeated.''

He frowned. "What, then? Must we change canon law?''

"No, merely put it aside." She shrugged. "Besides, it is an old Byzantine ruling. No one takes seriously the laws of Constantinople.''

"As you say . . .''

"Why so hesitant, my love? Do you doubt it can be done?''

He looked sharply at her. "I have no doubt I can win the support of the Curia, but the people of Rome—they are another matter.''

"You forget I am senatrix," she reminded him. "Between my husband and me, we have them well seen to.''

"Ah, but your husband—''

"Don't fear, John. I can bend him to my will.''

"Even if he discovers—''

She placed her finger to his lips to quiet him.

"Even if he discovers." Again she smiled up at him. "We no longer share a bed, have not for years. If you ask me, he is incapable of jealousy, while I, as you know, am a woman of passion.''

"Yes." The smirk was prominent on his lips. "That I certainly know.''

Their favorite retreat was the Maritime Theater, a stately apartment where Hadrian used to go to read, write and paint. The marble building stood on a small island in a moat. A drawbridge on rollers provided the only access.

Inside the Maritime Theater the chamber the handmaidens had arranged for Theodora was warm and simple. Camel skins captured from the Saracens were stretched on the floor to form a thick carpet, and the single canopied bed was covered with fine silk. From the bed beneath the

chamber window the lovers could gaze out on the hills of
Tivoli.

Bishop John's body was lean and sinewy with dark
hair across his chest and shoulders. As Theodora raised her
arms to him, he knelt and lifted off her delicate white
cyclas. Beneath it her skin had the warm tint of summer gold.
Her breasts were firm and full, a mature woman's breasts,
with dark round areolas that he touched with his tongue.

She quivered and seized his head, pressing him between her breasts. For a moment he was held there. Then
as if in anger he lunged for her, throwing her back against
the coverlet.

A thin, sharp cry escaped her and she closed her eyes
in an ecstasy of longing while his greedy hands reached for
her, smoothing the length of her flank to her taut buttocks
and thighs.

Hungry for him, her hands searching and clinging,
she reached out, touched the moist, soft tip of his manhood.
He shrank away as if he had been stung, so sensitive was he
to her touch. But an instant later with something like rage
he spread her wide and plunged into her.

She clung to him, shocked, almost terrified. Why this
violence? Why this brutal attack? And then her body understood what her mind could not explain, as lightning streaks
of pleasure spread through her, emanating from that single
core of response, the measure of her excitement, the thrill
she could not control.

Suddenly nothing was separate, nothing distinct. His
body and the hungry attack on her senses turned to warm
waves, tangled with her aching need for him, with the
breeze from the window and the hiss of his hot breath in
her ear, with the moistness of her skin and the perspiration
of his loins. Arching, they seized one another and held,
throbbing with pleasure, crying aloud in the sunlight.

*   *   *

At dawn's pink glow the mists rose from the moat, from the fields and hillsides. Now he was prepared to go. She was not sure when she would see him again.

Resplendent in the yellow robe, he bent over her, kissed her lips, then her nipples, her navel. She reached out for him.

"What must I do to obtain that thing we spoke of?" he asked.

"You must never stray far away nor for very long." Her black hair was spread on the coverlet. Her voice was soft. "And . . ."

"And what, my love?"

"Riches. You must send me such riches as I have never possessed before."

He smiled with all his cunning, cruelty and ruthless ambition. "Of course, my love. How could I deny you anything? Together we will possess the empire."

Chapter 10

During our summer's respite in Tusculum the pope remained in the city, driving the guildsmen mercilessly at rebuilding the Lateran basilica. I am told that Sergius would stride among the scaffolds, kilns and forges like a man possessed, shouting orders, berating backsliders, directing that lazy workers be dragged off and lashed or imprisoned.

Though the Lateran complex stands beyond Celian Hill, well away from the reek of the metropolis, still the heat and the vapors creep in. For the workmen slaving night and day, driven to the limits of their endurance, the suffering was unimaginable. Slaves dropped in their tracks and were crushed beneath marble stones.

Masons on narrow scaffolds in the clerestory would work to the point of exhaustion and beyond, sometimes remaining in place for days at a time. Food and drink were brought to them by carriers, but they found no relief from the relentless heat. They suffered attacks of delirium, praying aloud and conversing with the saints and spirits who were the subjects of their work.

Some could endure no more. They would lose all consciousness of danger. Poised on teetering planks as perilous as a mountain cliff, they would step away from their work, turn to the vision of a welcoming saint and leap to death below.

Such men had sacred burials. They were honored in their guilds. But those who malingered or begged to be relieved of their posts were disdained by their peers. Only a few refused outright to labor for the pope. They were tried by the chancellor of the Lateran and sentenced to the garotte.

As time passed the steady labor bore fruit of a kind more glorious than any of us had imagined. By the turning of the fall equinox at the end of September, Sergius had succeeded in completely rebuilding the basilica and restoring its votive gifts. What had been scarcely more than rubble was transformed into an immense edifice as splendid and well proportioned as any Constantine could have imagined.

To that emperor's original plan Sergius had added a portico of ten columns, and he divided the interior into five aisles. Ancient columns of granite and verd antique were restored, and the tribune was now ornamented with gleaming mosiacs. Light from the clerestory windows shone on the faces of the saints and martyrs, and the tesserae of glazed ceramic seemed alive with glorious color.

In a new annular crypt accessible to pilgrims rested the sacred skulls of Saint Peter and Saint John; the remnants of the Savior's garment lay in a separate niche. Sergius also had encased in magnificent reliquaries the Ark of the Convenant, the Tablets of Moses and the Rod of Aaron. To these riches were added an urn of manna from heaven, the Virgin's tunic, John the Baptist's hair shirt, the five loaves and two fishes from the Feeding of the Five Thousand and the dining table used at the Last Supper. Surrounding these precious relics were golden ampullae holding balsam and sacred oil. The pièce de résistance was the splendid polyptych that hung above the altar.

Over the principal doors were graven the words of Pope Sergius III, claiming just credit for the rebuilding of the Lateran. To the surprise of all Romans the work was dedicated to the glory of Saint John. For this reason the basilica would be known henceforth as Saint John's Lateran.

The dedication of the basilica was a triumph for Pope Sergius. Even the most conservative of patricians, those who looked back to past glories of Rome with aching nostalgia, were forced to acknowledge the soaring achievement of the papal architect. There were whispered comparisons to the Forum of Augustus and the Temple of Venus Genetrix, which was sinful, since no pagan edifice could rival a Christian work. However, such comparisons meant something to the people of Rome, who cherished their history, and they flocked by the thousands to Lateran to see the towering achievement of their own guildsmen.

Now Sergius' popularity rose as never before, and his sins were forgotten. Adding to his triumph was the bounty of a plentiful harvest. The summer had been a good one, both for grapes and for grain. Every freeholder owed the pope a tenth of the harvest. As the papal storehouses filled to overflowing, Sergius ordained that the abundance be disbursed among the people. Carts and carriers jammed the streets. Queues in front of the storehouses turned into festival entertainments with drunkenness, music, the banging of tambours. Merchants and guildsmen prospered as never before. Praise of Pope Sergius III was on everyone's lips.

In the house on the Aventine our return from the country was followed by days and nights of hectic activity. Marozia was in her fifth month and must take care, and her condition was visible to all. Neither she nor Father had sent word of this to my mother at Tivoli—nothing the whole summer long—and when she returned Theodora was furious. My father bore the brunt of her rage and as usual, was stoic in the face of her wrath.

I see now that our mother was changed in many ways by that summer at Tivoli. She had assumed what can only be called the arrogance of power. In times past I had seen her fly into a tantrum when she was crossed. That demanding nature was still there, but now it had hardened, matured. She was no longer a woman protesting her impotence. Now she had filled the role to which she had been elected. She was a senatrix, demanding respect, and her commands were immediately obeyed.

This was curious to me, but to others I believe it was frightening. I saw the servants glance at one another in terror when someone slipped or dropped a goblet or served a guest from the wrong side.

Their fears were justified. Frequently Theodora would order a handservant flogged for some slight misdemeanor. Even guards were punished at her command. And a slave from the kitchen who had saved forty-one draconae to purchase her freedom was returned to lifelong servitude for leaving her post too soon after dinner.

My father was dismayed by all this, but there was little he could do. Rarely had anyone been punished in his service; the guards especially had never been disciplined. Now my mother took the opportunity to remind him of his laxness. The household was in a shambles, she scolded. The Theophylact militia was useless. If Gaius was too softhearted to correct the situation, she would see to it herself.

A perceptible change came over the household. Meals were served on time and more orderly. The guards showed more discipline and I noted that their halberds, which used to show signs of rust and age, now gleamed with daily honing and polishing. Even old Tiberon, my father's chancellor, looked more alert these days—though alarmed might be the better word. Whenever my mother entered the room, he lifted his bowed head a bit higher and his shifting grey eyes took on an expression of nervous anxiety.

The change had an effect on city matters as well. Applicants who used to linger all morning in the atrium, gossiping and imbibing while they awaited a leisurely interview with my father, now were confronted with short, brief messages from Theodora. The least of them were simply told to go away. Threats, bribes and cajolery did them no good; if Theodora refused to see them, they had no recourse. Those who remained on legitimate business were quickly interviewed and dispatched.

Visitors also noticed a change in the material prosperity of the Theophylacts. This too was my mother's doing. Almost from the moment of her return carts began appearing at the door, piled high with tapestries, serving vessels, carved chairs, fine chaises with ivory devices and camlet cushions with gilt tassels. Four new litters with staves of ironwood were borne through the foyer to the atrium. Our old ones were given away, their curtains used for rags.

Even the taste of our food and the aromas of our private chambers were enriched by signs of wealth. Instead of plain capon we were served Apullian duck with carob seeds, minced tarragon and fennel and a glaze of cherry wine. Where country balsam in cambric packages had once lain near our pillows, we now had silver-lace sachets freshly stocked with Eastern frankincense and myrrh from Byzantium.

And now when Theodora saw visitors she wore beryl and sapphire rings, a fur-lined surcoat and a white lynx plastron with jeweled buttons. Whereas a modest woman would have worn wimple and cowl, she bound her head in a white satin cornet and a silver fillet. The fillet was encrusted with polished gemstones of topaz, ruby and amethyst, and her thick black curls were braided through with chains.

It was a style we had never seen before, a magnificent array. The most sophisticated patrician would gasp in amazement when Theodora entered the room, and even I, her own daughter, was awed by the spectacle of her haughty radiance. I felt it must be a sin to touch her hand, much less kiss her cheek, that I must humble myself even to speak with her.

Of course there were those who whispered against her. Her style, they said, was borrowed from the Saxons, from the court of King Alfred the Great, dead only ten years. They said the ostentation was unbefitting a Christian woman—and of course they wondered about the source of this newfound wealth.

My father was distressed by the talk. When at last the petitioners were gone, when no one but I and a few servants remained in the house, I often overheard their arguments.

"How can you shame us this way, dressing like a strumpet?" he stormed. "You are the talk of Rome."

"At least I am not a laughingstock," she answered coldly.

"Don't be so sure. How do you know what people are saying behind your back?" There was a pause. I could only imagine her expression. "Listen to me, wife. I have striven to build the Theophylact name. I am respected by the people, honored by the Senate. Through my efforts, at last there is peace in Rome. But now with your flaunting of riches and your arrogance you dishonor us and drag our name through the mire."

"You forget, husband, that I too hold senatorial power." Her voice was cold.

"So much the worse."

"I will not grovel and scrape to make a false show of

modesty. I am a senatrix. I deserve respect and I shall exercise my power as I wish."

"And defy the wishes of your husband."

"Yes, if I must to live in a manner befitting my station."

"We have always had enough."

"We have lived like paupers."

"We have lived simply and well." The fury was breaking through his voice now, his frustration bordering on outrage.

She was indifferent. "You may live as you wish, husband. As for me, I believe I shall have the comforts of my station even if you are too miserly to provide them."

His open palm resounded when it struck her face, hard, like a carpenter's mallet striking wood. From my mother there was only a sharp cry. I heard a jangling, clinking sound, as if some piece of jewelry had fallen to the floor. Then came a tense silence and I knew the heat of wild emotion that must be flooding through their veins. Closing my eyes, I prayed that neither would strike to kill.

Finally I heard my mother's voice as from a long way off. "You will be sorry for this." Then there was nothing but her rapid, retreating steps.

In the days that followed I behaved as if both guilty and aggrieved, avoiding their looks and passing with downcast eyes whenever either of my parents was near. It was foolish of me, I know, and yet I felt great tragedy lying in wait for these two people whom I loved and honored. I had witnessed the first act of their private drama, and nothing could be done to turn aside the course of disaster.

Chapter 11

For a time after we returned to Rome Marozia remained with us at home. Servants and attendants were warned not to let it out that she was back, for she had no wish to be summoned to the Lateran.

Marozia's presence made my mother uneasy, that I could see. Theodora spoke little to her daughter, and I caught her now and then eyeing Marozia with hostile envy. It was clear to me that a confrontation was bound to ensue. It happened one afternoon when my sister was in the loggia embroidering a shawl.

Marozia looked up as Theodora came into the room. Theodora had entered by mistake, thinking no one would be there. She was about to rush off when my sister's voice stopped her.

"Stay, Mother, and tell me why you avoid me."

Theodora assumed a haughty pose. "You accuse me wrongly, daughter. The harvest accounting is upon us. I am much occupied with matters of the estates."

"Yours and Father's?"

"Yes, of course. Why do you ask?"

"Come, come, Mother." Marozia laid down her embroidery. "Everyone knows where you spent the summer and in whose company."

In spite of herself Theodora could not still the flush

that crept into her cheeks. "Who knows? Of what are you
accusing me?"

Marozia shook her head in disbelief. "Surely, Mother,
you do not still consider me a child."

"Make yourself plain," Theodora demanded.

"Bishop John."

The name hung in the air. "What of him?" Theodora
said shrilly. "What slander have you heard?"

"For God's sake," Marozia burst out, "look around
you, Mother, at this flow of wealth, this sudden ostentation.
Do you believe anyone thinks it comes from our coffers?
No, Mother, until now the Theophylacts had only two
possessions—humbleness and modesty."

Theodora's face was suffused with rage. "You are no
one to talk. You, the pope's concubine."

"No, Mother." Marozia's voice was ice. "Do not
take that tone with me." She rose from her seat. "You
and I understand each other, I believe—even if Gaius does
not. He thought a simple trade was possible: his daughter
for the pope's favor. But you and I, Mother, we realize
that women are not so easily swapped. What we bring to
men comes at a far greater cost, does it not?"

Marozia laughed at Theodora's look of surprise. She
continued, "Yes, I have made peace with myself, but it
comes at a price. Do not forget this, Mother: Father
bartered me, but it was you who led me to market."

"I rue the day I did," Theodora confessed.

"I warrant you do, but that will not negate the action.
Now, what is to be done?" Marozia touched her belly. "I
bear the papal heir. The child of Sergius is about to
become a Theophylact. Father intends I shall be pawned
off once again, this time on a patrician. What do you
think, Mother?"

Theodora could not look into her daughter's eyes.
"You must not bear the child."

Marozia's laugh was taunting. "Ah, you and Sergius think much alike, I see." She studied her mother a moment. "Perhaps you do not know that Sergius sent his abortionist to my chambers."

At this Theodora looked up swiftly, but her expression did not change.

"Yes," Marozia went on, "but as you can see, he failed. It cost him his life. Believe me, Mother, I will not allow anyone to harm this child."

Theodora came a step closer. "You are unreasonable. Surely you know that all women have times when they should not bear children, when they must—"

Marozia would not let her finish. "When they must violate the womb and destroy the life within?" She shook her head slowly. "Not all women, Mother."

"Marozia, be sensible," Theodora pleaded. "Whose child will it be? Who will care for it? You cannot expect the pope to take custody."

Her daughter smiled, "No, I myself will do that—and whoever will marry me thereafter."

"Yes, but—I beg you, reconsider."

Theodora's voice quivered and faded. Suddenly she found herself at a loss for words. For a long moment Marozia studied her mother. Then she nodded, understanding at last.

"This Bishop John is a restless man, is he not? Perhaps he yearns for something more than the Exarchate of Ravenna." A glance told Marozia she had guessed the truth. "Bishop John will not stop at murder, and he knows he can count on one member of the Senate in his pursuit of higher office. As for you, Mother, no scruples stand in your way. None, that is, but this: it would cost you your soul to subscribe to the murder of the father to your grandchild. Better for you if the child were never born, even though its soul go straight to damnation."

"No," Theodora burst out, "that's a lie."

"Nothing of the kind," Marozia replied impassively. "Only bear this in mind, Mother. I am aware of your intentions, as I am aware of your passion for Bishop John. I shall watch and wait. I will not give up the child."

The day after this conversation Marozia was abruptly summoned to the Lateran. Armed guards arrived at the house to accompany her. She went unwillingly, I know, dreading her first encounter with the pope after a summer's absence. She gave sharp orders to Tasha, and her leave-taking from my parents was brusque and formal.

I could see there was some hesitancy in her manner. She took great care, dressing in a white surcoat that covered her swelling form. Just before she left I caught a glimpse of her looking in the glass, turning this way and that as she straightened the tucks and folds of her mantle. When she saw me watching, she seemed embarrassed.

"May I come to see you?" I asked.

She dismissed my question. "I don't expect to remain long. The pope does not want the baby and I expect him to renounce me. I cannot imagine why I have been sent for."

"Perhaps, after all," I ventured, "he will accept it as his."

Her face turned bitter. "I doubt that." She straightened her shoulders. "In any case, it is not his to claim. Whatever happens, this infant is mine."

Deterred by the grim set of her features, I chose not to argue with her. There was one question I had wanted to ask ever since that day in Tusculum, and I feared to let the opportunity pass.

"What of Alberic?"

She paled. "Why do you mention his name?"

"Marozia, please, I can see that—"

She turned away. "No, Lena, it's out of the question.

He made eyes at me at the Palio and that is all. The man is a bounder. You saw the servant he sent, that Gallimanfry, wretched creature.'' She would say no more.

At the Lateran palace things did not go quite as Marozia expected. The summer had worked a change in Pope Sergius. He seemed older, greyer and more serious. Any man who erects buildings and inscribes them with his name must by nature begin to think of his future; and so Sergius had at last stopped to consider who would follow him.

There was restlessness in his domain. Frankish warriors and marauding hordes of Magyars had again crossed the Alps. Berengar, the Lombard king, was fighting furiously to hold them off and to strengthen his hold over the northern provinces. In the south the Saracens grew increasingly restless, their attacks on wayfaring travelers bolder. A number of landholder bishops had acceded to the infidels' crushing demands rather than risk the sacking and pillaging of their benefices.

When there was restlessness in the Papal States, Sergius knew, the tremors would reach the Lateran. He must make a show of securing his power in order to maintain his grip on the papacy. As yet he had failed to come to a decision and now the idea of inheritance occurred to him.

True, he had not wanted a child, but if it were a son, Sergius would have an unprecedented opportunity to name him as the successor to Saint Peter's Chair. It would shake the church to its foundations to establish a blood line where none had existed before, and the uproar in the Synod would be enormous; but if Sergius succeeded in such a bold move, his primacy would be assured.

"I wish your lying-in to take place here at the palace," he told Marozia when she appeared before him.

She laughed. "You have already made one attempt on the child's life, Your Holiness. Do you expect me to offer a second opportunity?"

At Marozia's words hatred flickered in Sergius' eyes, but he could not deny her point of view. She had every reason to fear for the life of the infant.

He considered a moment, then rose from the ornate Byzantine chair where he had been sitting. "I will strike a bargain with you, Marozia. You shall choose your own midwife and handmaidens. Even the guards may be Theophylact's if you wish. If the child is a girl, I will renounce all claim and you may return to your father's house. If it is a boy, however—" He paused. "I shall announce the lineage and proclaim him my heir. Afterward you may marry whomever your father chooses."

Marozia did not hesitate. "Whether girl or boy I shall require forty thousand ducats, the House of Hadrian on the Via Lata near the Church of the Apostles, and the quitrents of the Province of Perugia."

The pope glared at her. "Any whore's mother could give me a child," he muttered.

She nodded. "Certainly, my liege, but not a Theophylact child—and no Theophylact comes cheap."

"Your suggestion is unconscionable."

"It is you who want the child," she reminded him, "yet you have me to thank for its life. Surely you would not expect the source of your greatest treasure to be left empty-handed."

The pope eyed her coldly, then shrugged. "As you wish, but if it is born dead, you receive nothing."

She smiled. "It goes without saying, my liege. I will inform my father of our agreement."

She knelt before him, then rose as easily as if a great burden had been lifted from her.

*　　*　　*

All Marozia's belongings were sent to the Lateran palace. A midwife from the neighboring house of Thelonius —Vespasia, who had helped my mother through labor —moved into the room next to Marozia's. As the pope had allowed, she posted her own guards. No one of Sergius' household was allowed to enter or leave her quarters without permission.

Tasha, of course, was Marozia's constant companion, and I made it my bound duty to call from time to time. However, apart from me Marozia had few visitors. She again took up the delicate embroidery she had begun during her early days at the Lateran.

She also renewed her acquaintance with Sister Teresa. Often I would find them together in the garden, strolling arm in arm.

They were there that day in late October when I came bringing news of a fateful arrival.

Alberic the Lombard at last had come to Rome.

Chapter 12

He was here at the request of my father. He entered through the east gate of the city, where the Via Praenestina and the Via Labicana are joined. Wearing plain mail that reached to the knees covered by a green tabard with a gilt lion rampant, Alberic was accompanied by forty men with broadswords by their sides and brass-studded reins in their black-gloved hands.

The arrival of the Lombards spread profound uneasiness through the city. Had the Roman militia not been forewarned by Gaius, the soldiers would have been alarmed by this sudden infusion of military strangers. But the casual pace of the Lombards on their chargers and their almost childlike curiosity about the sights of the city soon stilled the fears of most Romans. By the time the troops arrived outside my father's house, they had a large train of curious onlookers.

Alberic's name was soon on everyone's lips. Young boys rushed forward to touch the bridle and pluck the mane of the black stallion that had won the famed Palio. Alberic good-naturedly brushed them aside, but the high-spirited stallion was not so patient. Twice the great black rose on his hind legs to thrash out with his forefeet, and one of the boys was knocked unconscious by the flailing hooves.

Of course I was impatient to see this man—so much

so that I quite forgot I might come face to face with his messenger, Gallimanfry. Welcomed by Gaius and Theodora, the Lombards streamed into the atrium and I suddenly found myself confronted by the shaggy figure with his shambling gait and crack-toothed smile.

"Well met, well met, Sister Lena," he murmured, his smile increasing to enormous proportions. I drew back—involuntarily, I must admit, for I had no reason to fear him. "There, there," he continued. "I don't bite—'cept where biting gives pleasure, and that's more nibbling than gnawing, and certainly not poisonous. Unless poison be a pleasure, or vicey versy. Ah, but I see I have offended you. My talent, it seems, more's the pity." And still muttering, he passed by, downcast, as if I had hurt his feelings.

Alberic had already entered the atrium, warmly escorted by my father and mother. He and Gaius were soon involved in close discourse, and I remember how intense he seemed. Though my father was a tall man, Alberic had to bend his head to speak to him. That posture in such a powerfully built, broad-shouldered figure gave him the appearance of an eagle, as if he might at any moment swoop forward and clutch his prey in his talons.

I noticed uneasy stirring among his men from the moment Alberic entered. One in particular—Lambert, his second-in-command—followed Alberic with his eyes and seemed constantly poised to respond to the general's bidding.

Whatever my father had to say to Alberic held his attention. They passed the soldiers, moving on through the atrium and into the council chamber, never once breaking stride, in the manner of men who have immediate and urgent business. As they passed, however, Alberic gave an almost imperceptible signal to Lambert, who immediately bowed and murmured to the soldier.

Relegated to a secondary position, my mother bore a

sardonic expression. I thought at the time that she must already be scheming. As for Gallimanfry, he had completely vanished and I did not see him again for several days.

Save for a single detail the outcome of the meeting was most satisfactory. Gaius agreed that Alberic would be formally presented in the Senate. His claims to the duchies of Spoleto and Nepi, which he had taken by force, would be recognized. Of course there would be some opposition from Marcellus and the patricians, but my father could assure Alberic that it would be overcome. Gaius had promised a particular favor to Petronius the son of Marcellus and could now be certain of Marcellus' support in the Senate.

It took only a moment for Alberic to realize what Gaius hoped to gain from an alliance with Lombardy. The Saracens were an obsession with my father. Day and night he talked of nothing but the infidel horde that had invaded the shores of his beloved land. Every traveler, every visitor who had escaped the hands of the brigands was brought before him and subjected to the same interrogation. Where was the encampment of Caliph Husayn? How strong were his forces? How many ships? How many horses? How many bowmen and cavalry?

Each reply strengthened the deepening hatred in my father's spirit. Yes, the Saracens grew stronger each day. Their arrogance was boundless. They raped Christian women and pillaged the church's prized benefices, thieving precious relics and exacting tribute from people who could not even pay tithes to their own bishops.

As my father listened, his cold wrath would grow to unbridled fury. He would pace, clasping and unclasping his hands. I knew the image before him—the horrible sight of my Uncle Paul's crucifixion. Gaius longed for vengeance, which Alberic seemed instantly able to appreciate.

"Honored Princeps," he said, "it seems we share an enemy. The Duchy of Spoleto reaches far to the south. The Saracens are clawing at our borders, and soon they may come knocking once again at the doors of Rome." He peered into the atrium, where his soldiers were lounging, playing dice and talking. "My men are used to battles and long marches. I have no doubt they will prevail when they are called to do battle against the infidels." He turned again to Gaius, looking serious. "But our conquests will be futile unless the pope is behind us."

Gaius smiled triumphantly. "I can assure you of his complete cooperation. The favor of my daughter has sealed a certain trust between us."

Alberic frowned. "Ah yes. That is the final matter I wish to discuss."

"What is that, General?" Gaius rubbed the top of his head.

"Your daughter Marozia. Is she spoken for?"

"Please, Alberic, we must not—" He glanced at the young man. "Do you not know? She is expecting to bear a child and has gone to live at the Lateran."

Alberic paled. "But surely Sergius cannot take a wife."

"No." Gaius rubbed his head more furiously, his eyes flitting about as if to find some means of escape. "Still, the pope wishes for a son . . . as a device—"

"That's outrageous," Alberic exploded. "The Chair of Saint Peter cannot be inherited. That defies the very principles of the church, canon law, the teachings of Saint Peter."

"I'm afraid canonical tradition has no bearing on the state of affairs." Gaius shook his head. "Pope Sergius is concerned, quite understandably, with the longevity of his reign. Given the brevity of his predecessors' rules, you must admit the man has reason to fear."

"But surely, if you support him—"

Gaius shrugged. "My family's influence extends only so far as the lay powers invested in the prefecture of Rome. We cannot control clerical disputes or intrigues surrounding the papacy."

"Still, if the pope should marry Marozia. . . ." Alberic's voice trailed off.

Theodora, who had been listening to all this, stepped in. "He will not marry," she said harshly. "He only wants to have an heir who will live at the palace. Pope Sergius has one goal and one goal only—to preserve his power." Theodora looked from Gaius to Alberic. "If you want his support in your campaign, you must act like subordinates. Pope Sergius, as we have seen, cannot bear rivals."

Neither man attempted to argue with her, for both recognized the truth.

It was Alberic who replied first. "Nonetheless, honored Theodora, I must ask you to consider the fate of your daughter. She cannot continue to live with this man, bearing his children."

"What are you suggesting, General?"

Alberic bowed. "I hereby present my suit, with the knowledge and full consent of my liege Berengar, to make Marozia my wife."

Theodora could not help smiling. Suddenly this lean, fair man seemed almost like a peasant making a formal request for an indulgence.

"Your offer cannot be considered," she began.

Gaius cut her off. "Marozia has been spoken for. It is already settled. Petronius the son of Marcellus has made a suitable offer for her hand, and I have accepted on behalf of the Theophylacts." He paused and again there was that look in his eyes as if he wished to escape. "I cannot go back on my promise."

After a long silence Theodora sighed and turned to Alberic with a smile that was almost triumphant in its bitterness. "You see, my husband has settled the matter for us all."

Alberic's bow this time was short and quick, a gesture of anger rather than honor. "I would not be so sure." He looked from the senator to the senatrix, his blue eyes piercing. "Now if you will excuse me, my men and I are worn out from our travels."

"Of course, of course," Gaius breathed in relief. "My household and the best of Rome's are yours. You will join us at the feast table tonight. Rome has been abuzz with talk of your victories. Our citizens are impatient to meet you."

My father ordered the servants to show Alberic and his men to their lodgings in the Castel Sant'Angelo. Then, excusing himself, he began preparations for the night's entertainment. All the while, I warrant, there lingered in my father's mind the image of those piercing blue eyes, so mild and yet threatening—the eyes of a young, proud general who had suffered his first defeat.

"But why here?" demanded Marozia when I told her all that had transpired. We were standing in the Lateran garden with Sister Teresa nearby.

I had expected from the moment of my appearance that Marozia would dismiss Teresa, but she seemed to have won my sister's confidence. She remained only a few paces off, arms folded beneath her cassock, her eyes downcast, listening to every word with consummate interest. Throughout my story, while Marozia moved about in agitation, asking for details of the conversation and particulars of the man's dress and appearance, Teresa remained immobile.

"Clearly, Father had a reason for inviting him," I

continued. "Surely you have observed how the Saracens have become an obsession with him."

She nodded but did not speak.

"Nothing concerns him but to drive out the infidels and avenge Uncle Paul's death."

"And that evil little man, that Gallimanfry, what of him?" she asked. "He appeared only briefly, spoke to me and then was gone. I cannot say what has become of him."

At the chancellor's name I thought I saw a flicker of response from Teresa, questioning, almost fearful. Then she turned away.

As for Marozia, her agitation could not be disguised. In every word she said you would have heard anger and distrust, as if Alberic, meeting her only once, had offended her. I knew better and my heart ached for her; she was trapped in her private torment, powerless to change her condition.

"And Petronius? Father told him that I was betrothed to Petronius?"

I nodded again and Marozia heaved a great sigh. "Oh, Lena, how stupid and foolish it all is. If I live I shall be mother to a bastard, wed to a fop and the slave of Rome. But what am I saying? I shall die. I know it, Lena." She touched her abdomen, now large with the child. "I know it. God will not permit me to live. Oh, Lena—" She burst into tears, flinging herself away.

I started after her, but I felt a hand on my arm and heard a gentle, restraining voice. "No, let her be."

I looked in astonishment at Teresa. These were the first words she had uttered today.

"I must help her." I pulled my arm away. "Can't you see she's distressed?"

"God will heal her distress."

I was a nun, and I knew the platitudes. The curl of

my lip must have given me away, for Teresa turned to her true purpose. "There is something I must speak to you about."

"What is it?"

"This Gallimanfry you mentioned. What kind of man is he?"

I described him as best I could, noting Teresa's reaction. Her eyes widened and she assumed a haunted look, as if some dark memory had returned to shatter her repose.

"Then you know the man?" I inquired at last.

Her expression astonished me: she blushed red. Though I had paid little attention to her appearance up to now, I realized that under the wimple and cowl she was quite pretty, dark and slight with long lashes and deep amber eyes.

"There was such a man," she murmured at last. "He belonged to Saint Basil's rule. But he went off to become an adventurer."

"Perhaps it is a different person," I offered.

"Perhaps," she replied, but the faraway look in her eyes told me she did not think so.

It was several days after this conversation that I once again encountered Gallimanfry. I was on my way to Saint Peter's and had just crossed the Tiber on the bridge leading from the old south gate to the Castel Sant'Angelo. In the shadow of that grim circular fortress the beggars would congregate, pleading for alms from the pilgrims. Though I could offer them little, I felt it my duty to greet them.

On that morning I scarcely had time to say a few words when suddenly that man with his shambling gait and crack-toothed smile came wandering out of the fortress. He seemed startled to see me and I thought if I gave him only a nod I could escape. He recovered at once, though, and stepped in front of me, bowing profoundly.

"Let me pass, sir," I said.

He smiled and bowed again. "I cannot, sweet sister. If I let you pass, I let opportunity pass, and opportunities come to me so rarely I must hang on to them with all my might."

"Sir," I pleaded, "the sacraments at Saint Peter's are already being read. I am late."

"Your mission, signorina, is it not Christian?" He looked me up and down. "What could be more Christian than to show mercy for the helpless? I am not always helpless, but in your presence I certainly am so, and if you absent yourself rudely, I shall be ruined."

At this I blushed. "I am not being rude, sir. I do not wish to ruin you. I just do not wish to speak with you."

"Ah, I ramble on too long."

"You certainly do that."

"Rambling is my chief fault."

"Apply yourself to cure it."

"I cannot cure it but with your help, sweet nun."

"Then please be brief."

"I am."

There was a pause.

"Gallimanfry!" I was so impatient I nearly shouted his name. Several beggars turned around, amazed, I am sure, to hear me raise my voice.

"What?" he answered. "Oh, yes, signorina. You speak my name. Oh, bliss! Your beauty, you see—I fell to musing."

I seemed to be sinking into a vortex. "Gallimanfry, I beg you. I do not wish to be uncharitable or rude. Merely say what you must and be gone."

"What I must say is that I have fallen in love with you. I am entranced. Bothered. This is a pickle. I came on my master's mission to woo your sister, and here I sabotage the enterprise, pining for your sister's sister, whom you know well and I would know better.''

"Please, sir." My face was burning with shame, and I could hardly keep my hands from trembling. "I am a nun. I cannot permit you to go on like this or to offer the least prospect—''

"A nun, yes. I see by your drab robes, your cowl, your sandals. Yes, I see what you mean. That ring weds you to Christ. Too bad." He scratched his head and appeared completely put out. "Well, I've done it now. Overlooked the virgin. Seen only the woman, whose radiant beauty—''

"Perhaps you remember another nun," I said sharply. "One named Teresa."

I expected him to be shamed into silence, but apparently there was no such thing as shame in his character.

"I remember Teresa," he said dreamily. "I remember sweet sauce. I remember the singing sparrow and the lark on the hillside. There is the stuff of life and then there is the sauce that goes on top. Teresa, I must confess, I will remember for her sauciness. You, signorina, from what I can discern, are the very stuff—''

"I grow weary of your hyperbole," I interjected. "Will that be all?"

He sighed. "I wish only to say that I hunger for perfection, which is so close now I could touch it, were I allowed. There is a refinement here that defies my understanding and a feeling in my heart—for I do have a heart, whatever blubber you may see layered on top of it—a feeling that I am in the presence of that which I should not let pass, but which, out of courtesy, I will." He stepped aside.

"I thank you."

"Look at me, rather. Just once."

I did so. I cannot say what I saw there, for I suddenly felt as if I had been seized and hurled into an abyss of wantonness.

"And now I thank you, signorina."

"You may call me Sister Lena," I said stiffly.

"Sister whatever," he replied.

He spoke no further word but watched motionless as I passed by and continued to Saint Peter's.

Chapter 13

Alberic was presented in the Senate and his speech was a great success. Proclaiming the loyalty of Lombardy and its determination to protect Christendom, he spoke eloquently but humbly of his conquests, mentioning by name the generals and captains who had aided him in his enterprises. All who listened understood the implications of his words.

It was time for the Romans to accept the Lombards in their midst. The years of dissension must be ended. No longer were these the barbarian hordes who had once spread fear through the countryside and disorder all across the kingdom. Now, with Alberic's acceptance of the laurels of the Senate, he became a subject of Rome, entitled to all the privileges and honors the city accorded her leading citizens.

It was inevitable that the Lombard have an audience with the pope. In early November a summons arrived, delivered to Alberic in his quarters at the Castel Sant'Angelo. Donning his green tabard and iron crown, Alberic rode through the streets to the Lateran palace. There he was greeted by the full assembly, for the Curia had just convened, and he passed through the four antechambers into the throne room.

Following the Byzantine style, Alberic prostrated himself at the foot of the papal throne. Above him sat Sergius, wearing the tall white Phrygian cap with its imposing array of golden adornments.

"So, Alberic, we meet for the second time." Sergius gestured for the Lombard to rise. "It seems there is no limit to your conquests."

Alberic spoke the respectful formula: "Everything I have belongs to the church. It is mine only in accordance with your will."

Sergius laughed. "Come, come. We will expect small ransom from you—only that you leave our bishops in peace."

Alberic's face was impassive. "As you know, Your Holiness, we have not interfered with the functions of any church holdings."

Sergius nodded. "See that you don't." He brushed the issue aside, but there was an edge to his voice. "You do us a service by protecting our borders," he continued.

"I would do more than that." Alberic lowered his hand to the hilt of his broadsword. "The Saracens threaten my lands as well as yours. I stand ready to launch a campaign against them whenever the word of Christ calls me to the cause."

Sergius considered the young man. "And what do you hope to gain from such a crusade?"

"Safety for myself, for the Lombard people and for the lands of the church."

Sergius allowed him a thin smile. "I see you have been speaking with Theophylact."

"A noble senator. Rome is fortunate to have him."

"But perhaps he is much too obsessed with vengeance."

Alberic stiffened slightly. "Vengeance is something I can understand. The murder of a brother is not an easy thing to accept."

Sergius studied him for a moment, looking preoccupied. "Very well," he replied. "I shall consider the matter with my advisors. What benefice will you require in return for your services?"

"None, Your Holiness." Alberic paused. "However, there is a manner of reward I have discussed with Theophylact."

"What is that?"

"I wish to take the hand of his daughter in marriage."

Sergius looked mildly surprised. He could hardly conceal his smirk. "As you will," he replied. "To me she appears plain of face, but her manner is kind and simple, and perhaps that is best in a wife. Of course, Lena has taken a nun's vows, but I shall gladly release her from them for your sake."

"It is not Lena of whom I speak."

There was an audible gasp among the advisors and chancellors who stood about the room. Lambert, rapidly moving forward, touched his general's sleeve as if to restrain him, but it was too late. The pope regarded Alberic with burning eyes, his face flushed with anger. When he spoke again, his voice was heavy with derision.

"Lombard," he rumbled, "you are dismissed. We have no need of your services until you have learned to curb your tongue or your desires."

Alberic hesitated as if to argue, then thought better of it. He bowed. "As Your Holiness wishes. Only I warn you, the Saracens are gaining power. If you should change your mind, I stand ready to serve as before—with only the single condition."

"Your condition is unacceptable." Sergius spoke with tight-lipped fury.

"I regret that it seems so to you. My lords and bishops—" Alberic bowed to the rest of the company, which was stunned into silence by his boldness. "I take my leave."

And with a final prostration before Saint Peter's Chair, Alberic left the throne room.

News of the Lombard's insolence spread like wildfire through the city. The buzz of gossip in the streets was limited to speculation on the pope's revenge.

In the meantime Alberic made preparations for departure, but it was obvious he felt no great urgency to leave. A week stretched into a fortnight and still the Lombards remained in their garrison at the Castel Sant'Angelo.

Their presence was an insult to the Lateran guards, and there were occasional street fights between Lombards and Laterans, small tiffs that arose over a cockfight or a dice game and escalated into brawls. A Lateran guard was killed and one of Alberic's men castrated in an alley behind the church of Santa Lucia in Septem Via. And still Alberic refused to leave.

I had to pass each day by the looming fortress of the Castel Sant'Angelo. How could I ignore the Lombards who lingered about the battlements and passed along Hadrian's Aelian Bridge? I could not very well speak to the paupers and beggars at the walls of the mausoleum and ignore the rude greetings of the Lombards. I wished them gone, all of them, knowing that Sergius could not long endure Alberic's insolent presence.

One morning several days after Alberic's audience with the pope I was again approached by Gallimanfry. I tried to flee, arguing that I had pressing business at Saint Peter's, but he pursued steadfastly and finally induced me to listen to him.

The matter he wished to discuss was quite simple and utterly impossible: Alberic desired a meeting with Marozia. More, Gallimanfry confided, his master refused to depart from Rome until a tryst was accomplished. Who was there but I to accomplish the deed? I could come and go past the

Lateran guards; I was sufficiently trusted by Marozia to gain her confidence.

I was horrified. Marozia's distress I already knew, for Alberic's intentions were now public knowledge. If they were discovered, both would be ruined.

There was no help for it. It was clear to me that Alberic meant to remain until he could meet my sister. Day by day tensions in the city increased as the Lombard presence turned into a political factor in both the Senate and the Lateran. Marozia, who could not very well be kept in the dark about these events, walked about in a kind of daze, her life poised on a tightrope of irresolution.

But worst of all was that man who dogged my footsteps, pleading for my mercy, pleading for his master's sanity, for his own happiness—promising all if I would only carry out this simple matter. I would discover him in church, sneaking down an aisle to accost me, or again in the street, begging for my attention. I cursed the man, called out my father's guards to threaten him, and still he would not stay away.

Finally I gave in. Whether from weakness, shame or frustration I cannot say, but my resistance at last softened. I could no longer persist in my denials. I carried word to Marozia that Alberic wished to see her.

"Is this a ploy?" she demanded when I first broached the subject. "Does he think he can taunt the pope with my name and then beg mercy from my hand?"

I tried to calm her. "Marozia, please, you must meet with him. He has assured me by Gallimanfry that he asks for nothing. He only wishes to see you, to know whether you love him or not."

She shook her head. "Oh, Lena, if only he had not taken his suit before the pope it might have been possible, but now that he has already spoken to my father and to

Sergius, everyone knows what his intentions are. And I—what have I done? I have said nothing, nor given him the least sign of encouragement."

"I see now that I was wrong to bring you this message." I lowered my voice, ashamed at what I had done.

"Wrong? No, Lena." She took me by the arm, and it seemed her whole mood had changed. "I feel drawn to him, Lena—drawn by a strength as powerful as God's will. Ever since that day in Siena I have not been able to put him out of my mind. And yet we have never been alone together. Is it not strange how one man . . ."

I looked at her in sympathy, my heart softening. The raging, impetuous Marozia had momentarily disappeared. Here was only a sorrowing, vulnerable woman, desperate and in love.

She removed the ring from her finger and gazed at it, turning it slowly in her hand. "Tell Alberic I will see him. No—" She raised her head and looked at me with searching eyes. "No, tell him I must see him or I shall surely die."

When he refurbished the Lateran palace, Pope Sergius did not neglect the aging baptistery. It was an octagonal chamber adjacent to the basilica and could be entered by either of two doors. The first, of carved bronze, led into the sacristy; the second, of oak studded with brass, opened onto the main courtyard of the papal palace. The baptistery itself was small, scarcely thirty paces across, but it rose to a peak as high as the eaves of the church. Its proportions, therefore, were those of a narrow tower, tall and elegant, its vaulted clerestory surrounded by a rank of high windows that allowed the sunlight to pour down on the sanctuary below.

The chamber was stately and beautiful. At the center

in a circular sunken area of the floor stood a gold-encrusted baptismal font surrounded by a low wall that was capped by a series of columns. The ambulatory was of travertine marble. Both the walls were covered with mosaics of the saints.

Despite its beauty few clergy or parishioners ever visited the baptistery. It was used only for christenings and for formal assemblies announcing the pope's special ordinances. At night the tapers in the dark echoing chamber were never lit, since no one ventured in. Even during the busiest times of the church tribunals, when the nearby basilica echoed with shouts and disputations, no sound penetrated the thick bronze door and massive walls.

This was the place I had chosen for the meeting between Marozia and Alberic. It seemed to me the only choice. By day Marozia could not travel far outside the Lateran walls without being recognized, and by night a woman could not proceed far alone and heavy with child. As for Alberic, there would have been the utmost danger had he crept into the Lateran fortress.

I now see that it was rash and preposterous on my part to believe they could meet so close to the papal palace and remain undiscovered. At the time, though, perhaps because my mind was fevered with the urgency of this meeting, I could think of no better place of assignation.

Alberic would be dressed as a pilgrim, wearing a plain brown mantle. Coming to the basilica at nightfall, he would mingle among the penitents and wait until I appeared near the reliquary of Saint Michael. He would then rise and slip through the baptistery door, which I would unlock for him. Marozia, in the meantime, would have entered from the outside, through the banded oak door, which was left unbarred. I planned to remain within the basilica to rap out a warning if anything untoward should befall. Tasha would stand as a second guard by the oaken door.

On the night of the meeting I visited Marozia in her chambers to bring her the mantle, wimple and couvre-chef she would wear as a disguise. I wish I could say she showed courage that night, but on the contrary she seemed struck with fear. She could not keep her hands from trembling as Tasha and I helped her out of her maternal bliaud and into the nun's weeds.

"I must not do this," she whispered as I adjusted the wimple around her neck and brow. "He will betray me and I shall be ruined."

I brushed back a stray lock of her hair. "Marozia, my sister, be still. You have already chosen. Alberic waits in the basilica. Even now he may grow impatient at this unseemly delay."

"Lena, I cannot." She clutched at my wrist, clinging fiercely, her fingers like the claws of a falcon. "You go. Tell him he must leave at once. I cannot see him. If he insists—" She paused, her face flushed with the heat of despair. "If he insists, tell him I am in danger. Tell him the pope has threatened my life. Because he will, Lena." She looked at me with burning eyes. "Oh, he will destroy me if he should hear of this."

I pulled myself free. "No, Marozia. I cannot send Alberic away. You have already given your word. The time has come." Without allowing further room for argument I pulled the couvre-chef over her brow. "Say what you must to him, but be quick." I turned to Tasha. "Stay with her. I go now to the basilica. Remain here for the saying of three paternosters, and then you may come. Do you understand?"

Marozia was not listening. Standing mute, she twisted

the horsehair ring that encircled her smallest finger. I glanced at her only a moment to see that her wimple and cloak were adjusted in the proper style, but that single glance left a lasting impression, for I was struck by how radiant she seemed, how glowing. All fear had left her. She resembled some long-fasting nuns in that ecstatic moment before a divine vision appears.

This was no Christ she was about to see, but a man, lusting to know her, who touched her with something like divine fire. Seeing her dressed in my own simple garments, illumined, her beauty blazing with the power of a love I would never know, I felt a jealousy so piercing that I was forced to flee her presence.

I rushed down that dim corridor where the Theophylact guards nodded drowsily at their posts, out into the dim night and on to the basilica where the Lombard warrior awaited my signal to unite him with the object of his most passionate desire.

Chapter 14

As I crossed the open courtyard toward the basilica, I cursed myself a final time for my lack of caution. The moon was high and bright that night, the beams of its light pasted white as snow on the crenelated peaks and buttresses of the gigantic building. Even the pigeons seemed to think it was day. A whole flock of them, hunting and pecking in the courtyard, rose in a single mass, fluttering madly, only to settle again like a cloud as I passed.

It was an ill omen. For a moment I thought of turning back, rushing to Marozia and telling her everything was lost. But then I thought again of Gallimanfry and how he would persecute me if I failed in my duty. I grimly marched on, determined to carry out my task and see this ill-fated venture to its end.

As fortune would have it, the bright moon had wrought its effect on the populace. As happens every month at full moon, the waxing stirred masses of these souls from their homes. Cloaked in their penitential weeds, they moved like sorrowing creatures called to a tomb in ghostly files through the night, bowing, moaning and praying as they shuffled along. Inside the basilica the flickering tapers lit their faces as they passed one by one before the reliquaries, their limbs bent, voices singing, praying for relief from their suffering.

So dense were the crowds in the nave that I could not

well distinguish which monkish figure might be Alberic. I knew he would be watching for me, and I hurried to the reliquary of Saint Michael. There I swiftly knelt and rose, momentarily allowing my face to be lit by a votive candle.

From the corner of my eye I caught a glimpse of a lean figure dressed in monk's garb. He stepped out from behind a tall column and his shadowed face turned for a moment in my direction. I nodded and he withdrew behind the column.

My heart pounding, head dizzy with panic, I hurried down the aisle and stopped in front of the baptistery door. Though I looked around myself, no one seemed to pay any heed to my presence.

As I leaned forward to turn the key in the door, I silently gave thanks to Sister Teresa. How she had come by the key I did not know, but her generosity in giving it to me was far beyond the call of a nun's duty to her sister.

To slip the bolt and open the door required only a moment. My heart leapt at the grating sound as the great bronze panel swung wide. To me it was like a scream in silence, though it must have been only a thin squeal, for none of the penitents seemed to hear it.

Then Alberic was beside me, his tall figure hunched beneath the cowl, whispering, "God bless you, Lena."

After he passed by me and entered the baptistery, I pulled the door closed, leaving it unbolted, and moved away. Though I scanned the crowd for any signs of curiosity, neither clergy nor parishioners gave any sign of interest and I began to breathe easily, the more fool I. I was wrong to feel even a trace of relief, for in my worse imaginings I could not have construed the events that took place that night beyond the thick bronze door.

On entering the baptistery Alberic stood still, allowing his eyes to adjust to the cold white light that filtered down from the clerestory windows. He heard no sound. It took him only a moment to ascertain that he was alone.

He began to pace the ambulatory, his steps echoing hollowly like a mallet's hammering amid the vaulted rafters. Moonlight gleamed on the blue and scarlet mosaics.

Suddenly wood creaked as the oak door was pressed open. A shaft of light appeared, then vanished. A latch clicked against iron. Then silence ruled.

Neither knew how to begin. Now that they were alone together, the strangeness oppressed them. They should have known each other well; they should have rushed into each other's arms, and yet each waited, hesitant as a night creature, watching and waiting.

It was Alberic who came forward, pushing back the cowl that hid his features. "Marozia?"

"What would you have with me?"

"You said nothing, you sent no word." He could distinguish a sharp intake of breath.

Then she said harshly, "You are insolent and I am not at liberty."

"You have come—"

"I have come because my sister insists. Your suit to Pope Sergius has shamed me. How could you?"

Alberic struggled to see her face, but she was a shadow on the wall that moved away from him, eluding him. "Why are you torturing me in this way?"

"I could well ask you the same." Her voice was almost a sob. "You know I am not free. You know I carry his child—which he wishes to claim if it is a son, albeit the babe is a bastard." She paused. "Then what am I to do?"

The pleading in her voice was torture to him. Alberic reached out for her. "Only let me see you," he replied softly.

"I have told you," she moaned, "it is impossible. You must leave me in peace."

"No." He stood by the door, blocking her way. "No, I will not allow it. Not until I know your heart."

She laughed shrilly. "Is that the way you tribesmen go wooing? Know my heart, you say. Know the heart of one who feels nothing."

"I do not believe you."

"Believe what you will, Duke Alberic. I wish only one thing, that you may leave Rome and me in peace."

"No," he repeated. "I refuse to believe that such is your true desire."

She laughed again. This time there was a kind of frenzy in the sound. "I am mistress to one man, betrothed to another. And now you would rescue me from all my ills." The words seemed to catch in her throat, and when she continued it was in a hoarse whisper. "I would that you had that power."

"I will have that power." He was near her now. "Only I must know that you love me. You have given me no answer, no sign—"

"How can I know you?" she burst out. "We had but one encounter before you sent that wretched man to woo me."

"He is only a messenger. He delivered a small token into your hand." The question in his voice was unmistakable.

"Yes, that is so."

"Marozia, I beg you. Only let me see your hand— whether you wear the ring."

Her reply in the darkness was muffled. "I have lost the ring. I threw it away the moment it came to my hand."

He was even closer to her now, reaching out through the shadows. She had to step into the light to evade him. There was a rustle from her cassock and the moonlight streaming in from the clerestory lit her white couvre-chef.

"So this is your disguise," he whispered.

"Do not laugh at me, sire. I am in grave danger "

"Your hand."

"I must not—"

"Only let me see your hand and I will go." She hesitated, but she could see by his determined pose that he would not give in until she obeyed. Her long fingers were pale as a skeleton's, and he unmistakably saw around her finger the black horsehair ring.

With a sweeping, triumphant gesture Alberic stepped forward to lift her couvre-chef. For an instant he had the impression of dark panic in her eyes. Then she was in his arms.

His hungering lips kissed her cheek, her brow. Leaning down to her, he was gentle, towering and firm, his hands holding her head as his lips traced their course to hers.

She did not stir. She could not. But her eyes closed at his touch and she felt the molten fire, its hot fingers reaching to the depths of her, even to where the baby lay.

"No," she protested again. "No, Alberic."

"You must say that you love me, Marozia."

"No, we cannot. You know—"

"I will know nothing until you say the words. Beyond that everything will be plain."

He lifted her hand between his fingers and touched the ring. "Why do you wear this?" he demanded. "Why?"

Her voice was so low it was almost lost to him. "I cannot say. I cannot say."

It was then that they heard the furious knocking at the oaken door.

If Tasha had received the least warning, the tragedy might have been averted. I am certain she was fast in her duty and remained alert at her post. Fear alone would have prevented any sentry from drowsing off, but how could she suspect that the pope would come without guards, moving stealthily along the dark wall of the baptistery?

She had no warning. One moment she stood alone in the doorway, gazing into the night. The next he was upon her, rushing out of the shadows like one of those jinn she so feared. Her warning knock—that mad, sudden pounding that was heard by the lovers within—was too late and altogether futile. It was all she could do, as Sergius was already upon her.

The pope knocked her unconscious as he flung her aside. In a single motion he heaved up the latch and pushed open the baptistery door.

What did he see? Were the lovers still in each other's arms? Did the moonlight award that jealous and brutal man a tableau—a mockery of his tenderest affections, his most carnal desires—my sister and her proud Lombard sharing their first vows of love?

In an instant he was across the baptistery, his sword in his hand.

"So, Marozia, this is how you reward me."

With a triumphant, horrible gleam in his eye Sergius raised his broadsword, fully prepared to end my sister's life.

But men long used to warfare can act with the speed of gods, and so Alberic leapt forward, drawing his own sword through the opening of his cloak.

The clash of steel, the grinding of blade upon blade were followed by a scream of metal as the two swords parted. For an instant Sergius staggered, hurled backward by the Lombard's attack.

"No, Alberic," Marozia called out. "Leave me. Flee for your life. He will murder you."

Neither man heard her, for already they had set at each other again. The moonlight glinted from the blades of their weapons and the vaulted chamber echoed with their shrill clanging. Sergius plunged ahead, the broadsword slashing back and forth as he bore down on Alberic. With each sweep of the sword a great roar like the cry of a maddened bull escaped him.

Alberic was borne backward, gripping his sword in both hands. His blade was too light to withstand the battering strokes of Sergius' heaviest weapon. With each matching of steel against steel the man in the monk's robe was losing ground.

For a moment Marozia was transfixed by the madness in the steady, hard rhythm as of a terrifying martial tambour, a clatter of singing steel that could only end in death.

To her horror she saw the very blow that was meant to kill. Sergius leapt forward, the sword raised above his head, bellowing in triumph. The blade swept down, but this time there was no steel to meet it. Hurtled off balance by his foe's attack, Alberic staggered like a man thrown from a horse, toppling, falling . . .

At the last possible instant he spun and twisted away. Sergius' cry of victory turned into a howl of frustration as his blade met stone. The ring of metal ended in a jangling sound as the tip broke off on the stone floor.

The lopped weapon was no less effective. Without a moment's hesitation he turned to meet Alberic's ready sword. There was a change now, though, as if the greater part of Sergius' strength had gone into that final blow, as if he must fight with skill instead of anger.

Alberic was toying with him, meeting his strokes, then backing quickly, disappearing in the shadows, where the sweeping, blunt blade could no longer find him. Like a mouse luring a cat into a hole Alberic edged away toward the wall of the baptistery, where the shadows were dark as pitch.

Sergius followed blindly, possessed by his intent to

kill, heedless of danger. The two men were on the far side of the baptistery, close to the wall of the basilica, where the black night enveloped them. Marozia could see nothing, could hear only the steady battle noise of the two creatures lost in darkness. Then suddenly the clatter reached a fever pitch and the rhythm was broken. A man's voice roared triumphant . . . and ended in a wail.

Other sounds followed, bleak and horrifying, more shocking than the violence of battle: the thick, despairing thud of a body meeting stone; the slurp of the withdrawn sword.

Nothing moved in the darkness.

"Alberic," Marozia called softly.

Someone was lurking in the shadows, his breathing slow and labored. As he staggered toward her out of the black shadows, Marozia stood petrified. She gripped the stiletto beneath her robe.

Then she made out a monk's robe, the front darkened with blood. Alberic was clutching his side. He staggered and almost fell, the sword clanging on stone as it dropped from his nerveless fingers.

"Alberic . . . Alberic."

He stopped, his body swaying, and peered through the shadows toward her, almost as if he did not know who she was.

"Marozia?" His voice was clear. "Marozia, my love, what have I done?"

I waited in the basilica, never stirring far from the bronze door. At any moment I expected Alberic to emerge and make his way past me to be swallowed in the crowd of murmuring parishioners. Time passed and he did not appear, so I resolved to investigate. I slipped inside and closed the panel behind me.

Silence filled the chamber. At first I thought it

was empty, for across the way the oak door stood slightly ajar.

"Marozia?"

There was no answer.

I had turned and was about to leave when something in the shadows caught my attention—a shape sprawled against the wall. As I watched in fixed amazement, I thought I saw the slight fluttering of a white object against the floor.

Drawing closer, I was forced to acknowledge what I feared to believe—the moving object was a hand and the shape was that of a man who yet stirred with life. I bent down and touched him.

His hand was so cold and clammy it was like some underwater creature. The fingers quivered beneath mine. I felt the crusted jewel of the papal signet.

"Who . . . who?" The unfinished question, torn from the racked lungs of a dying man, unnerved me.

"Marozia?"

My face was in shadow. I wore the twins of the cloak and wimple she had worn in disguise that night.

"Pray . . . pray for me." His voice choked and his fingers, which I still held, trembled with the force of his dying strength.

"I will," I said softly.

"I . . . have . . . loved you."

A shudder ran through my body. I could not well restrain myself. I knew I must tell him what he longed to hear.

"And I you, Sergius."

The words acted as a balm on his tortured limbs. Through the dimness I saw the whites of his eyes, the lids fluttering, and heard the sigh of his voice. There was a low stirring, a groan, and his whole frame shook as if some ghoul had clutched him, wringing the last drops of life from his body. Then he lay still.

BOOK II

Chapter 15

Most Reverend Sir:

This messenger brings with him news that has shocked Rome and plunged the Holy City into turmoil. Pope Sergius III is dead, no one knows by what hand. He was murdered in the baptistery last night and his assailant fled without being discovered.

I realize this news will cause you to think of matters we have discussed. Be warned, it would be unwise to proceed. In its present state of disorder the Curia will be forced to act in haste in choosing a successor. I assure you, we have nothing to fear. My advice is to bide your time for both our sakes, and to remain in Ravenna.

When she had done dictating, Theodora made her scribe read the letter back to her. She sorely wanted to say something more personal, more private, but there was always the chance that such a message would fall into the wrong hands. For this reason it was necessary to leave some subjects implied.

She might also have added more emphasis in cautioning John to stay away, but she did not want to be too

vehement on this point. The bishop might glean information from her, but he would not take direct orders, no
matter how strong his respect; of that she was sure.

In the end she added only one minor change to the
message:

> Marozia has moved to the House of Hadrian with
> her servants. The pope made her a generous
> donation, the terms of which have been honored
> by the Curia.

To this too she might have added more details: that
Marozia had inherited all the church holdings of Perugia
and forty thousand ducats in addition to the most prized
house on the Via Lata. She did not, for she knew such
information would only enrage the bishop. Indeed, to Theodora herself it was a sore wound. This sudden prosperity
coming so soon to her daughter was almost more than she
could bear. However, there was nothing to be done about
it—except, as she had counseled Bishop John, to wait until
the time was ripe.

The Curia was thrown into chaos. Each faction of the
high church council eyed the other with suspicion, and no
man dared turn his back. The bishops were on edge,
expecting at any moment to be struck down by the same
hand that had wreaked murder in the baptistery.

As the funeral procession wove its way through the
streets of Rome, crowds of mourners wept and hurled
themselves to the ground, but their manifestations of grief
were short-lived. Pope Sergius III had scarcely been settled
in his crypt beneath the basilica when rioting broke out.
Crowds of looters stormed through the gates of the Lateran
palace, seizing whatever came to hand. Furniture, tapestries,
golden icons—even the pope's own clothing was pillaged
by greedy marauders.

Fortunately, Marozia's sinecure had been committed to paper. The pope had issued a cartulary, attested to and witnessed by the chancellor of the Lateran, which accorded to his mistress her forty thousand ducats, the House of Hadrian in the Via Lata and all quitrents owed by monasteries in the March of Perugia. It was an enormous inheritance, granting Marozia status that could not be disdained by any Roman.

When the chancellor read the cartulary aloud, he was derided by the Curia. Two days later he was found murdered, his body left by the Aurelian walls, his throat cut from ear to ear. Still, the cartulary was legitimate, bearing the pope's unmistakable seal. The inheritance could not be disavowed.

Marozia wasted no time before she asserted her rights and moved her belongings from the Lateran to the House of Hadrian. Within a week she had demanded tithes and had received emissaries from the Bishop of Perugia, who swore his oath of loyalty and paid a tenth of his holdings to the new liege. If he bridled at being ruled by a woman, he did not publicly give voice to his resentment.

Alberic had escaped without detection. On the night of the pope's murder the Lombard's disguise proved fortunate. Losing himself among the pilgrims, he slipped from the Lateran grounds and made his way through the streets without being recognized. When news of Sergius' death was brought to him at the Castel Sant'Angelo the next morning, he feigned astonishment and dismay. Later he joined the funeral procession on the Via Tiburtina and followed the cortege to Saint Peter's. In honor of Sergius he commissioned the glaziers of the atelier of Saint Cristobal to create a likeness in colored glass to be installed in the south clerestory of Santa Maria in Trastevere.

Alberic could not long remain in Rome. As the rioting and looting went on and the Curia continued to dispute the ascendancy, he took advantage of the confusion to slip quietly from the city.

There was no announcement, no warning. One morning the Lombards were posted in their castle, going about their business as usual, and the next, they were gone. The distracted Romans, who had greeted them with such a flurry of interest, scarcely noticed their departure.

Only I had any knowledge of Alberic's plans—and this from that gadfly Gallimanfry. He approached me outside Saint Peter's shortly after the funeral mass.

"I have a message from my master, dear Lena."

Still shaken, I was in no mood to indulge my tormentor. "I want nothing more from your master," I responded. "And as for you, Gallimanfry, I would be pleased to see you in hell."

He honored me with his crack-toothed grin and bowed low. "There are times when I share your wishes, dear Sister Lena. These nights are cold."

"Your chills do not interest me. Be off."

"My chills and my master's chills are the same, only we long for different heaters; he for a coal fire, and I for the molten glow of religious fervor."

"I have done enough for you and your master. For God's sake, let me be."

"I?" he demanded. "What have I done but bring lover to the arms of lover? Is that a punishable offense? Then punish me, for I'll do it again and again. But wait—"

Though I had turned away, the man leapt to block my passage.

"Wait, signorina. Hear only this: Alberic and I and all his men must leave tomorrow, but he will return for Marozia. Tell her this: she will not marry Petronius. She must not despair. Will you tell her?"

"I will tell her nothing, evil man."

"Then you wrong her, as you have wronged me."

I could feel the flush spreading to my cheeks. Had there been a weapon in my hand, I would have struck him down.

"How have I wronged you, pray tell?"

"By loving God more than me, dear Lena."

I looked about me then and my flesh turned cold. Never had I heard such blasphemy.

"Who are you," I asked angrily, "to compare yourself to God?"

He scratched himself beneath the chin and was silent for a moment. "My errors are fewer, my wit is greater, and I am not so fickle in my love. These are small advantages, I warrant, but still, you should count them when you think of me."

"I shall never think of you."

"Then think of my master," he murmured, "and deliver to Marozia the message I have given you. Tomorrow we'll be gone, more's the pity. Try to endure the days until we meet again, for I shall have to endure the same number. When next I see you, we shall be equals in longing."

And then with a grin he skittered away from me to be lost in the crowd.

The House of Hadrian, originally constructed during the second century of the Christian era, had been rebuilt many times. Recently Byzantine frescoes and ornaments had been added and the mosaics were of unparalleled brightness and beauty.

Marozia had chosen well when she selected this payment from Sergius. Now that it was hers, she spared no expense to create an elegant palace. Through its halls and antechambers carpets were spread, tapestries hung with care, chipped pilasters repaired and columns restored to their former grandeur.

Much of this work Marozia had to direct from her private chamber. She was now heavy with child and the midwife Vespasia had ordered her to stay abed. Growing restless at her confinement, Marozia seized every opportunity to defy Vespasia. However, this large-hearted woman could be as domineering as she was gentle, and she did not hesitate to decree what Marozia should eat and drink, when she should sleep and even whom she should see.

So it was to Vespasia that I first had to address myself when I came to visit Marozia. The midwife was a commanding presence to say the least, almost as wide as she was tall, with thick forearms and a head of wild, straggly hair. She blocked the doorway like a boulder, demanding to know what I wanted. Only when I promised not to distress Marozia and not to remain beyond the appointed time did Vespasia agree to let me pass.

Given the depth of the midwife's concern, I might have expected to find Marozia distressed, pale and sickly. Instead she was sitting up on her divan, chattering with Tasha. The room was bright with sunlight and Marozia was wearing a pale blue surcoat that draped gracefully over her swelling form.

I came to her side and took her hand.

"What news, Lena?"

I shook my head. "I promised Vespasia not to disturb you."

Marozia laughed. "She treats me as if I were an invalid. It's all so ridiculous. Still," patting her stomach, "I wish I were free of this burden."

"God grant you be, and that it be a healthy child."

I strove to be cheerful, but I saw that Marozia sensed my unease. Finally she asked, "What is it, Lena?"

I avoided her eyes, but there was no use delaying the news. "Alberic left Rome this morning with all his men." I glanced at her, but she seemed unmoved. "He had a final message for you."

I recounted all that Gallimanfry had told me, omitting, of course, his lurid overtures to my own person.

"Then he is certain to return, as he has promised," she replied firmly.

"But what of Petronius and your betrothal?"

She gestured impatiently. "It is nothing but a mockery. I shall not marry him no matter what happens, even if I must refuse him on the steps of the church. I could not endure such a creature."

"But Marozia," I cautioned her, "think of the consequences. You are already betrothed. Even now Petronius could demand his rights."

"Do not remind me," she burst out.

"I must remind you," I insisted. "You have set your heart on a man who will never be accepted in Rome, casting aside a perfectly respectable marriage—"

"To a perfectly despicable creature," she finished for me. "Thank you for your advice, Lena, but I don't need it. I do appreciate your kindness, though." She said the last warmly, but I could tell she wished for no further discussion of the matter.

I bowed my head and would have left, but she spoke again. "Wait, Lena. There is another matter that concerns me."

"What is that, Marozia?"

"On the night of my meeting with Alberic someone betrayed us."

I touched the cross at my waist. There was a cruel look in Marozia's eye. "How do you know you were betrayed?" I asked. "Perhaps the pope had spies looking out for you."

Marozia shook her head. "No, I was not followed, and Tasha will tell you that Sergius came by himself. Someone informed him."

"But who could know, Marozia? Only you and I were privy to our plans."

"You told no one else?"

"No one," I replied. Then a thought occurred to me that made my blood run cold. "Except—"

"Yes?"

I hesitated.

Marozia leaned forward. "Lena, you must tell me."

"I needed to obtain the key to the baptistery. I did not say for what reason, but I suppose it's possible that someone who knew you did surmise—" I stopped myself.

"Yes, Lena, go on. Where did you obtain the key?"

I shook my head. "I am surely mistaken, Marozia. You must forgive me for mentioning anything."

"Who, Lena?"

"No."

"You must say." Her dark eyes flashed. "If this person has betrayed us once, it will happen again. You know that is so." She paused, her eyes boring into me with a look of fierce concentration.

"Yes, Marozia, I know." I could not meet her gaze.

"Then who? Who gave you the keys?"

"It was Sister Teresa."

Marozia looked stunned for a moment but immediately recovered. "Teresa, of course," she said in an undertone.

"Please, Marozia, do not be angry. It is only surmise on my part. I do not know for certain. No one knows."

An odd look passed across her face. "You are right, Lena," she mused. "No one knows."

"Think how it has worked for the best. Sergius, whom you hated, is dead, and you are free—"

She cut me short. "Enough. Whoever informed Sergius could not have predicted the outcome. She is a traitor."

"Marozia, please, you do not know. It is only that she gave me the keys. She could not have been sure what they were for."

"You think not?" Marozia surveyed me coldly. "Perhaps you are right." She smiled. "Perhaps you are right. We shall see."

"What do you intend to do?"

"I intend to let Sister Teresa speak for herself."

I was horrified. "Not a tribunal. It would all come out."

"Oh, no, nothing so public as a tribunal." She went to the door and called for a messenger.

Tasha glanced at me, and I could see suspicion mingled with fear in her eyes.

Marozia spoke to the serving man in a low voice. "Send for Sister Teresa in the convent at the Lateran. Tell her I wish her to come for an audience tomorrow."

I heard the messenger's quiet reply. "As you wish, signorina." Then he was gone. I wondered even then at the great evil I had wrought.

The outcome was not long in doubt.

In the morning Sister Teresa arrived at Hadrian's Palace. Whether she suspected anything I do not know. Her interview with my sister was brief, and then she departed, having drunk a single cup of wine.

In the litter on her way back to Saint John's Lateran she suddenly turned ill. At the sound of her screams the bearers put down the litter and tore open the curtains.

It was already too late. Her face was black, her eyes bulged from her suffering and vomit ran from her lips. She died cursing Marozia. The guards, terrified out of their wit, left the litter where it had fallen and fled for their lives.

Sister Teresa was buried with honors in the third crypt of San Crisogono on the Via Aurelia.

Chapter 16

To the despair of Vespasia Marozia had frequent visitors at the House of Hadrian. My mother and father came at regular intervals, bringing special treats—oranges from Spain, fine wines from the valley of the Loire, Moorish silk damasks from Vienna and the rare mottled cheeses of the Visigoths in Roquefort.

In addition there were archbishops, deacons, dukes and messengers from Perugia who came to plead special favors or ask for immunity from the usual tithing. For the first time Marozia discovered what it was to have power, to mete out charity or justice, discipline or indulgence.

In the month of December, five days before Christ Mass, she celebrated her fifteenth birthday. Though Vespasia would not allow a major celebration because of my sister's condition, it was an opportunity for dozens of Romans to call at the house, leaving flowers and gifts in the atrium. Late in the day Marozia left her chambers and visited the indigo chapel in the north wing of the domus, where a mass was spoken for her patron saint and candles were lit in her honor. Bishop Lutense from Saint Peter's presided, and I led the prayer to Saint Cecilia.

Among the visitors that day—and one of the few admitted to Marozia's presence—was Petronius the son of Marcellus. It was not his first visit, but on all previous occasions he had been accompanied by my father, as if he could not quite muster the courage to see his betrothed without a chaperon.

In truth I felt sorry for him. Scarcely eighteen years old, he was pale and sickly with a sallow complexion and lank brown hair. Raised in the hothouse atmosphere of patrician society on the Via Lata, he had acquired all the worst traits of our inbred Roman nobles. His manner was affected and he spoke Latin with a slight lisp, curling his lip to emphasize his scarcasm.

He thrived on gossip and gloried in the downfall of others, relishing each new rumor that came to his ears. With my father he was respectful, but I believe this was only because he had never heard any evil gossip about Gaius. Toward his own father, Marcellus, he appeared surly, but beneath that surliness was a certain fear. I had no doubt that Marcellus had many times threatened his son with disinheritance, excommunication or worse.

If so, it had done no good. The youth failed to show any promise. His prowess as a sportsman and warrior was nil, and he was notoriously lazy. He could gossip, debate endlessly and woo women; that was all. As statesman, leader, arbiter or merchant he was useless.

Apparently Petronius regarded Marozia as a suitable wife, but I think he began to be troubled when she showed no interest in his wild claims of importance. His trivial revelations of social improprieties made no discernible impression on her. Her coldness he found unsettling, even intimidating. And, like most men when intimidated by a woman, he responded with exaggerated braggadocio and absurd demonstrations of wealth.

For Marozia's birthday Petronius brought her a gift of a large bas-relief, which was borne into her room by three sweating porters. With immense pride he launched into a lengthy speech praising the beauty of his "beloved" before he finally unveiled the work.

It was a tasteless bit cast in silver, portraying a number of the ancient gods and goddesses in obscene positions of copulation and fellatio. Gazing at the thing, Petronius ran his tongue over his lower lip and laughed mirthlessly. He seemed delighted at Marozia's discomfiture.

"Is it not wonderful, what these pagan workmen can do?" he asked. "Mind you, this can never be blessed. It will never be seen by any eyes but your own, my sweet Marozia."

"I thank you, Petronius," she replied stiffly. I doubt that any woman ever felt such revulsion toward a man as Marozia's for Petronius just then.

She would have sent him away at once, but Petronius chattered on and on. No rumor was too trivial for him. There was nothing in church or state that did not catch his attention, and yet he seemed to reduce everything to petty feuding, lusting and backbiting jealousy.

Following the death of Sergius, two bishops, both considered eligible for the papacy, had been murdered on their way to Rome. Petronius laughed as he recounted the manner in which they were assassinated. He did not believe for a moment that it was the work of Magyars—nor, for that matter, did anyone else. As a result there had been few able candidates for the Chair of St. Peter. The least likely of these, Anastasius, a little-known cleric from the diaconia of Santa Lucia in Septem Via, had been unanimously elected and approved by the Curia.

"He won't last long," Petronius laughed.

"Who do you think will take his place?" asked Marozia.

Petronius looked at her with mocking eyes. "Surely you can tell that better than I, my sweet. After all, Theodora is your mother, not mine."

"Theodora has nothing to do with papal matters," Marozia replied curtly. "She is only a senatrix."

"Only a senatrix, of course." Petronius touched his lower lip with his tongue, leaving a glistening streak of saliva. "But a senatrix with certain . . . ah . . . preferences among the clergy, wouldn't you say?"

Marozia fixed him with a chilly look. "Please speak clearly. I don't care for your innuendoes."

Petronius opened his eyes wide in mock horror. "Oh, my sweet Marozia, I did not mean to offend you, but surely you must realize that everyone is talking—"

"And you, Petronius, must realize that I don't care what people say."

"That may be so. Still, Marozia"—he leaned forward, his eyes lit with anticipation—"this liaison could have a most profound effect on the affairs of Rome. As we all know, your mother has certain ambitions for her lover."

Marozia continued to glare at him. "It would serve you well, Petronius, not to cast slurs upon my family."

"Slurs?" He raised his hand to his cheek as if she had slapped him. "Hardly that, Marozia. After all, Bishop John is a noble and well-respected man. But we all know that Ravenna is very far away, a long distance for two people to travel when they are in love."

She stood up. "You are beginning to weary me, Petronius. Shall I summon the guards?"

"Oh, very well, very well." He pouted. "Though it won't be so easy for you to dismiss me once we are man and wife."

"We shall see," Marozia replied distantly. "You forget that in a household the woman holds the keys."

He grinned and touched his crotch. "But the man holds another thing every woman wants." He stepped closer. "By our rights as a betrothed couple we have no need to wait for the wedding day."

She flushed. "I am fully aware of that, sir. Still, I prefer not to rush things."

"Have it your way, have it your way," he sighed. Then he looked at her with darting eyes. "We shall have a brilliant future, Marozia. Just think, the son of Marcellus and the daughter of Theophylact, the two great families of Rome, now combined in a single household." Winking, he pointed to her belly and grinned. "If that is a son—with Saint Peter's bloodline—who can stand in our way?"

He stepped back, one hand fondling the obscene bas-relief. "Won't it be splendid?" he lisped.

"Yes," replied Marozia without looking at him, "it will be splendid."

In the month of January Rome endured a steady, driving rain. It was a cold torrent that continued endlessly, filling the basins and fountains of courtyards pouring through open gutters into the great sewers that lay beneath the streets. From the Cloaca Maxima the water gushed forth into the Tiber, and soon all the lower plains were flooded, bringing misery and suffering to the inhabitants of the lands near the river.

In the ancient timber and brick insulae, which teetered perpetually on the verge of destruction, there was constant fear as the walls trembled and stones shook loose from their foundations. In all the rooms and terraces of the tenements the inhabitants huddled by smoking braziers, praying for the rain to cease. Few ventured into the streets.

The marketplaces were empty. In the storehouses of the diaconiae monks strove to feed those who came begging, but the grain rotted in its hulls. In time it swelled; occasionally it burst the very walls of the storehouses.

Passing through the streets, I could hear the screams and moans of starving creatures who cried out in their misery, calling on Mother Mary to help them through their trials. One night I also heard a tremendous roar as an ancient insula collapsed, crushing those who could not leap from the terraces in time. The next morning the hospices were full of the crippled and maimèd survivors to be cared for, and too many of the sobbing children were left orphaned in the streets.

Only one bit of news penetrated the darkness and isolation of those days. Despite the torrential rains, or perhaps aided by their cover, Duke Alberic had led a campaign to the city of Fermo, on his way conquering one town after another with ruthless determination. Then he moved on to wrest the coastal cities Macerata and Ancona from the hands of their Byzantine overseers.

At each conquest he placed his own dukes in power, Lombards who had distinguished themselves in battle. From each benefice and township he sent a messenger to the House of Hadrian to announce that the warring Lombard pledged his fealty and love to its mistress.

Inevitably Petronius heard of these visitations. He silently raged, but there was nothing he could do to prevent them. As for Pope Anastasius III, it was a sign of his waning authority and possibly fear that he did nothing to stand in Alberic's way. In the Curia they whispered that Benevento was slipping completely from the pope's grasp while Anastasius remained indoors, sheltered from political strife as he was from the rain, praying that his moment of trial would pass.

As for Marozia, she received the messengers, who arrived almost daily, with a secret smile on her lips. They cheered and sustained her during winter, lighting up the darkness, dispelling the rain and the chill.

It was shortly before dusk on the eighteenth day of February that a message from the House of Hadrian to me arrived at the Convent of Saint Peter's. On hearing the news, I hastened across Hadrian's Aelian Bridge and up the Via Recta to Marozia. The rains had subsided and everywhere there were citizens in the streets, wandering about as if dazed, talking quietly and striving to repair the damaged tenements.

Vespasia greeted me as soon as I arrived and for once seemed glad to see me; she was pale and fraught with anxiety.

"It is breech," she said as I came in the door.

I knew the danger, for many women died from such births. As if to confirm my fears I heard a howl of anguish, a voice that had I not known, I would never have recognized as my sister's.

I hastened to her room and found her clutching the counterpane, her face twisted in agony.

"I am dying," she whispered as I came to her bedside.

I took her hand. "No, no, Marozia. You must pray."

"How can I pray, when I—" She could not finish. Another piercing cry shattered the air, and she writhed beneath the sheets.

Vespasia had ordered Tasha to bring unguents and basins of hot water. Now, baring Marozia's swollen belly, the slave bent over her and slowly massaged the taut skin. Then, following the midwife's directions, she prepared a concoction of vinegar, sugar, powdered ivory and eagle dung. This she fed to Marozia between contractions, spoonful by spoonful, as the long hours of her labor continued.

Toward morning an iron magnet was placed in Marozia's hand and a chain of coral fastened around her neck. By then the contractions were frequent and intense, and it was clear that my sister's strength was waning. Vespasia had lifted the counterpane above my sister's abdomen, and I saw a single small foot emerge. It hung between Marozia's thighs as if suspended.

But Vespasia was prepared. She had mixed a decoction of flaxseed and chickpeas, into which she now dipped her hand and forearm. With a gentle motion, her eyes on

Marozia's face and one hand pressed to her wrist, Vespasia reached out with her moistened arm.

Her hand disappeared and into Marozia's eyes came a look of utter fear and horror. How my delicate sister could endure such pain I did not know. Her voice had become that of another being, a shrieking beast possessed of a woman's body.

Then Vespasia's hand emerged with two legs as tiny as twigs. She gave a sharp tug and the baby spilled onto the sheet as swiftly as a catapulted stone. There was a wail and I crossed myself.

"A boy," announced Vespasia in triumph. "A fine, healthy boy."

Marozia turned her head away and wept, but when the cord was severed and the child placed on her breast, she looked down and suckled him.

"God has blessed you, Marozia," I whispered in her ear.

Her face was damp with perspiration, the wet hair plastered to her head; her eyes were hollow from the long night of suffering; but there was blessedness in her eyes. I believe I felt closer to her then than I ever have before or since.

Chapter 17

During the following weeks many visitors came to view Marozia's newborn son. With squinting eyes, clenched fists and kicking feet he forbore all their attention, now and then bursting into tremendous yowls. He was a small baby, less than one hundred twenty drachmae in weight. His hair was fine gold-colored down that shimmered in the sunlight.

Marozia herself fawned over the child. She insisted on keeping him in her room and refused to relinquish him to a wet nurse. She would boldly uncover her breast and suckle him in front of guests. Of course, this was unseemly in a noblewoman. It was for peasants to nurse their own children; the daughter of a senator could well afford a slave to spare her sleep and preserve the beauty of her breasts.

I think Marozia's behavior was a form of defiance. Look, she seemed to say, this child is mine and mine alone. If you want him, you must tear him from my breast. She seemed to gloat at the effect on her visitors, above all Petronius, who grew squeamish at the sight of her bare brown nipple leaking milk. When the child began slobbering at her teat, Petronius would look around as if asking, What am I to do with her? Then he would seize the earliest opportunity to leave.

Marozia's defiance was more than symbolic, however,

for among those who came to visit there were many who looked at this child with unabashed curiosity, not free of envy. He was, after all, the son of Sergius III, a pope whom many had regarded with fear and loathing.

From the very first day, even before his christening, Marozia called the child Sergius. She seemed to take special pleasure in speaking the name in front of my father, reminding him of everything she had endured. The connection was not lost on any of her visitors either. Here, born to a Roman noble, was the son of a man whose name graced the highest portal of the Lateran palace. If ever there had been an opportunity for succession by inheritance, this was it.

Such succession would pose a danger to many. Their lands, their holdings, their fiefs and monasteries and benefices would all prove forfeit to a single liege if this young Sergius should ascend to power.

True, the canons of the church forbade it. The Curia, so far, still held control over Saint Peter's Chair, and who should occupy that chair was determined not by bloodline but by common vote.

In all of the Western Empire the Curia alone retained some semblance of democratic power. The Roman Catholic Church had done everything it could to obliterate the vestiges of Greek and Roman paganism. Even so, by now the church synod resembled nothing so much as the ancient Roman system. If it lost its hold on Saint Peter's Chair, the papacy would become a succession of kings and queens; the Frankish order would replace the Roman; and this squalling blond brat named Sergius would rule them all.

Four days before the christening I visited my grandfather Eusebius in his scriptorium on the Aventine. I loved Grandfather dearly and I sometimes turned to him for advice. Even if many of his views were outmoded, I could enjoy his rambling discourses on history. His harangues against the deplorable state of Rome were always lively and vivid.

My grandmother died when I was only four years old. After that Eusebius took up a monastic existence. To all appearances he mourned his wife's passing, but I think secretly he was glad to be free of household affairs and daily obligations. At last he could turn all his attention to his work.

A descendant of that famed Eusebius who chronicled the life of Constantine, my grandfather had long cherished the hope of continuing the record of church history from the death of the emperor to the present. In striving to achieve that goal he kept nine scribes hard at work in a north-facing chamber adjacent to the diaconia of Santi Bonifazio ed Alessio.

The scribes sat on hard wooden benches, their feet perched on stools, bending over the desks that held their copybooks. Beside each one was a small table with quills, ink, knife, erasers, compasses and ruler. Their work was conducted in absolute silence. They wrote on the finest vellum made of dried calfskin, and as they finished each quaternio they set the four finished sheets aside to be bound into a sixteen-page folio.

Whenever I came to visit, Grandfather would lead me among the scribes, allowing me to peer over their shoulders and listen to the faint, distant scratching of their quills. There was one scribe in particular, a thin, mournful-looking young man called Thetus, who always amused me. Though his quaternio was always neat and clean, he had a wax tablet where he would scratch down random thoughts: "The aching in my back sets my head to pounding . . . Margarita, I shall meet thee yet in holiest conjugation."

Grandfather looked on these asides with some consternation, but there was little he could do about them. Thetus would always strive to erase his tablet when he saw Eusebius coming.

"Perhaps you should allow him to compose," I suggested when Grandfather had led me from the room.

"Compose, indeed," he replied, pouring me a small chalice of wine. "The boy's thoughts are full of nothing but women and dancing."

"Still, Grandfather—" I hesitated. "Someone must take up your work when you are gone."

Under his skullcap his forehead reddened. "There is time enough to see to that, I'm sure."

He changed the subject. "What brings you to see me this chill day, Lena? I would have thought your duties at Saint Peter's would keep you occupied."

"So they do, Grandfather, but there is something I must speak to you about."

"What is that, my dear?"

"Since the birth of Marozia's baby you have not been to see her."

He avoided my eyes. "There is much to do here. My mind is on other things."

"Do you disapprove of her?"

"Disapprove? No, why should I?" He waved his hand vaguely.

"Then why do you keep away?"

He struggled to his feet. "Must you really know?"

"Yes, Grandfather, I must. You hurt Marozia by your absence."

He glanced at me almost as if he might dismiss me. Then, relenting, he sat and poured himself a draught from the amphora.

"Very well. You must know." He sighed again, puffing at his lips. "Well, it is this, then. I am not sure I can bear to look on the son of that man."

I had to laugh. "If you could only see him, Grandfather—he's nothing but a baby. All little fingers and toes and squealing energy."

"Yes, I know. Of course I know that. But never—" He paused. "Never in the history of Rome has there been such a man as Sergius. His wars, his intrigues, above all, his trial of Formosus. The Synod Horrenda was unspeakable."

"But Grandfather," I said softly, "that's over and done. This child lives now. He is part of our family."

"Do not remind me." His face was distorted.

I found myself growing angry. "I *must* remind you, Grandfather. What would you have Marozia do, kill the baby?"

Eusebius' face hardened. "That was the way of the ancient Romans. He is, after all, a bastard."

"Grandfather"—I fell to my knees before him—"if you could only see her, how happy she is. She hated Sergius as much as you, Grandfather, perhaps more, but Marozia's son is born afresh. He is sprung from God's will."

"He is of man's seed," he said bitterly, "and other men do not forget."

Tears sprang to my eyes. "Grandfather, I beg you, relent. It would mean so much to her."

He shook his head.

"Please, Grandfather, please. In God's name."

He began to shake his head again, then looked down at me, and I could see that my pleas had had some effect.

"What would you have of me, then?"

"Come to the christening."

He looked away. "Must I?"

"Yes. Please, Grandfather, if only for my sake."

He gazed at me again as if in great pain. Then at last he nodded. "Very well. I will come. Only do not ask me to touch the child."

*   *   *

The christening was held at the nones of March. Already spring was in the air; it was a bright sunny day when the Theophylact family rode in our litters to the basilica of Saint John's Lateran.

The high mass was performed in the baptistery by Pope Anastasius himself. Nobles and clergy crowded into the ambulatory, and though the christening itself was undertaken in a spirit of hushed reverence, many matters of business were discussed before and after the ceremony.

Marozia seemed shaken when she entered the chamber. She had not, of course, been there since the night of Sergius' death, and I do not think she was fully prepared for the memories that came flooding back. Still, the baptistery was brightly lit this day, crowded with people. With the wailing child in her arms, the new pope waiting and a dozen greetings to be given, Marozia did not have time to brood.

The ceremony was elegant and simple. Marozia looked radiant in a splendid white silk gown specially sewn for the day, and she carried the baby with pride.

Though he arrived late, Eusebius did come. Marozia's face fairly glowed as he kissed her on the cheeks. As he had sworn, he did not touch the child, but Marozia did not seem to notice the oversight, and the christening took place with no unpleasant incident.

Only as we were leaving the baptistery did Marozia glance at me, and I saw then how much she had kept hidden throughout the long service. For despite its innocent aspects, that room still held ghosts for her—the shadowy form of Alberic, the clash of weapons echoing through the darkness, the bleak cry of a dying man.

As for me, I had never told her of those final words from Sergius' lips. As I observed her cuddling the infant in her arms, swaying back and forth to soothe him—and the stricken look in her eyes—I knew there was more than one secret I was loath to tell her.

At the christening my father and Marcellus settled on a date for the wedding. Marozia and Petronius would be married on the first day of June, the lucky calends. Preparations for the ceremony and feast began immediately.

As befits two senatorial families, the wedding would be held in the basilica of San Adriano, which had been reconstructed from the Curia Senatus. From there the procession would take the Via Lata past the Baths of Nero and the Baths of Agrippa to the Pantheon.

The feast would be held there, for no single domus was large enough to accommodate the number of guests who were expected.

In the piazza of the Pantheon there would be trained bears and elephants, mock tourneys and a parade of lions with braided manes. Captive Muslim dancers would perform alongside Rumanian minstrels and court players.

For the feast itself, which would fill the whole Pantheon, each family would provide fourteen hundred goblets and enough wine to keep them constantly filled. On each side one hundred oxen were to be slaughtered and roasted. There were to be fifty suckling pigs, a table of sweetmeats as long as the rotunda and pasties of every description.

The skylight was to be covered with a screen and songbirds released into the air. Forty falconers would send their birds of prey to catch them and deliver them to the cooks below. The birds would then be plucked, dressed and roasted.

Marozia was informed of all these preparations. Marcellus and Petronius even asked her advice on a few trivial matters. For the most part, however, she held aloof from the proceedings, listening with vague interest as one ser-

vant or another told her of some delicacy or entertainment
that had been scheduled for the wedding day.

As time passed Marozia grew even more distracted. I
alone knew what troubled her. Alberic still had not returned,
and in spite of herself she was beginning to lose hope.

She was short with Petronius. He might be chattering
on about the most innocuous subject in that lisping, sarcastic
manner of his, when suddenly she would interrupt.

"Go away. Please leave me." To his astonishment,
she would rush off, holding her head in her hands.

What was she to do? Where could she turn? Day by
day the dreaded event drew closer, and still no rescue
came. The news from Benevento dried to a trickle,
then ceased entirely. Apparently Alberic had vanished off
the face of the earth.

Messengers reported the movement of Lombard troops.
There were short missives from the duchies and benefices,
but from the conqueror himself, nothing.

With each passing day I could see Marozia's hope
waning. Even the baby, as dearly as she loved him, was
not enough to distract her from impending disaster. Suckling the child, she would gaze down at him, lost in a
dream. But as soon as she stopped and handed him over to
the nurse for his nap, she would appear lost, desperate,
once again overwhelmed by the dread that pursued her.

Her impatience and restlessness grew. I saw a Marozia
I never had before, a woman weakened by love. When a
messenger appeared at the door, she would rush to the
atrium to greet him with trembling hands, begging for
news. She would almost scream with impatience as she
listened to the humdrum tallies of accounts, engagements
and tribunals.

"What of Benevento?" she would ask. "What news
of Alberic the Lombard?"

The messenger would shrug, lifting his brows in a

sign of simple ignorance. No one knew where Alberic was. The conqueror of Spoleto, Benevento, Fermo and Aquino seemed to be thoroughly lost.

In time Marozia's anxiousness turned to resignation and finally despair. Now she appeared to tolerate Petronius. She listened without protest to his endless gossip. Having lost all hope, she went through the motions of daily life with dazed persistence, as if nothing had meaning for her anymore.

April turned to May, and Rome came alive as her streets filled with travelers, merchants and pilgrims. Marozia remained indoors. Her face turned pale. Her headaches grew more frequent. She looked as if she had taken on some wasting sickness. I began to fear for her life.

Only her love for Sergius seemed to sustain her. There seemed to be some special communication between them, an understanding that held her apart from the world and all its troubles.

I must admit I could not quite share in her despair, for there had occurred certain encounters that gave me cause for hope.

On two occasions I had met Gallimanfry on the street. Each time I found him disguised in ridiculous garments: once wearing the cap of a guildsman and again clad as a hunter in a knee-length cloak with red hose clinging to his spindly legs. He looked so ridiculous, like an actor in costume on the streets, that I laughed aloud to see him. His response on both occasions was to stick out his tongue and hasten on his way without a word.

After his many overtures to me I found this behavior astonishing. I must confess I was more than a little disappointed to find his interest had waned. After each encounter I gave pause to wonder what business could have brought this extraordinary man to Rome.

Chapter 18

Marozia awoke early on the calends of June, her wedding day. I found her pacing her bedroom, still in her nightgown. She looked distraught.

"He has failed me," she said at once, then, bitterly, "He is like all other men. He wanted only to woo me, to know that I loved him, Now he has what he wanted and more. He is a murderer besides, and he has seized the patrimonies of Benevento. I have no doubt he's only biding his time until he shall seize Perugia from me as well."

Against this onslaught of denunciation there was little I could say. I strove to reassure her, but my words seemed empty. In fact, I shared some of her bitterness toward the Lombard. It grieved me to see my sister so ill used.

As in a dream we did our morning rounds: ablutions, the prayers at prime followed by a small meal of cheese and dried fruit. All around us the servants were in a flurry, and I could imagine the chaos at my parents' house as they strove to make last-minute preparations. Only Tasha maintained her calm, and it was strange to see her move among the others, serene, commanding, speaking not a word that could be overheard.

When we returned from breakfast, Tasha had laid out the wedding clothes, which Theodora had chosen. The undertunic was of silk woven with purple linen threads, so soft it made no rustling when Tasha lifted it. The hose were white with the finest tracings of colored silk. In defiance of custom Theodora had bought the bride a brilliant-colored gown from one of the Persian merchants at Venetia. It was worked with whorls and cross-patterns of gilt and turquoise thread and hemmed round with silver-flecked ermine. For all its richness and weight, the garment seemed to flow loosely around her, undulating with sparkles of brilliance as she moved. Marozia wore a jeweled chaplet, from which hung silver threads braided into her shimmering black hair.

I had only an instant to glimpse her features, for she did not pause to display herself before she slipped a light veil over her head, pulling the fabric close around her cheeks and down over her brow.

All morning long well-wishers arrived at the door, bringing gifts and bouquets and garlands. Every bishop, abbess and deacon in Benevento was represented, either in person or by proxy, and each must be acknowledged. This duty fell to Marozia's chancellor, a young, scatterbrained Tuscan by the name of Guillaume, and he dispatched it to the best of his ability, striving to remember the visitors' names for a later accounting.

As for me, it was all I could do to look after the guards and litter-bearers and see that the trappings were in order. We were late leaving, and the party from the House of Marcellus was already well on its way by the time we stepped from the door.

I knew that the citizens had taken this as a holiday, but I was not prepared for the sight of so many people. They jammed the streets and avenues, craning to get a glimpse of the bride. Cheering citizens threw dried rose petals and garlands of spring laurel and jasmine from housetops all along the Via Lata.

Marozia was unprepared for such a vast number of well-wishers. She lingered on the threshold, casting her gaze over the crowd, and the color sprang to her cheeks. The enthusiasm, the aura of expectancy, the celebration in the air almost overwhelmed her. Only a moment before she had been full of care, memories and sorrows. Now she was a public figure, standing before the people, her gown shimmering in the sunlight.

With a sudden, defiant gesture she threw back her modest veil.

That more than anything appealed to the crowd. At the sight of her jeweled chaplet, her beautiful face, her raven-black hair aglitter with silver threads, a great roar went up. Flowers fell all about us, a storm of scented petals and whirling leaves.

Even the litter-bearers appeared stunned for a moment, baffled by the multitude. They had to be ordered three times before they finally lifted their staves to bear the bride on her palanquin toward San Adriano on the Forum, where her groom awaited her.

It is our custom before the wedding ceremony to stand at the church door with bride facing groom and with the families of both gathered about. There on the steps of the church with nobles, clergy and citizens assembled, family matters are settled before the couple enters the sanctuary to make their vows. In this case the dowry was to be settled between my family and Petronius' with the exchange of many benefices.

Looking uncomfortable in an unbecoming rose tunic that reached to his ankles, Petronius was waiting beside his father Marcellus on the steps of San Adriano. Facing them, Gaius and Theodora stood together, casting sidelong glances at the crowd that thronged the Forum. At the first appearance of our litters Theodora turned to my father and spoke to him. They both looked much relieved, as if they had half expected Marozia to fail to appear.

The masses in the Forum roared.

"Make way, make way!" The guards shoved and shouted to clear a passage for the procession.

The crowd parted. Children got caught in the crush and screamed. A howl of anger rose as a fight broke out near the Arco di Settimio Severo.

Then a sudden hushed silence fell as Cardinal Celestine, Pastor of San Adriano, stepped forward, his hand upraised.

Marozia dismounted from her litter and genuflected at his feet. The cardinal made the sign of the cross above her bowed head. As he reached out and raised her, a single loud shout of approbation broke from the crowd.

And so the ceremony began. Close by the cardinal, high on the steps of San Adriano, the two families conferred in a huddle, sealing their agreements. From my position behind my parents I could hear much of the discussion. There seemed to be perfect understanding between Marcellus and Gaius. For once the two men, so opposite in their political views, were in complete accord.

My attention was soon distracted by a commotion on the edge of the crowd. Expecting to see that another fight had broken out, I looked toward the Tempio di Cesare, from which came the sounds of discord. They grew louder as I watched. A dark, churlish figure in the midst of the throng bobbed up, then disappeared, only to emerge again a few steps later. Pushed and reviled, taunted by those he passed, the man persisted, drawing ever closer until finally a way was cleared for him.

His hair was long and dark, his face bearded. He moved with a distinctive gait that seemed oddly familiar. Still striving to keep one ear attuned to the cardinal's words and the voices of the senators, I could not keep my eyes off him. As he drew nearer, having battered and cajoled his way through the milling crowd, I realized to my horror that this persistent stranger was none other than Gallimanfry.

His eyes lit up when he saw me. Then, springing free of the closest bystanders, he leapt up the steps of the church, waving a rolled parchment.

"Hold, hold," he shouted. "Cease these proceedings; they are illegal."

There was a moment of shocked silence; then Marcellus stepped toward him, his face blotchy with rage. "What say you, churl? Illegal? By whose authority?" The senator reached forward to snatch the parchment from Gallimanfry's hand, but the gleeful messenger was too quick for him.

Gallimanfry darted aside and tucked the parchment beneath his cloak. "By the order of Pope Anastasius," he announced loudly, "these proceedings are null and void and against the decree of His Holiness' word."

Petronius looked bewildered. Marozia's face I could not see, but I glimpsed her hand, clutching a fold of her gown. Only Marcellus seemed capable of action. Here, in front of all Rome, his only son's marriage was suddenly being challenged, his moment of triumph about to be shattered.

"Churl," he shouted, "I demand to see that document."

Gallimanfry took another hop away and waved the scroll before the crowd, grinning from ear to ear.

"Guards," Marcellus cried, "guards, seize him." He drew his sword and descended a step.

Gallimanfry spun to face the senator, the scroll firmly clutched in his hand. Still shouting, Marcellus raised his sword. Another moment and it would all be over.

But then with a sudden bow Alberic's chancellor fell to his knees. Only someone who knew him would recognize it as the gesture of a buffoon, not that of surrender. Nonetheless, he performed the role to perfection, holding out the scroll in his hand while he knelt quivering on the marble steps.

Dropping his sword, Marcellus lunged forward, seized the scroll and ripped open the seal. Unable to read it himself, he shoved it at the cardinal.

"There, read it to me. Tell me what it says."

Before the cardinal's lips began to move, another ripple at the edge of the crowd caused a fresh disturbance, crowding out of everyone's mind all thought of the papal decree.

On this festival day the gates of the city had been left open. Drawn from their posts by the state wedding, the guards had left their towers early. But even if there had been guards, even if the alarm had been sounded, it is doubtful that anyone would have thought of danger.

The man who rode in through the gates that morning was unaccompanied and he wore only a light sword at his waist. He carried no banners, sounded no trumpets. Mounted on his black charger, wearing only a green tabard over light mail, he rode at an easy pace, as if he had not a care in the world.

It was only when he came within sight of the milling crowds that his pace quickened. Alarmed by the noise of the people, his charger sidestepped but was soon under control.

Now the stranger was drawing attention. As he rode closer to the church, his head high above the multitude, the citizens turned about in alarm. Finally they recognized him.

"Alberic! Alberic has returned!" Like a breeze that gathered force to become a storm, the murmured words swept through the crowd, reaching at last the ears of those who were assembled on the steps.

I saw Marozia turn. Her hand flew to her throat and

she looked about her in panic, gazing as if spellbound at the green-clad figure riding his black horse across the Forum.

The crowd drew back, making way for Alberic. Watching him, Marcellus knelt and lifted his sword from where it had fallen. Beside him, Petronius did not stir. He sneered as if by habit, but there was fear in his eyes.

Then Alberic was before us, his mount restless beneath him. He bobbed his head once and I saw the iron tiara that bound his golden locks. There was a flash of blue; the penetrating eyes looked only at Marozia. And then, as if satisfied, he turned to Marcellus.

"You have received the decree?" the Lombard demanded.

"What is the meaning of this?" Marcellus held his voice in strict control. He stepped forward, the sword clutched in his hand.

Alberic looked down at him. "The decree from Pope Anastasius," he repeated, as if explaining a simple matter to a child.

"You cannot stop this marriage," Marcellus replied, his voice rising. "It must go forward. We have declared—"

"It cannot go forward without the pope's consent," Alberic interrupted. "If you read the decree, you will find that this matter goes against you."

Marcellus glanced at the cardinal, who now held the document at full length in his outstretched hands. "Cardinal Celestine, is it true?"

The clergyman looked up in fear. "Yes, Senator. The marriage of Petronius and Marozia is blocked by decree of Pope Anastasius III."

"On what grounds? I demand to know the grounds, Cardinal." Marcellus' face was still flushed.

The cardinal looked down at the scroll. His voice was faint with fear. "Honored Senator, I hesitate to speak—"

"Cardinal, I insist," Gaius interjected. "If there is an injunction against this legal marriage, it must be heard."

"Please, Senators, please, I beg you—" The parchment trembled in the cardinal's hand.

Gaius and Marcellus exchanged glances, as if each sought to find some weakening in the other, but only for an instant. When Gaius looked away, his voice was clear enough for all to hear.

"Cardinal Celestine, read the injunction."

Once again the pastor raised the scroll. A hush fell over the crowd.

"In the name of God and Jesus Christ . . ." He paused to clear his throat. "I, Pope Anastasius III, holder of the Chair of Saint Peter, duly elected by the Holy See, do find Petronius the son of Marcellus guilty of the sin of sodomy and do hereby intercede to prevent—"

The crowd would not let him finish. The Forum was filled with shouts, hoots and catcalls. Petronius was bewildered and shaken, as if struck from behind. His lips moved in feeble protest: "It is not true!"

"Calumny, falsehood! You vile, lying monk—" Marcellus tore the scroll from the prelate's hand.

The crowd was laughing at his rage, shouting and clicking their tongues.

"Senator." Alberic stepped forward. "Do nothing rash. This is the pope's decree. It cannot be reneged. Marozia is no longer betrothed to Petronius."

At the mention of her name the crowd grew hushed again. All eyes were focused on my sister.

"Subject to her father's consent," Alberic continued, "Marozia is now free to choose whom she will marry."

The crowd was spellbound as Marozia stepped forward. There was a gasp as she swept back her veil and looked into Alberic's eyes. For a long moment there was no sound, no murmur, as she surveyed him.

Then suddenly she lifted her hand and leapt. The motion was as swift and sure as if they had planned it forever, although it was perfectly spontaneous. She seemed to float waist-high as the Lombard's arm came down to meet her, and then he caught her and swept her onto the withers of the stallion.

How did she know the precise moment when his arm would reach out to take her? How did he on his charger know when she would fling herself into his embrace? At such times love is unison in motion. This flight was breathless and splendid, and none who were there will ever forget how Alberic carried the beautiful Marozia up onto his charger.

All heads turned to see them, and the crowd parted as the high-spirited steed plunged forward, eyes wide, head rearing as he fought the reins clenched in his master's hands. Around the Via Sacra they rode, through the Arco di Settimio Severo, past the ruined foundation of I Rostri. They passed the columns where the Basilica Giulia once stood, rounded the front of the Tempio di Cesare and the Tempio di Antonio e Faustina.

At each step of the way the roar of the crowd grew louder. The cheering and clapping rose to a high pitch of intensity as the citizens surged forward to touch the hems of the magical pair, then pulled back in fear as the charger stamped. From the craggy ruins of the monuments and statues the people strained to catch a glimpse of the fearless Alberic and the beautiful Marozia.

They seemed oblivious to it all, the lovers—Alberic tall and straight, hands locked on the reins, eyes fixed on the Via Sacra; Marozia riding easily, one hand on the horse's mane and one on the arm of her lover, her veil blown off her forehead against his chest. Not a soul in the

Forum could take his eyes from that couple as they completed their circuit and returned to the foot of San Adriano.

Alberie's lieutenant Lambert waited there smiling. A few steps away, the poor cardinal, still clutching the papal decree, glanced surreptitiously from Gaius to Marcellus. Gallimanfry had already climbed down to be lost among the crowd, and Petronius, I'm afraid, had turned quite silly with confusion. His mouth gaped as he stared over the heads of the multitude at his would-be bride, kidnapped by this Lombard. As for Marcellus, I thought at any moment he would take the sword to my father's throat. Only my mother remained unperturbed. She whispered in my father's ear, incomprehensibly to all appearances.

At last Alberic and Marozia stood before us again. The strong Germanic voice could be heard clearly above the roar of the crowd.

"Gaius Theophylact, you have heard the pope's decree. Marozia is free to marry. Will you permit me to take your daughter to wife?"

I knew what my father would say. Clearly the Lombard had committed an outrage. Every noble Roman would be offended if he prevailed. The Senate would be split, the coalition with Marcellus completely shattered. The marriage to Alberic would have to be denied.

It was then that I learned the true power of the people. The citizens gave my father no opportunity to reply. With one voice they shouted, "Yes! Yes! *Yes!*"

They went wild. They knew high romance when they saw it, and romance was always suitable. They wanted the noble German warrior and the equally noble Roman beauty locked in love's embrace. It was vicarious passion that spoke from the throats of the citizens. There was no denying them.

Passing his eyes over them all, not daring to look at

Marcellus or Petronius, my father turned his head until at last his gaze came to rest on Marozia.

It was she who convinced him. With a single graceful gesture she submitted her plea.

Gaius dropped his eyes. When he raised them again, he was half smiling.

"I consent to the marriage," he declared.

He spoke loudly enough for only the closest to hear, but the words carried through the multitude like a wave gaining power, and the roar of acclamation swept away any possibility of objection.

Chapter 19

Throughout that day and night Rome was in a frenzy of celebration. The ceremony of marriage was performed at once in San Adriano. Cardinal Celestine presided. Out of respect for my father even the patricians were forced to attend, and none dared murmur against Alberic.

Once the marriage was made, Lambert rode to the Nevi gate and sent a messenger to the Lombard encampment. Alberic's men were waiting not ten miles from Rome, and they made a triumphant entry into the city.

Already the wine was flowing. All restraints were cast aside. If on their previous visit the Lombards had been regarded as strangers, they were now welcomed as heroes. It was as well Gaius had given Theodora her head with the preparations; no feast would have been too lavish.

Cast into the shadows like lurking felons, Marcellus, his son and family were exiles in their own city. Surely it was an unlucky day for them, but not one among the hilarious crowd gave them a moment's thought.

Bacchus' revels were unleashed. This was the thing that Romans best knew how to do. They poured into the piazzas and courtyards and thronged the streets, plundering the storehouses, drinking and carousing; they seemed to be in thrall to the god of celebration.

For Alberic and Marozia the revelry of the citizens was only background for the calm delights of their love. In the sanctuary of the Pantheon, where the feast was spread and the speeches read aloud, the young couple lounged at the high table, their faces glowing, hardly noticing the bounty, the praise and the gifts that were offered on every hand.

How I envied Marozia her happiness. All fears, hardships and suffering appeared to be banished as if by a miracle as she stretched in the arms of her bold lover. None but I could tell of her misery and heartbreak; none but I knew of the dread secret she and Alberic shared.

The knowledge was safe with me. I would not betray them.

Finally, a wet nurse had been found for the infant Sergius. She was Annette, a good woman from the Hospice of Saint Clement. That night after she had suckled the baby, swaddled him and laid him in the crib, she sat by the window, listening to the sounds of merriment and watching the revelers pass to and fro with flaring torches. Once during the night the baby awoke and she comforted him.

It was not until nearly dawn that Marozia and Alberic returned to the House of Hadrian. Marozia spoke quietly to the nurse, inquiring if all was well, but apparently the woman's reply did not satisfy her, for she insisted on looking in on Sergius herself. Only when she had seen him sleeping peacefully did she return to Alberic.

Dawn's light was just breaking when they retired to her chambers.

It was only then that she realized he was a stranger to her. In all the months of waiting, while her despair grew keen and her passion waxed, Marozia had loved an image of a man.

Now that he stood before her in the flesh, she found that he was much different from what she had imagined.

This was no immortal, but a man, strong and rough, smelling of leather and sweat and the heat of travel. Even his rough Germanic voice sounded odd and foreign to her. She felt a moment of panic, as if she had made a terrible mistake.

She watched him set the iron crown on a chest by her bed. Reaching through the fitchet cut in the side of his tabard, he unfastened the sword and scabbard and placed these next to the crown. Then he lifted the tabard over his head.

"Marozia," he said softly, coming to her, "why do you watch me this way?"

"I do not know you," she whispered.

"You are my wife."

"You have saved me," she said. "I am grateful."

He smiled and touched the circlet on her brow. "Nobility . . . beauty . . . love," he murmured, as if the three words described her completely.

"I am afraid," she said.

"Of what?"

"Alberic, we are murderers."

"We did not seek death." His voice was even. "It came seeking us. It was kill or be killed."

"Still, I am afraid."

"Marozia." He took her hand. "That is all behind us now. There is much to be done." His grip grew firm. "Your city will have to make room for a Lombard. There will be anger and resistance at what we have done. The people will not always applaud us as they have tonight."

"But you have conquered so many cities." She looked at him with shining eyes. "Surely there is no greater Lombard—"

"Stop!" He put his finger to her lips, but he was smiling. "I still owe fealty to Berengar." She looked bewildered and his smile broadened. "I see there is much

you must learn about our Lombard ways." He grew serious.
"But you must believe me. I cannot betray an oath of
allegiance. Whatever happens, I will not be disloyal to
Berengar."

"Then I too am his vassal."

He nodded. "But whatever I hold is yours. I have
already declared it this day."

She turned away.

"What is it?" He came close to her, his hands on her
shoulders.

"My Sergius," she began, but her voice broke. Then
she turned back, a pleading look in her eyes. "I know you
must hate him, the son of that man."

"I bear him no ill will."

"Swear," she insisted suddenly. "Swear you will not
harm my son in any way."

He gave her a long, searching stare. At last he replied,
"Of course, my love."

At this, she reached up and drew his fingers to her
breast.

"Come," she said softly. "It is dawn already, and
we are not yet man and wife."

His cheeks were rough with a dry stubble of beard,
his hands hardened by long hours of riding, the nails
broken. His body was long, lean and sinewy. Naked, he
appeared like a standing trunk of ironwood, a cold figure
cast in bronze. What was it then to close her eyes and feel
him touch her? She expected disappointment. Her heart
cried out, What have I done?

It was that—the aching of needless remorse—that he
had to heal.

When he had lifted the silk tunic from her body and
she too stood naked, he took her in his arms and kissed
her. Then she understood the hard muscles and the rough-

ened hands, but only vaguely, as part of a strength that enveloped and held her. All that mattered was the softness of his lips, the heat of his chest held to her breasts, the struggling animal fury. She felt his power flowing to her and then returning multiplied as intensity built. Suddenly she leapt and caught his neck with her arms. Riding him like a bearcub on a tree, she pressed her lips to his as he stabbed into her.

She sank only slightly, poised in wonder, her body impaled. Between her thighs everything was heat, a single point of sensation that spread, becoming pain and then pleasure. He cradled her against him as easily as a giant would cradle a baby.

"Lie down," he said softly in his foreign, guttural tone.

He laid her on the bed. She twisted away from him, stretching, and then he was covering her body with kisses.

"My queen, my queen," she heard him murmur. Her head was filled with images: sunlit fields, men's roars, charging horses, crenelated cathedrals, sweet music. . . .

Then there were no images, only kisses. His lips on her breasts, her stomach and thighs. His lips at the hollow of her neck. His breath hot, coming fast now. The pleasure rising slowly as he entered her again.

It was more than she could bear, this gentleness. She turned her head away almost in pain, tears coming to her eyes. It was splendid to have him inside her, to be allowed this tenderness at last.

The pleasure rose again and suddenly she was frightened. She had only wanted to satisfy him, and now it was she who demanded fulfillment. She was reaching for him down there in the heat, and yet she wanted to stop herself.

Wouldn't he be angry? This clawing—her hands around him, pulling; her voice rasping, calling to him—wouldn't he despise her for this desperate hunger? This was animal, beast, devil . . .

Then she was gone, the waves of pleasure rolling from her depths. She tried to stop herself, to still the fury—but too late.

In the fading of her passion she was certain he would hate her, beat her, punish her for exercising the devil's lust. Already the punishment was beginning. He thrust, then thrust again. Hard punishment, yes—but it did not wound her. It intensified what she had felt before, the need to seize him, possess him, twist her pleasure from him.

His voice hissed in her ear. She waited—only a moment—and then it was over for him, the seed spurting into her, the sheltered sigh. Over. No punishment.

He lay on her still, kissing her.

"Alberic, Alberic, my love. . . ."

She waited for him to hurt her, but he never did.

Chapter 20

Their happiness seemed boundless. There was no end to their love. It was a miracle to see them together, young creatures full of health and joy. Their household was a cyclone where fleet-footed messengers came and went and servants were constantly in a flurry. The smell of baking pasties and richly herbed dishes filled every corner of the grand old mansion.

I do not know why God is so equivocal, why one person living in the depths of loneliness and despair can suddenly be raised to a pedestal of happiness from which the world appears transformed and beautified. So it was with Marozia.

She had been given everything she desired. Those of a selfish nature, who expected nothing less from life, might have accepted such happiness as a matter of course, but long, bitter months of anger, fear and torment had taught my sister the value of this happy time. The radiance she bore was a kind of thanksgiving, humble and sure, without self-righteousness or self-denial. If she ever felt that her happiness would be transitory, the only effect was to make her cling more fiercely to what she had, to enjoy what God had given her.

Still, Marozia had been a Roman too long to turn her back on the dictates of society. She knew that in marrying a Lombard she risked inciting jealousy and anger on the part of Romans who hated the influence of foreigners. Out of judiciousness if nothing else, she did everything in her power to secure the position of her husband.

Within a week of the wedding she invited Pope Anastasius and the prelates of the papal palace to the House of Hadrian for a great evening feast. High merchants, bishops, senators and reigning nobles were also in attendance.

Whether from curiosity or a sense of duty, all came to this feast—all, that is, except Marcellus and Petronius. The guests were served roast suckling pigs and game birds, sweetmeats and cheeses, along with the best wines of Lambrusco. Muslim dancers with bare bellies and naked thighs performed throughout the night. The revelers went away satisfied long after lauds was rung.

It was apparent that these Romans did not quite know how to accept Alberic. To them his ways were rough and unfamiliar. To show affection, for example, he clasped a man's forearm or hugged him tightly about the shoulders, manners that jolted the haughty, sophisticated Romans.

Alberic's guests soon began to appreciate that there was more to his hearty good nature than met the eye. A surly bishop, feasted and entertained at the head table, would hardly realize that by the end of the meal he had given up half a year's quitrents in exchange for the Lombard's protection. A cynical senator, arriving with doubts about his host, would listen in astonishment as Alberic recited line by line the complex and just laws of the Lombard people.

Marozia observed all this with a half smile, flushed with conquest. Her fellow Romans had taken this man for a barbarian, a threat to their civilized way of life, but now they found him entirely different. In Alberic they were faced with a force, a presence, a proud and powerful man who was oblivious to the backbiting and gossip that these effete Romans valued so highly.

Nor was his triumph over them secured only by the strength of his personality. The one thing above all that bred respect in the heart of every Roman was military power. Alberic's troops were well equipped, well disciplined and faithful, bound by tribal trust and loyalty.

Since Alberic's marriage to Marozia his soldiers were seen everywhere—in the streets, guarding the bridges, in the Castel Sant'Angelo, within the churches and diaconiae, even along the city walls. Their presence was now an undeniable fact of life.

Despite his success, or perhaps because of it, there were small things Marozia did to change the man she loved. Each morning she required him to endure the ministrations of a voluble Roman barber who used rose-scented soap to shave him and who trimmed his blond curls close around his forehead.

His dress changed too. At first he wore his mail and green tabard at all times, but for special audiences and religious occasions Marozia soon persuaded him to put these aside for a dark velvet surcoat with Byzantine braiding. His plain iron brooches were replaced with gold, specially worked by the artisans of Ostia, with a lion rampant on each. Marozia even taught him snatches of Latin—not enough to make him eligible for the Curia, but sufficient for greetings and partings on high church occasions.

He endured all this with gentle good humor, but I sensed growing restlessness in him. Clearly he was not a man to remain long inactive, and I could see that Roman life was beginning to wear on him.

In truth, the conquered cities of the countryside suffered in Alberic's absence. While the dukes remained loyal, and messengers from the conquered marches made regular reports, some vassals grew uneasy.

In Spoleto there was an uprising, quickly suppressed

by Lambert and six legions, but only at the cost of two days' fighting and the loss of sixty men. In Aquino the bishop's militia resisted the duke's collection agent, and the abbey was burned to the ground in the ensuing battle.

Alberic heard of these events with deepening concern. Day by day he grew moodier, until he could no longer hide his anxiety. All this came to the fore when he and Marozia were out riding.

To mount a palfrey and take part in falconry was not considered seemly for a Roman lady, but from the first Marozia had insisted on joining the hunt with her husband. She loved the hard ride, the wind in her face, her shawl blowing. As often as not she rode without bow and arrows, and she usually returned empty-handed, but she loved to watch the falcons in flight, to risk her neck galloping across the campagna. Besides, of course, she loved to be close to Alberic.

On this day, however, he seemed uneasy with her. Pursuing quail in a low valley, they got separated from the other riders. At a barrier of thick bracken they were finally forced to rein in.

Her face flushed, hair in a tangle, Marozia came alongside him. "We have lost them."

"So we have." He appeared indifferent.

She confronted him with his silence. "Something has been troubling you, my love. Please tell me what is wrong."

Alberic was mounted on a big roan. Seeming to sense its rider's unease, the horse shifted nervously.

"There is trouble in the duchies," Alberic replied at last without looking at her.

"I know, of course. But why are you loath to speak of it?"

He glanced at her guardedly. "It means I must soon leave."

"I have already thought of that."

He nodded. "There is something else. To hold these duchies I must be willing to defend them."

Her blood froze. "What do you mean?"

"I am a Lombard. I cannot always send Lambert to do my fighting for me. The trust between me and my dukes must be sealed in battle. There is no other way."

"I have understood that from the first," replied Marozia, trying to keep her voice steady, "but you must not leave me behind—not now, when we have so much."

"The duchies—"

"Forget the duchies," she stormed. "Think what we have, what we have conquered, you and I. Did you come to Rome and steal my hand only to give it up so soon?"

He shook his head. "You must see, Marozia, that everything will be lost—"

"I see clearly that I have been happy. I cannot live without that happiness."

She stared off into the leafy green depths of the forest. The sunlight glinted in her hair, the golden light turned violet among the black strands.

"I beg you, Alberic, do not leave me so soon."

His voice, when he replied, was soft with the anguish of his choice. "This is most bitter."

"I love you."

There was a long silence in the forest. Then from afar came the sound of the falconer's voice.

They looked up. Wheeling high above them was the soaring, graceful bird, its talons extended.

"The cities sleep," muttered Alberic, "but their enemies do not."

Marozia gazed at him steadily. Now she smiled. "Oh, my warrior husband, the simple pleasures of the hunt are not enough for you."

Her amusement seemed to annoy him. "I cannot abide Rome much longer."

"Nor can I."

He looked at her in astonishment. "What then of these feasts, these parleys and saint's day celebrations? Are all these for display only?"

"I would give them all away to ride with you into battle," she replied flatly.

"Into battle?" He was astounded.

"Isn't that the way of the Lombard queens? Of Hilga and Irmengard and—"

"You are a Roman, Marozia."

"Yes," she said firmly, looking deep into his eyes, "but I am married to a Lombard, to a man who should be king."

Marauding bands of Magyars had made inroads in the north of Italy. Wherever they went they left a path of rape and pillage, burned cities and villages, looted churches and monasteries.

Now the Magyars were at Fano, a beautiful seaport with one of the finest castles in Italy. After a short siege they took the city by storm, slaughtering many of the inhabitants. With the fortress secure they were preparing to make advances into the Duchy of Spoleto, which was held by the vassals of Alberic.

Alberic summoned his loyal subjects to stand to arms in service to their duke. From Camerino, Aquino, Spoleto, Teano and Fermo the freemen were mustered. Crowds of militia thronged the roads on their way north from Spoleto. Every royal leader and his sworn soldiers responded to the call. Major landowners appeared at the muster with mail shirt, shield and lance, riding their chargers. Minor landowners wore no mail, but they too brought shield and lance. The common soldiers, traveling on foot, carried only their shields, bows and arrows.

Every fit man between the ages of sixteen and seventy

answered the call to battle. With them they brought provisions—flour, wine and pork as well as hand mills for grain, adzes, shovels, axes, planes, augers and slings. At the head of each train was an ox-drawn cart, the *carroccio*, fitted with a staff bearing the knight's battle flag.

News of the great levy of troops swept through Rome, and travelers returning from Ravenna along the Via Flaminia spoke with awe of the number of men-at-arms they had seen.

On the eve of her departure with Alberic Marozia went to the House of Theophylact on the Aventine to bid her parents farewell. Theodora immediately took her into a private meeting chamber.

"You must stop him," she said without preamble.

"I cannot," Marozia replied. "The *arrière-ban* has already been pronounced. The march to Fano begins tomorrow."

Theodora turned on her daughter in fury. "Don't you realize what this means? Fano borders on the exarchate of Ravenna. Those lands belong to Bishop John. If the Lombards seize the seaport, he will be forced to demand fealty."

"Fealty? From Alberic?" Marozia looked at her mother in astonishment, then laughed. "That's ridiculous. My husband will honor the church benefices and the tithes will be paid, but when he conquers, Fano will be his."

Theodora's eyes were blazing. "I warn you, Marozia, Bishop John will not permit this invasion."

"Let him try to stop us," Marozia snapped. "You forget, Mother, I ride with Alberic. Any man who acts against him will have to deal with me as well."

"You are a fool."

Marozia shook her head. "I am content. For the first time in my life I shall be proud of who I am, proud of the man I love. I'm sorry, Mother, but Alberic will not change his course to suit your will—nor that of your lover."

Theodora stared at her daughter. "You have taken on the barbarian's ways," she said grimly.

"That may be," Marozia retorted, "but I am not ashamed of them—and I certainly am ashamed of Roman ways."

Theodora drew back, offended, but she said no more.

As Marozia made her farewells to Gaius and Eusebius, she wondered how far Theodora would go to oppose her. If Bishop John truly dared to match his forces against Alberic's, the result would be a civil war, and that would embroil every churchman, every Lombard, Roman and Frankish warrior in Italy—every person in Italy, for that matter.

That thought was strangely reassuring. Theodora might be impetuous, but she was not without reason. Her aspirations for John would be realized by means other than civil war, of that Marozia was certain.

Marozia's parting from Gaius and our grandfather Eusebius was made difficult by their disapproval. Never before had any Roman woman, let alone one of the noblest, gone riding off to war. Though they tried to hide their dismay, the two men seemed overwhelmed with shame.

Their feelings hardly touched Marozia. Indeed, she seemed slightly amused by their reaction, knowing that her father and grandfather were more worried about prestige than about her safety.

If that parting from them was merely awkward, however, the separation from her son was almost unbearable. Sergius was out of swaddling now. He could crawl and climb, uttering loud cheerful howls of conquest whenever he overcame a particularly difficult obstacle. Annette had to follow that curly blond head everywhere, sometimes dashing to catch her charge before he tumbled to the floor.

When Marozia came to see him, Sergius had just succeeded in raising himself to full height at the foot of a chair. He stood laughing at her, his face flushed with happiness and pride. She swept him into her arms and hugged him, but he enjoyed the embrace only a moment before he twisted to get away.

"Good-bye, Sergius," she whispered, "good-bye."

He looked at her in puzzlement, then grabbed her hair in his fist. She winced, then laughed as she tried to untangle the strands from the grappling, chubby fingers. When she had succeeded, he wriggled to be set free, and she reluctantly put him down.

I saw tears in her eyes. "Marozia, are you sure?"

"No, of course not, Lena." She looked me full in the face and I could see the determination there, some ambition deeper and more lasting than anyone could comprehend. "What Roman woman has ever done this before?" she reminded me, echoing, I knew, my father's very words. "I am his wife, Lena. I am not wed to Rome. As a Lombard, I shall ride by his side." Her voice faltered; then she added with resolution, "Other Lombard queens have followed the battle, and so shall I."

"But Sergius—" I was loath to remind her of the child by her knee, now clinging to her, begging for attention.

She lifted her eyes to me. "I must trust you, Lena. Can I do so?"

"Yes, of course, Marozia." I picked up my nephew. Surprised, he wrenched himself around to look at me in astonishment. I touched his nose with my forefinger, and he laughed. When I looked around again, Marozia was gone.

Chapter 21

The long march was worse than any ordeal she could have imagined. Refusing the litter, Marozia insisted on riding her palfrey with only a veil to shield her face and head from the dust and the blazing sun.

On the first day she thought she would drop with fatigue. At each step she expected to slide from the saddle to the stones of the Via Flaminia, to be trampled under the relentless tread of men's feet and horses' hooves. She could not afford to bow her head or show her tiredness, though, for all around her were the leaders of the Lombard duchies, each anxious to get the measure of Alberic's new queen.

She felt a surge of pride when these sworn followers came to pay their respects to her husband, mounted high on his black charger. As they bowed and withdrew murmuring among themselves, she struggled to hold herself erect in the saddle. They were praising her beauty, her strength. She must not fail.

Somehow she survived that first day on the road and the next and the next, until almost without realizing it she no longer had to fight a desperate battle of endurance. Hours passed in the saddle without her noticing, and the rhythm of each day's passing took on a quiet force of its own. She learned the soldiers' pleasures: a brief gulp of water and a few words at midday, the deep sleep of real fatigue, the renewal in the cool air of dawn, when she mounted up again.

On the day before their arrival at Fano as the afternoon drew to a close Alberic glanced over his shoulder, then slowed his charger to come to her side. He looked at her curiously.

"I have seen men who fared less well on a long march," he said quietly.

She felt an unaccountable stirring of resentment. It was the first praise he had given her. It would almost have been better if he had said nothing. His grudging words held unmistakable condescension.

"Did you think I would fail?"

"You would have been prudent to ride the litter."

She glanced at her hands. They had turned hard from holding the reins and the knuckles were red.

"I would have been prudent to remain at home with my embroidery."

"Yes," he replied, "but if you had done so, I would not have believed it possible for you to endure such a march as this." He spurred his mount and rode to the head of the column without waiting for a reply.

It soon became apparent that an immediate assault on the castle at Fano was impossible. Only a token garrison manned the abutments and donjon, while the main body of the Magyar tribe had deployed itself in the cover of the surrounding countryside. As soon as the Lombards were within a league of the city, the hidden Magyars launched their assault from the rift valleys and steep hills that lined the road.

Stocky horsemen clad in leather garments with steel scales, they rode with terrifying speed. Their mounts were small saddle horses, unsuited for close combat but as fast as the wind. Descending along the slopes and narrow passes, the Hungarian warriors unleashed their arrows, then wheeled and with fierce, shrill cries retreated among the trees.

It was only luck that saved Marozia from being cut down in the first volley. The moment the Magyars appeared—seemingly out of thin air—panic and confusion spread among the Lombards. Horses reared; carts were overthrown; the infantry scurried for cover.

A Magyar arrow passed so close that it touched the mane of Marozia's horse. As her mount reared, she clung desperately to his back, throwing herself forward. That alone saved her from the next volley, which skimmed above her as she fought to control her palfrey.

After the third such attack Alberic called a halt and made camp, ringing his army with a barrier of sharpened timbers. All night long sentries with torches kept watch, driving off raiders who strove to break through.

By morning Alberic had settled on a plan. In the dim mists of dawn he sent lines of infantry moving stealthily into the hills that flanked the Via Flaminia. As the sun rose high, the main body of the Lombards moved forward. The Magyar raids commenced once again.

This time, though, when the tribesmen returned to the hills, Alberic's infantry rose from their positions in the forest to slaughter the Hungarians, halt their retreat and create panic and confusion among their ranks.

It was a costly maneuver. Hundreds of Lombard infantry were lost once their positions had been discovered by the Magyar riders. But the road was cleared, and soon Alberic's army was within reach of the city of Fano.

Alberic ordered a direct assault on the castle doors. The Magyar defenders stood on the ramparts above, pouring hot pitch on the attackers, but new axmen quickly took the places of those who had fallen, hewing at the great oak beams. Finally Alberic's men set the doors on fire.

While the massive timbers blazed and crumbled around them, the knights who had been chosen to lead the attack rushed through the breach. Wielding two-bladed Frankish battle axes and Roman spears with long, sharp points, they hurled themselves on the Magyars at the gates of the castle, mowing them down in waves.

Unaccustomed to weapons and untrained for battle, Marozia was forced to observe the action from the brow of a low hill overlooking Fano. The din of battle, the grunts, howls and curses of the soldiers who rushed to the attack washed over her. She trembled with frustration. Her blood was pounding, her head dizzy with sights and sounds, but she herself was helpless.

From the distant height she watched as the first wave breached the defenses of the castle gate. She caught a glimpse of her husband, helmet glinting in the sunlight, sword flashing, bright green tabard vivid among the plain-clothed troops. Alberic leading, men poured through the charred remnants of the wooden doors, horses, bodies and battle gear charging with the momentum of a single huge engine of war.

After he disappeared a strange lethargy seized the troops in the rear guard. Separated from their leader, the generals of the second wave seemed thrown into confusion. The Magyars on the parapets, recovering from the first rush, took advantage of this hesitation. The rain of arrows resumed with deadly effect.

On the bare plain before the castle all was confusion. Leaderless, halted, the Lombards were helpless, picked off like flies by the expert Magyar bowmen.

Then Marozia saw what had happened and understood. The carroccio carrying Alberic's banner had come to a stop before the gate. One wheel broken, an axle shattered, it tilted crazily to one side. All around the cart the mounted guards were milling about, horses rearing. Frantically the men shouted out to one another, struggling vainly to free the pennant.

"Fools, fools, attack!" Marozia shrieked, but her voice was lost in the din.

Then without a second thought she pounded down the slope toward the broken carroccio. Foot soldiers turned in astonishment as she swept past mounted knights, jolted into action by the sight of their queen galloping into battle, wheeled to close ranks and protect her.

A great shout went up from the troops as Marozia leapt from her horse onto the carroccio. For a moment she was oblivious to everything—the shouts and screams, the clatter of hooves and the Magyar arrows that sang about her ears. She saw a soldier's bloodied hand, the nerveless fingers touching the base of the pennant. She heard her own breath in her ears, her groans as she lunged to free the banner from its iron flange.

"Saint Michael, help me." The prayer sprang unbidden from her lips. At once she felt a shadow descend, strength enter her arms, and then the pennant was free, the standard waving.

It was heavier than she had thought. It wavered and started to topple.

Then suddenly there were soldiers all around her. "For Alberic! Alberic!" Strong arms steadied the battle flag and gave it the momentum to lead the charge. In their midst she felt the headiness of victory, the frenzy of triumphant attack.

The wave of men and horses carried her and the banner of Lombardy across the mounds of hot pitch, already cooling to softness on the hard ground. Then they were inside the walls, she among them, lost, tossed aside.

The banner went on, seeming to march with a life of its own to the center of the courtyard. The rear guard rallied around it, storming the bastions, galleries and parapets as they fought for the glory of God and the honor of Duke Alberic.

Afterward, as Marozia wandered through the smoking timbers of the courtyard, dismay overwhelmed her. Everywhere Lombards were looting the bodies of the fallen Magyars of jeweled knives, swords, rings and armor. Naked bodies were tossed in heaps on the oxcarts.

By the shelter of a wall a Magyar raised his hand in a plea for mercy. Cursing harshly, a Lombard slashed at the upraised hand. It fell among the cobblestones, blood spewing from the stump.

Then she saw Alberic. He was descending from the parapet along the inner stairway. His hand was pressed to his tunic near his throat. Blood seeped between his fingers.

Marozia ran toward him. "Alberic!"

His eyes glittered. "It's nothing," he said. He paused at her side. "We have conquered. Fano is ours." Then he looked down into her eyes, brooding, fierce, intense.

"I saw none of it," he said hoarsely, "but Lambert has told me all."

She was almost afraid. Then she saw fierce pride and acceptance: she was not a maid but a soldier who had performed well in battle.

She lowered her eyes and turned toward the smoking ruins.

Chapter 22

The arrow had pierced the muscles of his neck and shoulder just above the collarbone. The wound was not serious, but the shaft of the arrow had broken off, leaving the barbed tip inside.

The army physician, Gerrardo, a short, squat man with a froglike face and pudgy fingers, offered Alberic an anesthetic made from the juice of opium, but the duke declined. With a shrug Gerrardo ordered his patient to lie prone. As Marozia held Alberic's hand, the physician plunged his knife into the general's shoulder.

Fortunately, the arrow point was near the surface. Gerrardo cut an opening and pulled the tip through the muscle with a pair of iron pincers. Gleefully he held up the bloody object, then spat on it and hurled it to the ground, muttering curses to drive away infection. Throughout the surgery Alberic made only one sound, a short, sharp groan when the barbed tip was pulled free.

Marozia prepared a poultice of mustard and saltpeter and bound the shoulder with strips of linen. Gerrardo watched her with satisfaction. From his pouch he drew a small counter and rolled his eyes back, calculating quickly.

"Saturn and Mars are in conjunction," he reported. "It will be slow to heal but successful."

"I thank you," said Alberic. "How many wounded do you count?"

"Eight score, by my reckoning," replied the little man. "I have been kept busy all this day."

Alberic nodded. "You will be rewarded."

Whether from unfavorable alignment of the planets or from wrong treatment in the hands of his physician, Alberic was indeed slow to heal. The wound festered, but he tried to ignore it. After all, there were matters to attend to. He must award manors to loyal lords and donate holdings in the countryside to the freemen who had performed well in battle. Finally, a suitable duke, Conrad of Siponto, had to be appointed to rule over Fano.

Once all this was done, Alberic could no longer ignore the fever. A chamber was prepared in the donjon of the castle and Marozia forced him to go to bed.

For three days and nights the fever raged. Delirious, Alberic cried out against the poisonous devils and clawed imps that tormented him. Seated by his bedside, Marozia bathed him with cold water and swabbed his lips and cheeks with rosewater and vinegar. Gerrardo prepared pills of powdered stag's horn, of garlic, myrrh and finely ground pearls, but they had little effect, and the physician soon left, grumbling under his breath against the cursed stars.

This was when Marozia came to know Lambert, the black-haired solemn Imolan general who had served so long at Alberic's side. Day or night she could count on him to be standing by, drowsing in a corner of the room or pacing fitfully in the hall outside. At her slightest gesture he would be at her side.

Like a servant Lambert hastened to refill the buckets of cold water, helped Marozia turn the general on his bed, and changed the pomanders that hung about the room. He seemed never to sleep or grow restless, and the deep concern in his eyes somehow lessened Marozia's fear.

Through his care he helped carry the burden that she otherwise would have borne alone.

On the fourth day, when the fever finally broke, Marozia and Lambert stood together at Alberic's bedside. The general was sleeping fitfully. Droplets of perspiration clung to his brow.

Marozia leaned down and brushed the hair from his forehead. His eyes opened. "Marozia," he whispered.

She tried to keep the tears from her eyes and failed. He smiled and touched her cheek. Then he looked past her to where Lambert stood. Alberic tried to stir, but Marozia pressed him back down.

"Are . . . are the troops in order?" he asked.

"They await your command, my liege."

Alberic closed his eyes, then opened them again. "Tell them . . . tell them . . . a full review . . . tomorrow."

"Of course, my liege."

The eyes closed and Alberic's breathing grew heavy. Marozia looked up to Lambert, who was smiling with infinite relief.

"He is sleeping soundly," said Marozia.

Lambert nodded and suddenly they found that they were laughing and weeping.

Within a fortnight Alberic was prepared to leave Fano, satisfied that its affairs were fully settled and the city was in loyal thrall. For many of his fiefs the forty-day term of obligatory service was almost finished, and it was time for them to return to their respective duties. Payment was arranged—three *solidi* per day for cavalrymen, one for infantrymen—and the troops were dispatched for the return journey along the Via Flaminia. Only the arrival of Bishop John of Ravenna and his half-brother Peter, Deacon of Bologna, delayed Alberic's departure.

The day of Fano's conquest Alberic sent assurances to Ravenna that the bishop's holdings would not be tampered with, but apparently that was not satisfactory. The bishop and his brother needed further assurances, or perhaps a greater donation, and so they arrived at this most inopportune moment at the Abbey of San Andrea Catabarbara outside the castle walls. Alberic, Marozia and Lambert were invited to a feast there, and they deemed it unwise to decline.

Bishop John greeted them with impeccable good manners, congratulating Alberic on his many conquests and assuring him of the support and blessing of the exarchate of Ravenna. Marozia knew from the outset that John was up to something, but it was close to dawn and the feast nearly over when she realized what he had in mind. It was his half-brother Peter who gave the game away.

A sharp-faced man with an ill-cropped, bristling beard, Peter had an unctuous smile and a seemingly endless store of ribald jokes. Early in the evening he had attached himself to Lambert, evidently trying to endear himself to the man. Having failed utterly, he later approached Marozia, and after exchanging the usual pleasantries and drinking an inordinate amount of wine, he hinted broadly that he would soon be visiting Rome and would not be averse to seeing her in private.

Marozia found him repulsive, but she humored him, striving to fathom the motive behind his words. At last her patience was rewarded.

"You wouldn't think it," Peter grumbled, "but John is displeased."

"How so?" Marozia kept her voice idle and incurious. "He seems content enough."

"Appearances, appearances." Peter coughed. "The fact is"—he lowered his voice confidentially—"he is not certain that Alberic will—ah—show proper respect for the clergy.''

"You mean to say he will not send Bishop John an unreasonably large ransom," Marozia replied sharply.

"Ah, signora, signora." Peter gestured in dismay. "You take offense where none was meant. Of course he will demand nothing beyond the normal tithe, but you must understand, a clergyman of his influence could do a great deal to—ah—further your husband's career."

Marozia eyed John where he sat at the head of the table. His long slender diamond-ringed fingers were poised on the lip of his chalice. He laughed heartily at some joke he had just told.

"What amount does he wish from Alberic?" she demanded bluntly.

"Amount?" Peter looked astonished. "Why, nothing but what is seemly in the eyes of God. Church and state remain congenial. Surely you recognize that, signora. But what am I saying? Who knows more of the church than you yourself?"

For an instant Marozia thought she would strike him, but she controlled herself. Best to get away, though. She rose and groped for a civil farewell.

Peter appeared utterly abashed. "I beg pardon if I have offended you. I did not wish—"

"Take care," Marozia said coldly, "that you cling to your half-brother's skirts, Deacon Peter, for it is certain you will get nowhere on your own. Now if you will excuse me, I am ready to retire. I have already heard the cock's crow."

What transpired between Bishop John and Alberic later that night can only be conjectured. It is certain, however, that Alberic held his rule over the city and lands of Fano. Bishop John retained only the abbey and a few small benefices adjacent to the ducal holdings. He was accorded a tithe, or tenth, in compliance with canon law, but no more.

The parting between the two men was not amicable. The bishop left Fano the next afternoon, watched warily by the assembled troops of Lombards, and returned to Ravenna in high dudgeon. Thereafter he did not refer to Alberic in private except as "that ambitious upstart." As for Peter, he dismissed Marozia as the wife of a barbarian and made no attempt to see her when he came to Rome.

Chapter 23

In Alberic's absence events in Rome had taken a turn for the worse. It all arose out of Marcellus' feelings of injury. From the moment Alberic appeared at the Forum, putting an abrupt end to the original wedding plans, things seemed to have gone against the senator.

Poor man, he suffered the injury to his dignity more deeply than did his own son. In the end Petronius might even have been somewhat relieved that he did not have to marry Marozia. She was not, after all, a woman to enjoy his ceaseless gossip and idle pastimes and she obviously intimidated him.

I do believe that from the moment Alberic seized Marozia in his arms, Petronius felt as if a great burden had been lifted from him. Whining constantly, complaining to all who would listen that he had been dealt with unjustly, he nonetheless easily returned to his old ways. He regaled his drinking partners with stories about Marozia—all untrue, of course—and they had a lot of laughs at her expense. And he purchased at the slave market three pagan girls who were kept at Marcellus' house on the Via Lata to minister to Petronius' various lusts and appetites.

Marcellus could not endure the slight with such light-hearted ease. His honor had been insulted in public, his family affronted. Worst of all, a pope's decree had an-

nulled the legal betrothal of marriage between two noble
Roman families.

Marcellus tried to make an issue of the matter in the
Senate. In long, impassioned speeches he called for his
colleagues to censure the pope. Between the consuls who
ruled Rome and the prelates of the papal palace there was
only a tenuous connection; however, a common vote of
censure in the Senate might influence the Lateran cardinals
and force Pope Anastasius to step down.

Day after day Marcellus returned to the Senate with
new charges to levy against Anastasius III. Of course
Gaius, Theodora and their followers spoke against him,
refusing to countenance such action. Eventually even his
fellow patricians, who were at first sympathetic, grew tired
of Marcellus' ceaseless diatribes. They hid their faces
behind their hands and laughed among themselves when he
stood up to speak.

With everyone opposing him, feeling like the laughingstock of the city, Marcellus began to lose his senses.
Citizens found him wandering the sordid back quarters,
waving his arms and muttering to himself. As often as not
his sharp-nosed little chancellor had to scurry off to find
the senator and bring him back home.

Finally Marcellus turned silent. For many weeks he
gave no speeches in the Senate. He attended only a few
feasts, and when he did make an appearance, he observed
the proceedings without participating. At last he requested
an audience with Pope Anastasius.

Ignorant of Marcellus' state of mind, Anastasius agreed
to see him and welcomed the senator to his chambers.
Even then, disaster might have been averted had the pope
been shrewder, but he was a good-natured, innocent
man.

When Marcellus asked Anastasius if he recalled a

certain decree regarding Petronius, the pope hesitated for a moment.

"Decree? Ah, the unfortunate matter regarding—" He glanced at Marcellus and cleared his throat nervously. "Yes, I remember it now. I found it hard to believe myself, but there was quite a body of evidence against him."

"Evidence? Of what kind?" Marcellus' watery eyes looked inflamed.

"Why, witnesses. A priest gave testimony, as I recall, and there was a little man with an odd name." He thought a moment. "Gallimanfry."

"I see. I see." Marcellus could no longer control himself. His cheeks quivered. "And on the basis of these lies—this calumny—you insulted me, degraded my son before all the people of Rome. My name is besmirched!" Marcellus staggered to his feet. "They hoot as I pass! They laugh and point!"

Pope Anastasius was growing alarmed. "Marcellus, dear Senator, control your emotions. If there is anything—"

Marcellus leapt at Anastasius with a bared dagger, plunging it to the hilt into the heart of the man who had brought so much misery into his life. He must have acted in a frenzy, for he stabbed the pope seven times before the guards could drag him away. Had Marcellus ceased struggling, the soldiers might have shown mercy, but the senator continued his frenzied attack even after the pope had perished and at last the papal guards were forced to cut the assassin's throat.

Marcellus was excommunicated and his body dragged out into the campagna and left for the ravens.

The Curia, fearing a repetition of the looting that had taken place after Sergius' death, immediately went into seclusion. For two days and nights they conferred. On the morning of the third day they reached a decision. A cloud of white smoke rose from the chimney of the Lateran palace as a signal to all the citizens of Rome that a new pope had been elected. For three days the people thronged the streets in drunken celebration.

They soon realized, however, that the new pope was no better than his predecessor. Bishop Lando of Fermi was a mild-mannered and pious man whose main mark of distinction was his tolerance of Saracen rule in his own district. Plainly his selection was the result of compromise, and there were few in Rome or elsewhere who respected him sufficiently to pay him honor.

As for Petronius, he dismissed his father as an over-emotional madman and did everything in his power to dissociate himself from his parent. He even went so far as to joke about Marcellus' "ridiculous behavior." Throughout the funeral orations and the public grieving he drank steadily and intensely, going from house to house on the Via Lata in a stupor of oppressive merriment and cynicism. Nonetheless, the patricians took pity on him, and he was elected to the Senate to fill his father's place.

This was how things stood when Alberic, Marozia and Lambert returned to Rome. Of course we welcomed them home with open arms, and the House of Hadrian was once again a place of celebration.

Sergius had grown since Marozia left, and she appeared delighted with him, watching him walk and listening endlessly as he babbled and chattered, repeating the few words he had learned.

During the campaign Tasha and Annette looked after the boy and he was attached to both of them. That odious man Gallimanfry was left behind to run the household, a task he seemed to manage surprisingly well.

In the meantime I was much occupied with my studies and with caring for the pilgrims. I managed to find time whenever possible to visit the House of Hadrian and look in on the boy. This brought me into contact with Gallimanfry more frequently than I might have wished, but it was my duty to see that all was well.

Upon Marozia's return I took her aside and made her tell me all that had occurred. When her story was done, I related what had happened in Rome in her absence. I could see that she was deeply troubled by my news. When I was finished, we sat close, clasped in each other's arms.

There was one woman in Rome who privately rejoiced in the assassination of Pope Anastasius. This of course was Theodora.

Not long after Alberic and Marozia returned to the city she visited Gaius in his private bedchamber to discuss the matter that had been so long in her heart.

Husband and wife now lived apart. Gaius Theophylact's life was much changed. He frequently entertained concubines, indulging in a taste for athletic women with strong thighs, flat stomachs and small breasts. Passing through towns in the campagna on festival days, he would pause to watch the games and dancing, then select the wenches who pleased him most and bring them home to the Aventine.

Despite them, however, his chambers had the aura of bachelor quarters. They came and left without leaving a trace. My father's surcoats, clean and dirty, were piled helter-skelter on the chest; half-read cartularies lay open on the table where Tiberon had dropped them; chains and brooches of office were piled at the foot of the unmade bed. All betrayed the signs of a man distracted from life.

Tiberon, of course, was astonished to see Theodora appear at Gaius' chamber. Always droopy-eyed and shuffling, the faithful servant had recently grown a long grey beard that did nothing to improve his appearance.

As Theodora entered Gaius' private quarters, she had a moment of déjà vu. The wall hangings, the icons, the tapestries and furnishings all were familiar, yet all from a distant part of her life.

Two of the athletic wenches were with her husband now. Stripped to the waist, they waited on Gaius, pouring his wine while he watched. From tiredness or indifference his eyes were half closed. He was leaning back on the divan.

At his wife's entrance he jumped up. "Tiberon, I thought I commanded you—"

"Your mercy, Senator. The lady insisted." The poor man shrugged helplessly.

Gaius turned and spoke sharply over his shoulder. "Imogene, Francisca, be off. That's enough."

Glancing curiously at Theodora, the girls snatched up their shifts and left the room. Seeing that he was no longer needed, Tiberon bowed and departed.

"Wine?" Gaius gestured toward the amphora. Theodora could see from the flush in his cheeks that he had already had a great deal to drink.

"No, thank you." She shook her head. "I will be brief."

He gave a weary sigh. "That would please me."

"We see little enough of each other as it is."

"That was not my choice." His bleary eyes glistened with resentment.

Theodora met his gaze and continued. "Nonetheless, husband, you must acknowledge that we have profited by my arrangements."

"In some ways, yes," he replied, "but the name of Theophylact is not what it once was."

"Perhaps that can be changed."

"I don't see how." He ran his fingers through his hair. Then with a quick, sharp gesture he seized his chalice and tilted the amphora to fill it again. A few drops of red wine spilled on the floor. "My wife a bishop's concubine. My daughter the mother of a bastard and wife to a Lombard. The pope I chose murdered, as well as his successor, and the Saracens—my brother's killers—once again clawing at the heart of Rome."

He took a quick gulp from the chalice and with an unsteady hand set the cup on the open cartularies. The wine around the lip of the base left a ring on the parchment.

"Perhaps your ambitions were too high, husband." There was a note of unaccustomed gentleness in Theodora's voice. "Do not try to change what cannot be altered. My love for Bishop John—"

He winced visibly.

"Yes, husband," she repeated, "I love him. Marozia's feeling for Alberic is real as well. These things cannot be altered." She came a step closer. "Why oppose a woman's passion? You have already seen what damage can be done. Forcing Marozia to become Sergius' whore, attempting to marry her off to Petronius; what have you to show for these vain efforts?" Her tone was cutting. "Sergius is dead, Anastasius murdered, and a senator has been slain in the act of assassination."

"None of this was my doing," Gaius growled.

"No?" Theodora's eyes flashed with anger. "Not your doing? Now you would abrogate responsibility because your efforts failed. You could not turn your daughter's will to suit your diplomacy, and you will not turn mine."

Gaius made a motion as if to speak, but Theodora intervened, her voice cruel and sharp. "You have the courage but not the will for these times, Gaius. You expect men to act with honor and women to obey their husbands and fathers. Unfortunately, that is a dream of a time gone by. You have proud illusions, Gaius, but they are only that. I can respect you for them, even if I cannot love you, but they appear to me childish, inconsequential. All I ask of you is that you abandon this game of politics. It is *my* game, a game for realists. Give your interests over to other matters."

"Other matters?" Gaius replied vaguely. "If I do not have Rome, then I have nothing."

"You lost Rome long ago," Theodora spat. Her voice was hard with frustration. "Can't you see we are not a Roman but a Christian kingdom? The emperor cannot be seated by the Senate. His throne is in the Lateran. You bowed to that fact the night you sent Marozia to meet her destiny with Sergius. Yes, that one time you allowed the truth to intervene, even though you did not acknowledge it."

At this Gaius stood and came close to Theodora. His face seemed craggy, his eyes gleaming as they bored into her soul, searching, searching. She felt a moment of fear and unconsciously touched the stiletto at her waist.

She had mistaken his expression. He was not threatening, only curious, probing, as if by fathoming her will he could understand what had become of their marriage. "What would you have of me?" he asked.

"Do what you do well, husband," she answered, her voice hushed and insistent. "Give your speeches in the Senate. Inspire your Romans to think of grandeur. It is time you settled this aching in your heart. Paul is gone, but his murder is not yet avenged. You must take up arms, lead these Romans against the Saracens."

His eyes glittered. "How inspirational that sounds. Do you not think I would have marched against them long ago? Every alliance I have attempted has been shattered by misfortune—or by meddling women. Look what I am left with: the twelve *portae* of Rome with their unruly militia, hardly able to keep the peace in the city; this foolish pope, Lando, a stripling without power, and his few Sabine bowmen; and in the Senate nothing but gossips and social climbers. These are the men who tax the patriciates to feed their appetites, men without the will or the patience to organize their brigades, much less bear arms against the infidel. And consider the Papal States. There is such treachery and discord among them that fully half the bishops of Capua and Apulia have signed deeds of trust with the Saracens, treaties with the devils, in exchange for protection. What am I to do? Attack Husayn and his hordes with my housecarls and servants? No doubt that would satisfy my passion for revenge, but it would do nothing to stop the man I hate above all others.''

''You see it, then,'' Theodora replied firmly.

''What do you mean?''

''There is no other way.''

He shook his head. ''Speak clearly, wife. I cannot follow you.''

Suddenly Theodora reached up and touched Gaius' chest. Her hand lingered there like a pledge. ''You forget that the Lombard is your son-in-law.''

He snorted. ''That is useless. The upstart will not obey me.''

''He will oblige Marozia. Lombard he may be, but he has a barbarian's taste for the power of Rome.''

Gaius shrugged. ''He cannot unite the renegade bishops of Capua and Apulia.''

''No, only the pope can do that.''

''Lando?'' Gaius started to laugh.

''Lando's successor,'' Theodora said crisply. ''Think, husband, what would happen if the man who rules Spoleto and Benevento were to combine his power with that of the Archbishop of Ravenna, the Deacon of Bologna and the leading senators of Rome.''

Gaius withdrew from her hand as if it held poison. He eyed her from a distance. ''Oh, woman, you would have me approve my wife's lover as Bishop of Rome, pope over the Holy Roman Empire? All this while a reigning pope still lives?''

Her hand fell. "Yes."

"Bishop John of Ravenna," he murmured, "the man I have reason to loathe above all others. Peter of Bologna. Alberic the Lombard. All allied with Gaius Theophylact."

"These and his wife Theodora."

"An unholy alliance."

"These are unholy times."

He turned away and for an instant Theodora felt something like pity, but she stifled her feelings. He had no right to his illusions. Those empty Roman titles that he lavished upon himself with such abandon all might have meant something in times gone by. But now? Power was for those who could use it.

He turned to her. "We have no grounds for censuring Lando."

"Don't concern yourself with Lando." She paused. "When the name of Bishop John comes up for consideration, the Curia will argue that he cannot be Bishop of Rome, since he is also Bishop of Ravenna."

Gaius nodded. "The grounds on which Formosus was impeached."

"Exactly," she replied. "I will see that those objections are overcome, but it will require a unanimous vote in the Senate to ensure that his nomination is approved. To have the senatrix who introduces the motion opposed by her husband will make a farce of the proceedings."

Gaius hesitated only a moment. "I must have his oath to make war on the Saracens."

Theodora bowed her head. "I shall obtain this pledge."

There was a silence. Then finally Gaius spoke as if the words pained him greatly. "So be it," he said. "I shall support his nomination to the papacy."

Chapter 24

Within a month Bishop John arrived in Rome for the meeting of the Holy Synod. His appearance caused considerable astonishment, for unlike the other clerics, who brought only their private guard and small detachments of the militia, the bishop came with a full six regiments of armed and mounted troops.

Many of these wore captured Frankish helmets. With the dingy conical steel caps clamped down over their heads, the low, protruding flanges pressed over their noses and the draped mail panels dangling behind their necks, they looked very fearsome indeed. Their weapons too were Frankish. Many carried the enormous *francisca* with its curved, axlike blades, while others bore javelins that resembled the old Roman spear. Behind Bishop John rode his brother Peter with his regiments from Bologna, similarly arrayed.

The display was enough to strike terror into the heart of any enemy. Coming so suddenly upon Rome, the show of troops served to spread confusion and panic. Tenement dwellers gaped at the ranks of soldiers. Hagglers, priests, nuns and pilgrims poured from the churches and diaconiae around the Forum. In the Forum itself everything came to a standstill as people stood and stared. Everyone wondered what it could mean, this display of power from a cleric who by the Donation of Constantine was sworn to be faithful to Saint Peter's City.

But the populace was not to be left wondering for long.

On the first day the Synod met, Bishop John rose to condemn Pope Lando for heresies performed in the name of the Holy Office, acts of defilement in the eyes of God and perversions of Saint Peter's love and might. He produced witnesses as well, abbots from the Sabine monasteries and servants of the Lateran who stood ready to attest that Lando had indulged in bestiality and idol worship. A priest from the Hospice of Saint Gregory in Nocera swore that he had seen Lando deny the sacraments. A young nun of the Diocletian order testified with lowered eyes that she had witnessed Lando dancing by firelight, engaging in sodomy with a succubus. She broke down in hysterical sobbing and writhed on the floor when she recalled this event.

As the charges were raised against him, Lando struggled in vain to plead his innocence. His arguments withered as one by one his allies turned against him, recounting moments when they had seen him murmur the name of the devil or spit on the cross. The final and deciding testimony was given by his private chancellor, who testified that during Lent the pope demanded that the ashes of dead infants be applied to his forehead as the mark of penance.

In the end Lando was glad to escape with nothing worse than banishment and excommunication. On the night after the trial the poor man fled through the south gate along the Via Appia and hid in the catacombs. Theodora had set a close watch on him, however, and when he continued his journey the following day, he was set upon and murdered within sight of the Castel Gandolfo.

There was no question as to Lando's successor. Even as the deposed pope was fleeing through the night the

Curia met in closed chambers and John's name was put forward by his brother Peter. By morning the decision had been reached. Puffs of white smoke above the Lateran chambers announced the news, and the sacred tiara settled on the brow of John of Ravenna, now Pope John X, Bishop of Rome.

Senate approval came swiftly. Theodora spoke ardently, praising the strength and godliness of the new pope. She promised the assembled senators that John would soon deliver them from all their enemies. For his part Gaius Theophylact said little, but he did not oppose the nomination, and when it came to the vote, his voice joined the thunder of "ayes" that resounded through the chamber.

To honor the coronation and succession the papal storehouses opened and many festival days followed. This all occurred near Christ Mass, at the Feast of Fools, and the ascent of a new pope only increased the fervor and drunkenness of the populace. A priest from San Martino, a man with a grotesque red nose and a walleye, was elected Lord of the Revels and installed as the Abbot of Fools. The crowd shaved his head, turned his ragged cassock inside out and led him to the altar of his church, where he was made to bend over while the drunken citizens simulated lewd acts upon his person.

The priest took it all in good spirit, as the Lord of Revels must do, and recited a benediction filled with doggerel and gibberish while wenches and their companions played at dice on the altar behind him. The air stank with the smell of burning sandal leather, swung in the air by acolytes who held their noses. Priests wearing beast masks, dressed as fools or women, danced in the nave.

Later all rushed from the church into the streets, dragging the fool with them. While naked men in carts hurled manure at the crowd, the Abbot of Fools continued his lengthy prayers and benedictions, issuing indulgences to all who demanded them. It was a memorable feast, and by the time the revels came to an end all were in drunken high spirits.

Beneath the raucous celebration there was a mood of uneasiness. By now the news of Bishop John's mistreatment of his own fiefs had spread far and wide. All knew how he had taxed the peasants, driving many of them to their graves. Though the populace of Rome glutted themselves from John's storehouses, there was an edge of desperation to their joy, as if this might be the last great festival before the bad times began.

For many, I am afraid, the prophetic dread proved all too real. As if some curse had been laid upon the city, an outbreak of malaria seized Rome soon after the passing of Christ Mass. In the weeks that ensued it was all I could do to trudge from one hospice to the next, treating the sick with doses of aloes and praying for the dead and dying as Rome's recurring blight took its toll on her citizens.

The coronation of Pope John was a triumph for Theodora. Casting aside all restraint, she moved into an annex of the Lateran palace, which became her sole residence in Rome. Far more than concubine, she was at least for a time Pope John's most trusted advisor. It was she who realized the danger of the epidemic, for she understood the superstitious nature of her people.

"They are restless and uneasy," she warned him. "Because of this outbreak of sickness they are murmuring against the choice of the Curia."

They were in John's private quarters when she spoke of it. He seemed annoyed. Already matters of government pursued him everywhere—and now even to his bedchamber.

"What of it?" he snapped dismissively. "They saw my troops; they know the strength of Ravenna."

Theodora flushed. "You cannot turn Ravenna against Rome." Then, moderating her tone somewhat, she came close to him and took his arm. "John, John, these are Romans. I know you think that means nothing. They are only creeping, filthy beggars, merchants and foot soldiers. But there is in the soul of these people—yes, even in the lowliest—some pride." She noted his look, as if she were speaking nonsense, and went on hastily. "They can endure only so much and then they will rebel. There are times when all Romans speak with a single voice. It is a great mystery to me, but it happens."

"How am I to fathom the emotions of these mysterious people?" Pope John inquired bitingly.

"Think how they feel," she insisted. "Berengar in the north is king of the Lombards, crowned at Mantua. They know he fights furiously in Tuscany, Lombardy and Aquileia to repel the Franks and Magyars. Here they see Alberic gathering Spoleto, Benevento and many other duchies under his reign. But whom do these Lombards serve? To whom are they beholden? If the pope does not bestow their crown, then who is their master?"

"Bestow the crown—on a *Lombard*?" Pope John wrinkled his nose in disgust.

"You are a ruler now," Theodora reminded him harshly. "Behave as such. Ravenna is only a country town, a way station between the Papal States and the Byzantine Empire, Rome, need I remind you, is the heart of the kingdom."

She turned on him, her eyes burning. "Do not make me regret my choice, dear John. Either you scorn your prejudices and welcome the Lombards' oaths of fealty, or I swear by all I believe, the fear of the people of Rome will drag you down."

John paced for a moment. "Will Alberic cooperate?"

"He is honor bound to Berengar."

"Then Berengar must be emperor."

Theodora smiled. "There is no other way."

After a long pause John nodded. "Very well. I shall send Berengar a summons . . . soon."

"Tomorrow."

"Yes, tomorrow."

"There is one other thing."

He shot her a dark look. "What is that, Theodora?"

"Your pledge to wage war on the infidels—you must announce that too, or my husband may begin to doubt. I have made my promise to him—"

"On my behalf?"

"On your behalf. My husband will be your ally as long as the Saracens are our enemy—*and we fight them.*"

"And after that?" There was sarcasm in the pope's voice.

"After that we shall see."

Soon after this conversation we all heard of the burning of the beautiful imperial monastery of Farfa in the Sabine. Every Roman was shaken by the news. Next to Nonantula, Farfa was the most magnificent monastery in all Italy. The abbey had a splendid church, dedicated to the sacred Virgin and surrounded by five basilicas. Its architecture, its riches, its invaluable ciborium and onyx columns, its magnificent colonnades were renowned throughout the land.

Most impressive of all were the walls and towers that protected the fortified palace, basilica and dwelling houses. An army of great and petty barons secured these holdings.

The Saracens breached these defenses, laid waste the estates, fortresses, churches and villas. The abbot held out bravely, marshaling his vassals to protect the magnificent edifice, but in the end the convent and monastery were taken, the ciborium of the high altar destroyed. Somehow the abbot managed to send a few of the convent's treasures to Rome. Then he and his flock buried the onyx columns and fled, leaving the shell of beautiful Farfa in the hands of the infidels.

Such tales of woe made every Roman shudder. Something must be done to stop the tide of terror that was sweeping toward the city. Thus when it was heard that Berengar was on his way south to be crowned emperor, the capital was filled with jubilation. Everyone knew how Berengar had stemmed the tide of Magyars flocking across the Alps; how he had usurped and blinded King Lewis of Provence; and finally, consolidating his power in Lombardy, Tuscany and Aquileia, how he had crowned himself king in Mantua.

In all of Rome, it seemed, only Marozia failed to gain satisfaction from news of the impending alliance.

"What will you do?" she demanded of Alberic one day when they were alone in the House of Hadrian.

"I will give my loyal support, of course," replied Alberic. "Berengar is the general I serve. He has fought long and hard. I will not try to diminish his moment of glory." He smiled. "After all, Marozia, this is a victory for all Lombards."

"I rejoice in that," she replied. "But it is also a victory for my mother."

"What do you mean?" he asked. "And why speak so of your mother?"

"Because I know her mind," she answered coldly, "almost as well as I know my own. You are a threat to her."

"I? How?"

"First, you are my husband and through me privy to

the secrets of Roman life. Second, you are a general, so you threaten the power of the one she loves most." She paused. "I mean, of course, Pope John."

"She is beholden to him, then?"

"She is his paramour," Marozia reminded him.

Alberic nodded and rose to his feet. "I detest that man."

"That too she knows, I assure you, and that the only way John can win your loyalty is through your fealty to Berengar."

"Whether Berengar is my king or my emperor, I will serve him." Alberic studied Marozia closely. "You must do nothing to steal this honor from my liege."

"But Alberic, don't you see—"

"I see everything," he snapped. "I have seen all the politicking, backbiting and petty insult that Rome can offer, and I tell you, Marozia, you do not understand the oath of fealty that binds me. Do what you will with your mother and her wiles, but I will not betray Berengar. Nor shall you."

Marozia considered him sullenly. In spite of herself she understood what had drawn her to him from the moment she saw him in Siena to now. It was integrity, simple, uncomplicated, like a curious foreign gem delivered to her hand.

She wanted to shout at him, to make him wake up to reality. He would never understand Rome; that she could see. He could never compete with the treacherous alliances that came and went as quickly as a handclasp or a salute.

His sense of honor and justice came from another world, and because of that she could not argue against him. To do so would be to oppose the very force she admired, that strong simplicity of character. Even so, she did not share his illusions. She knew that before much more time passed she would have to speak with her mother, if only to defend Alberic's interests and her own.

"I have been expecting you," Theodora said when Marozia entered the Lateran audience chamber.

"I will not detain you long," her daughter replied coldly. "You have acted fast to summon Berengar."

Theodora shrugged. "It was necessary. Pope John's predecessors left the issue in doubt far too long."

"Nonetheless," Marozia went on, "Alberic must remain in Rome."

Her mother raised a graceful hand to her neck to toy with her emerald necklace. "I do not see how that concerns me," she replied vaguely. "Berengar and Alberic may find it inconvenient to reside in the same city."

"I am sure they will. That is why Berengar must return to the north."

"Return?" Theodora appeared startled. "But my dear Marozia, that is impossible to predict. When Berengar is emperor, he may do as he desires."

Marozia shook her head. "I don't wish to banter, Mother. We both know that Berengar will obey the pope's wishes."

"Marozia, I have so little influence over—"

A short, sharp laugh cut off her words.

Theodora let the necklace fall to her breast. "This Alberic of yours," she said sneeringly, "does he aspire to greater things?"

"He will obey Berengar," replied Marozia.

"But will he obey the pope, my dear?"

"Within limits."

"And who will define those limits?"

Marozia did not answer. There was a pause before Theodora continued. "I see. I would be extremely careful if I were you, daughter."

"I intend to be."

"I am not sure you understand the consequences—"

"That is why my suit is especially important."

Theodora stiffened slightly. "Oh? What suit is that?"

"To become a member of the Senate."

Her mother smiled. "I fear you aspire too high—and too soon."

Marozia did not return the smile. "As I understand it, you desperately need Alberic's support."

"Desperate would be the wrong word."

"Then I leave it to you to find the right one. The fact is, neither you nor Pope John—and least of all Father—can marshal the forces you need. There is only one man in this city who has proved his military might. If he is to serve Rome, he must be privy to the decisions of the Senate."

"Marozia, have modesty. You are a woman—"

At this, Marozia did smile. "You too are a woman, Mother. But I warrant you see the situation more clearly than the rest. To arouse Alberic's enmity at this juncture would be most dangerous."

Theodora did not look at her daughter. Finally she muttered almost to herself, "Three Theophylacts in the Senate. It would not look well."

"To whom?" demanded Marozia. "To Pope John?" When her mother did not reply, she added very softly, "Are you so afraid of his wrath, then?"

"Certainly not," Theodora replied brusquely.

"Then you will humor me?"

Theodora studied her daughter's eyes. "Yes," she said at last, "I will humor you."

"I shall be honored to serve as senatrix," Marozia murmured, "and I can assure you that Alberic will show his profoundest thanks as well."

"See that he does," Theodora replied sharply. She left the audience chamber without a word of parting.

Berengar the Lombard, famed warrior, conqueror of the northern marches, slayer of the Magyars, was an imposing presence, a man who immediately attracted respect. Broad-shouldered, dark-featured, with lowering brows and a gruff voice, he seemed perpetually angry, but his bursting laughter was thunderous and appealing, an expression of easy good humor that affected all those around him. It was impossible to dislike him.

He and Alberic greeted each other like long-lost brothers. To honor Alberic and Marozia the Lombard king chose to take up residence in the House of Hadrian until the coronation.

The banquets they gave for him were in the Lombard style, with meats and fish in pairs: suckling pigs with crabs, hares with pike, partridges with trout, ducks and heron with carp, beef with eels. For entertainment there were many displays of strength and prowess. Castrated weightlifters hoisted marble slabs above their heads, and athletes tested their skill at hurling and the javelin.

On the final day before the coronation Berengar ordered his horsemen to display the newest war sport. Mounted knights bearing long, unwieldy lances raced their chargers toward spinning quintains. The crowds cheered indiscriminately as the riders were unhorsed and the quintains broken asunder.

In comparison to these celebrations the rites of the coronation seemed solemn and dreary. The nobles of the Senate, accompanied by Roman militia, greeted Berengar on the steps of San Adriano and read long speeches in his honor. All around stood a forest of lances ornamented with images of eagles, lions, wolves and dragons. Teachers from all the schools were present, with a poet to record the event in lines of hexameter liberally adorned with quotations from Virgil.

As a sign of unity the pope's brother Peter, now a cardinal, accompanied Petronius and Gaius to greet Berengar at the Senate. They followed him in respectful procession to the steps of Saint Peter's. There Pope John, who was seated on a folding throne, rose ceremoniously at his approach. When Berengar had tendered to the church his oath granting protection and justice, the doors of the basilica opened.

A wave of applause burst from the crowd as the chancellor brought forth the domed golden crown and the emperor's tiara to replace the steel one of Lombard. A papal lector read the diploma of the new emperor and Berengar confirmed the Roman Catholic Church in her possessions. Finally Berengar called for a train of ox carts to be drawn up. They bore a hoard of treasures that he presented to the pope, the clergy, the nobility and the people. At the sight of his bounty cries of joy erupted from the crowd.

On that same day amid the proclamations it was announced that Marozia would join her mother and father in the Senate. By papal decree and with the consent of the emperor, Duke Alberic was formally ceded all the benefices and allodial holdings that had fallen under his sword, excluding only convents and monasteries belonging to Pope John.

I know for certain there was something that gave Alberic greater joy than any of these ceremonies, for this was the day Marozia chose to tell him she was pregnant again. She had already consulted a soothsayer, a man found by Gallimanfry. The egg of a pheasant, dropped into a liquid of sacred oil spiced with mint and pepper, had turned red and floated to the surface. It was a boy.

Chapter 25

Shortly after the coronation Emperor Berengar returned to
Mantua to restore unity among the northern Lombards.
Almost at once he was caught up in a fresh campaign
against the Magyars, who had taken advantage of his
absence to cross the Alps and make inroads toward Cremona.
Fierce battles raged along the River Adige and the River
Po.

Meanwhile, Pope John and Duke Alberic launched
separate successful campaigns against the Saracen stronghold of Saracinesco, in the mountains beyond Tivoli, and
Ciciliano, that treacherous rocky fortress in the Sabines.

To my father fell the task of rebuilding the Roman
navy at Ostia. Such a grand enterprise might take years,
but my father was undaunted. He knew the necessity of
amassing a strong fleet for this of all campaigns.

The Saracen dromons were powerful and well armed.
From their bases on the island of Sicily and their strongholds
along the coast the infidels dominated all the sea travel
west of Italy. For decades no Roman ship had dared
venture into the shipping lanes without fear of Saracen
piracy. As a result the Roman navy was in a shambles, its
great galleys rotten with neglect. Its skilled seamen had
been dispersed and were now fishing the coastal waters or
engaging in petty trade with Tuscan sea towns.

It was a formidable challenge that awaited my father,

but he did not flinch. Freed at last from the politics of Rome, he used his authority to impress seamen, craftsmen and outfitters to his service. They at once set about restoring the strength of the Roman fleet, determined to hone it into a fine weapon capable of withstanding the savage Saracen attacks.

Ships were commissioned. Hundreds of men were set to work laying the keels for the great double-ended biremes with their paired masts and two ranks of oars. The great strategist of the day, Nicholas Picingli, was recruited to retrain the mariners in the fundamentals of warfare at sea.

During these months, when Alberic too was often away on campaign, the midwife Vespasia returned to the House of Hadrian to bully the servants and handmaidens into submission. Concerned for Marozia's welfare, I often came to see her.

In the course of these visits, much to my dismay, I frequently met Gallimanfry, who never ceased to remind me of his intentions toward me. I must say I was not so repelled by the man as I used to be. Having given up his ragged traveling clothes, he now dressed in the Roman style, a short white tunic fastened at the waist with a suede belt trimmed in gold.

If he drank to excess he could not quite be blamed, for his conversation only turned more animated, his gestures more emphatic. At odd moments he would even betray signs of remarkable learning. This intrigued me, since I could not fathom where a servant had acquired such knowledge. I sometimes found myself involved in lengthy and not unpleasant discussions with him.

One day, I know not how, we found ourselves in the dressing chamber adjacent to the indigo chapel. This room was set aside for the comfort of visiting prelates, and like the other sleeping chambers in the House of Hadrian, it had a luxurious lounge with many bolsters.

As we were expecting a visit from the Bishop of Benevento, I had come to this room to see that all was in readiness. Gallimanfry, having followed me there, began to regale me by reciting long passages from *The Flies*, an ancient Greek poem, quite obscene. As I went about my chores I pretended not to be amused, but in fact his antics as he acted out each part were so ingenious and bizarre that I found myself laughing heartily.

At my outburst he stopped in midsentence, approached me and looked at me closely, as if I were some interesting specimen of bird or leaf.

"What is the matter, sir?" I inquired, uneasy at his scrutiny.

"You laughed," he replied simply, as if it were some sort of phenomenon.

"Well, yes, I am capable of laughter."

"If you are capable, why don't you indulge more often?"

"I am afraid I find little in life that warrants amusement."

"That is because you seal yourself away with churchly matters."

"Perhaps, but it is God's work."

He grinned. "You forget, Lena, that I too did God's work. Among the monks of St. Basil's I lived like a pauper. I did nothing but beg and pray—and I gained nothing from it."

"Perhaps you should have persisted," I said stiffly. "To reach a state of grace requires constant toil."

"No." He shook his head. "To reach a state of grace requires a fortune in gold to grease the hand of the bishop. Offices do not come cheaply these days."

"They are only the outward signs of inward grace."

"I am finished with grace. No better act did I perform than the walk from that den of soul-killing poverty, when I returned to life."

I was horrified. "Oh, Gallimanfry, you are mistaken. Please believe me, you have made a grievous error, forswearing God's orders."

"Have I, then?" he demanded. I noted that his face was quite flushed.

It was then, without warning, that he took me in his arms and pressed his lips to mine. This was something that for all his admiring words to my person, I had never expected him to do. For the duration of that kiss such bewilderment overcame me as I had never suffered before.

Oddly, I did not feel endangered, but a great swooning took hold of me, as if I were being possessed. His lips, to my astonishment, were quite gentle, as were the hands that sought my body beneath my habit.

I would rather draw a veil over this scene, but that which men and women have done cannot be hidden from God. Shall I not freely admit, then, that I let this man have his way with me? For all his blunt manners and unfeeling postures, Gallimanfry showed the virtues of a devoted lover.

True, I cried out when he broke into me, but that could have been from surprise or fear. I know I had a sudden vision of Saint Peter, and I thought, Now the world has opened and I am his.

Whether I was thinking of Saint Peter or of the manhood that stirred inside me, I cannot be sure. I know only that our clothes lay around us on the floor, while from our mingled heat came an indescribable ecstasy. Many times he receded, then rose again, each arousal culminating in a violent explosion and shaking of his body; there were several moments when I joined him in a similar, mysterious kind of frenzy.

I was glad, when at last we passed from that chamber and went our separate ways, that the world had opened. Such a strange pleasure, to be kept so long from a woman.

It seems to me most peculiar that Marozia's child was born that same night; indeed, her labors coursed with ours during the long passionate dark. The chamber where we lay was quite distant from my sister's room, and we heard nothing of the servants' commotion or of her birthing cries. Such was the power of our passion that we heard only the beating of our own hearts.

As for the child, it was a boy, just as the soothsayer had predicted. Marozia named him Anthony.

BOOK III

Chapter 26

The waters of the Mediterranean glittered azure, and dappled patterns quivered on the white houses surrounding the seaport. On this day in April the town was bustling with slaves, soldiers and freemen, all trudging down to the harbor. Their carts were laden with armaments, tackle and baskets of food for the waiting ships. Shouts and cries mingled with the clatter of weapons and the clopping of horses' hooves.

Gaius Theophylact pushed his way through the crowd, followed closely by Tiberon and a small band of guards. The senator passed nearly unnoticed among the soldiers, shipwrights, merchants and farmers who thronged the streets. Now and then someone would take a second look, startled to see a Roman general walking about like a common guard, but Gaius seemed oblivious to stares as well as to the mad bustle of activity that surrounded him.

Passing carts laden with dried figs, olives and hard bread, Gaius paused only to give an order. At his command the peasants scurried about, moving even more rapidly for the harbor.

Merchants, craftsmen and peasants all seemed to benefit from this ambitious campaign. Excitement as well as mercenary ambition could be seen in their eyes.

There was something more besides, if Gaius judged it right: relief. The great military adventure had finally begun. Saracen tyranny was coming to an end at last. If all went well, new ports would be opened, new roads made safe for every citizen.

It had been many years, Gaius reflected, since his famous speech in the Senate, when he vowed that church, Romans and Lombards would combine forces to overthrow the infidels. The senators had cheered him then, and the people had reinforced those cheers with their own approbation.

The destination of Gaius' great fleet was no secret. High on a hill overlooking the boggy plain of the River Garigliano was a Saracen fortress that was reputed to be impregnable. Its walls were of closely fitting granite, constructed without mortar, standing twenty-six feet high. At the gates were spiked doors of tree-thick solid timber faced with bands of steel.

Behind those gates, as every Italian, especially every Roman, knew well, were ranks of the finest horesmen on the continent. From the fortress on the Garigliano poured a seemingly endless flood of mounted Saracens armed with their bows and arrows and deadly curved scimitars. So far these horsemen had repelled every force that had been thrown against them.

From Ostia to the Garigliano was nearly one hundred seventy miles by sea. To make the journey Gaius Theophylact and the strategist Nicholas Picingli had assembled the largest fleet of ships since the time of the Caesars. Eighty-one biremes fully manned with oarsmen stood offshore in the cramped harbor.

A second fleet of fishing boats equipped to carry men and armaments had been gathered from ports as far north as Genoa.

A large army of mounted soldiers with thousands of reserve horses had already departed from Rome along the Via Appia. Led by Alberic, the land force would await the fleet at Gaeta, less than fifteen miles north of the Garigliano, for the final assault on the Saracen fortress where Caliph Husayn held sway.

Husayn—how many times had Gaius Theophylact uttered that name during the past ten years? And still the image it conjured made him shudder with fury.

"Gaius! Gaius! Gaius!"

The shouts thundered in his ears as Gaius Theophylact mounted the long plank to the first galley. The oarsmen, their sweeps standing, joined in the acclamation as the senator strode to the forepeak and mounted the steps to the captain's chair.

Gaius turned to Tiberon, who was close behind. "Is Alberic's position known?"

The old secretary nodded eagerly. "The runners just arrived. They report him three miles from Gaeta."

"Very good." Gaius allowed himself a broad smile. It was extraordinary news; for a large force to move with such speed was unprecedented—and the Muslims had harassed the advancing troops every step of the way.

Still smiling, Gaius scanned the galleys that flanked him. A dizzying array of standing oars, masts and bowsprits hugged the wharves like a single drifting forest. On the adjacent ship, the pope's own bireme, the ermine-covered captain's chair was empty.

Gaius' smile vanished. "Where is Pope John?"

"He—" Tiberon cleared his throat. "I believe he is still in consultation."

"With whom?"

There was a moment's hesitation. "With Senatrix Theodora, my lord."

Impatiently Gaius jumped up, and the roar of acclamation reminded him of the crowd's presence. Hang them, they would not be ignored.

Despite the clamor Gaius' mind was elsewhere. Pope John was meeting with Theodora in one of the ecclesiastical merchant houses on the wharf. Even at this moment of triumphant farewell she chose the pope rather than her own husband.

It was not her disloyalty that perturbed the senator; nor was it jealousy. It was the empty seat on the adjoining galley that annoyed him. All the efforts to demonstrate unity between Senate and church, all the preparations for a victorious campaign were somehow threatened by the omen of that empty seat.

As Gaius stood brooding, the crowd continued to shout for him, the frenzy in their voices building.

He could delay no longer. It was fourteen years since Paul bled to death in his brother's arms, his last words a curse upon Caliph Husayn. In the fortress on the Garigliano the Saracen leader waited, supremely confident. For more than fifty years the Romans had been unable to drive the Muslim invaders from their land. Now the time had come.

Gaius raised his hand and an instant hush settled over the crowd.

"Fellow Romans, Lombards, defenders of the pope and the crown." They stirred around him, acknowledging the courtesy of his address. "For generations we have been plagued by a pestilence that feeds upon our crops and livestock, that threatens the lives of our women and children, devours our kingdom and gnaws at the very heart of the Roman Empire. These are not men we set out to fight, but fleas and lice that crawl about the face of our kingdom, sucking our blood and poisoning our country."

Gaius took a step toward the bowsprit, high above the heads of the crowd. Faces strained to see him. Swords unsheathed and ready, eyes shining, the soldiers seemed to sway as one.

"Who among you has not lost a friend, a loved one, in battle against these creatures? Who has not heard their ungodly chants howling from their pagan throats? It is an insult to every Christian." He held up a hand. "You all know my own story. You know how Paul the Roman was captured by Caliph Husayn, how they severed his feet and crucified him—not to die as a man but as a living carcass, fit only for the birds of prey.

"Yes, that was my brother. When I found him, he still knew my name. Romans and Lombards, Christians and soldiers, he called on my honor, he whispered with his dying breath that I was to avenge him and save Rome for our people.

"My countrymen, I pass that pledge on to you. I ask you, will you avenge—"

His voice was drowned by a great roar of hoarse cries and wild cheering. The soldiers crowded around the wharves, ships and warehouses, their steel headpieces and shoulder mail flashing in the sun. Spears, swords and halberds waved above the surging mass.

Gaius cast his gaze from ship to ship, along the ranks of shouting soldiers. Did they have the strength? The skill? After all these years of suffering, enduring the Saracen hordes, was this the turning point for Rome, the beginning of a new era? Or was it false courage, the empty crowing of inexperienced men who would turn and run at the first scent of blood?

Here and there Gaius saw a man whose lips were closed, whose face bore the stony look of a creature battered by war. He thought, There is an experienced soldier; that one will stand in battle. These silent ones were few, though, and all around them were the anxious, cheering enthusiasts who gained courage from the frantic demonstrations of their neighbors.

Called to arms by pope, Lombard and senators, these men needed to pass no test, prove no skill to become soldiers. The drudgery of their lives, the sameness of their daily toil were a burden to them. In each of these men—peasants from the fields, servitors in the courts and churches, apprentices and merchants—was a fierce, wild cry, half-god and half-animal, sprung from the yearning to take vengeance for humiliation. Theirs was a blood quest, need and greed for victory, and they turned to Gaius to lead them to glory.

Suddenly a change came over the crowd. Heads turned. Fingers pointed at the high balcony of the church granary.

Pope John X had appeared, adorned in a magnificent robe edged with purple braid. Its pearls and gold glistened in the sunlight. John's headpiece also glittered with a mass of rubies, emeralds and amethysts as he bowed to acknowledge the cheers of the crowd.

Directly behind him, furtive eyes scanning the masses, stood John's brother, Cardinal Peter. His white robe almost blended with the stucco wall of the granary. Moving like a vole trapped in a cage, he darted to one side of the balcony and then the other. Always behind the pope but never hidden, his hands reached out nervously to touch the railing.

"Senator." Tiberon touched Gaius' arm. "Look there, your wife and daughters." We caught his gesture and nodded back; we had just taken our places of honor on an adjoining balcony. On this occasion Theodora had summoned us together as a family to say farewell to Father. Of course it was for the benefit of the crowd, to show them the pope had the full support of the Theophylacts, but I believe Mother was sincerely proud of him. Much had been accomplished. If the campaign was successful, we would all deserve many honors.

My head was covered and I wore a simple grey gown. Gallimanfry stood nearby. He had become the boys' tutor and was now their constant companion.

Marozia took her place in the forefront, alongside her mother. The two senatrices, proud of their position, drew cheers too. Near me, in attendance, was the dark-eyed Tasha.

Suddenly little Sergius darted forward to peer over the edge of the balcony. Without hesitation Gallimanfry made a lunge and pulled the boy away from danger.

A short tussle ensued, fists flying, as Sergius attempted to beat his way free of his tutor. Then the younger boy, Anthony, seemed to catch his brother's yearning for independence. Shaking free of Marozia's hand, he lifted an arm and waved to the crowd of soldiers.

His gesture brought more cheers and good-natured laughter. The little boy jumped up and down, delighted in his moment of triumph.

I glanced at my mother. Theodora seemed magnificently dominant over all, her proud head raised in bold profile, the grey-streaked black hair pulled high on her head. Brooches, necklaces and gold pendants glittered in the sunlight.

I saw that she had not yet looked at my father. Instead she turned toward Pope John. Their eyes met, and some tacit, serious admonition passed between them, leaping the narrow space that separated the two adjacent balconies.

Had any one else seen that secret look?

Gaius turned toward Tiberon. "We have been delayed long enough. Order the soldiers aboard. We leave in half an hour whether the pope is ready or not."

"Yes, Senator." Tiberon was looking past him again,

out toward the balcony where his family stood. "Gaius Theophylact, if you please, your wife—"

Following the direction of his secretary's gaze, Gaius saw that Theodora was looking at him, her hand raised in the gesture of a fond and gentle parting. Her abstracted air had been replaced by an almost abashed signal of wifely concern.

He returned her look without stirring. He admired her as one might admire a statue of marble, appraised her beauty, the fineness of line and the grace of her pose. How he had longed for her once, with what passion clung to the memory of their first good years together; but it had all faded like a passing dream.

He recalled how she found him that day years ago when she came to his bedchamber. He shuddered. The dissolutions and debaucheries he had turned to in despair, in a vain attempt to forget, were things of the past. Before him lay the greatest expedition of his lifetime, the most ambitious Roman enterprise within memory. This was no time for regrets.

Chapter 27

"Guttersnipe. You twisted, wretched, hunched ogre of a man!" Sergius' voice was piercing. "In front of those soldiers you—you made me look the fool."

"Apologies, apologies, signorino," Gallimanfry muttered, head down. "Now put your cap on and look to it. The cart's about to leave."

"To hell with the cart." Sergius hurled his velvet cap into the dust and turned on his tutor. "I deserve better than that. You saw Grandfather give his speech, did you not, Gallimanfry?"

"Yes, that I did."

Sergius puffed out his chest. "Well, someday I shall give speeches far better than that one."

"Not unless you study your Cicero as I have urged and—"

"Cicero!" The boy spat in the dust, narrowly missing his hat. "He's old and disgusting and boring besides. Now, speeches—why, I can make up speeches right off the top of my head. Listen—"

"Come along, Master Sergius, you can give all the speeches you want on the way back to Rome. Mount up there."

"I refuse to ride in that bumpy cart. It's a disgrace. A cart is for commoners, peasants." He spun and called to his mother.

She smiled and looked up. "Yes, Sergius?"

"May I ride in the palanquin? I hate this old cart."

"Certainly, if you wish." Marozia turned to her younger son. "Anthony, would you like to go with Gallimanfry in the cart?"

"Behind the horses?" The boy's eyes shone. "Yes, Mother. Oh, yes."

"Very well, then. You boys change places. Gallimanfry, you see to Anthony."

"Yes, of course, signora."

"Sergius, you will ride with Tasha."

Sergius made a face, but hastened into the servant's palanquin. Up ahead, Anthony seized his tutor's hand and Gallimanfry hoisted the boy to the seat behind the driver.

Theodora traveled in the lead, alone in a litter surrounded by guards. Immediately behind her was the cart with Gallimanfry, Anthony and a driver. This was followed by the double chair in which Lena rode side by side with Marozia. Last came the palanquin with Sergius and Tasha. Dozens of guards surrounded the entourage, with watchmen riding ahead, alert to bandits.

"I was a great success, was I not?" demanded Anthony, looking up at his tutor.

"Yes, I should say so," replied Gallimanfry. "You had them cowering at your feet."

"Do you think I will be a great leader someday?"

"I wouldn't be surprised." Gallimanfry, unsettled by the movement of the cart, belched noisily.

"Why do you do that?" The boy's eyes were wide with appreciation.

"Do what?"

"Why do you belch like that?"

Gallimanfry snorted. "To clear the alimentary canal and make room for better things to come."

"What better things?"

"Wine, lamb, roast suckling pig, freshly baked fig pudding. Shall I go on?"

The boy wasn't listening. "Sergius says you are a common drunkard."

"Oh ho, is that true?" Gallimanfry leered. "What do you think?"

"I cannot tell." He hesitated. "You are a tutor. How can you be a drunkard?"

"I'm a man of many parts. Some of them"—he belched again—"whole."

Anthony continued to stare, and Gallimanfry, finally responding, stirred uncomfortably.

"Sergius does not like you," Anthony said finally.

"More's the pity."

"Do you like him?"

Gallimanfry shifted in his seat, spat over the side of the swaying cart and stared up at the cloudless sky.

"Well?"

"An odd thing, Master Anthony, a very odd thing," Gallimanfry mused.

"What is?"

"The way we are born."

"What is so odd about that?"

"Not the birth itself, but what's born into us. That brother of yours, he is always the one for pomp and ceremony, but he cannot bear to be interfered with. You tell him to do a thing and he won't. But you set him up on a little stub of a pedestal and he'll lecture everyone on the way it should be done. That's not what you or I or any Roman taught him to do. It's born to him. He can't tolerate the voices of others in his ears."

"Do you think he'll be a senator one day?"

"Oh, no doubt of that. No doubt, no doubt." Gallimanfry wiped his lips and looked about as if aching for a drink. "Mind, you'll be more than a senator yourself."

"Me?"

"Just the way they cheered you was a fair sign of that."

"But my brother is older."

"Older, yes, but no wiser. Did you hear the voices of the people?"

"Oh, yes." Anthony bounced up and down on the seat. "Everything. It was wonderful."

"Your brother, I warrant, heard nothing, only his own demands speaking in his ear."

"I don't understand you."

Gallimanfry shook his shaggy head. "If I make myself clearer, this day may become cloudier."

Anthony stared at his tutor. "You still haven't answered my question."

"It must have slipped my mind."

"Do you like my brother?"

"I am his tutor."

"That is no answer."

"Some questions should not be answered."

Anthony looked at his hands, then at the back of the driver. Gallimanfry rubbed his chin. The two continued their journey to Rome, each buried in his own thoughts.

I had pulled the curtain aside and was watching Gallimanfry and young Anthony by his side.

Something in my expression must have caught Marozia's eye, for she asked, "What are you thinking, Lena?"

I was startled. Though we saw much of each other, she rarely showed any interest in my thoughts. Always, it seemed, she was preoccupied with her own affairs—politics, the Senate, her estates and the business of Rome.

"I was listening to their voices," I replied.

Marozia laughed. "Lena, you are always listening, always so quiet. What passes through your mind?"

"Just . . . things I imagine."

"What sorts of things?"

"There are times when I have visions."

Suddenly she was looking at me as closely as if I were a stranger, and I realized that Marozia must know very little about me. There was a kind of sadness in that, for there were many reasons why we sisters would be drawn together.

"Yes," I explained, "there are times when I see the world, this very time and place, from a great distance, as though I lived apart from it all."

"I don't know what you mean," she said.

"I can't describe what I mean, but it is a sense that I have lived my life before and will live it again through those around me."

Marozia looked distressed. "Are you sure it is good for you to think in this way, Lena?"

I could only shake my head. "No, it is ungodly; I know that, but what am I to do? I cannot still the thoughts that come to my mind."

Marozia pondered me for a moment. Once again I parted the curtain and looked ahead of us at the two figures on the cart.

My sister's voice drew me from my reverie. "And what of him whom you regard so intently?" she asked.

"Him? Anthony?"

"No, of course not. Gallimanfry."

I blushed strongly, but she did not take her eyes from me.

"What of him?" I asked. "Why should I hold any regard for him?"

"Oh, Lena, please do not try to hide it. I know what you feel for him." She touched my shoulder, and when I leaned toward her, she held me in her arms. "It must be cruel to keep your passion a secret for so long."

My eyes brimmed with tears. "Yes, Marozia, but I fear discovery."

"How is it you have not had a child?"

"There was one, but I miscarried early."

"Oh, Lena, and you have suffered all this without me."

"I did not want to tell you." I did not go on, for I could see I had hurt her. In many ways we had become strangers to each other.

Striving to breach the gap, I asked, "What of you, Marozia? Aren't you afraid when Alberic goes away on campaign?"

She glanced at me guardedly. For a moment I feared a snub, but her response when it came was gentle enough.

"I would far rather be at his side," she replied, "whether to live or die." She raised her head and studied me closely. "But Rome cannot be left unattended. If we are not to lose all we have gained, Alberic's position must be protected as well as my own."

"Protected from whom?"

She glanced at me sideways. "Do you not know?"

I met her eyes, then looked down at my hands. Yes, I knew, but the answer was an arrow of grief. The breach between my mother and Marozia had never healed, much as I prayed it would. Like feral cats they stalked each other still, each grasping, hoping for some advantage over the other. Power. It was all power that they sought, and their prideful souls would not bend to forgiveness or love.

With an impulsive motion Marozia flung back the curtain on her side of the palanquin. The bearers looked up, startled, as the cloth flew aside. Then they respectfully lowered their heads.

"Marozia," I laughed, "what are you doing? You will have them staring at us."

"Oh, let them look their fill," Marozia burst out.

"God knows, I have nothing to hide. Look, Lena, what a day it is."

Glorying in the rush of air, the warmth of sunlight, she drank in the sights. I had to share her impetuous joy, for the countryside was coming to life with the first growth of spring. Wild gentian with brilliant blossoms of orange and purple dotted the light green of the fields. Olive trees with their glistening, waxy leaves seemed to shimmer like new leather buffed by springtime's polish. The air was fresh and cool, flavored by a sea wind, alive with the finches' songs.

As if delighted with some discovery of life, Marozia turned toward me and laughed aloud. I could not help smiling in return. For a moment we gazed at each other. How long had it been since we looked this way, sharing secrets? Not since we were girls, surely.

I wondered if Marozia could erase the nun's face in front of her and see again the Lena she had known. Could she understand that I longed for the same things other people wanted? I too could keep secrets locked in my heart. I was not just a dutiful worker, going from convent to diaconia on my appointed rounds.

Marozia's smile of joy gradually faded to a shadow of pain and she turned away. I seemed able to see all her thoughts, for I too felt the sudden fear that gripped her heart.

What if she had grown blind? Consumed as she was by her own ambitions and desires, what if she was no longer capable of seeing the lives of others? In many ways she had passed out of my life into another, and she felt the passing as strongly as I.

Hooves clattered on the road behind us. Marozia looked around as the guards stepped aside, allowing a horseman to pass.

A moment later Cardinal Peter appeared, riding a

white charger with gold-studded reins and bridle. The stocky, steady-paced horse had been retrained by Peter himself, reduced to a high-stepping showy trotter.

Erect in the saddle, resplendent in velvet riding breeches and an embroidered silk tunic, the cardinal cast his eyes down and held the reins aloft as though he entertained the fastidious hope that the road's dust would never touch him.

He looked up, however, as he passed the litter, and he seemed startled to see Marozia and me peering out at him. For a moment I thought he would spur his horse to a canter and escape, but he reconsidered and politely slowed the charger to a walk.

"Good day, signora, signorina." He wore a hard white skullcap rimmed in emeralds. The jewels glittered absurdly around his lean, angular features.

"Good day, Cardinal Peter," Marozia replied. "Why is it you're not going with the troops?" There was an edge of sarcasm in her voice.

If he noticed, he gave no sign. "My poor stomach," he laughed. "Seasickness is my curse. I would never make it alive through the voyage."

"In that case you should have accompanied my husband by land," Marozia observed.

"Certainly, of course." A look of distaste flickered across his face—clearly Cardinal Peter would never consider traveling with a Lombard under any circumstances—but quickly changed to a wan smile. "Unfortunately, that occurred to me too late. Besides," he hastened to add, "someone must look after the Curia while the pope is off to war."

Marozia gave him an answering smile. "Yes, I expect so. Well, good day to you, Cardinal Peter."

"Good day to you, fair ladies." With a quick touch of the spurs he was gone.

feeling the warmth of John's embrace, his arms around her, his body pressed close to hers. She had ruled him, and that power gave her a thrill that made her flesh burn with excitement.

Yet there was always the danger that he would suddenly blink and see an older woman before him, turn cold and disgusted. Each time they met there was the same slow circling toward the center of their shared desire. They were fierce lovers, enemies in passion, victorious only in the moment of union and then again hating each other, their minds consumed by the necessity of playing their fierce folly to the end of time.

A pope had been killed for the sake of these lovers' ambitions. It was something Theodora could never forget. The love that survived had a monstrous guilt to feed. Each look, each meeting, each moment of passion was a sacrifice of flesh to justify a man's murder. How could they part and make it all for naught?

She trembled. The love of Pope John, to her that was life itself.

Gaius—John. Again she recalled the parting at Ostia, confused by the emotions that raged through her. If one had to die—she could not finish the thought. She had imagined that there would be two farewells, the public one with her husband and the private parting from John.

Instead there had been none, just two men going to war and a woman on her balcony, aching for a touch, alone with whatever world she had created.

Chapter 28

Gaius Theophylact looked with pride at the fleet that emerged from the harbor channel between the two lighthouses of Ostia. The long, blunt prows of the biremes were reinforced with oak sheathed in iron. Each had a forecastle built on the prow above the main deck, where catapults were mounted for assault. Amidships there was a second castle overhanging the gunwales on either side. Heavy weights suspended from the overhanging projections could sweep the decks or crack the hulls of enemy ships that came alongside.

The most powerful weapons were concealed below-decks. These were precious caskets of naphtha laced with sulphur, pitch and quicklime. Each warship carried a dozen barrels of the explosive mixture of flammable oil.

Every foredeck was mounted with a long wooden tube lined with bronze, its open barrel trained on the sea. From the base of the tube a slender pipe ran belowdecks to an enormous bellows. On each ship Gaius had placed a small select guard to operate the bellows and flame thrower.

Secrecy had been maintained. Throughout the weeks of lading and boarding, while workmen and soldiers came and went, there had been many whispers and questions about the curious devices, but so far all was speculation. None but a handful of men knew that it was the deadly Greek fire that would be aimed against their foe.

The Egyptian-built Saracen ships were well constructed and thoroughly armed, but in all the history of Arab sea battle, Gaius had never heard of the Saracens using Greek fire. He had taken every precaution to insure that no informant divulged the Romans' secret weapon. In the fighting to come it might be the only advantage Gaius possessed.

The two lateen-rigged sails amidships were filled now. The northwest wind blew a steady six knots, making the oarsmen's chore easy. Off the port beam was the coast of Italy, her hills a hazy green in the afternoon sunlight. Here and there the sail of a small fishing boat could be seen, a flicker of white outlined against the shore.

The Mediterranean waters glinted turquoise flecked with silver. The ship creaked with each steady stroke of the oars as the steersman marked time.

Gaius descended the galley stairs from the bowsprit and strode along the catwalk. Mounting the aft deck, he nodded to Timius. The small, knobby-kneed steersman held the sweep in his muscular hands with easy familiarity. At the senator's greeting he grinned, exposing several gaps in his front teeth.

From his vantage point on the stern deck Gaius surveyed the fleet, spread out like a flock of geese heading south. Sails gleaming white in the afternoon sun, oar blades flashing as they met the water, the great ships formed a single phalanx that turned the sea to foam.

He had done all he could. The training of the troops and sailors, the years of preparation and tactical planning had been carried out to the utmost of his abilities. To be finally embarked on the campaign gave him a curious feeling of freedom. His ships were sound, his weapons strong, his men well trained. His leaders . . .

Looking back, Gaius frowned as the ship behind him

swerved off course. The small artemon sail at the forepeak flapped and jibbed, and Gaius saw several crewmen rush forward to adjust the tackle that had fouled in the lines of the bowsprit sail.

It was a foolish error. The ship's master would have to be disciplined. Glancing at the pennant that fluttered from the mainmast, Gaius felt his face grow hot with anger. The vessel that had swerved from its course was Pope John's.

Gaius quickly descended from the aft deck and made his way along the port catwalk toward the forepeak. The sense of emancipation was gone. His responsibilities had returned, as close and confining as the grey stone walls of Rome.

Pope John was no better a sailor than he was a general, Gaius reflected bitterly. A man at ease in the Curia, admired for his high, regal deportment and his flattering manners, he was not a man to lead soldiers into battle.

The pope was a necessity and an affliction. Displaying all the condescension of a superior intellect learning a barbarian language, he had listened to Gaius' and Alberic's plans for a joint sea and land attack. Time and again he had passed along orders to his generals with sloppy imprecision, so that tasks that should have been performed in days or weeks had stretched into months.

In political or clerical matters he was keenly perceptive, capable of understanding the motives of an opponent and undercutting his attack before the subtle assault had even begun. When it came to military matters, however, the physical and strategic problems of moving men and materiel from place to place, he was a literalist. He understood the task that needed to be performed, but he could not comprehend how it fell into the larger scheme of the campaign. His participation was adequate but never exceptional and his imagination was weakened by boredom.

Even now, Gaius reflected, Pope John regarded the campaign as little more than an afternoon lark. Many times he had referred to the Saracens as "those tribesmen," little understanding the power and might of the enemy.

Nor did he understand the mind of the Roman soldier. For instance there was the simple matter, trivial in itself, of the naming of the ships. While the shipwrights, caulkers, riggers and stevedores worked assiduously to see that the vessels were properly fitted and loaded, Pope John had concerned himself primarily with christening them, changing their names from pagan gods to Christian saints and martyrs. Gaius' vessel, chosen by him for its seaworthiness and speed, had originally been named after Leda, the consort of Zeus the Swan.

The pope himself rode a bireme that the sailors used to call Thor until John objected. Christians could not go to war in ships named after pagan gods, so they had duly been renamed *Sant'Angelo* and *San Giovanni*. Likewise, the other ships of the fleet had acquired Christian names as the pope and his cardinals went about their daily rounds.

The sailors resented this intrusion of ceremony on tradition. They were superstitious, attached to the past, impatient with any myths but their own. *Leda*, the fastest and most beautiful ship in the fleet, could not lightly be renamed *Sant'Angelo*. Her identity could not be torn away from her with a few drops of holy water and the sign of the cross.

In rechristening these ships Pope John had fallen measurably in the sailors' estimation. Whether he could regain their respect through a demonstration of his fighting spirit and seamanship remained to be seen.

On the western horizon the sun reddened, turning a deep velvet carmine as its path stretched on the surface of the darkening water. The hills were etched in hazy colors, as still and beautiful as a bas-relief.

Gaius signaled to Tiberon. ''Order the aft lantern lit. Mind it's on the seaward side.''

Guided by the stars and the telltale lead of the flickering stern lanterns, his ships would glide on their course through the night. With luck they would be standing off Gaeta, only a few miles from the Saracen stronghold, by the break of day.

Chapter 29

Once the pride of the Roman Empire, the Via Appia had fallen into ruin. By the time Alberic's troops passed, it was little more than a treacherous track consisting of ruts, crevices and gulleys, dangerous for horses, wagons and men alike. Where once there had been a solid, hard-surfaced road stretching from Rome to Gaeta there was now only the remnant of a great highway. Spring rains had washed away stones and foundation, leaving gashes of mud as wide and slippery as riverbeds. Many of the stones had been taken for other construction. Embankments had been destroyed and mounds of silt covered the bricks.

Horses slithered in the ooze. Men had to fling aside their weapons in favor of picks and shovels to repair the damage rendered by decades of neglect. Carts floundered; axles broke; the wheelwrights worked throughout the night to mend spokes and splines shattered by each day's travel.

Throughout the march they met urgency and danger. The journey was fraught with nightmarish encounters with Muslim warriors. Each step of the way Alberic's troops were harassed by marauding bands of Saracens who swept down from the hillsides, attacked swiftly and galloped away into the forest on their fleet horses. Hundreds of Lombards were killed on the road.

Throughout the journey Duke Lambert led the advance guard. It was a well-deserved honor, for in a decade of training troops and defending territory against Saracen advances Lambert had more than proved his worth as a general.

No campaign could compare to this one. If Lambert's men failed, the land expedition would end in disaster. Gaius would arrive at the Garigliano without cavalry, without support troops and—most critically—without an open supply route to Rome.

Now safe in Gaeta, only a few miles from the Garigliano, Lambert should have slept easily. Certainly his exhausted troops provided an example worth following; their snoring rumbled and hissed all around him. Only Duke Lambert was restless. The sea waves breaking on the shore close to hand carried a message to him, a constant reminder that the Saracen fortress was all too near.

Casting his blankets aside, he got up and pushed aside the flap of his tent. A sleepy guard jerked erect at the sound of his exit, but Lambert passed by him quickly, making for the headland. On a low rise overlooking the broad bay of Gaeta he stood among the tall grasses, feeling the steady northwest wind against his cheek.

A shining pattern of stars, the sign of Scorpio, hung close to the southern horizon. As he turned toward it, the one familiar sight in this strange landscape, Lambert had the uneasy sensation that something was wrong. A low bank of clouds seemed to be creeping from the south, obscuring the lowest stars in the sign.

Lambert soon realized that the stars did not vanish completely. Instead they flickered, appearing and vanishing at regular intervals. Squinting, he stared for a few moments longer, feeling his heart begin to pound. These were no clouds, but ships, Saracen ships, leaving the shelter of the bay and heading out to sea.

Lambert turned his head sideways—a trick taught by

Alberic to help soldiers see in the dark—and now by the thin gleam of moonlight he could make out the vessels— seven, eight, nine—passing across the waves with their triangular foresails set—twenty-eight, twenty-nine— He continued counting, his body motionless. He kept expecting to hear a shout, the creaking of oars, the call of a foreign boatswain's chant, but there was only the wind in his ears, blowing steadily. It carried away any sound that might have drifted toward shore. Those were phantoms passing in the night. . . .

Sixty-eight, sixty-nine, seventy—at last the sign of Scorpio held steady, its gleaming stars unimpeded by passing sails. How many had gone by before Lambert arrived? He could not even guess. It was a large fleet, of that he could be sure, quite possibly even larger than that of the pope and Theophylact.

Why sail at night? Why straight out from shore, headed south rather than west? Could it be that they had heard of the strength of the Roman fleet and turned tail? For a moment Lambert was thrilled by a vision of the Saracens in flight, ships loaded, soldiers in panic, fleeing from the coast of Italy to find refuge in Sicily.

Even as the image sped before him Lambert realized it could not be true. What he had seen was no disorganized, hasty departure but a carefully planned silent maneuver.

Turning on his heel, Lambert descended from the hillock and made his way through the sleeping camp to Alberic's tent.

For a moment they seemed to be repeating a scene from the past, so many times had they plotted and planned their campaigns together. Leaning on the wooden table, hands spread on either side of the chart, Alberic glanced at Lambert with a tight-lipped smile. "More difficult than Spoleto, eh?"

Lambert shrugged. "At the time nothing was more difficult than Spoleto."

Alberic studied the other man. Battles, the pressure of leadership and the ever-constant rigors of court life had added more than ten years to his face. Scars of experience were deeply etched around Lambert's eyes and mouth. Some of those lines were from laughter, for despite his responsibilities Lambert had lost none of his enthusiasm and sense of adventure. Nor had he shaken off his restlessness, Alberic reflected. To be walking the headland at night after a march that would have crippled most average men was typical of Lambert's valiant nature.

"Caliph Husayn, it appears, is considerably wiser than we expected," Alberic remarked.

Lambert frowned. "This fleet, then. You think—"

"I do not know, except that Gaius will have his hands full."

"Certainly," Lambert agreed, "with seventy ships— more than seventy, perhaps. But why set sail southward when they could make their way to the west and meet the fleet?"

"West would take them into the prevailing wind," Alberic said shortly.

"Yes, but if they wish to surprise the fleet, to meet them before dawn—"

"Perhaps they seek a different advantage." Alberic bent over the chart, his mind full of dreaded possibilities. If Gaius didn't arrive, if the fleet were destroyed, he and Lambert would be left in the heart of Saracen country, hampered by their extra horses, carts and ox wagons, far from the safety of Rome.

With an effort Alberic turned his thoughts to the present. "It is certainly no later than midnight," he mused. "Two hours' sail with only the artemones on their sprits, and they will be seven miles from shore."

"Yes, but our ships—"

"Our biremes hug the coast, bringing them on the swiftest course to the bay of Gaeta. Before dawn the Saracens will be there." He pointed to a spot off the coast. "They will stow sail and row north, bringing them here." Alberic's finger rested on a location well offshore, directly northwest of the bay.

"Very well." Lambert was growing impatient. "They have made a mistake, then. The harbor will be open, unprotected. Gaius and John can land and bring their troops ashore unhindered."

Alberic shook his head. "No, not in time. You forget something vital about the Saracen fleet. Their ships have two mainmasts, some three. From this point off the coast they will bear down with the westerly full off their beam. Our fleet will have to come about, back wind and face them with only oars to power them."

"And the Greek fire—" Lambert blanched.

"If we try to use it the flames will be in our faces." Alberic turned from the table, walked to the opening of the tent and flung the flap aside. For a long moment he stood silhouetted in the triangular opening, his back to Lambert. Finally he turned.

"Gather ten of our pennants," he said, his voice clipped and hard. "Send them with your swiftest riders along the coast. Send out loyal fishermen with the pennants on their masts. They must intercept Gaius and deliver the warning. It is our only chance."

Chapter 30

It was a speedy fishing smack from Terracina that made first contact with the Roman fleet shortly before dawn. Gaius was just climbing from his hammock when he heard the clatter of footsteps overhead and the cry, "Hold oars! Bear off!" A moment later Tiberon appeared in the galleyway, out of breath and panting.

"There is a smack off the port bow bearing the pennant of Alberic," he reported. "The fisherman says he has a message. Shall we let them board?"

"No, I will speak to them where they lie." Seizing his belt, Gaius buckled his sword to his waist and made his way up on deck, Tiberon close behind.

The sun was not yet up, but pale pink light spread its glow behind the distant eastern hills. Before them, dimly visible as a grey looming mass in the distance, was the headland of Gaeta. They had made fair progress during the night, but now the wind decreased and the waves calmed in that eerie, breathless repose that settles over the sea just before dawn.

Off the port bow the smack wallowed and swayed in the lee of the great galley. Four fishermen stood on deck, clinging to a line from the *Sant'Angelo*. As Gaius watched one of them made the rope fast while a tall, curly-haired fellow in a white smock, apparently the captain, saluted.

"Noble Theophylact," he shouted, "we bring a message from Alberic."

"What proof?" called Gaius.

"His pennant." The sailor pointed to the slim blue cloth that fluttered languidly at the tip of the mainmast.

"Lower it at once," Gaius shouted, "and give it to my man." As one of the sailors leapt to carry out his bidding, the general continued, "Now then, quickly, what is your message?"

"Alberic's first general, Lambert, has seen the Saracen fleet pass Gaeta, heading southerly in the night. Alberic believes they are now behind you with the wind at their stern."

Theophylact's jaw hardened. His hand gripped the rail. "How many ships?"

"He counted seventy; there may be more."

Seventy. Gaius wheeled and said a few words to Tiberon, who nodded and went below. Meanwhile, the pennant, furled into a tight ball, was hurled from the fishing smack to the deck of the *Sant'Angelo*. A soldier caught the bundle and delivered it to Gaius. When he unrolled it, he saw the familiar emblem. On a background of indigo stood a lion rampant with three arrows in its paw, and adjacent, a suckling cub. The sign of Alberic united with that of the House of Theophylact, a German and Roman alliance. The pennant was genuine—whole silk, not muslin, and there was Marozia's mark stitched into the corner.

Tiberon returned carrying a pouch of gold, which Gaius tossed to the deck of the smack.

"You have done a service to Rome," he called. "Fair winds and prosperity."

The captain's face lit with pleasure as his sailors scrambled for their newfound wealth.

"Cast off," came the shout. "Back sails and round."

Gaius mounted the lookout platform and squinted astern. Across the expanse of sea to the west the horizon was a grey inscrutable line, yielding no movement, no clue to the enemy's position. There was a clatter overhead as the lateen sails picked up the freshening wind. Somewhere out there the Saracen armada was lurking.

Aware now that the eyes of his soldiers and crewmen were turned upon him, Gaius scanned the horizon once again. This time he saw them, the Saracen dromons, their broad-stretched sails forming a single dense line on the western sea.

Everything had changed. The Romans had been the pursuers; now they were the pursued. They had held the element of surprise; now the Saracens were prepared to catch them off guard.

A nearby movement of oars distracted Gaius. Pope John's ship was approaching the *Sant'Angelo*. In a moment it would be alongside, demanding to know what had happened, why the fleet was at a standstill. Gaius would have to tell him, but he could not afford to spend precious hours in consultation. Now every moment must be used to the best advantage.

On impulse Gaius leapt down from his post on the bowsprit and strode aft along the catwalk. As he passed, the oarsmen looked up, their faces white, mouths open in expectation. There was a shout as the signalman on the *San Giovanni* hailed the *Sant'Angelo*, but Gaius ignored the pope's call. With a single bound he marched the gangway steps to the steersman's position. Old Timius tipped his white-haired head and peered up at the senator. For an instant as Gaius looked into those onyx-black eyes he was reminded of a parrot.

Gaius spoke quickly. "If we drive into the heart of the Saracen fleet, can we evade them and pass?"

Timius twitched, grinned and spat over the side. "If

you have yourself the right steersman, master, it can be done."

"You have done it?"

"Many's the time. Not in recent years, but I warrant the hand's still there." He patted the gnarled fist that held the sweep.

"Once past," Gaius continued, "we shall have to come round to catch them from behind. All the same way, mind you, or we'll collide with each other."

Timius glanced up again, Gaius thought with sardonic admiration. "Aye," said the steersman, "but try and teach these young fellows to act in unison, and you'll have yourself a task, I warrant."

"Not me, Timius. You."

The steersman frowned. "Bah! The lads I've tried to teach—"

"We haven't much time. Look there."

"I've seen them already." Timius spat again. "The infidels"—he sniffed—"and their dung on the winds."

"Two hours?"

"Not more," Timius agreed.

"We shall lie to and the other steersmen will come aboard. Then you will instruct them."

Timius' face contorted with misery. "Nay, Senator, I'm no hand at teaching."

"Our weapon is fire," Gaius said brusquely. "Do you wish to lay it aside or to blow it into the face of the wind?"

The steersman grunted. "Well, then." He paused, looking at the enemy fleet growing ever larger on the horizon. "Hell and damnation. Get a youngster to man this sweep and tell me what's to be done. Yourself will have to deal with the admiral over there." He nodded with no sign of respect toward the pope's ship. "I've been watching him, and he appears to take his orders direct from on high, never mind the wind and the tides.''

The sails overhead billowed and snapped, catching the light wind that came in with the dawn.

''And damn,'' the old man muttered, ''lower them things afore they flutter themselves out. We won't need 'em, standing by.''

Silence held the fleet. Ranged in a single line, the oar blades of one galley almost touching those of the next, the Roman ships faced west. The catwalks were clear, soldiers below. Iron shields had been hung along the gunwales to protect the oarsmen's ports.

The slender cylinders were ready on the foredecks, their long wooden barrels pointed out to sea. Below, the crewmen of the special guard stood by the casks of naphtha and the man-high bellows. On the aft deck of every ship the steersmen were poised, tensely awaiting the order to advance.

From the afterdeck of the *Sant'Angelo* Gaius could observe the *San Giovanni*, where Pope John X walked among his oarsmen, blessing them individually as he passed. Timius stood beside Gaius, his hand on the sweep, but if he noticed the actions of the pope he gave no sign. His black bulging eyes were fixed on the sea ahead, measuring the narrowing distance between the waiting Roman ships and the Saracen fleet that approached on the wind.

Sails set and oars churning the water, the great Saracen vessels presented an awesome sight. In contrast the Roman ships, spars bare and oars stirring listlessly, were like rabbits trapped in a warren and awaiting the deadly, swift dive of the ferret.

''How many more?'' Gaius asked Timius.

''Four beats,'' the steersman replied without hesitation. Again the Saracen oars touched water. Gaius' gaze flickered. The distance was closing rapidly, too rapidly. He glanced doubtfully at his steersman, but he had followed Timius this far, trusting the old seaman's instincts. This was no time to betray him with a countermand.

Two, three—

The blades touched the sea again, each moment a vanishing interval between enemy fleets. Gaius could see the enemy themselves, their dark faces rising over the bows, their shrieks carried on the wind.

"Now," said Timius, in a voice so low and calm that Gaius nearly missed the single syllable.

He raised his hand and let it fall.

The response of the Roman fleet was instantaneous and simultaneous. With a roar of voices as though a great thunderclap had sounded the oarsmen bent to their task. Hulls creaked and muscles strained against the stout timbers of the biremes.

For a moment it seemed the ships would crack and splinter. The powerful vessels stood frozen in the water, unable to stir. Then gradually, almost imperceptibly they began to drive forward, a thin lace of foam lifting from their bows. The sweeps roiled the turquoise water.

Gathering momentum, the fleet that had been a single line began to spread like talons. The farthest ships turned away, driving toward the outside, and soon only Gaius' vessel remained on true course, steering into the center of the Arab fleet.

The Saracens were slow to respond to the change. With confidence inspired by full sails and a favorable wind they held firm, giving no sign of pursuing the dispersed Roman ships. Gaius' heart sank as the Saracen fleet continued to advance, bearing down on the single vessel that remained in the center, the *Sant'Angelo*.

"Come, little swan," he muttered.

"She'll fly, captain, she'll fly." Timius glanced up from his oar. "Look there."

The Saracen ranks finally broke. Alarmed by the swiftly moving ships that threatened their flanks, the attackers began to fan out. Farther and farther they stretched their line until more than a beam's worth of room was between them.

"Well done, Timius," murmured Gaius.

"Not so fast. There's a matter to be finished yet," the steersman growled.

Gaius stepped forward. "Decks clear! Ramming course!" he commanded above the creak of the oars. "Signalman, dip the pennant."

The line was stretched to its limit, the farthest bireme scarcely visible from the *Sant'Angelo*. The signalmen were ready. As the pennant fell and then rose again, the order was passed from ship to ship, each changing course, prepared to ram.

Baited by the attackers on their flanks, the Saracens spread in scattered ranks across the glittering sea. Their keening cries swept downwind toward the Roman ships and turned to howls of anger as the Romans, bending to their oars, plowed directly toward the bows of the oncoming ships. Like hedgehogs ducking into burrows the Saracen soldiers dashed sternward, bracing for the moment of impact.

One Saracen ship was headed straight for the *Sant'Angelo*. The Arab vessel had all the advantage of speed and the wind behind its sails as it held to a ramming course. Gaius glimpsed the enemy bowman leaping for cover and seized the rail, glancing at Timius, fully expecting to feel the great bireme shudder as it met head to head with the enemy warship.

The steersman was unswerving in his concentration. Timius stood riveted to his post, feet planted wide, the sweep an extension of his lean, hard body. He wore an odd half smile as of a glutton whose appetite is about to be satisfied. Without a quiver of motion, never taking his eyes from the approaching ship, he managed to wink at Gaius.

"Starboard to starboard it will be," he said.

"Excellent." Gaius turned to the mid-deck crew. "Soldiers, the starboard catapult!"

The artillerymen rushed to obey his order. Laden with stones and arrows, the enormous, cup-shaped lever was pulled hard against the deck. To the fusillade in the catapult the soldiers added clay jars filled with naphtha and saltpeter. A pair of hatchetmen stood poised on the planks of the catwalk, axes upraised, ready to sever the cords that held the device drawn back.

As the Saracen vessel bore down on them, cleaving the waves with its bow, Gaius could see the enemy bowmen scrambling along the sides and clambering into the rigging, prepared to rain arrows on the deck of the bireme. Head to head the two ships drove toward each other with rash speed. The howls of the Arabs were fierce triumphant ululations, biting through the wind. In another moment it would be too late.

With a sudden spring Timius pushed the sweep hard to starboard. For a fraction of a second the bireme failed to respond, and so for one horrifying moment it seemed the Saracen ship would catch the *Sant' Angelo* by the bow. The massive vessel groaned, then finally responded, yawing to port.

Gaius caught a glimpse of the Saracens' faces. Braced for the impact, they chattered with astonishment as the bireme veered past their bow and scraped along their beam. Then almost at once the Arab archers saw their opportunity.

Arrows sprayed the deck of the *Sant' Angelo*, and the ship swayed as wounded oarsmen screamed and fell. Even as they tumbled from their benches, coughing blood, their places were taken by crewmen who sprang from the hold. The rain of Saracen arrows continued without pause, felling the new recruits as well, but at last the *Sant'Angelo* pulled away.

"Fire the catapults," Gaius bellowed, his arm stroking downward to signal his men.

At once razor-sharp axes sliced the hempen ropes. Like some monstrous arm suddenly released from bondage, the long pole of the catapult with its cupped load arced across *Sant'Angelo* toward the Saracen ship, spraying arrows, stone and flaming naphtha. Rivers of fire poured over the Arab decks.

On the enemy vessel men fled before the leaping flames. The wounded thrashed about, trying to escape, their screams turning to shrieks of agony as the hot oil boiled over their bodies and clung to their clothes. Some threw themselves into the sea, only to be sucked under by the churning between the two ships.

The Saracens were unable to stop the rush of their downwind attack. With oars shattered and sails in ribbons they hurtled past the Roman ships.

Once they were by they began clearing the decks, tossing their dead and wounded into the sea, pouring water on the flames that licked along their bulwarks. Men scrambled to the rigging to drop sails as the ships turned on their own wake.

On the *Sant'Angelo* crumpled oarsmen lay where they had fallen, bodies tilted against the bulwarks. Soldiers dragged the corpses from their positions, wrenching free the fingers that still clung to the sweeps. The dead were hurled below, while the living waded through the arrows that lay everywhere to take their places in grim acceptance of their fate.

Gaius felt a pain in his right hand and glanced down in amazement at the blood that was streaming from his wrist. The shaft of the arrow that had grazed him was embedded in the wood by his fingers only inches from his side.

There was no time to rejoice in his good fortune. "Now to starboard," called out Timius. He threw his weight against the sweep, pushing it hard over.

"Back, starboard! Forward, port!"

At his command the oarsmen to starboard backed water in unison, hurling themselves against the massive sweeps. The port oarsmen also bent to their task, plowing their blades to pivot the massive bireme like a leaf turning slowly in a stream.

Gaius rapidly marked the position of his other ships. All along the line the Roman vessels pivoted, their banks of oars flashing in the sun like birds' wings.

Gaius heard a grunt from the steersman, then a hoarse laugh. "Damn youngsters! Taught 'em a thing or two."

"That you did, Timius. There'll be a gold wreath for you." Gaius paused. Here and there he could see ships that had failed to make the pass—spars tangled, their sweeps fouled with those of the Saracen. Where the Arab grapples had taken hold, warring vessels stood beam to beam, locked together in the water.

Above one of these ships fluttered a purple pennant with the emblem of the cross and the sword. It was the flagship of Pope John.

"Timius, mark you the pope."

With a growl of disgust the steersman took in the plight of the helpless vessel. Senator and sailor shared glances, instantly understanding what had to be done. There was no alternative. The pope's flagship must be saved.

Barking commands to alter course, Timius swerved to

bring the bireme round. Oars bit the water as the *Sant'Angelo* surged toward the struggling ships.

Leaping from the aft deck, Gaius strode forward until he reached the bridge below the forepeak.

"On the bellows there, make ready." At once the special crew seized the crosspoles that worked the lungs of the bellows. From where they stood a stitched-leather tube snaked up to the flame tube on the foredeck.

"Stevedores," Gaius bellowed, "four caskets, and a dozen in reserve. Quickly now. Torchmen, stand by."

The foredeck swarmed with activity as soldiers and seamen crowded the gangway, handing up barrels of naphtha and quicklime. Scanning the water ahead, Gaius measured the rapidly closing distance between the *Sant'Angelo* and the stern of the Saracen vessel. The papal ship was locked fast against the foe, and Gaius caught a glimpse of the pope, standing well protected on the aft deck, haranguing his generals. In the center of the pope's vessel the catapult stood useless, fixed in position, its hempen ropes bound fast to the blood-spattered stanchion.

"Damnation," Gaius swore.

There was no time to be lost. Already the gap between the *Sant'Angelo* and the Saracens was closing. The enemy guard had observed the approach of Gaius' ship, and the howling bowmen sprang to the stern, mounting high on the gunwales to unleash their deadly rain of arrows. On the foredeck of the *Sant'Angelo* a stevedore carrying a barrel of naphtha suddenly screamed and clutched his chest as an arrow killed him. Gaius leapt forward to catch the casket before it fell.

"Move up there, move up!" All along the line men were shouting as others fell, passing the barrels hand to hand. Through the gaping bunghole on the bronze-lined tube the liquid naphtha poured in a steady stream, filling the reservoir of the cylinder until it could hold no more.

Glancing astern, Gaius waved a signal to Timius. Now only a ship's length remained between the *Sant'Angelo* and the aft of the Saracen vessel, and with each passing moment the hail of arrows increased.

"Back water," Timius called. With a shudder the bireme strained, the leatherbound oarlocks screeching as the weight of the men bore against the crushing momentum of the moving ship. The wind was behind them now, steady and strong, carrying them on toward the enemy.

"Bellows," Gaius shouted, raising his voice above the sound of creaking and splintering wood. "Torchmen, ignite!"

Two men leapt from under the foredeck, flourishing fiery brands that hissed and smoked as they scrambled to light the Greek fire. The Arabs saw them at once and a renewed fusillade of arrows traced their advance. One searing brand fell to the deck as its bearer spun away, the angled shaft of a spear protruding from his throat. The second torchman had already reached the incendiary tube. As the bellows below pumped wind, sending a powerful rush of air through the shaft, he lowered his torch to the touchhole.

The *San Giovanni* had seen, too, and pulled free just before a long stream of flame shot from the mouth of the tube, advancing like the breath of a dragon as the *Sant'Angelo* bore down on the struggling Saracen ship. Carried downwind, the crackling tongue of yellow and blue licked at the bulwarks of the enemy. With wild cries of anguish burned men tumbled back from the rail.

Timius signaled to his oarsmen. The sweeps dipped once, twice. Now the Romans were bow to stern with their prey, the stream of fire a single line between them. The *San Giovanni*, having evaded the Greek fire, was bringing her own might to bear on the Saracen, picking off the hapless defenders.

Helpless against the tide of flames that poured into their vessel, the Saracen bowmen climbed the mizzenmast, angling for position as they trained their arrows on the foredeck of the *Sant'Angelo*. When the volley came, Timius stumbled and leaned against the sweep. For a moment the steersman lost control; the ship wavered. Then the sturdy, short legs found their footing again, the hands clenched on the steering oar, and the *Sant'Angelo* eased around to the beam of the Saracens' ship, the mouth of the flame-throwing cannon now turned to blast a path of searing heat across the narrow, twisting deck.

Attacked by the *San Giovanni* on one side, the *Sant'Angelo* on the other, their ship eaten by the flames that gnawed at the blackening hull, the Saracens flung themselves toward the high forepeak, their last hope of sanctuary. Marksmen toppled from the rigging, twisting and howling as they fell. Desperate oarsmen surrounded by fire huddled for safety behind their leather shields, unable to move as the flames surged toward them.

"Quench the fires! See to the wounded!" Striding the catwalk, Gaius surveyed the damage that remained in the aftermath of battle. On the enemy ship bodies were draped over oars and rails. Fire licked at their indifferent limbs and clothing. The few Saracen survivors, now crouched in the forepeak, watched in horror as the hold of their ship turned to a blazing inferno, incinerating the bodies that lay strewn about the walks.

On the *San Giovanni* men leapt with arms and weapons raised, consumed by jubilation at their victory. A victory at great expense, Gaius thought bitterly as he eyed the carnage. He touched the wound in his wrist. It was barely bleeding now, but the pain was worse.

Around him Roman soldiers and sailors moved along the catwalks, helping the wounded down into the hold.

Others worked at clearing debris from the cluttered deck and poured sand on the spluttering fires.

Gaius squinted to see the other Roman ships. All along the line flames leapt from the Saracen galleys, the black smoke writhing upward to form a pall against the sphere of the morning sun. The Greek fire had done its work. The Saracen fleet was nothing much more than charred wood and ashes.

Suddenly the *Sant'Angelo* lurched beneath him as if the steering sweep had been jolted. Gaius turned and saw that Timius was draped over the oak shaft, head bowed and arms hanging.

In a single bound Gaius was at his side. He gently lowered the steersman to the deck. In his leg was a Saracen arrow, fired in the earlier fusillade; but the mortal wound came from a bolt driven deep into the steersman's side. It was a Roman arrow, misfired by one of Pope John's bowmen.

The eyes opened and Timius grunted. "The gold laurels. . . ."

"You will live to take the wreath in your hand."

Timius coughed and turned his head away. "Nay, I'll be gone. Here is the measure of my reward, Senator. Deeper than the laurel it grows." He touched the shaft that protruded from his side.

"Tiberon," Gaius called out, "two soldiers to help this man."

"No!" The old steersman's voice was sharp. "Give me the laurels here and let me. . . ." He waved his hand. "Look you, Gaius," he muttered, "I've heard His Holiness praised, but you and I—" He winked. "We know better now." There was a pause while the old man's eyes closed. Gaius touched his hand and Timius started as if suddenly awakened. The eyes flickered. "Were we victorious?"

Gaius glanced at the Roman biremes, now fanning out from the smoking pyres of the Saracen ships.

"Yes," he said softly, "victory is ours."

Chapter 31

I will never forget the sight of that messenger riding through the Borgo toward Saint Peter's. Face flushed, hair flying, he shouted the news.

"Victory! Victory at Gaeta!"

Pilgrims and merchants poured forth from the houses, courtyards, shops and porticoed streets. Servants and waiters left the inns and lodging houses, all chores forgotten, oblivious to the fat aproned tavern-keepers who bellowed for their hirelings to return to their duties. In the basilica the money changers in their forty-nine stands seized their purses and slipped away, anticipating the riotous celebration that was to come. Straw vendors and booksellers in the atrium pulled in their wares and closed their stalls. Goldsmiths, rosary makers, cobblers, cloth merchants, sellers of purses, vendors of religious souvenirs, all shut their doors in haste and rushed into the streets to add their voices to the roar of acclamation.

Amid the confusion it was all I could do to make my way through the throng to the messenger. The rider was surrounded by eager questioners. Garlands of flowers were tossed about his neck. A painter of religious keepsakes had seized his palette and was drawing the scene with rapid, sure strokes.

"Please, sir—if you please." I had to tug at the

messenger's leg to draw his attention. When he turned to me, I said, "I am Lena, the daughter of Gaius Theophylact."

At that the crowd backed away, giving us room. The rider looked down at me with respect.

"Fair sister," he said, "you belong to the noblest family of all. Gaius Theophylact has won a great victory." He told me all that had transpired, waxing eloquent when he realized that the whole crowd was listening.

"Victory! Victory over the infidels!" cried the mob when he had finished.

I had heard enough; I slipped away to tell Marozia.

In the House of Hadrian Marozia took the news calmly enough, but the boys were ecstatic.

"Grandfather! Grandfather is a hero," they shouted, jumping up and down and clouting each other on the back.

Eventually, of course, Sergius hit Anthony too hard and the younger boy took offense, going after his elder brother with a broken battledore. Gallimanfry had to pull them apart, but by then there were other distractions.

An enormous crowd had gathered outside the door of the house, awaiting a speech from the daughter of Gaius Theophylact. From the small window that overlooked the piazza the boys peered excitedly at the sea of faces. Stretching from San Ciriaco north to San Marcello and east to Santi Apostoli, the mass that swarmed the Canapara was restless.

"Gallimanfry," the boys called to their tutor, "what do they want? Why have they come here?"

For an instant Gallimanfry glanced at me, a smile on his lips, and I felt a twinge of sadness that I could not openly take him in my arms and hug him for joy at this moment of triumph. He must have understood, for he turned to the boys.

"Dolts, this is your first public appearance and you're dressed like stall-muckers. Go on, get into your finery."

"Damn good, damn good," Sergius proclaimed, using the only curse he could pronounce with impunity. "I'll damn well wear my helmet."

At that Anthony looked crestfallen. It would be another year before he received his iron training helmet for battle practice.

"Never mind," Gallimanfry told him when Sergius had rushed away. "I'll find you a shield to carry on your arm."

And so the boys appeared before the crowd, Sergius looking like a beetle with his helmet pulled low on his brow. Anthony was fiercely proud, almost dragged to the ground by the enormous shield that bore Alberic's lion rampant and suckling cub on a field of indigo.

As decreed by my order, I covered my head with the cowl at this public gathering, but I could not hide my excitement. Only a few days before we had stood in Ostia watching the fleet depart—and now, so suddenly, this tremendous victory.

As for Marozia, her speech was inspired. Resplendent in her finest robe trimmed in lace and gold, she stood poised, proud, her head flung back, her voice strong. When she was done, the cries rose around her.

"Princeps! Senatrix! All hail!"

How powerful she was at that moment, how suffused with splendor. My heart swelled with pride at her glory.

Only when we had returned to the house did I realize that Marozia's mind was already grappling with the consequences of this news. She immediately called Gallimanfry and me to her side.

Marozia's confidence in Gallimanfry had grown. Perhaps this was a consequence of Alberic's regard for the chancellor, and yet it seemed to me that Marozia respected certain qualities in his advisor that even Alberic did not fully appreciate. Gallimanfry played the fool, it was true. Over the years his manner had changed little, and yet his value as an effective emissary and informed source of knowledge could not be matched.

There were also dark depths to him, areas of fear and grim loathing. Beneath the idiotic aspect was a stark prescience of doom. Marozia had come to rely on him to tell her the worst along with the best, to share her anxieties with no fear that her weakness would be betrayed to anyone else.

It had been inevitable, when the time came to select the boys' tutor, that Gallimanfry would be chosen. In some inexplicable manner I suppose he had made himself tutor to us all.

"Was there no mention of Pope John?" Marozia asked me on this occasion.

"Not that I heard."

"What think you?" She turned to Gallimanfry.

"I only know what Picingli the strategist has told me."

"And that is?"

"There are popes fit to bless ships and popes fit to sail them. Rarely do the twain meet; in this case they do not even approach from a distance."

"You think, then, that he failed to distinguish himself?"

Gallimanfry coughed. "Let us give thanks to God that his right-hand man didn't bollix the works—and sorrow that he'll have a second chance on land. A bad general is a worse danger than a host of enemy archers."

"He is so poor, then, at arms?"

"A man who has pearls to look after cannot be thinking of strategy."

Marozia tossed her head in annoyance. "I suspected

as much, but Mother had to push him forward to share in
the glory.''

Gallimanfry shrugged. ''It was not his name they
called in the streets just now. All I heard was 'Gaius,
Gaius,' till my ears rang with the clamor.''

''Yes, and that is what I fear.''

''Marozia,'' I interrupted, ''Father deserves the praise.
Why begrudge it to him?''

''I do not, Lena,'' she replied swiftly. ''He deserves
it all and more. God knows, he has lived for this campaign.''
She stopped herself, putting a close to her bitter thoughts.
''I fear his name being raised above Pope John's. The
pope is a jealous man, and ruthless. I fear that if Gaius'
name is proclaimed aloud, and Alberic's too—''

She paused, unable to continue, but we understood all
too well.

''What do you suggest?'' she asked Gallimanfry.

He didn't hesitate. ''A speech in the Senate from the
daughter of Theophylact praising the noble deeds of Pope
John. From there the rumor of his triumph will spread
through the city. I myself shall help it along, a task I can
perform with honeyed words to the citizens.''

I stared at them. ''Won't Father be resentful? A
speech from his daughter praising Pope John?''

''He may be resentful, perhaps,'' answered Gallimanfry,
''but your mother will be grateful.''

Marozia nodded. ''A speech then—tomorrow. Send
the messengers to call a meeting of the Senate.''

Chapter 32

We expected that the Saracen fortress on the Garigliano would be quickly captured after the swift triumph at sea, but an easy victory was not to be. Despite their losses the Muslims had more than enough men to meet the Roman forces.

The first battles were fought in the muddy lowlands beneath the fortress. There the Roman and Lombard cavalry foundered in the quagmire, while from the heights above the Saracens poured down a murderous hail of arrows. In a month of hard fighting the combined forces of Pope John, Duke Alberic and Gaius Theophylact gained scarcely a quarter mile.

Then came disaster. In the second month after the equinox the rains flooded the Garigliano. The river overflowed its banks and our hard-pressed troops had to retreat to the north, giving up all the ground they had gained. Camped on the lowlands with their provisions beginning to rot and their water turning bad, the soldiers suffered those greatest scourges of war, yellow fever and dysentery.

As spring dragged into summer the heat and stink of the camp became intolerable. The Lombards and Romans were forced to retreat even farther until by July they were encamped on a grassy knoll well to the north of the Garigliano. From this spot the soldiers could see across the valley to the Saracen fortress. Grey, formidable, appearing more impregnable with every passing day, it stood as a monument of resistance to the Christian army.

For the generals in the field the situation was made worse by the disloyalty of some dukes and bishops in the nearby provinces. Striving to protect their churches, benefices and baronial lands, many of the local potentates had struck bargains with the Saracens. These truces were written under duress, for the dukes knew they would be slaughtered if they mustered their forces against the infidels. They lived in fear, and when the pope summoned them to the camp on the Garigliano, they came very reluctantly in small bands, disguised as merchants or pilgrims so as to avoid discovery by the enemy.

Finally Pope John was forced to travel by ship to Terracina to conclude a formal treaty with the provincial lords. Under its terms he renounced several claims of the church in the southern Campania, including the patrimonies in Traetto and the Duchy of Fundi. These were large concessions, but they were necessary in order to win the cooperation of the terrorized dukes. At last as the ides of the month approached the southern nobles mustered at the camp to witness the final cartulary agreement.

Gaius Theophylact signed at the top of the document, then Duke Alberic on behalf of Berengar, High Emperor of the Lombards. Then Petronius signed for the Roman Senate, followed by Gratian; Gregory; Austoald; Lambert; the Secundicerius Stephen; Sergius de Eufemia; Adrianus; Stephen, Primicerius of the Defensors; and the Arcarius Stephen. Seventeen other nobles also swore to the treaty at Pope John's command.

Overleaf the document bore the signatures of the princes and generals of the league: Nicholas Picingli, Stratigus of Greek Lombardy; Gregory, Consul of Naples; Landulf, Imperial Patricius, Duke of Capua; Atenulf of

Benevento; Guaimar, Prince of Salerno; and John and Cocibilis, the duke and consul of Gaeta.

It was Theodora's privilege to announce the successful conclusion of the treaty to the Roman Senate, which she did on the third day following the signing, when Pope John's messenger brought the news to Rome.

The announcement produced only a mild flurry of interest. In the *calcararium*, where the lime-burners worked, and in the *scorticlaria* among the skinners and tanners a day of rest was called to celebrate the accord. A few pilgrims paused at the hospital at Santa Maria in Aquiro to bless the wounded and wish them a safe return to battle, but otherwise the news caused hardly a ripple in the daily affairs of Rome.

There was reason for this indifference, for Rome was once again under the scourge of dysentery. There were too few beds for all those who lay about the abitato, feverish and moaning.

As always during these times, fear of the disease led to an increase in strange pagan practices and harsh measures of penitence. At night secretive bands could be seen traveling through the Piazza Aracoeli or the Porticus of Octavia, hastening past with tapers to light their way. Like fireflies that bear the souls of unborn infants, these scurrying mourners darted through the night to gather in foul hovels and insulae, where they worked their magic. Dancing by torchlight, they mingled strange brews of goat's milk, eel, ox head, powdered ram's horn and animal blood. Lambs were found sacrificed, their entrails strewn in mystic patterns.

By day there were flagellants in the streets. They beat each other with thorn-tipped crops and sticks, their howls of repentance mingling with the cries of the sick and suffering.

To this sorrow was added our own private grief. In

the third week little Anthony was seized by the dread illness.

There is something in God's justice that I do not understand, for I wonder how a sinless child can be subjected to such misery. I do not doubt this was God's work, for something greater than man had taken hold of that small body and was tearing it asunder. He lay doubled up on his bed, shivering and moaning, his thin limbs all atremble.

Marozia sent word to Alberic that his son was ill. She took turns with Tasha and me at the bedside, but there was little any of us could do except change the wet cloths on Anthony's forehead or hold his trembling body when he was racked by fever. Sometimes Gallimanfry would have to come and grasp his wrists, or I am certain the poor child would have torn his own body to shreds, so great was his agony.

Whenever I left Anthony's bedside, I would go to the indigo chapel and pray most fervently, even past the hour of lauds, but as hope dwindled, I gave up prayer. When I saw the poor boy suffering, his face grey, his eyes scarcely open, the beads of cold moisture on his forehead, I wondered at the Maker who would wreak such cruelty.

If this was blasphemy, God must have forgiven me, or perhaps he wished to show me the way, to prove that He has a greater power. I do not know.

All I know is that I longed for a miracle, that a morning would come when the boy would awake with clear eyes and turn his head to greet me. Dear God, how I also longed to be gone from the sickness and grief of Rome.

Chapter 33

For many nights after the news was brought to him, Alberic slept fitfully, tormented by anxiety for the sick child. Worst of all was the delay. At any time of the day Alberic might be reminded of his son's suffering without knowing whether Anthony's condition had changed.

Lambert asked after the boy, and that night, when they had both drunk too much wine, Alberic confessed his fears. The two men talked until dawn.

One morning several days later a messenger galloped into camp and dismounted in front of Alberic's tent. At once the general was standing at the flap, his face creased with concern.

"How fares he?"

"Better. He has eaten his first meal."

Alberic went back inside his tent. Out of sight of the messenger he stood for a moment as if confused. By his empty cot lay the sword he had thrown down the night before. An icon was pinned to the leather flap. His leather *carbatines*, splattered with mud, were hung to the tent pole by their thongs.

It took Alberic a few seconds to realize that his hands were trembling. Suddenly his eyes filled with tears.

As the days passed and Alberic received news that his family had safely departed Rome for Tusculum, his mind gradually returned to the campaign. The restlessness of the soldiers could be felt. Time and again Gaius and Alberic put forward plans that were countermanded by the pope. Like nodding pigeons, the pope's followers always agreed with His Holiness' decisions.

The pope had no plan of his own. Instead he seemed intent on delay. Nightly under the papal canopy there were inebriated celebrations that lasted until dawn. Women were seen around the campground—Roman whores, Lombard concubines and even Saracens. Discipline among the papal guards was almost nonexistent, and the disarray of John's troops was beginning to infect the other soldiers.

A plague of lethargy spread through the air. The demoralization could be felt growing stronger every day. There was grumbling, discontent—and still no plan of action from the generals.

His own restlessness increasing, Alberic awoke early one morning and made his way through the crowded campground. It was not yet dawn. To the east above the valley of the Garigliano a tinge of pale blue light could be seen on the horizon.

In that bewitched time of morning filled with solitude, when the earth seemed to be enveloped in a breathless void, the campground looked peaceful. The soldiers slept on in the dark brown tents crowding the grassy highland. A few sentries paced the perimeter, their spears probing the thinly lit sky.

Alberic threaded his way among the tents, his feet sliding on the dew-slick grass. As he passed the last of the sentries and descended toward the river, he could make out the low, swooping gulls, the stark outline of a few bare trees. His feet were chill now, soaked with morning dew. By the river the spongy, thick clay clung to his steps. This was the mud that had ruined them, clawing at their horses' hooves, dragging them down until every Roman cursed as he floundered in the endless bog. Always the Saracen arrows had rained about them, spreading death.

Alberic heard the river, the dim lapping of waves. Ahead the grey waters faded into mist. Beyond them was the unseen far shore with its treacherous boggy terrain, and to the south, high on a hill stood the Saracen fortress.

The small field of vision made Alberic more acutely aware of his yearning. He could almost see his son Anthony, the clear blue eyes that seemed full of knowing and wonder. Then there was his young stepson Sergius, pouting and furious, insisting on having his way.

Gradually the boys vanished and there was only Marozia. He heard her soft voice ordering Sergius to obey his stepfather. She turned now, the profile of her slim, lithe figure outlined through the silk tunic. She came from her bath, her flesh glowing with warmth, her eyes filled with welcome. . . .

Something awakened Alberic from his reverie. He looked about him.

The fog was burning off the river. On the distant shore a mother goose led her gaggle of goslings up the bank, scolding them raucously when they fell behind.

The sun rose, casting flecks of gold on the flowing river. From where he stood Alberic could see every line and contour of the distant Saracen fortress. A stout Byzantine castle, thick-walled and forbidding, it had been built to repel the very invaders who now held it in their grasp.

A sudden movement startled the geese. Hissing, the mother flailed the air with her wings. The goslings tumbled around her.

Alberic ducked behind the cover of the underbrush. Peering through a thin screen of leaves, he studied the opposite shore.

A dark, slim Arab emerged from the trees on the south embankment. Hesitating, he glanced furtively up and down the river, then made a signal to someone behind. Immediately there was rustling among the trees. A second Saracen emerged, then another and another until there were twenty men on the opposite shore. One by one they crept stealthily toward the swiftly flowing river.

Their weapons were strange—no curved scimitars or massive strongbows. Instead they carried long, needle-sharp spears with slim shafts. They were shirtless, wearing only black turbans and pantaloons with dark sashes.

Crouched at the water's edge, they waited motionless, staring down into the shallows. Then suddenly a spear shot out, stirring the surface. Ringlets of tiny waves rippled out from the bank.

Alberic saw a gleam of white teeth as the hunter flashed a triumphant smile. The Saracen raised his spear, showing off his prize to the others. It was a large bullfrog, thrashing and kicking on the point of the weapon.

Alberic breathed a sigh of relief. What he had taken for an advance guard with a secret mission was nothing more than a band of frog hunters out on a morning foray. As he continued watching, the silent, darting figures resumed their hunt. Frogs were speared, lifted, then dropped still wriggling into the bag that hung at each man's waist.

Finally, when all their pouches were full, the Saracen leader gave a signal and the hunters withdrew into the trees, vanishing as quickly as they had come. Once again the river was silent and still.

Easing from his hiding place, Alberic retreated into the forest behind him until he found a tree with thick foliage and high branches. Shedding his tunic, he clambered hand over hand to the topmost branches.

Between the riverside forest and the castle was a wide plain split by a series of shallow gullies. From his vantage point Alberic could make out the dark turbans of the hunters as they crossed one of these gullies and emerged on the open plain. Skirting the corner tower, they approached the east wall of the fortress. In front of the gate the leader came to a stop and raised his spear to signal the watchman. A moment later the hunters moved swiftly through it and disappeared.

Alberic's mind was racing as he climbed back down the tree. The Arabs must value frogs' legs very highly to risk such a daring foray.

How long had these expeditions been going on?

The Lombard sentries were lax in their duties. They would have to be punished. As for the Arabs, their precious breakfast would cost them dearly.

Chapter 34

Inside the leather campaign tent the air was close and ripe with the smell of unwashed bodies. A single table stood in the center of a thick carpet, and around it were seated Pope John, Gaius Theophylact and Alberic. Lambert stood near Alberic's right hand, Tiberon near Gaius. Young Senator Petronius hovered behind the pope.

Along the periphery of the tent were the lesser dukes, bishops and generals who had declared themselves allies in the campaign. Some seemed to be half drowsing, leaning on their shields or spears. Others sat on the carpet, slumped forward with elbows on knees. Despite their apparent lack of attention all were aware of the tension that invested the three men at the table.

"A daring plan," Pope John observed. He glanced at Alberic with mingled condescension and scorn. "Very daring. Nonetheless, it would be rash to proceed in haste."

"Proceed in haste?" Alberic could hardly contain his rage. As he surged up off the camp stool the other men in the tent looked up in alarm. Alberic leaned over the table, his face eerie in the light from below. "My men have been waiting two months," he said harshly. "Thousands have been killed in futile cavalry charges across the plain. How much patience do you think they have?"

"Ah." The pope raised his hand. "It is your men

who concern you, then?'' He smirked at the other dukes and generals, inviting them to share his disdain.

"Of course," Alberic snapped. "We cannot expect them to sit idle all through the summer or to keep flinging themselves into a sea of mud. They have already felt the bite of the Saracen spear, the sting of infidel arrows—"

"Alberic is right," Gaius interjected.

The pope glared at the senator, but Theophylact remained firm. Finally John shrugged and straightened the folds of his robe.

"Very well," he huffed, "I can see I am outnumbered. Perhaps we should look more closely at the Lombard's plan."

Biting back anger, the young general shot a quick glance at Gaius and began. "It will take a small force, perhaps twenty men. They must blacken themselves and wear turbans."

John snorted and glanced at one of his captains, shaking his head. Ignoring him, Alberic continued, "The frog hunters cannot be recognized from the top of the walls and I have observed their signal to the gates."

"And if your men *are* recognized?" John cut in.

Alberic gave him a steady look. "Then I will be the first to fall, for I shall be leading them."

"No." Gaius leaned forward. "Absolutely not. I must insist—"

"There is no other way, Senator," Alberic interrupted. "His Holiness does not believe in the soundness of the plan. I do. Therefore it seems imperative that I prove it can be done. I must lead the men myself."

"And darken your skin like a Saracen?" There was no mistaking the sneer that twisted John's lips.

"And blacken myself? Yes." Alberic looked from one man to the other. "If the plan fails, twenty men will die, I among them. The gates will not be opened. My legions will be left with orders to pledge their loyalty to Your Holiness and''—he turned pointedly to Gaius—''to obey your commands.''

The pope scowled. ''That is most generous,'' he muttered, ''but you still have not said what we shall do if the gates are opened. Will you and nineteen other men storm the fortress on your own? That would be a majestic feat indeed.''

''We will fight to the last man to keep the gates open,'' Alberic replied evenly. ''That is all I can promise. I leave it to you to take advantage of the breach.''

''It will take time to cross the Garigliano. You will have to hold the gates for several hours,'' the pope said dismissively.

''Nonsense.'' Theophylact's voice was harsh. ''Alberic clearly has a plan for that as well.''

The general nodded. ''To the east of the fortress there is a gully abutted by a line of trees.''

''A deathtrap,'' commented John.

Alberic nodded. ''If we are caught there, yes. But if we can move in during the night—''

''We shall be seen by first light of day.''

''Not if the men keep still and cover themselves with brush.''

''Disguises again.''

''Better disguises than death.''

''We shall all be dead if we are seen.''

''We shall all die of plague and foot-rot if we huddle in this camp much longer.''

''Ah, then you admit this is a desperate plan.''

''It is a plan, the only one. We have an opportunity we cannot ignore. If Your Holiness is too obtuse—''

''Romans,'' roared Gaius, ''are we allies or are we not?''

For a long moment there was silence in the tent. The

...man had other plans." He laughed.
...oung general's daring, but I have not
...s turned out as they did."
...erals are arrogant," Alberic admitted.
...ink favors are their due. In time even an
...general can learn to be grateful, though."
...lied the Lombard with some amusement.
...ral with the brown dye, my son-in-law." He
...the tent flap, then paused. "And wrap your turban
...y. You have played a Roman well. I see no reason
...you cannot play a Saracen to perfection."

generals were deeply shocked by the open disagreement among their leaders. Glaring, Pope John turned his eyes away from Alberic as if the Lombard were a hound dismissed to his kennel. The pope glanced sourly at the senator. "Gaius, you find this plan appealing?"

"I agree with Alberic. It has the virtue of surprise."

"We shall use frog hunters in disguise to take the Saracens." The image—the indignity—seemed to cause the pope the utmost pain. He surveyed the tent, looking for some confirmation of his feelings among the dukes and bishops. Did they not see how ridiculous it was? Some stirred uneasily, but none stepped forward to speak against the plan.

"Very well." John shrugged and stood up. "I see that Rome has found new methods of war. Our children's children will sing of the frog hunters' campaign." He looked around again. "Though I oppose this, I believe I am outvoted. When do we move?"

"There is no moon tonight." Alberic looked at Gaius.

The senator nodded. "We go tonight then." Rising, Gaius gestured to his captains to step forward. "Have the troops prepare for departure—and silently, mind you. We must not be detected on pain of death. Dispatch the skiffs four miles upriver and lash them end to end. The men will cross there and hold to the forest until they reach the gullies to the east of the castle. Pope John, yours will be the second rank." The pope made no reply.

Gaius glanced at Alberic. "How far from the gullies to the gate?"

"Nearly a mile," Alberic replied.

For a moment Gaius' confidence seemed to waver, but a look from Alberic made him recover. "Very well. It will be several minutes from opening the gates until we can get there with reinforcements."

"We can hold out."

"Once we begin the attack, the gates must remain open," Gaius declared emphatically. "If we find ourselves on the open plain with the fortress barred, the legions will be slaughtered."

"The gates will be open," Alberic assured him without hesitation.

"Good. Then all that's left is a blessing." Gaius hesitated.

Every man in the tent waited. With deliberate reluctance, as if the very effort cost him dearly, Pope John raised his hand, his fingers extended.

"In the name of the Father, the Son and the Holy Ghost, a blessing on our legions and this campaign." Without pause he added, "I go to my men, where I await your orders, Gaius Theophylact." And brushing past the table, he made his way from the tent.

Only Gaius and Alberic remained behind.

"I have done you a disservice by making an enemy of him," Alberic muttered.

Gaius waved his hand. "I have more reason than you to call him enemy." He sighed. "Perhaps infidelity is not so terrible after all. That my wife should love another man, that I can bear; but that it should be he . . ."

"Do not underestimate him," Alberic said coldly. "His weakness is dangerous."

"Weakness always is. Still, his power—"

"Was obtained through a woman and likewise can be taken away."

Gaius snorted. "You assume she will still obey me."

Alberic shook his head. "I assume only that she can be made to see reason." He leaned forward. "Gaius, the popes have ruled too long; you and I know that. The Papal States they wrested from the Emperor Constantine, those vast lands from Lombardy clear to the Sabine Hills, how

have they managed [...] their monasteries, t[...] bishops, through [...] and give them w[...] the afterlife?"

Alberic's [...] marched throug[...] duchies. I have rulea [...] have not been able to win [...] why? Because of that puppet in By[...] of the temporal and spiritual authorit[...] them like *this*"—the Lombard clenchea [...] grip of fear and superstition. Did you see ou[...] now, when he hesitated to give the blessing? [...] them tremble, fearing to march into battle unble[...] they might go down to death and be damned? Gaius, h[...] only a man, as you and I can see, a mere mortal who fi[...] in his robes, hesitates to take action and thinks only of h[...] self. They see the same man, but they see him as a god. H[...] weaknesses are invisible to them, his unwisdom ignored. They perceive his power as that of the Almighty."

"And Theodora," Gaius said quietly, "what is it that she sees?"

Alberic avoided the eyes of the elder man. The question was almost too painful to answer. "I cannot say," he replied at last.

"I must remember to ask her." Gaius' voice was bitter. He passed his hand before his eyes. "These are not good thoughts for the night before a battle."

"Then perhaps we should talk of other matters."

"Yes, perhaps."

"Of a statesman who saw a young general, a foreigner from another tribe, and overcame prejudice to welcome him into his family."

Gaius smiled. "That would be a pleasant topic. I can

Chapter 35

A bullfrog plopped into the water; leaves rustled faintly. Alberic reached out and his hand touched a shoulder.

Lambert's face, dyed dark brown, was almost invisible in the predawn darkness. Only the whites of his eyes, intense and questioning, were clear to his leader. The general glanced up toward the rustling leaves. Lambert nodded and gripped his dagger more tightly. The Saracens were approaching.

The first of them was only a few yards away now, crouched low, his sharp, slim spear at the ready. Then at his signal the others appeared around him, rising from the bushes and slipping down toward the river. They passed so close that the hidden Lombards could almost reach out and touch them.

Quick splashing sounds as spears clove the water were followed by low grunts of satisfaction.

Alberic nodded at Lambert and together they went into fluid motion.

Alberic's blade flashed. The nearest Saracen turned, but his cry died with him; his throat was cut. The spear flew from his hand and floated down the river, spinning in the current.

Out of the corner of his eye Alberic caught a glimpse of Lambert. One of the Saracens lunged toward him, and as the Lombard spun away the thin tip of the hunter's spear lodged in his side. Somehow Lambert twisted free, splintering the shaft, and flung himself forward. His stiletto found its mark between the ribs of the Saracen.

Alberic was racing toward Lambert when a scream from behind brought him up short. Spinning round, he saw a dark figure topple into the river, followed instantly by a Lombard who swam in pursuit, thrashing with his knife.

The death blow caught the Arab between the shoulder blades. He hesitated for a moment, then raised his arms and sank beneath the surface. Cursing softly, Alberic's soldier ripped the turban from the Saracen's head and swam to shore, the dark cloth clutched between his teeth.

The ambush ended as fast as it had begun. Some were up, some were down, and that was that. Alberic gave the men a quick once-over, appraising the costs of battle.

Twenty feet away a Lombard crouched over a body, relieving it of turban, robe and spear. Another soldier knelt by the river, fastidiously wiping his blade with sand. He held the tip up to examine it for stains.

Alberic strode to Lambert, who was standing in an awkward position, examining his bloody side. Probing the coin-sized wound with his fingers, Lambert found the broken spear tip and pulled. At once he doubled over, his mouth distended in a silent howl of pain.

Clutching his friend's shoulder, Alberic helped him to rise. "It will have to be cut out," said the duke. "Remember, their weapons are barbed. You must return to camp so Thaïs can perform the surgery at once."

Lambert shook his head. "No, there is little pain now. I will go on."

Alberic gave him a skeptical look. "You will lose a good deal of blood."

Again Lambert gestured denial. "If I fall behind, you may leave me."

Alberic stared him in the eye to appraise his strength; his aide returned a clear, steady gaze. To send him back would shame a man of great courage.

Alberic nodded. "I must see to the others."

Aside from Lambert's there were few wounds, for the Lombards had moved swiftly and caught their prey by surprise. Only one other Arab spear had found its mark, leaving a Lombard dead on the riverbank. Its owner lay nearby, felled by a blow from behind. As was critically important, no Arab lived to give the alarm.

One of Alberic's men was crouched beside his fallen comrade. He looked up as the general approached.

"What was his name?" asked Alberic.

"Clementis. He was a Spoletan."

The general touched his companion on the arm. "Leave him. He will have a Christian burial."

"He wanted to reach the gates."

"He has reached other gates now," Alberic replied gruffly. "Come, strip the Arab and leave him with the rest. We must hurry. Dawn is breaking and the guards at the gates will be suspicious if we are late."

In a matter of minutes Alberic's men emerged from the final gully and loped toward the enormous gates of the fortress. With bent heads and swift trotting gait the Lombards perfectly resembled the Saracen huntsmen.

Still, as Alberic glanced at the looming castle walls, he felt the first edge of concern. The penetrating eyes of the watchmen were upon him and his followers. Moving across the open plain, his band posed easy targets for the archers on the parapets.

Any moment the Arabs might notice something amiss, the unfamiliar stride of the leader, a turban badly tied or the odd way a spear was held. Even now some young

Saracen might be looking down at the small troupe of frog hunters and wondering why one of them did not give an expected wave, why he did not call out to his friend.

Coming abreast of the east gate Alberic threw back his head and raised his spear, signaling the watchman. There was a cry from within, and he braced himself, expecting to see arrows fly from the battlements and put an end to this charade.

Instead the immense doors creaked open. The crack between them widened, slowly revealing the courtyard within.

Keeping his head low, pretending to shield his mouth from the dust, Alberic strode forward. He swaggered, twirling his heavy frog pouch as if to show off the weight of his bounty.

Now he could observe the interior of the fortress. In the bare dusty courtyard a few Arab soldiers lounged by the barracks sheds. Women with water jugs waited in line by a bubbling fountain. Thin smoke rose from cooking fires at the base of the battlements. He could smell hot spices, hear laughter.

Alberic looked up swiftly. Someone was calling out to him. An Arab soldier, obviously a leader of some importance, was advancing across the courtyard, grinning broadly, holding out his hand for the sack of frogs.

Alberic glanced around. Behind him the disguised Lombards had filed casually through the open gates. There were only two watchmen below, and already they were surrounded, lost in the confusion of turbaned heads. The plan was working smoothly.

Only Alberic heard the low, sharp grunts of surprise and pain as the two Saracen guards were dispatched. Only he knew that just outside the fortress, unseen by those in the courtyard, Lambert would be waving a red pennant as a signal to Gaius Theophylact.

The Saracen leader came closer, his hand outstretched, his wide grin flashing a welcome. With ten paces still between them Alberic gave his pouch another whirl. Playing the heft of it in one hand, he suddenly released his hold and slung it straight at his approaching enemy.

The Saracen reached out for the bag. Expecting a few pounds of soft frogs, he caught many pounds of hard rocks. He stove his fingers and sprained one wrist before the booby-trapped bag slammed into his upper chest and knocked him over. Dazed, winded, he shook his head and was starting to get up when all hell broke loose.

The whole party of frog catchers was laying into the soldiers by the barracks. The women were screaming, dropping their jugs, crushing the shards as they fled.

The tower watchmen shrieked an alert. The Roman attack had been spotted as it rose and came out of the woods.

The still-bewildered Saracen glanced up at the tower, then looked at Alberic. On his feet now, he was suffused with wrath as it dawned on him that the enemy was within the gates. Then the knife entered his stomach and cut upward. He lurched into Alberic's arms, went limp and fell for the last time. Alberic unceremoniously dropped him and leapt for a torch. He wedged it against one side of the gates and rushed to burn the other side too. The Saracens would not bar the Romans this day!

Half-clothed warriors raced from the garrison hutches, donning shields and helmets, poising their weapons. At first they did not realize what was happening. They saw only the frog hunters standing over their recumbent comrades and a turbaned man lying in the center of the courtyard. Then they realized that the men in the dust were dead. Then they understood.

As the shrieking Arabs hurled themselves forward, Alberic's soldiers yanked their swords from scabbards hidden inside their pantaloons. Most tossed aside their stone-filled frog pouches and light hunting spears.

In a frenzy the Saracen bowmen rushed for a position on the battlements, but the first of Theophylact's troops were already at the burning gates. The combined ranks of Lombards and Romans thundered through the breach.

The barracks had to be cleared. From their windows the Saracen bowmen poured deadly rain into the courtyard. The heavily walled rooms were a fortress within a fortress.

If Pope John had brought up his reserves as planned, this might have been quickly accomplished. The Lateran Guard was noted for its marksmanship, and the papal guard also numbered many expert sling-throwers. But John and his troops had not appeared. It was futile to speculate over what had deterred them; none of the messengers sent out to the east gully had returned.

Without the support of Pope John's archers Alberic, Lambert and Gaius had no alternative but to plunge ahead through the barracks, fighting to take them room by room, at great cost of valuable foot soldiers.

They had just cleared a long open gallery when Alberic lost sight of Lambert. It happened so quickly that he scarcely had a chance to realize what had occurred. First Lambert was locked in combat with a tall warrior; then suddenly both had vanished through an open door to the passage beyond.

There was no time to follow, for the attack had to be pressed. The next room was a dense confusion of howling, slashing Arabs.

It was all close fighting now, short, hacking sword strokes, burning with fatigue. A thrust of the knife, a parry—in the narrow, confined chambers, the weapons of friend and foe were dangerously mingled. The screams, the clangor of sword, ax and stiletto, the howls of dying men, all were intensified by the closeness and rapidity of movement and the echoes that sprang from the walls. It was a vision of hell, demonic grunting, twisting and sweating, men elbow to elbow and shoulder to shoulder, turning just in time to deal death—or be dealt it.

For what seemed like forever uncertainty ruled the mass of writhing figures. Then the balance tilted and the attackers swept through the room. Furious in their triumph, Romans and Lombards cut down the survivors, though the last defenders continued to fight furiously. Archers slumped at the windows, killed at the moment of firing.

"Bardolf," Alberic called out to one of his captains, "on to the next room. Advance!"

Even as he gave the order, Alberic found that his way was blocked by a Roman soldier, his jerkin tattered and streaked with blood, his face streaming sweat. The man's eyes burned and his chest rose and fell in great heaving gasps. His sword hung from his fist as if a great weight bore it down. Its blade leaked a slick of blood.

It took a few seconds for Alberic to realize that this panting, blood-drenched specter was Gaius Theophylact. "The rooms are clear to the east," announced the senator, his hot eyes fixed on Alberic.

"To the west as well. Now all that remains is the battlements. Where is Pope John?"

The senator shook his head. "Still hiding, it seems." Stepping into the gallery, he surveyed the nightmarish clutter of fallen corpses and wounded men. "Where is Lambert?"

Alberic glanced at the open doorway through which Lambert and the foe had disappeared. Gaius followed his gaze. They looked at each other and Alberic nodded. "It leads to the tower."

*   *   *

Footing in the dim corridor was treacherous. The only
light came from window slits high above. It was poor
and irregular illumination for spiral stairs that wound their
way upward. On the first landing Alberic noted a single
bloody handprint on the sill.

Everything was muffled here. Only distant groans,
shouts and rattles of weaponry reached them. As they
followed the stairway, the light gradually brightened. Then,
strangely, the sounds of fighting grew louder. At the top of
the steps was a door, and from behind it came shouts and
the ringing of swords.

Alberic glanced at Gaius. The two generals sprang
forward, their swords at the ready. They crashed the door
open before them.

It was a large round cell with broad windows overlooking the main gate. In the center over a smoking fire
hung an enormous cauldron. The stink of hot pitch filled
the air.

Scarcely ten paces away, back to the wall, hand
clutching his side, Lambert fought desperately to fend off
a broad-shouldered Saracen, his sword at an odd, defen-
sive angle as though he could scarcely support its weight
in his hand. The Arab's scimitar was raised for the death
blow.

"General," Lambert called out, but his desperate
plea was too late. A shudder passed through his body and
he looked down helplessly as the Saracen blade plunged
into his belly.

With a feeble, agonized stroke Lambert brought his
sword around one final time. The blade glanced sideways
off the Arab's leatherclad sleeve, slicing through to the
skin. With a shout of pain the Saracen leapt backward,
clutching his wounded arm. Then Lambert lurched and
sank, fingering the blade that was lodged in his abdomen.

"Husayn!" The name sprang to Gaius' lips an invocation.

At the sound of it, the Saracen whirled. Suddenly realizing he was weaponless against two armed men, he seized the hilt of his sword, striving to wrench it free from Lambert's body.

But the death grip was too strong. Struggle as he might, Husayn could not release his scimitar from Lambert's desperate grasp. He looked up as two swords came to rest against his throat.

"Mercy!" The whites of his eyes were rimmed with pink.

"Husayn." Gaius savored the name this time as if it were a term of affection.

The Saracen backed away, clawing for the knife at his waist, but Alberic's sword slashed down at his fingers.

Husayn clutched his bleeding hand. "My soldiers will swear allegiance." The words of the local dialect stumbled on his tongue.

Gaius smiled. "And become Christians."

"Christians?" Husayn raised his head. "No, never."

"A proud Muslim," Gaius said hoarsely. "A murderer."

"I am no murderer. I am a soldier."

"No decent soldier cuts off a man's feet and hangs him to die, a carcass for the birds."

There was an electric silence as Husayn stared at Gaius with new eyes. "You—you are his brother—Theophylact?"

"I am Gaius Theophylact."

The Saracen's face was tense. "You and I—" He signaled. "Peace between—"

"No." Gaius shook his head. "Justice before peace."

Alberic glanced at Gaius, then away. Some ugliness long hidden in the senator had crept to the surface, distorting his features, turning his face into a mask of vengeance and cruelty.

"We have a punishment for murderers." Gaius seized Husayn by the hair and hurled his old enemy to his knees. Panting, the senator freed the knife from his waist.

Husayn screamed as Gaius hurled him backward and planted his knee on the Arab's chest. His knife punged down.

A horrible, unearthly cry echoed about the room over and over again.

At last Gaius rose from his victim and the Saracen rolled over, blood streaming from the empty sockets of his eyes. Slowly he raised himself on his hands and knees and crawled away. His fingers touched the hot coals of the open fire and he cried out in anguish again.

Gaius touched Alberic's arm. The Lombard looked at the senator and saw that his eyes seemed empty now, his face swept clear of all emotion, almost as if he were a child again, wondering what he had done and asking for an explanation.

They heard cheering in the courtyard, and Alberic glanced through the window.

"The pope arrives at last."

Gaius appeared not to have heard. "We must see to our men," he muttered.

Alberic nodded. He looked at Lambert's lifeless body, crumpled against the wall, hands still clutched around the naked blade of the scimitar. "We took Spoleto together," Alberic said softly, "and now the Garigliano."

From a distant corner of the room beyond the cauldron of simmering pitch came the sound of fingernails scratching stone and a low, agonized moaning.

"I will finish him," said Alberic, "and then carry Lambert below."

Chapter 36

Only Marozia made the journey from Tusculum to Rome for the victory banquet. Gallimanfry and I remained in the campagna with the two boys. The ravages of disease continued to be felt in the city, so neither Marozia nor I thought it wise to return the household to the capital.

At the time I deeply regretted missing the thanksgiving festival. This was a great victory for Christendom. At last the hated infidel had been driven from our shores. I knew there would be acclamation for those I loved most dearly, for Mother, Father, Marozia, Alberic, and even our scholarly grandfather Eusebius.

The night of the celebration I went into the house chapel and gave a prayer of thanks. As I knelt in the darkness, Saint Cecilia came down from the altar. She was dressed in a white robe and her hair was girt with a crown that shone like the stars. I know I was deathly afraid, but I saw a look of such gentle kindness on her face that I took comfort.

All around the saint were gathered the souls of myriad beings, living and dead, some evil and squirming in the air, others light as angels. When she herself reached out to touch me, I was transported by a kind of rapture and I swooned away.

I do not know how long I lay there before Gallimanfry

found me. He picked me up and carried me to bed, where he applied compresses to my forehead.

He laughed when I spoke of what I had seen. It was then I told him that I thought I was again pregnant and that I hoped to bear.

He ceased laughing, but he was still very kind and brought me warm broth. For a long while we lay side by side, both of us a little in awe, I believe, and afraid to speak.

Finally he asked, "Will you leave the order?"

"No," I answered. "The baby will be a foundling, given up to be cared for in one of God's houses. But I shall love you forever."

We slept very soundly that night, held close in each other's arms.

Just before vespers several days later the church bell in Tusculum began a loud clamor. We could hear shouts and the rattle of cowbells down in the village.

Sergius and Anthony burst helter-skelter from the house and went dashing down the road toward town. Midway they met Alberic and Marozia. The two were mounted, followed by a great crowd of peasants carrying crosses, banners and garlands of flowers. Alberic dismounted and caught up the boys in his arms. It was a wild troupe of celebrants that entered the courtyard, and we served food and wine to all, with many prayers and blessings and toasts.

Some time later I drew Marozia aside and asked her how matters had gone in Rome.

"Alberic has been made consul," she replied, "and he has won the patrimony of Laurentiopolis."

"And Father?"

"Tivoli, Ostia and the Trastevere."

I caught my breath. "Those are high honors indeed."

Marozia nodded. "Too high."

"But Sister." I touched her arm. "You should be jubilant."

She sighed. "Lena, I am afraid. Perhaps it's unreasonable, but the campaign . . . You see, something happened."

"What is that?"

Marozia looked over her shoulder before replying, but our guests were too consumed with drunken revelry to pay any notice.

"Pope John did not comport himself with distinction," she said in a low voice.

"What do you mean?"

"When Father and Alberic took the fortress, Pope John was to bring his troops from the forest to reinforce the attack. But he failed to appear until the fighting had ended and the stronghold was secure. Then he entered the fortress in triumph." She hesitated again, almost overcome by her feelings. "If he had arrived earlier, then Lambert and scores of others might not have died in battle. Now the soldiers talk openly of Pope John's cowardice."

"All the more glory to Father and Alberic, then."

She frowned. "Yes, for now. But I do not believe the pope will tolerate their popularity."

"But surely, with the troops they command and the backing of the citizens he would not dare act against them. Besides, Mother would intercede."

Marozia shook her head. "I wonder whether Mother retains her influence over His Holiness. I suspect he begins to tire of her."

"Marozia, you are always imagining the worst."

"Perhaps," she replied, "but there is something else. Petronius has the ear of the pope."

"And you fear he will speak against Alberic?"

"Of course. He was humiliated by him, by both of

us. It ruined his father. There's nothing he would like more than to have his revenge. I have no doubt, even now, that Petronius is spreading false rumors against our family.''

I took her hand. ''There is one thing you have forgotten, Marozia.''

''What is that?''

''Berengar, the emperor. Pope John crowned him, after all. The pope cannot take action against Alberic without insulting that same emperor.''

At this Marozia laughed. ''You think the pope sets great store by a crown? No, Lena, I think he would take it away from Berengar as swiftly as he gave it to him. Besides, Berengar is occupied with other matters.''

She did not need to explain further. I too had heard of trouble to the north. Rudolf, the king of Cisalpine Burgundy, had crossed the Alps to seize the crown from Berengar. Battle after battle ensued, and the emperor, short of his own troops, had sunk so low as to recruit Magyar mercenaries. This was a grievous error, for these same Magyars turned on him and burned Pavia, the ancient seat of the Lombard monarchy.

Already the northern kingdom was split. New leaders were emerging, most notably Hugo and Guido, two half-brothers, sons of the renowned Duchess of Pavia. Hugo, the son of Count Theobald of Provence, was a dissolute noble who had been given the Duchy of Pisa. Guido, the son of Thomas, Margrave of Tuscany, had taken over Siena. An intense, serious young man, Guido was already building up his militia. Either he or his brother was capable of unseating the emperor.

I had to admit that Marozia was correct in her appraisal. Berengar could offer little protection to the House of Theophylact.

*　　　*　　　*

It was far later in the night, past the hour of lauds, when I finally found courage to tell Marozia my own news. The boys were in bed, the fires burning low. Alberic remained at the head table with his lieutenants gathered around him, each trying to top the other with tales of battle.

As Gallimanfry went lurching by, he made bold to touch my rear parts in a most familiar way. I jumped and laughed, for the honey wine had gone to my head.

"Lena," whispered Marozia, "why don't you give up the order and marry him?"

I shook my head vehemently, blushing to the roots of my hair. "No, I could never do that. Father would never give his consent."

Marozia sniffed. "I'm sure it could be arranged."

"Of course," I replied, "but if it were ever discovered—"

"What?" she demanded.

"Must I tell you?"

"Yes."

Now it was my turn to take a fearful look around. When I spoke, it was in a whisper.

"I am bearing his child."

"Oh, Lena." She held me close. "But how will you manage it?"

"In two months' time I will go into retreat. A nun in Santa Maria in Trastevere has said she will take care of everything."

"And you will keep the child?"

"I mean to place the infant in a foundling home. Saint Petronilla's."

She looked at me closely, then shook her head. "I do not understand this vow that binds you to the church against all human nature."

For a moment I saw in her eyes the same expression

as in Saint Cecilia's—warmth and kindness so deep as to
need no instruction in Christian love.

"I do not understand, myself," I replied softly, "and
yet I am very glad."

Chapter 37

As the days of summer drifted toward fall, the weather in Tusculum remained unseasonably warm. There was an abundant harvest. The granaries were filled to overflowing; the ripe grapes seemed ready to burst their skins.

In these days Marozia was more content than I had ever seen her before. Alberic remained in Tusculum and the boys were under Gallimanfry's care. The days passed so slowly that we all seemed suspended in a timeless haze of prosperity.

The death of Lambert had been a bitter blow for Alberic. Marozia could see in her husband's eyes what it cost him to lose his friend. Now that Lambert was gone, she realized just how often Alberic had sought his companionship—riding the hunt, discussing the affairs of Spoleto and Lombardy, engaging in the long, hushed preparations for the Saracen campaign.

An image recurred to Marozia: Alberic and Lambert as she had seen them only once. They were seated on either side of a long, empty dining board littered with the scattered remains of a feast. It was dawn. All the other guests had left; only the dogs remained, snuffling around the bones and garbage that littered the floor. Marozia came upon them suddenly, facing each other with mugs of wine clutched in their hands, heads thrown back in laughter.

She could hear the laughter now; there was nothing mean or gloating in it, nothing drunken. It was the pure joy of survivors on broken earth, the heirs of a shattered empire, travelers together on a long journey.

She was jealous at the time. She turned away, closing the door on them. But now Lambert was gone and the jealousy could be discarded. With clearer vision she hoped to understand precisely what the two men had shared. And she hoped once again to hear that kind of laughter from Alberic's lips.

Alberic had a way of turning suddenly to face anyone who spoke to him. There was nothing calculated in the movement, nothing intimidating. His gesture seemed rather to imply that speech itself was a source of interest to him, as if he could not fully understand what a person was saying unless he turned, leaned forward and watched attentively.

At first encounter some Romans were embarrassed in his presence. They were accustomed to being confronted with haughty arrogance. They expected a duke or general to be aloof. To be approached by this tall, muscular man and held fixed in his gaze, full of interest or amusement, frequently unnerved them. Marozia had seen many a bishop or senator, expecting derogatory words and glances, rattled by this direct-speaking Lombard with his forthright manner.

Now she teased him about it, though he did not know quite what amused her. "Alberic," she would say suddenly as he passed her. As if he had heard a distant sound, hoofbeats or a church bell pealing, he would hesitate, then round on her, his brow furrowed, head tilted forward.

"Yes, Marozia?"

She would boldly survey him from head to toe, then shake her head, smiling. "Oh, nothing. There was something, but I've forgotten."

He would nod and turn away. "Well, if you remember. . . ."

Then her heart would go out to him, just when his shoulders straightened and he continued on his way. He would hesitate a little; it was as expressive as the change of gait in a fine stallion, showing something akin to anguished loneliness.

He always had pressing business; there were always things needing to be done. The interruption of the flow of matters, the pause that she threw into his motion by the mere act of calling his name, seemed to put everything in doubt. He could not decide whether to linger or to go on about his duties. For just a glancing instant he seemed to be in her hands.

She came to him one night in the middle of the harvest, when the warm air was filled with the pungent aroma of crushed grapes.

"Marozia?"

She stood at his bedside in a long white gown. When she sat down beside him, he made room, rising on one elbow.

She stroked his forehead, pushing the hair from his brow. There were drops of moisture on her fingers.

"Are you feverish?" she asked.

He smiled. "What do you think, my love? Should I not be?"

He pulled her down to him and kissed her in the hollow of the neck. She was suddenly unreasonably afraid, as if she did not know this man.

The kiss was familiar, though. His hand moved gently to her breast, and his touch was welcome. She felt his palm linger almost wonderingly, and then his mouth, hot against her nipple, his breath and his tongue soaking the cloth.

Under the coverlet he was naked. He often slept so on these warm nights. She slipped off her gown and lay down beside him.

For a long time he stroked her flank, waiting, soothing . . . for what? She didn't care. She could not bear the slightest distance any more. She wanted to be crushed, fulfilled, taken.

The gathering tempest was sudden but not brutal. It came first as a fleeting touch—the merest touch—to the fleece of her thighs, and then the pressure of his naked body against hers, the limbs strong, gathering her fiercely. She could not cling to him tightly enough. There was not enough strength in her entire body for the rage of possessiveness that overwhelmed her.

He entered her at once, the force of him stabbing into the blind warmth of her body, and she hurled herself against him, her embrace a plea. His lips were against her mouth, the weight of his body hard against her, and she wanted more, wanted all of him to bear her down and away into the liquid darkness where there was only his breath and the words of love and the scent of warm grapes fermenting to wine.

It seemed dawn's light never quite signaled the reality of full day. Awakening beside Alberic in the early morning, Marozia would sometimes turn to him while he slept to admire his profile and to attempt the impossible. She wanted to waken him without physical touch, to *will* him awake just by gazing at his sleeping form.

She believed she was capable of such power. Lying on her side without stirring, her body languorous and full from their lovemaking of the night before, she would press her cheek on her arm, watching.

He slept on his back, breathing slowly and heavily. The slightest clatter of weapons in the courtyard would have wakened him, but Marozia's silent scrutiny had no effect.

She even committed the blasphemy of asking God to intervene and rouse him, if only to prove the power of her indescribable happiness. But prayer too failed, and so she was forced to touch him, tracing the line of his brow with her fingertip, following the ridge of his nose down to the nostril. Her finger perched there like a fly. He wrinkled his nose, sniffed.

She had to bite her arm to keep from laughing. A fine soldier, teased in his sleep. Finally she could restrain herself no longer. She eased forward until her mouth was on his neck, kissing him in the groove of his collarbone, bare as baby's skin, where no hair grew. In that position she tightened her grip, her arms around him, holding him to her breast.

Their morning lovemaking had none of the suddenness of the night before. At night there lingered always the tensions of the previous day, the need to rip aside restraints and bury themselves in each other. There was sorrow to be healed, comfort to be given, a wild desire to be satisfied in the hot, lurid darkness.

Morning was innocence. The need had burned away. They awoke cleansed by the night air. He could have anything of her he wanted—her hair, her breasts, her thighs. His lips at her nipples, his body against hers and then the smooth flowing of his flesh into hers: it was all accomplished effortlessly, without the greedy, grasping haste of the night.

She could not have resisted even if she had wanted to. Long before he awoke, as she stared at him in the dimness, she was already submitting herself to him, allowing him to take her. At the moment she pressed her lips to his neck she became the supplicant, no longer striving to possess him, but instead merely begging that he awaken and love her.

She was loved. She knew that now. Some portion of Alberic's privacy had indeed fallen to her, but that was not all of him. She could not possess him fully. He would rise from the bed and leave her. What then? Would he think of her when he was away? Throughout the long day was there any single action that reminded him of her, some gesture that echoed the love and sensuality of this morning embrace, causing the memory of it to sweep over him?

She herself was a victim of such moments. They came to her unexpectedly. That reserve of sensual longing, the perfect remnants of the morning's passion, she had taken to calling it happiness. That was the wrong word, really. It was more like a softening of the edges, a folding inward until she thought she would cry.

Turning away from a servant or talking to Gallimanfry, watching the boys practice their riding or planning the dishes for the night's feast, she would pause, eyes fixed, and catch sight of a stray branch of oleander, or perhaps the far-off hollow clang of a cowbell. Suddenly she would be unable to resist the beauty of her life.

Always in Rome such a feeling remained just out of reach. Now she seemed to grasp it fully, to hold, finally, something so sweet it should last forever.

It was young Sergius who broke the spell, though indeed the accident occurred through no great fault of his own. It was simply youthful enthusiasm that took the upper hand.

The boys had been riding almost daily, staging races with Gallimanfry as their instructor. Though Anthony was younger than his half-brother, he was clearly the superior rider. Gallimanfry vainly attempted to even the competition between the two by holding back on the bridle of

Anthony's horse in order to give Sergius a lead. Though both boys raced full tilt, spurring their horses to a lather, young Anthony usually finished first, Sergius a length or two behind.

Sergius' frustration grew. He was too big for his small Arabian mare, he insisted. Anthony had all the advantage, being lighter. Finally one day Sergius insisted on riding his stepfather's roan. Gallimanfry forbade it. The stallion was too strong for a ten-year-old boy, and far too high-spirited.

Sergius had a domineering way among the servants and stable hands. By offering bribes and favors he soon had his way.

Late one afternoon, to the astonishment of Anthony and Gallimanfry, who had been impatiently awaiting his appearance, Sergius peacocked out of the stable on the big roan. Gallimanfry ordered the boy to dismount but Sergius ignored him. As Gallimanfry approached to take the reins, Sergius dug in his heels and the roan reared, hooves flailing.

Calling out his challenge to Anthony, Sergius spurred to the starting line, and before Gallimanfry could stop them the two boys were galloping down the hill at a furious pace.

Marozia emerged from the loggia just in time to see the roan disappear over a stone wall with Sergius clinging to the saddle like a flea on the back of a dog. She sent Tasha scurrying to fetch Alberic.

Both horses returned riderless, flying past the villa and on down the dusty lane toward the village. Alberic and Gallimanfry found the two boys lying in the brush several hundred yards from each other.

Anthony had landed on his back and the wind was knocked out of him. Otherwise he was unharmed, and he staggered to his feet, gasping for air.

Sergius was unconscious, his leg broken. When Marozia saw the limp figure cradled against her husband's chest, she felt certain he was dead.

At his mother's approach the boy's eyes flickered open and he began muttering imprecations against his half-brother, Gallimanfry and the stable hands, who in his opinion had caused the whole accident by mishandling the charger.

Alberic carried Sergius to his room and called for a surgeon. The leg was broken just below the knee, but the bone had not broken the skin. Alberic held the boy's shoulders while the surgeon pulled the leg straight and bound it to a pair of spear handles with strips of linen. Sergius screamed and fainted, and by the time he awoke again the apothecary had arrived with a draught to ease the pain.

It was almost sunset when Anthony trudged up the road clutching the bridle of the pony. The roan was still missing, and Alberic sent out several search parties.

Alberic refused to go to bed that night. Long after the servants had retired he lingered by the dining board, his brow creased in worry. Now and then he looked in on Sergius and laid his hand on the boy's forehead. Once he strolled out to the stable and gazed at the empty stall; the search parties had straggled back without his favorite horse.

He was returning, lantern in hand, when Marozia met him in the corridor.

"How is he resting?" she asked.

"He seems to sleep soundly."

She hesitated. "You care for him as if he were your own son."

"He is your son," replied Alberic. "That is enough." But he moved the taper away so she could not see his face.

"Do you ever think of the man who was his father?" she asked, her voice low.

"No." He shook his head. "Do you?"

"Sometimes when Sergius looks at me a certain way, I am reminded of him." She shuddered.

Alberic gazed at her in wonder. "And yet you harbor dreams for this boy."

Marozia lowered her eyes. "Perhaps it is only guilt. I would not wish to bring his father back to life. And yet"—she looked up—"it *was* murder."

"It was not our act but his that determined the outcome."

She sighed. "And yet I feel God had a part in it. Surely someone greater than mankind protects Saint Peter's Throne."

"I do not know," Alberic said gruffly. "All men are mortal."

"Women too." She tried to smile, but something had disturbed him.

"And Anthony?" he asked. "What of him?"

"He is my son and I love him," she replied.

"But?"

"Nothing." She shook her head, but he was looking at her closely now. She could not lie to him. "Only that I believe I am a little afraid of him."

Alberic laughed. "He is only a boy."

"He has his father's gifts. A formidable little boy."

Alberic studied her with a peculiar expression.

Marozia looked up. "Enough. Come to bed. You are tired and the boys sleep well. I'm sure the roan will turn up in the morning." She took him by the hand.

Chapter 38

In the days that followed Sergius was irritable, restless and often in pain. Whenever Anthony came near, his brother ragged him unmercifully, demanding that he bring him pieces of fruit from the garden or help him while away the hours playing backgammon.

Anthony soon grew restless under this barrage of demands. Sensing the boy's growing impatience, Gallimanfry one day suggested an outing to the village of Tusculum. Anthony readily agreed.

As they passed through the gates of the little town, Anthony's eyes brightened. No matter how many times he came here, there was always something interesting to see. Today, for instance, a peasant was having an altercation with a big-eared mule in the middle of the main street. Standing in the dusty road, the man shouted insults and beat the stubborn creature across the rump. A gathering of boys tormented him in turn, laughing at him and throwing pebbles at his legs with such force that he danced as he yelled.

On the far side of the street a clang of metal rang from the bronzesmith's shop. The scent of baking bread, an aroma laced with anise, floated from an open doorway. At the edge of the common grazing land a cloud of bees hovered on the branch of a mulberry tree. Three brown-cloaked monks with gloved hands and cowled heads gingerly raised a net to capture the swarm.

With sudden resolve, as if giving way to an impulse that had been in his mind for some time, Gallimanfry grasped Anthony by the hand and turned down a twisting side street.

"Where are we going?" Anthony almost had to run to keep up.

"I have a friend here, a man of extraordinary learning." Gallimanfry coughed. "Learning of an unusual sort."

Anthony looked with amazement at the houses on either side of them. They were now in the dingiest quarter of the town, where the buildings were cramped and twisted as if their closeness made them teeter precariously. Their stucco exteriors, long unwashed, were streaked with dirt and green slime like the walls of an underground grotto. It was a section of town that Anthony had never visited before. When asked about the place, people usually turned away, muttering against the pagans who lived there.

They stopped in front of a rickety door. Gallimanfry knocked three times, waited, then knocked twice again. After a long pause the door creaked open. Ferret eyes glared out from the gloomy darkness.

"Gallimanfry." The voice was husky. The eyes shifted to Anthony. The boy felt as if some spell had been cast over him. Those green, glowing eyes seemed to bore through him, questioning, threatening.

"Who is the boy?" the voice croaked at last.

"Anthony the son of Alberic the Lombard. His mother is Marozia of the House of Theophylact."

"Your fault, Gallimanfry, is that you provide elaboration where simplicity would suffice." The door creaked again and the figure stepped back. "Enter."

They went inside. The door slammed shut and all was darkness. Then there was a rustling sound. A shutter opened and a stream of light fell into the tight, airless room.

Against the left-hand wall, covered with a purple cloth, was a small altar that held an assortment of glittering objects. There were other objects hanging on the wall: small metal vials, miniature knives and shortswords suspended from their scabbard loops. Ranged among them were the limp carcasses of birds and rodents.

It was these that lent the room its peculiar odor of stale leather and rotting pelts, like a hunter's cabin that had not been used for months. That a man could live in such quarters defied belief.

Anthony rubbed his nose, trying desperately not to cough.

"Why have you come?" croaked the voice from the shadows.

"I wish to know something," replied Gallimanfry.

There was a high-pitched squeal of laughter. "So it is, so it is." A stubby, gnarled finger pointed accusingly out of the dimness. "Year by year they deride and abhor me. I am spurned, spat upon, kicked aside. Oh, the fine Christians of Tusculum have a merry time with Delphus."

The figure lurched forward. Thumb and forefinger fondled the edge of Gallimanfry's silk cloak. "You've risen in the world like a meteor, my old friend. Aye, thou beam of light streaking across the night sky. Mayhap I shall grovel and pray as your steps pass by." There was another cackle of laughter. "I remember you as you once were, how we gave 'em a song and a story for their money. Fine you were, Gallimanfry, and finer you've become." The shining green eyes narrowed into catlike slits. "You're a bit of a sycophant, wouldn't you say? There's a tad of a smell about you, from licking the fart-holes of them that treats you so well."

"Enough, Delphus."

The high, screaming laughter was unbearably shrill. "Touched a nerve, have I? Found the soft-boiled rag of your withered soul." He jabbed Gallimanfry in the ribs with his narrow thumb. "A pity then—all your monk's learning gone to educate the pig's drop of a Theophylact."

His words were cut short as Anthony threw himself forward, fists clenched. Howling in pain, the man retreated, spreading his hands to ward off the blows.

Powerful hands halted Anthony's attack. He was nearly lifted in the air as the hands pulled him backward.

"Let me go, Gallimanfry, let me go! He insulted—"

"Mind yourself," his tutor growled. "We are guests."

"Guests in a slop heap."

The blow across Anthony's face was sudden and shocking. His head spun and his ears rang. As he came to his senses, his anger mingled with disbelief. Gallimanfry had never before hit him, even when Anthony shattered the mead jar, ran away with the horse, reached up the kirtle of a serving maid.

Through the haze of his dizziness, as from a great distance, the voice lectured him. "The poor live as they must. You are superior to no one. You are both dust and gold, but you are not yet a man, certainly not more than a man."

Anthony stepped back, holding his head.

"Why have you come?" demanded Delphus. "Tell me why you've come."

"I have come for an augury," Gallimanfry replied.

"For yourself?"

"No, for the boy."

Suddenly Anthony's head was clear. Motionless, he listened, the nightmare of the past few moments replaced by understanding. Now it all made sense: the altar, the vials and implements and the hanging corpses of animals.

A pagan augur, the first he had ever seen. Oh, he had

heard of the lurking, outlawed fortunetellers with the stain
of forbidden rituals on their hands. Their practices were
said to be unspeakable. They were despised by every
Christian, and yet there were some who said, always in a
whisper, that the mightiest of the Romans, the heads of the
church itself, turned to such people in times of misfortune
and doubt.

"The boy, the boy," croaked Delphus, as if repeating
an incantation. "Of course. The son of Alberic. And what
would be in store for such a one as he?"

Delphus lifted Anthony's chin with his thumb and
forefinger. The glistening green eyes seemed to bore into
the boy. Anthony trembled.

"I will do what I can." Delphus indicated a place
near the altar. "Kneel."

Anthony hesitated. "Do as he says," Gallimanfry
ordered sharply.

The boy approached the altar and knelt. Glancing up,
he automatically began to cross himself, but the augur's
gnarled fingers clutched at his wrist.

"No," came the rasping voice, "and a curse upon it
besides. There will be no need."

Releasing the boy's hand, Delphus turned to a plate
on the altar, lifted a crust of bread and broke off a few
crumbs. With nervous, scurrying steps, he made his way
to the window, pulled open the shutter and scratched at the
sill. He dropped the bread crumbs on the rotting wood and
held a silent, expectant pose, staring up into the sky.

The silence was broken by a sudden flurry of wings
and a medley of cooing. Delphus' eyes flickered and he
smiled faintly as he surveyed the doves that gathered
around the proffered crumbs. With a darting motion he
reached out and seized one of the birds, startling the others
into flight.

When Delphus turned from the window, a white dove

was nestled in his hands, the bird's head jerking to and fro. As the seer approached Anthony, the bird seemed to grow calmer. Gradually its head settled onto the folds of its white feathers until finally it rested motionless.

In front of the altar Delphus paused, selected one of the hanging knives and with a quick, sure motion sliced off the dove's head. It fell to the floor in front of the boy.

Anthony stared down. The quivering beak opened and closed convulsively. A black, beady eye stared back.

At the altar Delphus worked rapidly. Having laid the body of the bird on a silver platter, he sliced it from neck to tail with a clean incision, hardly staining the white feathers. The chest cavity spread, he cut out and withdrew the still-pulsing heart. This he laid on a white cloth, which he placed in front of Anthony.

As if transfixed the boy gazed at the beating heart. The augur stood close beside him, muttering strange syllables.

After a moment Anthony felt himself losing consciousness. Time and place seemed to have no substance. He was hypnotized by the staring eye of the dove, the pulsing heart that lay before him, the delicate sprays of blood falling on the white cloth.

That dense, silently moving object enthralled his imagination. He felt himself becoming in some strange way a part of that tiny body, that heart pumping his own lifeblood. He could view himself from a great distance, a boy kneeling in a room, the two men around him, the town and the campagna, Rome and the boot of the peninsula, Sicily and the sea—a vast expanse of land and water. At the center of it all was the heart of the dove, pulsing, pulsing. . . .

He did not know how long he remained in that pose or what became of the two men nearby. The silence was so deep and the concentration so profound that it was only reluctantly and with a great pain that he saw the heart had finally ceased beating. It lay motionless, the blood rayed around it like spines from a sea urchin. The bird's eye was filmed and dim as if in mute recognition that death had come to it at last.

Then and only then did Anthony raise his eyes and meet the penetrating green gaze of the soothsayer. Fluttery dry lips moved in and out over toothless gums, and for a single horrified moment Anthony was again watching the inner workings of the heart, the breathing valves somehow transmuted to the quivering old face.

"What does it mean?" He was surprised to hear that his own voice was calm, deep and manly.

"The beak worked in praise of a ruler. The eye saw for a man of God. The heart beat for a long life. The pattern—" The augur gestured to the blood-speckled sheet. "The pattern is a ring of glory."

All derision was gone from the harsh, cracked voice. Delphus glanced at Gallimanfry. "The son of Alberic will prosper. But the cost . . . the cost." His voice faded in a kind of misery.

Delphus lifted the dove from the platter. Seeking sinew and bone with his gnarled fingers, he tore the flesh from the skeleton. The bloodied feathers and draped wings were hung on the wall alongside the others.

Delphus lifted the platter from the altar, strode to the window, pulled back the shutter and hurled the bloody remains into the courtyard. Returning, he lifted Anthony by his elbow, impatiently forcing him to rise. Gallimanfry said nothing.

Releasing his hold, Delphus bent down and took up the heart from the sheet. He glanced at Gallimanfry and spoke with sardonic mockery. "No prophecy is complete unless he—"

"No!" With an abrupt gesture Gallimanfry tore the

bird's heart from the old man's grasp. "Enough. He is still a boy." Striding to the window, Gallimanfry hurled the heart into the courtyard.

Anguish spread fleetingly across the augur's face, then vanished.

"Ah, Gallimanfry, I have served my purpose, have I? Come to old Delphus for a trick or two, then spit on his ways and revile him. Ah yes, I knew, I knew . . . but who's to say?"

He approached Gallimanfry, shaking a crooked finger beneath the tutor's chin. "Who's to say that my prophecy is truth? Pig's dung," he spat. "Nothing's true that's pagan, and naught pagan that's true. That's what they say, ain't it? God's truth." He shooed them. "Boils on a whore's ass and piss in your wind. Go on with you, and take the boy too. Pagans, they might lie, but the dove's heart don't lie. Go on, get!"

Delphus impelled his two visitors toward the door. Then suddenly had second thoughts. He tugged Gallimanfry by the sleeve.

"Serving man to the general, are you? Caretaker to a whore's brood. You've got a measure of wealth, I warrant. Now here, Gallimanfry, you monk's offal, how is a poor man to live?"

The prophet jammed his hand into the pouch that hung at Gallimanfry's side. His twisted fingers turned over the coins, searching for the heaviest. "I'll thank you for this when I've a mind."

"Double that for your silence," Gallimanfry added, fingering a second coin. The old augur stared at it greedily, his green eyes glittering.

Gallimanfry pulled the coin away as Delphus reached for it. "I pay you well. Let a word of this pass your lips and the bishop will soon hear of Delphus. Drawn and quartered, you'll strike a fine figure."

Delphus trembled. "Silence, I swear." As Gallimanfry handed him the coin, he cursed under his breath. "Swine's breath," he muttered. "Go, go!"

Already Gallimanfry and Anthony were through the portal, squinting in the sunlight. The door rattled shut behind them and a bar slammed home.

Chapter 39

The fall equinox was already a week past and we had begun our preparations for departure when one night a loud clatter in the courtyard woke me. I heard horses' hooves, then low, urgent voices. There were some final words and the horseman galloped off as fast as he had come.

Silence fell over the household again, but I could not sleep. All about me the villa seemed to wait breathlessly, as if in anticipation. As soon as I was up I threw a cloak around my shoulders, for the nights had turned chill.

I stepped into the hallway just in time to meet Marozia. She was coming toward me with a taper in her hand. Her hair was loose, her face pale and her steps agitated.

"What is it?" I whispered.

"Father has been called before the Synod. He is accused of treason."

"Treason?" I shook my head. It was impossible, inconceivable. "He has distinguished himself. He is a hero."

"No longer." Marozia's voice was bitter. "Pope John has an informant who claims that Gaius and Alberic have plotted to overthrow the papacy."

"But that's absurd. Why should they—"

"I know it's absurd." Marozia's eyes blazed with anger and impatience.

"Who is the informant?" I asked, almost afraid to learn the answer.

"The messenger could not say, but I have my suspicions."

"Petronius?"

She nodded, then seized my hand. "Father is being kept in the Lateran prison. I suspect the pope will want to try him quickly, before he can marshal his supporters. Alberic and I leave tonight for Rome."

"What will you do?"

"I must speak to Mother first of all. She must use her influence if any remains to her."

At this a chill crept through me. "But surely if Alberic is charged he too will be in danger."

Marozia hesitated, and all at once her mood seemed to change. "I begged him to leave," she said hoarsely. "If he could only get to Spoleto, he could assemble his troops. But he refuses." Her gaze fell. I felt her hand tremble. "He insists that he must speak on Gaius' behalf before the Synod. He is certain he can prove Father's innocence."

I gripped her hand. "Let him go alone, Marozia. Please stay here with the boys. I will speak to Mother."

Marozia looked at me sadly. "No, Lena, I must stay close to Alberic. Besides, you must care for yourself now, and bear your child in good health."

It was almost like a final parting, and suddenly a great fear took hold of me. There was such anguish in her eyes.

"I haven't much time," she said, glancing over her shoulder.

It was only then that I heard the servants rousing the stablehands. Soon they would be making ready the horses.

"Lena," she added, "you must care for Sergius until we return."

"Of course," I promised, "and Anthony as well."

"No." She shook her head and lowered her eyes. "If . . . if anything should happen to Alberic, I fear his son would be tainted with his father's guilt."

"Marozia, please, I am certain—"

She cut me short. "No, Lena. I too hope for the best, but we must take measures to protect the boy. That's why I . . . I wish to send him away."

I felt a sudden shortness of breath. "Away? Where?"

She shook her head again. "The time is too short. Someone must travel with him. They must leave tonight."

Finally I understood the reason for her distress. "Gallimanfry." The word slipped from my lips.

She raised her eyes, peering closely at me. I could not deny the depths of her plea.

"Of course," I said softly. "It must be done."

She grasped me with both hands. "I'm sure that Father will be vindicated—and Alberic. Every soldier in the ranks knows the truth. Anthony will stay in hiding for a few days, and when this has passed, Gallimanfry will bring him home." A sob rose in her throat. "Oh, Lena, don't look at me that way."

I blinked away my tears. "No, no, you are right, Marozia. This will all pass quickly. Then everything will be as it was before."

Suddenly we were in one another's arms, clasped in a strong embrace.

She drew away. "I must leave now."

I nodded. "God go with you, Marozia."

"And you, Lena."

Then she was gone.

In years to come Anthony would always remember the final hours at the villa as a fleeting blur of rushing servants, hushed voices and sudden, distraught expressions

lit by flickering torches. An indelible picture of it remained in his mind. Yet at the time there was no sense to
the motion, no explanation for the onslaught of activity
that seemed to throw everything into disarray. He wanted
to cry out, "Stop! Somebody tell me what has happened."
By the time it rose to his lips, the shout was distilled to a
tremulous plea, which went ignored or was brushed aside.
"Gallimanfry will explain it all to you. Now quickly, get
ready. There's no time."

Then too the intensity seemed unrelated to the mere
haste of packing and saying farewell. He had often been
separated from his parents. It was nothing unusual, but this
was different. In the desperate flurry of preparation there
were single moments of significance, moments that would
linger vividly in the mind.

He saw his mother's face close to his. Marozia's eyes
were filled with tears. Her hands brought his cloak up
around his neck to keep him warm. "Obey Gallimanfry,"
she said. "I know you love him, but you must respect him
as well. Respect him as your father."

He asked, "How long will I be away?"

"I cannot say. I hope it will all be over soon."

What would be over? What was she talking about? He
urgently wanted to question his mother, but just then a
servant appeared.

"Signora, the duke is asking for you. He wants to
know whether you wish his roan or the bay palfrey."

"The bay."

The servant nodded and disappeared down the corridor.

His mother bent down. She held Anthony by the
shoulders, peering deep into his eyes.

"Mother?"

She hugged him close, then straightened and turned
away.

*   *   *

Anthony went to his half-brother's room and pushed open the door. Sergius was sitting up in bed with a short oxhide whip in his hand, flicking at the moths that fluttered around the candle. He gave a short yelp of victory with every one that drifted to the floor.

"Damnit, what's up?" he demanded.

The sight of Sergius filled Anthony with an almost overwhelming sense of relief. Still resenting his long confinement, Sergius behaved as if nothing were out of the ordinary.

"I'm going away with Gallimanfry."

"And leave me lying here with this disgusting leg?" Sergius batted at his toe with the tip of the switch and winced. "Did you bring me any plums?"

Anthony hung his head. "No, I forgot." Ever since Sergius broke his leg he had demanded this daily toll, as if the younger boy owed him a penalty for his infirmity.

"Piss-brain." Sergius shifted angrily and lashed out with his whip. Anthony jerked aside and flattened himself against the wall. "You go off and leave me here forgotten, you measly little pimple. God and Christ, what a moron I have for a brother."

"I'll bring you twice the number tomorrow," Anthony began, then stopped, realizing his mistake.

"You know damn well you won't, because you and Gallimanfry are leaving and I'll be *all alone* with nothing but serving women and—Pah! Got him!" Sergius' flashing whip caught a large, colorful moth, sending orange and purple wings spinning.

Anthony edged away from the wall. "You won't be alone for long. Father will soon return."

"Your father, not mine," Sergius retorted. Anthony drew back again, stung as if the whip had actually touched him. "Well, never mind," his brother continued almost apologetically. "Only he doesn't care quite so much about me. It's true, you know."

"No, I don't. I mean, I never—"

"No, of course you wouldn't." Sergius flicked at the wall with his crop. "It makes no difference. He likes me well enough, I suppose.

"You'll be off to the Apennines, no doubt, ram-hunting or whatnot." He shook his head. "Oh, damn, damn stinking villa. Well, it's not your fault. I took my own fall, I expect, but at least I had the nerve to ride the roan." He looked at Anthony searchingly, a sarcastic gleam in his eye. "Big horse, eh? I saw you back away from him. Scared as a little vole, you were. You and your pony."

Normally Sergius' teasing would have thrown Anthony into a rage, but this time he was almost grateful for the chatter. Even now he could hear the servants running up and down the hall, calling to each other as they made their frantic preparations for departure. Compared to the storm outside the interior of Sergius' room seemed an island of normalcy and calm.

And yet the separation hung over them, ominous, threatening. Anthony wondered again what had instigated this sudden, tremendous upheaval in their lives. Why did he need to flee with Gallimanfry? And why didn't Sergius have to go too? He could travel if he had to.

Anthony hated to show his ignorance, but he could restrain himself no longer.

"Sergius, do you know what's happened?"

His brother gave a derisive sniff. "How am *I* supposed to know—lying here? I was hoping you could tell me."

"It's all so confusing," Anthony began. "A messenger came an hour ago. I'm certain he was from Rome."

Sergius' eyes narrowed and he rested the tip of the crop on his toe. "So. Trouble." He sighed.

"Sergius, you do know, don't you? You must tell me."

The boy in the bed sneered up at him. "Yes, you'd just like to know, wouldn't you? Well, go ask your precious Gallimanfry." Satisfied that he'd had the last word, Sergius resumed tapping the foot of his lame leg.

Just then a loud cry came from the hall. "Anthony, Anthony, where are you?"

Anthony looked over his shoulder, then at Sergius. He suddenly felt tremendously old and wise, as if his prospective journey gave him an enormous advantage of years and experience. Pale and restless, propped up in bed with the moths fluttering around his head and the whip tapping against his foot, Sergius was seen to be less threatening, more fragile than ever before.

The door to the room flew open and a servant appeared.

"Anthony? Ah, there you are. Come at once. Everything is packed and Gallimanfry is waiting. Come, you must be well away before dawn."

Anthony looked once more at Sergius, then without warning ran to his brother's bedside, flung his arms around his neck and kissed him on the cheek.

Sergius was so startled that for a second he could only stare in dumb amazement, but a glance at the servant brought him to his senses.

"Anthony, what the hell?" The invalid writhed free, pushing his brother away.

Already the refugee was in flight. Past the astonished servant, out the door, down the long hallway he ran pell-mell to the loggia, where Gallimanfry was pacing and grumbling. Feet skimming over the smooth bricks, tears streaming down his cheeks, he tore headlong toward the future, leaving behind everything that was familiar.

Chapter 40

Pope John had alerted the militia at the north gate, where the Via Flaminia enters Rome, and so as they crossed into the city, Alberic and Marozia were surrounded. While Marozia was held under guard, her husband was forced to dismount. He was gagged and bound and thrown into an oxcart.

In the early morning light citizens on their way to market gazed in astonishment at the sight of the Lombard general being hauled off to the Lateran. Cardinal Peter himself met Alberic at the door of the palace and ordered the guards to lock him up.

The trial of Gaius Theophylact took place at noon of the following day. It was held in the basilica of Saint John's Lateran with all the major primates of Rome and the cardinals of the Papal States in attendance. The Honorable Petronius son of Marcellus presented the principal evidence against his fellow senator. The night before the battle against the Saracens, he claimed, he and several others overheard Gaius Theophylact and Duke Alberic plotting in Alberic's tent. They spoke calumny against Pope John and schemed to overthrow him.

Gaius denied all the charges, citing the deeds of honor and sacrifice he had performed on behalf of Rome. Dozens of dukes, senators and officers of the troops stood outside the basilica door, pleading to be admitted to the proceeding. But the Synod was restricted to clergy, and all the laity were barred.

All, that is, except Petronius. When the trial had ended and Pope John had pronounced the sentence, Petronius strode proudly through the ranks of the clergy, his face flushed with triumph.

The trial of Alberic the Lombard would take place on the morrow.

Following the reading of the sentence, my father was taken into the Lateran courtyard and tied to a plank, his shortsword placed alongside him. Pope John administered extreme unction.

The clergy hoped Gaius would make a final confession of guilt, but I am told that my father said nothing except to respond to the reading of the sacrament. Even when red-hot stones were applied to his naked feet, he did not cry out.

As is the custom when one is sentenced for treason, his tongue was torn from his mouth with a goldworker's pincers. Then four chargers were positioned around the plank. Hempen cords were lashed to my father's limbs and then to their saddles.

At the pope's signal the riders urged their mounts toward the four points of the compass until my father's legs and arms were yanked from their sockets. Later his body was quartered by swordsmen so the frenzied horses could more easily draw him apart.

My mother remained in her bedchamber in the Lateran palace throughout the trial and execution.

Petronius was surprised to receive an invitation from Marozia to visit her that night in the House of Hadrian. It pleased him nonetheless, and he sent word that he would appear an hour from vespers.

He had no doubt of her intentions. It was his moment of triumph, just recompense for the public humiliation he had suffered at her hands. With her father tried and convicted of treason, her husband in the Lateran prison and her mother fallen from grace, Marozia had no alternative but to beg for mercy.

On his way to the House of Hadrian Petronius tried to imagine the coming encounter. There were many means he could use to exact his tribute, and the thought of each one was more delicious than the last.

He was led directly to Marozia's council chamber, where she rose to greet him. The servant was dismissed.

"My condolences," her visitor said at once. "I know what a terrible loss this must be for you."

"I thank you, Petronius, for your heartfelt sympathy." If there was any anger in her, the silken voice did not betray it.

Petronius studied her closely. Her head was tilted back, her dark lovely eyes heavy-lidded and sultry. She looked as if she had taken trouble with her toilet, for the caul on her hair was carefully netted with jewels and a silver chain glittered at her neck. As she touched the folds of her robe, he noted a plain black horsehair ring on her finger.

"You are lovelier than ever before," he said softly.

It was a tone he had used with many women, and always it had the same effect, the sharp intake of breath, the flush to the cheeks—surprise and gladness.

He was gratified to see that she responded with a kind of subdued modesty.

"You are most kind, Petronius."

He smiled. "Not kind, Marozia, only truthful. You forget that we were once betrothed."

"I have not forgotten."

"Perhaps the time will come to renew our vows."

She did not flinch. "That is why I have called you here tonight, to see what can be done."

He raised an eyebrow. It was all quite easy, far easier than he had anticipated.

"Alas," he replied, "an obstacle remains."

"Alberic's trial is tomorrow," she said tonelessly.

"Indeed."

"And then the final obstacle will be removed."

Petronius could no longer suppress his astonishment. "You wish—"

"You have the evidence against him?" she cut in.

"Of course."

"And you will speak out to condemn him?"

Petronius lifted his hands in a gesture of helplessness. "Why, I must. Surely justice must be done."

"I agree," Marozia said without hesitation. Her eyes fell. She twisted the cord of her robe almost as if embarrassed.

Petronius' heart pounded, almost deafening to his ears. So long he had waited, so long. He had missed nothing if he could have her now. Marozia was magnificent, more beautiful than any other woman he had ever seen.

The need swelled in him to possess her, to have her at last. Her willingness was the final spark to his passion.

"Then . . . you will be mine?"

She nodded without looking up.

He spoke in a whisper. "We shall seal it tonight. Now."

Suddenly she was looking at him, her eyes full of helpless love. "If you wish, my liege."

He stepped toward her and took her in his arms. For a moment he felt the smooth touch of her warm, full lips, smelled the sweetness of her breath. She reached out to hold him and he sighed, wrapping his arms around her.

He hardly knew what hit him. For an instant there

was no pain, only a sharp prick and a dull cramp that seized his body.

"No!" He backed away choking and saw the knife in her hand, yanked free, dripping with blood.

"No, no." He held his hands in front of him, fingers spread, but his plea had no effect on her.

"Die," she snarled. "Die, you wretched traitor."

Her eyes had turned horrible. The love, the helplessness, gone, but where? All feigned.

Her quick dagger was slashing at his arms, his wrists, but it was the stomach wound that doubled him up, made him helpless. Then she was upon him, the blade rising and falling, plunging into his chest, his throat, his cheeks and eyes until he was blinded, grasping, choking. The blood gurgled in his throat.

As Marozia rose, Petronius curled up, shuddered once and lay still.

The sliver of moon set early that night. After it touched the roofs, four trusted soldiers Marozia had selected from her household guards made their way through the silent streets of Rome to the Lateran palace. Some time after lauds they slipped in through the south gate, overcoming the single soldier who stood watch.

Marozia's head guard, Jordanus, knew every winding corridor and twisted alley of the Lateran compound. To reach the prison he followed a little-used alley that had once been maintained for the convenience of the servants.

Only two watchmen stood by the prison gate. Both were dead before they could speak and their bodies dragged into adjoining cells.

Jordanus and his men found Alberic in a windowless chamber. He had been left nothing but a pair of filthy breeches bound at the waist with a hempen cord. His feet and hands were lashed together with leather thongs.

Jordanus cut him free. Hastily he delivered the message from Marozia: Alberic was to flee to the castle at Nepi. Marozia would summon the Lombard forces outside Rome and meet him there.

The loyal Lombard Bardulf was waiting for Alberic outside the east wall of the Lateran. Jordanus guided him up the balustrade and lowered Alberic over the wall with a thick knotted cord.

As Alberic and Bardulf rode off into the night, Jordanus and his men attempted to return through the Lateran grounds the way they had come. Just inside the gate they were challenged by seven armed men of the watch.

Jordanus attempted to flee but was surrounded and captured. The other three of Marozia's house guards were killed. When it was learned that Alberic had escaped, Jordanus was dragged before the captain of the watch. The guardsmen prodded his genitals with spears until he confessed all he knew.

The fortress at Nepi was high on a hill overlooking the campagna some thirty miles north of Rome. Midway between the Via Cassia and the Via Flaminia, the mighty bastion was ideally equipped for defense. It housed a garrison of Lombard troops fiercely loyal to Alberic.

Alberic and Bardulf arrived at the fortress before dawn and by evening Nepi was provisioned for a siege.

In the House of Hadrian Marozia waited in vain for Jordanus and the house guards to return. The body of Petronius had been dragged into a small crypt beneath the chapel, but she was haunted by the presence of the corpse. She paced her rooms, starting up at every sound, expecting the guards to return at any moment.

By the time the first light of dawn touched the peak of the house, Marozia was in a frenzy of anxiety and despair.

Why didn't they return? What had happened? What had become of Alberic?

She roused the servants and stablemen. Her palfrey was saddled up and she changed into dingy riding clothes. Her intentions were vague. She had no plan. She feared the worst, but she knew that if Alberic was alive, if he had escaped, he would be at Nepi. THere was no reason for her to remain in Rome.

She had already delayed too long. When she emerged from the courtyard, Bishop Peter was waiting outside the House of Hadrian with the papal militia.

I am told that she attempted to break through the guards, but the men seized the reins of her horse and dragged her to the ground. She was held at spearpoint while Peter called her a traitress and a whore.

The House of Hadrian was searched and the body of Petronius found in the chapel crypt. Marozia was confined to her chambers and a permanent guard surrounded the House of Hadrian.

By the following morning Pope John had embarked on a campaign to invest the fortress at Nepi. Marozia in her isolation did not know whether Alberic was alive or what had become of the guards she sent to effect his escape. Throughout the siege Marozia was not permitted to step outside the walls of her house.

The messengers I sent from Tusculum were turned away at her door by the papal guards. When they persisted in trying to enter, they were brutally beaten and flung into the streets.

It was during this time, I believe, that Marozia first felt the visitation of demons—and no wonder, for she was sorely confined and must have suffered intensely. Separated from her loved ones, forced to endure the hours of isolation without any kindred spirit to share her thoughts, she roamed through her elegant and richly furnished house without any hope or prospect of relief.

I would like to think that she turned to God, but it cannot be so. Once the demons have possessed a mind, one can no longer witness the beauty and peace of our Maker's world. The beating of their leathery wings, the thunder of their horrid voices, the heat of their fires drive all faith from the human soul.

There was a further affliction to add to Marozia's burden of troubles. Pope John had tired of my mother, finding her age an impediment. He discovered in Marozia the youth that had fled from Theodora. Seeing Marozia confined, half-mad with her suffering, apparently added fever to the intensity of his desires. She had to be bound to submit to his pleasure, but still he would not relent.

And so while his troops laid siege to Alberic in the fortress of Nepi, Pope John misused my sister most horribly. Surely if there has ever been a time of darkness in Christendom it was this.

BOOK IV

Chapter 41

Along the banks of the Arno servant girls and peasant women, kirtles hiked up above the knees, bent over their washing. Children ran about in the shallows, splashing each other and howling with delight. Farther along the embankment, closer to the center of town, the quays above the river were crowded with merchants, sailors, clergymen and guildworkers engaged in animated transactions, hands gesturing wildly, their staccato voices drifting out across the flowing water.

To the young man standing at the bow of the freight scow the sound of those voices was like a welcome home. His dark eyes glittered as he took in the familiar scene of Pisans going about their daily business. It all seemed perfectly familiar, a painting unchanged by the years that had passed.

As the scow pulled alongside a quay and the young man mounted the ladder to the stone wharf, few paid him any notice. Heavily bearded, his face tanned and weathered from months at sea, he wore a loose-fitting leather jerkin and wool breeches. A heavy bag drawn tight with a cord was slung over his shoulder. Leather sandals were strapped and cross-tied around his ankles in the manner of sailors. In short, there was nothing to distinguish him from

any of the other seamen who mingled with the crowd—
nothing, that is, except the glittering gold ring with the
emblem of a Lombard lion that he wore on the third finger
of his right hand.

Making his way up the Via Roma toward the Piazza
del Duomo, he paused by a tanner's shop at the corner of a
side street. For a moment he hesitated, wondering whether
to turn or keep to the main course. Shifting his burden
from the left shoulder to the right, he glanced absently at
the tanner's shingle. Then with sudden resolution he turned
and strode off.

Either because the town was safe in the heart of
Lombardy or because its citizens had simply given up hope
of defending themselves, there were no walls around Pisa.
The narrow lane ended not in a barricade but in a broad
meadow.

Only two shepherds kept watch over the flocks at this
time of day. One, sprawled beneath a mulberry tree, was
obviously sleeping off the effects of the previous night's
wine. The other leaned wearily against his crook. He did
not acknowledge the sailor's greeting, but watched sulkily
as the young man once again shifted his burden and made
his way toward a cottage that lay on the far side of the
common land.

The place was hardly more than a shack, a whitewashed stone dwelling with a thatched roof, surrounded by
a muddy yard. A sow and four piglets moved sluggishly
through the muck. At the sailor's approach the sow cast
him a baleful eye and struggled up on all fours, the suction
of her body releasing a wet, slapping sound. The piglets
squealed as she nipped and prodded at their heels, driving
them safely away from the stranger.

Hesitating on the doorstep, the sailor set down his
burden and knocked once. When there was no reply, he
pounded twice again. Another silence followed, but at last

the door swung open and a pair of gleaming eyes peered from the darkness. Finally a face appeared, broadening into a grin. A bandy-legged grey-haired man stepped from the shadows, slammed the door behind him and yanked the young man by the arm.

"You're a year late," said Gallimanfry, "but no harm done." He looked up at the sailor and grinned. "Aye, and uglier by a boar's hair than when I saw you go." He gave a tug to the bristly beard. "It lends you majesty, but I've no doubt it carries lice. Come along, young Anthony, we have much to talk about."

Despite the wretched appearance of the hovel, the interior was clean and warm. That night as a hissing fire of faggots lit the whitewashed walls and cast a red glow about the room, the two men dined on ham hocks glazed with jelly, black bread and sharp cheese. And they talked.

Anthony told Gallimanfry everything that had happened to him during the past three years at sea. He painted a vivid picture of the great merchant ships with their square-rigged sails and flying pennants and of the far-off places he had visited—Narbonne; Barcelona; Tortosae; Valencia in Aragon; Ceuta at the mouth of the Great Sea; Oran; Bougle; Tunis; Tripoli; and Alexandria in Egypt. He had passed time in Acre, Gibelet and Antioch and a merchant ship had carried him to Constantinople and the mouth of the Black Sea. He described great battles in which he fought for his life against bands of Turkish pirates. He recalled times of great peace and beauty, as when he walked at night beneath the stars by the shores of the Bosporus.

As Anthony spoke, his eyes shone; his gestures gained animation. Gallimanfry listened with rapt attention, never stirring, only now and then interrupting to ask a question.

It was nearly dawn when they finally turned to the subject that was closest to their minds.

"In Alexandria," said Anthony, "I heard that my mother has married again."

"That was a year ago, to Duke Guido of Siena."

"It is only natural, I suppose." Anthony's face flushed. "Still, I find it hard to accept."

"I know, I know." Gallimanfry laid his hand on the young man's arm. "It was no insult to your father's memory, I am sure." He leaned forward. "Her position in Rome was precarious. With Pope John still in power and the Senate obedient to his influence, your mother was in jeopardy."

Anthony looked unconvinced. "This Duke Guido, what sort of man is he?"

Gallimanfry shrugged. "He wears sincerity about his shoulders like a surplice and takes the burdens of his office seriously. In Siena he organized the merchants, the guildsmen and the traders. You have perhaps heard of the Siena Company?"

Anthony nodded.

"His doing," Gallimanfry continued. "It bears all his marks: frugality, far-sightedness, conventional wisdom."

"And his troops?"

"Cut of the same mold. They perform to perfection."

"And this is Duke Hugo's half-brother," Anthony said musingly.

Gallimanfry snorted. "Half of a half-brother and then a quarter of that, if you want a truer proportion. They are as unalike as a strutting goose and a rutting pig."

"They are enemies?"

"Not so long as they avoid common ground. Here in Pisa Hugo holds court—as you know well, having served in it yourself."

Anthony nodded again, this time with a grimace.

"In Siena Duke Guido prospers in his own way," Gallimanfry observed, "reaping wealth from the merchant trades. His half-brother Hugo is dissolute by nature, and yet the people glory in his fabled excesses. Guido is frugal and judicious. His people are obedient to his will, but they can hardly be said to love him."

Anthony shook his head. "Still, I cannot see why my mother would choose to marry such a man."

"No?" Gallimanfry's eyebrows rose. "Consider, then. Upon her marriage to Guido Marozia brought the duke to Rome. His troops, numbering more than thirty score, are quartered in the Castel Sant'Angelo. To pass from Rome to Saint Peter's and the Borgo the pope must use Hadrian's Aelian Bridge, which happens to be guarded by that same Castel Sant'Angelo."

Anthony seemed greatly surprised. "But Pope John would not tolerate such a thing."

Gallimanfry smiled. "He has been forced to up to now. He knows that the papal guard would be far outmatched and outnumbered, were he to meet Duke Guido's troops in battle."

Anthony shot him a questioning look. "And now?"

"He arrives in Pisa in two days' time to form an alliance with Duke Hugo. According to the rumors he plans to crown Hugo King of the Lombards. But to tell the truth, it is the Lombard soldiers he wants, not the particular love of their duke."

Anthony pushed back the bench and rose to his feet. "Then if Hugo returns to Rome with Pope John, surely that would mean civil war."

"With Guido and Hugo in the same city, I do not see how it can be otherwise."

"And my mother? Do you think she desires such an outcome?"

Gallimanfry sighed. "I have never been able to read

your mother's mind, least of all now, when she plots an unknown course. I am certain that nothing will stop her from trying to ruin the man she hates above all others.''

Suddenly Anthony's eyes assumed a faraway look filled with burning intensity. "I too have every reason to hate Pope John," he said quietly.

Eleven years had passed since the day Anthony and Gallimanfry left the villa at Tusculum. For the young boy, dazed by the sudden parting from those he had known and loved, it was a time of hardship and confusion. With only the clothes on their backs and a few meager belongings he and his tutor wandered from town to town, never staying long in one place. Convents and monasteries gave them lodging, but when there was no benefice to turn to they crawled into the fields and slept under the furze with only their cloaks to cover them during the long, cold nights.

To all they met they presented themselves as pilgrims returning from Rome. If anyone wondered at Anthony's youthfulness, Gallimanfry simply explained that the boy, his son, had been prompted by a vision of Saint Jerome to undertake the holy journey.

At last they came to Pisa, a bustling port, brimming with life, crowded with seamen, traders and fortune-seekers. Here Muslims, pagans and Jews, Turks, Libyans and Parthians mingled freely with Christians from every part of the empire—Venetians, Genoese, Greeks, Cypriots and Cretans. And here for the first time Gallimanfry felt safe.

In truth they could not have gone on even if they had wanted to, for young Anthony had passed the point of exhaustion. By the time they reached Pisa, he was almost in a daze. Oblivious to his surroundings, he walked with downcast eyes, thinking only of each step that lay before him.

Gallimanfry quickly found them a lodging place. True,

it was only a pig-keeper's cottage, but at least there was a roof over their heads and a clean straw pallet to lie on.

The cottage and its pigsty, untended for years, lay within the domain of Duke Hugo of Pisa. Gallimanfry prostrated himself before Hugo and begged a freehold, winning for himself and his "son" the right to inhabit the pig-tender's land. He would owe three suckling pigs per annum, brought live to the duke's kitchen. In return he was given access to the granary and a guarantee of his holdings.

And so they settled in, the boy and his tutor, for how long Gallimanfry would not say. To Anthony it was like living on an island in a great sea of doubt and confusion. His lessons continued, but to these were added the chores of carrying feed for the pigs, mending the stall gates, carrying water from the well and digging the trenches they used for jakes. The bearded, careworn face of his tutor, the sounds of the pigs snorting through the mud outside the cottage, the shepherd's call from the hill nearby and the gossip of the women at the well became familiar to him, as familiar as the Roman mansion with its many guards and servants had been.

That other life was gone now, utterly finished, a boyhood dream that could never be recaptured. It did not leave him gradually but suddenly, with the abruptness of a falling sword stroke. One moment he had the past to cling to and the next it was gone. Even now Anthony could remember every searing sensation of that fateful day when he heard of his father's death.

It began with the women at the well, their screeched whispers betraying the glee that was mingled with their false astonishment and horror. To Anthony, their chatter was merely disjointed phrases, scarcely heard, meaning little until Alberic was mentioned. Then suddenly the boy was listening attentively, his body taut, every fiber straining to catch the faintest syllable.

"Nepi. Yes, my dear. The pope, they say—"

"But he was—"

"Yes, oh yes. Everyone *knows* Alberic was—"

"Reached too high—"

"Yes, that was it."

"And now—"

Tongues clucking, heads bowed, they drew away. The boy, overcome with terror, confusion and sorrow, flung his water jar aside and raced back to the cottage, tears streaming down his face.

Gallimanfry had heard nothing. He did his best to calm the child, then set out on his own to discover what he could. When he returned, his face was grim. He tried to break the news gently, but Anthony was wild with impatience. There was no comfort in delay.

What had happened was brutally simple. Alberic bravely defended the garrison at Nepi, but reinforcements from Spoleto did not arrive in time. Pope John used the captured Saracen mangonels to hurl fire into the castle and break down the gates. Nepi was taken, Alberic captured.

It was the last part that Gillimanfry did not want to tell, that he would have softened for the boy, but lies would do no good. Anthony could not be sheltered forever, and the truth would finally reach his ears. And so Gallimanfry was forced to be unsparing in describing the execution.

Alberic had been tortured in front of the Senate House. His head was severed and placed on a staff, which was paraded through the city before crowds of jeering citizens. For seven days the skull remained in the Forum, until the flies and the buzzards had picked it clean. On the eighth day Cardinal Peter removed it from its staff and threw it into the Tiber. It sank like a stone.

* * *

Now, remembering that day, Anthony realized how absolutely the dream world of boyhood had been shattered. At first he had only felt bitter resentment at his father's death. The unfairness of it all—to be left all alone, forgotten, with no one to turn to but Gallimanfry. As he dragged a big-teated hog from the mire or plodded with a cartload of cobs from market, he sometimes wondered bitterly what Sergius was doing now. In his mind's eye Anthony saw his brother as he had left him—contented, spoiled, well-fed, lying in bed nicking flies while servants hurried to carry out his wishes.

That was far from the worst. The worst was at night, when he could dream that all was just as it had been before. He saw his mother waiting for him, smiling, as he came in from riding. There was Tasha's firm touch as she crouched down to straighten his cloak. Quiet Lena, with her wide eyes and gentle manner. And his father . . .

Anthony saw the strong, handsome face. He felt again that rush of pride he had always felt in his father's presence. He saw the smile, heard the welcoming words. He rushed to his father's arms.

Just then the dream would end in horror. His father had no arms—no body at all. Only a head, and beneath it, dangling like tentacles, long bloody fibers that reached out to Anthony, tangling him in their grasp.

He would awake screaming. Gallimanfry tried to comfort him, but it was no use. Only time could make it fade.

Anthony knew without being told that he must never mention his parentage. What had happened to the great duke and general could also happen to his son.

To everyone in Pisa he was known as Odilo, the son of a pig-tender, vassal to Duke Hugo. As Odilo he mended the fences and fetched water from the well. As Odilo he became a page boy to his liege, helping to serve in the great banquet hall.

During all these years he never once used the name Anthony, nor did he ever refer to his mother, his father or the House of Theophylact. To all but Gallimanfry the son of Alberic had vanished from the earth, his place taken by a lad named Odilo who had learned to forget the past.

Now Anthony had returned.

"Do you remember the soothsayer?" Gallimanfry asked suddenly.

The two men sat on stools close to the hearth. The embers were burning low. Now and then the fire hissed and spat as a branch crumbled and fell into the grate. By Gallimanfry's side was a flagon of wine, now nearly empty.

"How could I forget?" Anthony looked curiously at his old tutor. It was the first time since they left Tusculum that Gallimanfry had mentioned the episode.

"Are you ready to fulfill the augury?"

Anthony laughed. "As ready as a man can be, but look you, Gallimanfry, it's a far cry from a sea adventurer to a princeps of Rome."

Gallimanfry shrugged and took a long pull at the wine. Wiping his lips with the back of his hand, he passed the jug to Anthony.

"Not so far as one might think," he replied mysteriously.

"What do you propose?" Anthony jumped up to pace. "I cannot suddenly appear in Rome and acknowledge my birthright. I can only imagine how pleased Pope John would be to see the son of Alberic rise from the dead."

"No—bolder yet," said Gallimanfry. "I have told you that John arrives in Pisa in two days' time."

Anthony's fists clenched, but he remained silent.

"Very well," Gallimanfry continued, "I would have

you appear in Duke Hugo's court in the presence of the pope himself and proclaim your identity."

"Here?" Anthony's eyes widened. "That would be sheer folly. Do you wish me to bait the lion—"

"Better here than in his own lair," Gallimanfry interrupted. "If you are to become Anthony again, to be known far and wide as the son of Alberic, what better way lies to hand?"

"They will slay me on the spot."

"I think not." Now Gallimanfry rose too. He approached the young man and studied his face. "Yes, you have his quality," he muttered under his breath.

"What do you mean?"

"There is something in some men that makes others obey them. Your father had that temper, and it is borne out in you as well."

Anthony did not reply.

"Duke Hugo is a Lombard," Gallimanfry went on. "He has no reason to bear you a grudge. However much the pope may wish to see you dead, he will not touch you in a Lombard court."

"After I have declared myself?" Anthony asked, speaking low. "What then?"

"There are men in Spoleto who still honor the memory of Alberic and Lambert. Duke Bardulf leads them. He will be ready to serve you."

Anthony snorted. "A single garrison of soldiers, no matter how loyal, cannot turn an empire to my bidding."

"No," agreed Gallimanfry, "but that is only the beginning. Move those troops to Rome, ally yourself with Guido, and you will find yourself with a greater force by far."

"And my mother? How will she stand in all this?"

Gallimanfry smiled. "I assure you, she will endorse any act that brings about the ruin of Pope John."

There was a thoughtful pause. Then Anthony sighed and raised his head. His eyes met Gallimanfry's.

"I will do it. Pray to God that you are right."

Gallimanfry clapped Anthony on the shoulder. "Good. You will show yourself at the first banquet. After that on to Spoleto. You must remember everything I have taught you. You will need to keep all your wits about you if you are to be a leader of men."

"And Mother? How will she learn of it?"

"The moment you announce yourself I will send a message to Rome with one of the pilgrims. I myself will follow soon thereafter."

"So we shall meet there?"

Gallimanfry grinned. "Yes, son of Alberic. We will meet in Rome."

Chapter 42

The banquet hall of Hugo, Duke of Pisa, was a magnificent square-ceilinged edifice of travertine marble, outranking in size and splendor all other structures in the city. It was large enough to hold six enormous tables with ample room between them for dancers, jugglers, wrestlers and strongmen to perform. From the main doors to the duke's own table was more than a hundred paces. Along every step of the way the visitor was flanked by some exotic ornament or monumental work.

The duke provided well for the comfort of his entertainers and courtesans. Window seats and divans on either side of the hall were furnished with enormous silk bolsters and covered with fine shawls, damasks and down pillows, and there was always plenty to eat and drink. At feast time the tables were crowded, and servants continually moved among the benches carrying dishes heaped with food. Music filled the air, the rhythms building as dancers hurled themselves about in a frenzy of motion.

During Anthony's boyhood stint as a page he developed an almost prudish dislike of the debauches and of the sordid aftermath the revelers inevitably left behind. Even now he recalled the voices of the women on the divans, who tried to lure him away from the feast to their luxurious darkened chambers.

Men would toss him about in jest, women tug at his

clothing, fondle his buttocks and tease his genitals. He was nothing to them, a pig-tender's boy who should feel privileged to serve in such a place, more so to draw their exalted attention.

He defended himself with apparent good spirits, but afterward there were times when he wept, raging at the humiliation and embarrassment, wept even as he swept the floor, scrubbed the long soiled tables and washed away the remains of the duke's great banquet.

Now all these years later the feeling returned to him, a wave of revulsion that almost drove him from the room. With a great effort of will he steadied himself in the doorway and looked out at the duke's guests. Surely they would recognize him, though he was a grown man dressed in a nobleman's tunic, and see him for the young boy who had crawled among the tables picking up scraps for the dogs.

Instead his appearance was barely noted at all. Only a few curious stares were cast at the tall bearded figure entering the hall. The diners needed only a glance to take in his fine clothing, his gold ring, the elaborate cloisonné on his sword hilt; this was obviously a world traveler, invited by the duke. Pisa was prospering from her sea trade, and many such adventurers were to be found here.

So Anthony was left free to make his way in unannounced. He immediately saw that Duke Hugo sat at the head table with Pope John by his side. They turned to each other as they joined in wild laughter.

Choosing a central location at one of the long tables, Anthony edged his way between a pair of jugglers. There were hoots and catcalls as he ducked to avoid their flying batons of fire. Finding a space between two of the pope's guardsmen, recognizable by the cross on their tunics, he seated himself on the leather-cushioned bench and reached for a platter of game birds.

Across the table a thin blond man regarded him curiously. Anthony pretended to ignore him, but several times during the next few courses he noticed that the fellow's gaze was still upon him. Finally, reaching toward the same platter, their hands almost touched. Anthony gestured for the other to go first, and the blond man took the opportunity to introduce himself.

"I am Duke Theobald of Lucca," he said brusquely. His eyes met Anthony's.

Anthony nodded politely and continued to gnaw on a ham bone.

"And you, stranger?" Theobald demanded. "Your name?"

"I seem to have forgotten." Anthony examined the gristly bone as if to find some choice meat that had so far escaped his attention.

At this the guards on either side ceased their lively conversation. They glanced at Theobald, whose face was suffused with anger, and cautiously edged away. Anthony continued to eat as if nothing concerned him.

Theobald rose to his feet. "That is an affront," he declared loudly. "I demand to know your name."

Anthony waved the ham bone dismissively. "I tell you, sir, I have forgotten it. If it matters so little to me, surely it is none of your concern. Though of course I apologize for the oversight."

The duke was not appeased. In a flash his sword was on the table, the double-edged steel crashing among the jugs and crockery. A hush fell over the hall. Even the rattle of the tambourines and the blaring of the krummhorn stilled as the diners turned to stare. Then everyone looked to Hugo, whose duty it was to settle the argument.

The Duke of Pisa surveyed the long table and the two men, one with trembling hand on the hilt of his sword, the other nonchalantly examining his ham bone.

"Theobald," called Hugo, "what manner of dispute is this?"

"A pardon, Your Grace," replied his guest. "This visitor to your hall refuses to produce his name." His sword point rose to the vicinity of Anthony's breastbone.

His words met with a low murmur as the diners turned to their neighbors. Such rudeness! Heads were shaken. Puzzled looks were exchanged. No one seemed to know the stranger.

Leaning to the advisor on his left hand, the chronicler-priest Luitprand, Hugo made a discreet inquiry. Again heads were shaken.

"Stranger," pronounced Hugo, "you are not known in our court. What is your name?"

Dropping his ham bone to the table and pushing aside the point of Theobald's sword, Anthony slowly removed himself from the long bench. He wiped his hands on the sides of his leather jerkin, glanced at Theobald, then turned to the head table.

Bowing almost imperceptibly, he asked, "Would Pope John also like to know my name?"

There was a low gasp as his insolence invested the very air of the hall. The papal guards looked toward the pontiff, awaiting a signal. The signal did not come; instead Pope John gazed at Anthony with a kind of rapt attention.

Once handsome, the pontiff had changed strikingly since Anthony last saw him. He had jowls now, and his hazel eyes had lost their luster. His complexion was an unhealthy grey. Only the silky brown hair remained the same. Anthony realized with a shock that it was a wig; the smooth, shining curls of a far younger man were absurdly incongruous beside the aging face.

The pope examined him now with silent intensity, as if Anthony reminded him of someone or something long forgotten.

"Should Your Holiness wish it, the varlet will be ejected from the hall," Hugo growled.

Pope John shook his head, never taking his eyes from the stranger. "No. Do not disappoint Duke Theobald. Let us hear his name."

The silence was profound. No one dared move or breathe. The revelers glanced from one to another. Would this man dare defy the pope?

Anthony considered the waiting guards; Duke Theobald of Lucca, his hand still on the sword; the concubines, jugglers and page boys. Finally his eyes returned to the head table, where Hugo and Pope John sat awaiting his answer. When he spoke, his words rang through the hall.

"I am Anthony, son of Alberic the Lombard and of Marozia of the Theophylacts."

As he spoke he felt a great burden lifted from his shoulders. What triumph, what joy to speak his name aloud, to make bold announcement of his identity at last.

He threw a long look about the hall, then pushed his way out through the crowd. He disappeared before any of the revelers could gather their wits.

Chapter 43

When Duke Guido married Marozia, a subtle but distinct change came over the House of Hadrian. Guido had the fastidious spirit of a careful merchant, and he believed that fine works should be displayed even if they were not used. His influence on the day-to-day running of the palace had not been profound, but in the quality and arrangement of the decor everything bespoke a man of means who wished others to be impressed with his status.

There were pedestals around the atrium now, each bearing a gold or bronze figurine. The worn Byzantine tapestries with their tired religious scenes had been replaced by silk hangings in brilliant colors, silks imported through Vienna and Genoa and traded by the Siena Company. The duke's propensity for comfortable furnishings was visible everywhere. Borrowing shamelessly from the Turks and Saracens, he had established the fashionable use of enormous bolsters for lounging and conversation.

Sometimes I scarcely recognized my sister in these new surroundings. Since her marriage to Guido, Marozia seemed more queenly in appearance. She bound her hair in a caul, a net of gold thread and precious jewels. She was slim and graceful still and according to some she was more beautiful than ever. To my eyes, though, the many jeweled rings on her fingers and the splendor of her gowns and robes did little to enhance her natural fairness. It seemed to me she sought only to hide the gentle sister I remembered behind all that brittle glitter.

One month before the season of Lent I came to the House of Hadrian, big with news from a pilgrim. A Sienese warden, one of Guido's staunch house servants, greeted me at the door.

Marozia had many visitors these days, and I was forced to wait for some time. When I saw Tasha, I told her I had an urgent reason for my visit and she ran to tell Marozia.

Several others were in the audience chamber when I entered, including a senator from the Quirinal and several envoys from Benevento. Marozia was dismissing them as I came in.

"Lena, welcome," she greeted me. "Boniface, I will speak with you later. You had better review your accounts. The tithe is considerably underpaid by my steward's reckoning." That pushed the last of them out the door, you can imagine.

Marozia's expression changed as she took my hands in hers. "Now, what brings you, Lena? We see so little of you. I do not know why you insist on living at Saint Petronilla's. You would be far more comfortable here."

"Marozia, please." We had engaged in this argument many times before. "You know I have my duties," I reminded her. "How would it appear if the abbess chose to live separate from her flock?"

Marozia shook her head. "It's so hard to think of you as an abbess." Then she studied me closely. "How radiant you look today. What brings you here, Lena? Is it good news?"

"The best of news." I glanced at our old servant. "Tasha will be pleased to hear it, too."

"What, then?"

I moved closer. "This morning a pilgrim from Pisa arrived at the convent and asked for me. He said he had a message he wished me to bear to Marozia, a message concerning her son."

"My son? Sergius is here in Rome, at the Lateran. Surely he did not follow Pope John to Pisa."

At this I smiled. "No, Marozia. The message was from Gallimanfry."

"But I thought—" Her voice was almost inaudible.

"Use your head, Marozia. It's Anthony."

"Anthony," she murmured as if the syllables were strange to her. And then, "Oh, Lena, could it be that he still lives?"

I nodded. "Lives and prospers. Gallimanfry has looked after him all these years."

In a moment we were in each other's arms, weeping with joy. An odd sight we must have made, Marozia with all her jewels and finery hugging a drab, dark-cloaked abbess. There was no one to see us except Tasha, and I doubt that she caught more than a blur, for she was as weepy as we.

When we had dried our eyes and wept again, I called in the pilgrim, and he gave a first-hand account of Anthony and Gallimanfry—how they looked and spoke, what they wore and on and on. When he had finished, Marozia made him say it all again and asked a score of questions he could not answer.

The pilgrim was dismissed with forty ducats, a tithe of which he vowed he would donate to Saint Petronilla's, and I was alone again with Marozia and Tasha.

"It was a dangerous action to declare his true name before Pope John and Duke Hugo," Marozia mused.

"Surely he had advice of Gallimanfry," I suggested, hoping to ease her fears.

"I have no doubt." She seemed lost in thought. I

stared at her, puzzled, until she favored me with her gaze. "What will you do," she asked suddenly, "now that you know Gallimanfry is alive?"

I blushed deeply and turned my head away. "I will wait," I stammered. "I cannot do otherwise."

"If he comes for you?"

"Please, Sister, do not remind me. I am an abbess now."

"What about the child? You will have to tell him—"

"Hush," I interjected. "I have only just now heard the news. How do I know what I should do or say?"

She studied me intently for a moment, then drew me toward the ottoman. "Tasha," she ordered, "fetch us some wine, please. Two goblets. And tell Margrita we will feast at dusk."

"Yes, signora." She bowed and left us.

There was a long silence, and it seemed to me that Marozia had forgotten my presence. Then she took my hand and smiled.

"I feel reborn, Lena. That night when we sent Anthony and Gallimanfry away, it felt as if part of me had been stolen. Through all that followed, I prayed—" She paused. "I prayed that Anthony would someday be found."

I laughed. "The man that pilgrim described—it's hard to imagine he was once our little Anthony."

The joke was lost on Marozia. "This is a new beginning," she said urgently. "I am certain of it. All that I have waited for and suffered—"

"Still, there is much to be considered," I cautioned. I could see the calculating gleam in Marozia's eyes, and it frightened me. "What will this mean for Guido—and for Sergius?"

"I do not see how there can be any difficulty," Marozia replied. "Sergius is well placed in the church; I have seen to that. But still, Rome needs a leader."

I stared at her. "What of Guido?"

"I must forge an alliance between them," she said as if there could be nothing more natural. "Surely Guido will see the wisdom of it. He knows he will need allies now that the pope has wooed the support of Duke Hugo."

Just then Tasha appeared with the wine. As she turned to leave, Marozia called her back.

"Don't go. I wish to call the senators to our table tonight. And send a messenger to the Lateran. Tell Sergius he must be here as well—without the knowledge of Cardinal Peter."

A raised brow was Tasha's only sign of surprise. She bowed and left us again.

"According to the pilgrim, Anthony has gone to Spoleto," Marozia continued. "He must mean to gather Alberic's loyal men before he comes to Rome." There was a triumphant look in her eye. "Then we shall see how Pope John teeters on his precious throne," she whispered. "And then we shall watch him fall."

The feast after vespers was well attended but not a complete success. At the news of his brother's reappearance Sergius turned pale, and the goblet in his hand trembled when he rose for the toast. A glance at his mother's face did not raise his spirits, either. Marozia was radiant, victorious; she could not have hidden her happiness even if she had wanted to.

As Sergius' pale eyes darted about the room, measuring the reaction of the senators who surrounded him, I thought how changed he was from the boy Anthony had known. It had been Marozia's decision to place him in the Lateran, and the young man had fast wormed his way upward through the ranks of sycophants who seemed to throng the palace. He was now a cardinal and a close associate of the pope's brother Peter.

Sergius' injured leg had never healed properly, and he continued to walk with a limp. Since this interfered with his activities, he was somewhat slothful by nature. He had also turned corpulent and his face was unpleasantly pudgy. He had the ruddy, curly hair of his father and his stocky build as well, but none of his father's fire. When he wore the scarlet surplice, as now, he looked more like a jolly jongleur than a churchman of some status.

"What do you know of this?" he demanded of me. He had taken me aside midway through the meal. I noted that he nervously glanced around, as if he did not wish to be overheard. Fortunately, the feast was at its height and no one paid any attention to us.

"No more than you, Sergius," I replied.

He made a gesture of annoyance. "What will happen now?" There was an edge of whine in his voice. "I know Mother always favored Anthony. I *know* she did. If he returns—"

"Sergius!" I did not feel like scolding him, but his childishness shocked me. "You know your mother was always fair, and look how far you have risen. What have you to be afraid of?"

His lips curled. "That man Gallimanfry," he continued as if he had not heard me, "that odious man. I hoped he was gone forever."

I could have smacked him. My nails dug into my palms and I had to bite my lip from spitting out my thoughts. Perhaps I should have thanked the arrogant young man for his insults, though, for he made me realize how strong were my affections for my long-lost lover.

"Your mother and I will want to see harmony between the two of you," I managed when I could speak again.

"I have been here doing my duty," Sergius complained.

"I didn't go wandering off like some idle adventurer. God knows what he's been up to all these years."

"It was not his choice to go wandering," I said stiffly.

Sergius laughed. "That's true. It was not. It's hard to show your face when your father's been branded a traitor." That reflection made him brighten, and he added, "At least the Romans will never forget that."

Another wave of anger seized me. "Sergius," I said fiercely, "you must heal this bitterness before Anthony comes. If there is rivalry between you, your mother will not be able to endure it."

There was a silent pause while he looked away.

"Sergius," I urged, "do you not love your brother? Can you not welcome him without fear or jealousy?"

He shifted uneasily to take the weight off his bad leg. "As long as he knows his place," he muttered, "I am perfectly satisfied to see him return."

So he said, but Sergius, always a poor liar, refused to look at me. He returned to the table, sourness written all over his features.

There was another unhappy face at the table that night, as I could not help noticing. Duke Guido of Siena was a noble-looking Lombard with angular nose, high brow and piercing black eyes. He had the bearing of a wise old scholar. When he listened, he tilted sideways from the waist, keeping his eyes fixed on some distant corner of the room rather than on the speaker, so he always seemed lost in distant thoughts.

His marriage to Marozia had been entirely my sister's doing, though of course he could see the wisdom in the match once it was proposed. At Marozia's behest Guido had come to Rome from Siena with pennants flying. There was quite a stir at the time, for unlike many nobles of the region, Guido maintained a full garrison of militia.

His men were superbly outfitted and expertly trained. Each wore a fine quilted gambeson covered with a hauberk, a tunic of chain mail reaching almost to the knees. Their sturdy iron helmets were of Frankish design, and each tabard had the emblem of the boar and the hart, Guido's family seal, embroidered in white on a background of scarlet silk. When they marched through the city, the thudding of their feet and the beating of their tambours made a frightful, steady din that drew the wonder and admiration of the citizens.

Guido and Marozia were married in the basilica at Santo Stefano Minore, adjacent to Saint Peter's. Pope John was absent from the wedding, a circumstance noted by all. Clearly he had no wish to give his blessing to such a match.

Marozia's alliance with Guido gave her power she had not possessed before, and though that power was secular, it might well pose a threat to the pontiff. As if to carry her defiance further, Marozia immediately nominated Guido to the Senate. He was duly elected and installed, and his first speech was a tremendous success.

Once Guido was established as a Roman, he showed no signs of wishing to return to Siena. His soldiers were housed in the Castel Sant'Angelo, the fortress at the critically important bridge that connected Rome to the Borgo around Saint Peter's.

Guido himself lived with Marozia at the House of Hadrian, but he did not neglect his troops. He inspected them daily, required them to be in full array and observed their exercises on the fields outside the Leonine Walls from the heights of the battlements. After a time it became a common diversion for the Romans to watch Guido's men engage in war games.

The significance of Guido's presence in the city was not lost on Pope John. His political power within the church remained as strong as ever, but his military strength had dwindled. If danger threatened, he could call out only a few men, badly trained and ill equipped for war.

Knowing he would have to seek alliances, John was reluctant to share his power. He waited as long as he could before making up his mind, but at last he turned to Hugo, Guido's half-brother and hated rival. It was a politically shrewd move, but it meant John would have to leave Rome at a most dangerous moment. If Guido chose to increase his garrison while the pope was away, the Lateran, the seat of the papacy itself, might be in jeopardy.

However, Pope John did not expect Guido to move quickly, and in this he was correct. For all his show of strength Guido was a cautious man who rigorously avoided taking unnecessary risks.

It was only after John's departure that Guido began to realize the danger that might lie ahead. If Hugo did indeed ally himself with the pope, they would certainly launch an attack on the Castel Sant'Angelo. Guido knew he could not afford to sit back and wait for that event, but neither was he ready to march forth and set upon his half-brother.

It was a stalemate. Guido waited, wondering what would happen next, as the time of decision grew closer. Then the sudden appearance of Marozia's son made that decision all the more difficult.

"What are your plans for him?" Guido demanded of his wife when they were alone that night.

"I will welcome him," she replied, innocently gazing up at him.

"And what then? He is no longer the little boy who toddled by your side." Then Guido checked, startled by his own loudness, and peered around.

The banquet hall was deserted except for a page boy collecting goblets as he made his way toward the scullery.

Marozia waited until he was out of earshot. "I promise you, dear Guido," she said softly, "I have no intention of raising Anthony above your own person."

"I had not even considered that," Guido snapped. "And in any case I would not allow it." He glanced at Marozia. "But how do you know what his feelings are? Will you ask the son of Alberic to bend his knee and kiss my ring?"

She smiled a secret smile. "If necessary, yes." Then, seeing his look, she came closer and laid her hands on his chest. She searched him with her dark eyes. "I know it is hard for you, dear Guido, that I have not been able to bear you a child. If you could only take Anthony as your son, accept his loyalty—"

Guido wrenched himself away. "You think he will readily forswear his father's memory?"

Marozia's eyes clouded. "No, nor shall I ask him to. All I want is an alliance between you. Whether you regard him as a stepson or only accept him as a vassal, that is between you two, but I cannot have enmity between you."

Guido considered this for a moment. "Perhaps if he were given Spoleto—"

"That's out of the question," Marozia exclaimed. "We need him here, and soon. If the pope is successful, if he returns with your half-brother in his pocket, we will have little or no time to make preparations." Her eyes burned as she pleaded with him. "John is still pope, Guido. I cannot abide that. We have waited long enough." Her hands were clenched and her body trembled with the fury of repressed emotion. "Don't you see, dear Guido? We have waited long enough."

Chapter 44

Two weeks passed before Pope John set out for Rome with the Duke of Pisa at his side. He blamed Hugo's legions for the delay. Years of lax rule punctuated by frequent debaucheries had given the men plenty of false courage. Their swaggering indifference was almost as dangerous as outright rebellion.

As they sharpened their weapons, repaired their chain mail and bartered for clothing and supplies for the campaign, the soldiers behaved like hagglers at a county fair. Fist fights broke out over the sale of leather breeches. Money was spent recklessly on razors, ornate drinking flagons and useless trinkets that would only encumber the army on the road. Women were everywhere, mingling with the men, showering them with flattery, luring them from their duties.

As a result marching orders were delayed and delayed again. Meanwhile, more recruits straggled in from the surrounding towns and villages—from Lucca, Pistoia, Pontedera, Sacina, Leghorn, and even as far away as Carrara, Massa, Prato and Florence.

Hugo knew full well that Guido had planted his Sienese spies among them, but there was nothing much he could do about it. There was no effective organization in his army, no firm hierarchy of command, no system of punishment and therefore no discipline. It was true that spirits ran high among the troops and his men bragged of their prowess, but the simple act of obeying a command—setting up a campsite, assigning work details or standing guard—seemed to escape their powers of concentration. Thus Pisa, supposedly preparing for war, soon came to be more like bedlam.

Then too, there were rifts between the papal guard and the Lombards. Though hardly in peak fighting condition themselves, Pope John's Roman militia had adopted an air of aloof superiority that offended the provincial soldiers. The Roman commanders and captains enforced loyalty and competence but no more. To aid in the preparations for the campaign was deemed beneath them. Remaining in their encampment, obeying only the orders of the pope and his lieutenants, they observed the frenetic scene with bemused indifference, as if it all had nothing to do with them.

On every hand these Romans were regarded with growing hostility. The exaggerated grandeur of the papal troops with their rigid marching routines, their well-stitched purple-emblazoned uniforms and their formidable bronze helmets seemed to bring out the worst in Hugo's Lombards. In sturdy leather jerkins, patched mail, rusted halberds and dented broadswords the Northerners flaunted their casual organization and crude manners as if in defiance of their allies. At times the two factions seemed on the verge of open confrontation.

Pope John found the disorganization, delays and internal strife to be maddening. Daily messengers from the Lateran brought him deeply disturbing news of Rome. Guido marched through the streets; Guido brought reinforcements to the Castel Sant'Angelo. Guido entertained the nobles in Marozia's palace. Guido spoke to the Senate and was well received. Guido, Guido, Guido! Why was only he, Pope John, tormented by this man? Surely the greater affront was to Hugo, whom he would crown King of the Lombards.

Nevertheless, Hugo seemed almost indifferent. At night the revels in the banquet hall continued as before, only now the jests and insults were almost universally directed at the Duke of Siena. Duke Guido was a ball-less coward, they said. He was a jester in Tuscan clothing—and some court sycophant would hop up on the table to demonstrate how Guido strutted and sashayed.

Pope John was not amused by such antics. One night he rose abruptly from his place, making brusque apologies, long before the banquet was finished. Crossing the moonlit square, he made his way to the army camps and wandered among his troops, conferring with the guards. Such restlessness was new to him, but he could not bear to loll among the banqueters while the hours ticked by and serious matters were buried in the debauchery of Hugo's court.

John was increasingly assailed by doubts, doubts he could share with no one. For the first time he regretted leaving Cardinal Peter in Rome. His brother would have understood. Of all the men who surrounded the pope, Peter alone could be trusted to refrain from sentimentality and partisanship. He was a thorough politician, a man who acted only in self-interest. For this reason John always felt easy with him. To win Peter's alliance one need only offer him the right price. He would drive a hard bargain and invariably keep it.

For that very reason it had been essential to leave Peter in Rome until the alliance with Hugo was sealed. Peter could manipulate the Curia; even the Roman Senate would be swayed by his will.

Most important, Peter alone had no wish to become pope; of that John was certain. Peter could see as well as anyone that the papacy was a position of exposure, and he had no desire to pay for glory with untimely death.

Pope John shuddered, whether from the chill air or from premonitory feelings he could not tell. Leaving the city by the Porta Nueva, he strolled along a dim path up a low hill through silver-bright pastureland. As he approached, a figure moved near a solitary tree, a shepherd, perhaps, roused from slumber. Somewhat below and to the east, almost lost in the shadows at the base of the hillside, a pig-keeper's cottage could be seen. Low grunting came to the pope's ears as he passed.

With startling rapidity a figure rose from the ground twenty paces ahead. The pope slapped his hand to the sword at his waist, but the figure made no threatening gesture. John caught the profile of a bandy-legged man, short and squat with wild hair and a flowing beard, his head tilted quizzically.

"Who goes there?" demanded the pope.

The head tilted farther to one side, but there was no reply.

John raised his voice. "Tell me your name, peasant."

A shrill laugh broke the silence. "You shall not know mine, Your Holiness, but I know yours."

John felt a chill along his spine. Even in the full moon's light he should not have been recognized.

"Retreat as you came," he said carefully, "and your life will be spared."

"My life is spare indeed, some might say sparse. And yet I live judiciously, having no lives to spare."

The pope stiffened. Apparently the man was insane, and yet it was somehow fitting, even amusing, to hear the cracked voice that addressed him in this fearless way.

"What madhouse have you escaped from?" he asked, still holding his sword.

"All madhouses but life," replied the voice, "and you?

I hear your Lateran is a fine place for a man to eat, sleep and pray. Yes, a fine place for lewdness and butchery.''

"Is that what they say?" The pope laughed. "Then get you gone, slave, before I butcher you."

"Better the pigs than me," the man retorted, skittering off a little, "though in truth the pigs are better than I. They only take what they are given and look to their young, while I am a grasping, thinking, sentient man and I want what only the pope can give me."

"And what can the pope give you?"

"What only he has to offer."

"What would that be?"

"Why, the papacy, of course."

John laughed and jabbed the point of his sword in the earth. "Just what would you do with the papacy, fool?"

"I would wear a crown, as popes do, and a ring. I would speak to God and man and distribute God's gifts. Better to tell you what I would not do."

"What is that?"

"I would not murder a senator nor make his wife my whore."

For a long moment there was no sound. Far away a startled sheep sprang to its feet and leapt away. On the waters of the Arno the moonlight sparkled.

"Madman," the pope gasped, "who are you?"

"Why, if I have my way, I am the pope and you are the madman, everything being topsy-turvy in the world of Rome."

John hardly felt the sword in his trembling hand, but the weight of it gave him solace, as if the weapon alone could save him.

"Answer me," he growled.

"I am a sage, Your Holiness, the sage that grows on a green pasture. Therefore I am part of the pasture and can safely be ignored." The figure was retreating, its bandy legs moving in a kind of crab walk, but the arrogant voice did not cease. "Or perhaps I am conscience, which is a type of herb that flavors your drink and makes it bitter." The man laughed. "I would not trade places with you for all the world, in spite of what I may say."

"Who are you, you fiend?" The pope's voice rose in a bellow of rage.

"Hush, hush, you will wake the sheep. The sheep sleep, here as in Rome, but there is a wolf who can waken them. This wolf is named Anthony. He is son to the man you slaughtered."

"Fiend, fiend!" The pope's rush was sudden and unexpected, but the bandy-legged figure was quicker. Leaping aside, he dodged over the hillock, easily evading the sword that sliced at him.

Pursuit was futile. The pope stopped where his prey had been only a moment before. Sword in hand, he squinted into the moonlight.

"Fiend," he called, an edge of desperation creeping into his tone, "where are you?"

"I am here, Your Holiness." The voice returned softly to him, all the shrillness of insanity now gone. "Soon I will be in Rome. Very soon. I and my charge, Anthony. We have many things to tell the Romans, tales that will fill them with wonder." The bandy legs were in motion now, the figure departing from sight. But the voice, though fainter, was still distinct. "Come swiftly, pope and father of the western empire. We shall all be awaiting you there—even I, Gallimanfry."

Then the figure was lost in silence among the dark ridges and gullies. Pope John stood shaking, still in the grip of superstitious fear. He was certain it had been a demon, but the name Gallimanfry was somehow familiar.

*   *   *

"Ah, Your Holiness, we have missed you." Clutching the edge of the high table, Duke Hugo forced himself to his feet. "You are pale, Your Grace. Where have you been?"

In the vast dining hall the remains of the feast lay strewn about. Bodies slouched over the soiled tables and half-clothed men and women lay intertwined on the couches and divans. The rank smell of roast mutton and rancid fish was mixed with the stink of vomit. Amid the wreckage mangy dogs roamed with their heads slung low, picking at the scraps and bones. Now and then a dog sniffed at a man's grease-lined face, only to be slapped away.

The pope shrugged off Hugo's drunken embrace. "Tomorrow—we must assemble the troops and leave tomorrow," he said thickly. "There is no time to be lost."

"Tomorrow . . . tomorrow." Hugo lurched closer and thrust his lean face forward. Repelled by his breath, John turned away, but there was no rebuffing the man.

"Your Holiness," Hugo carefully enunciated, "do not fear for Rome. It will be there in the morning and the day after that. You and I"—he staggered, barely catching himself from falling—"we are brothers. You are pope"—he thrust a forefinger at John's chest—"and I am king. I will be King of Italy. And pr—" he caught his breath—"and proud of it.

"In due time we will reach Rome, and then we will take that brother of mine, that Guido. We will squash him between our fingers." Hugo made a motion as if pinching a bug.

Then he hiccuped and looked pityingly at the pope. "But come, you are still pale, and that grieves me. No one in my court should look as you do. Wenches," he bellowed, "wenches!"

From a pillowed divan at the side of the hall several young women arose, rubbing sleep from their eyes. Hugo seized a dark, slim one with curly hair. His hand strayed over her breast and down to her thighs, but she did not look at him. Her eyes were on the pope.

"She is fine, fine," remarked Hugo, pushing her toward John. "Take her."

The pope closed his eyes as he felt her arms around him, her small breasts against his chest. The scent of her hair was sweet and delicate, blotting out the noisome odors of the room. As he lifted his hand to her head, he felt himself gliding in a rush down that infinite tunnel of warm darkness toward pleasure.

He opened his eyes. "Tomorrow, Hugo. Tomorrow we must—" The girl reached up. Her lips were against his, silencing him.

"Oh, yes," roared Hugo, laughing. "Tomorrow indeed. Tomorrow will be soon enough."

Chapter 45

During his years at the Lateran Sergius had become a collector of rare jeweled crucifixes, and his private chambers were a glittering shrine. Crosses of gold and silver set with jade, amethyst and lapus lazuli lined the walls of his bedchamber and audience room, and he prided himself on the rareness and value of these precious objects. Each visitor was regaled with stories of how Sergius had cajoled various traders and dealers of antiquities into parting with their treasures. He took enormous pride in his collection, and the appreciation of his guests gave him immense satisfaction.

In a curious way these jeweled relics were not only the symbol but also the tool of Sergius' rapid rise. To garner such rare pieces he had been forced to deal with many people in all walks of life, from the highest cardinals to the poorest Tuscan pilgrims. These dealings gave him a grip on the kingdom at large. Through the bargaining he kept in touch with greater issues—who was gaining power, who prospering, who failing. Because he paid well for his innocent hobby he had the reputation of a man of largesse, and the constant comings and goings of those who dealt with him made him seem very popular.

Today as he welcomed Cardinal Peter to his audience chamber, Sergius appeared anything but secure. He paced

the room, hands folded behind his back, his body rolling
as he favored his lame leg.

Cardinal Peter was gaunt but somehow ageless. The
grey surplice hung on his twisted frame like clothing on a
line. His cheeks were hollow and his ferrety eyes darted to
and fro.

"Look here," Sergius exclaimed the moment the cardinal entered. He stopped near the east wall, where a gold
crucifix hung by the window. It was as long as the span
of a hand, ornately worked. "Isn't that magnificent?
Magnificent! I tell you, those Venetians are unsurpassed
in their craftsmanship. Imagine attempting the body of
Christ in jade—and see how the rubies are placed on the
feet and hands and around the skull. Each a drop of
blood." He laughed triumphantly. "Can you guess what I
paid for this?"

"I cannot, I am sure," Peter replied, not quite keeping the boredom from his voice.

"Take a gamble. Guess."

"Truly, Sergius, I am sure I cannot attempt—"

"A trivial piece." In his excitement Sergius would
not let Peter finish. "It cost me the forefinger of Saint Paul
in an iron reliquary." Again he laughed shrilly.

For an instant Peter appeared startled, and Sergius
hastened to reassure him. "Oh, it isn't real, I can assure
you, though your brother complied in blessing the thing
and calling it so." He wrinkled his nose. "A pagan bone,
if the truth be known, dug up somewhere in the scorticlaria."
He waved his hand toward the quarter of the city outside
the abitato where the skinners and tanners toiled. "Poor
soul," he shrugged, "I suppose this cross was his life's
work, and a nice bauble at that. Well, he's happy now.
He's delighted with his relic, and no doubt Saint Paul
answers his prayers all the same."

"It is fine indeed," Peter commented. "Truly, Sergius,

your collection is unparalleled.'' The young cardinal beamed at the older man's flattery. ''But surely you did not invite me here just to see this.''

''No. Not at all, not at all. The truth is—'' Sergius hesitated. ''I have rather a delicate matter to discuss.''

Peter raised an eyebrow. ''You know I have supported you already.''

Sergius gave a slight bow. ''I do, I do. I thank you for your guidance.''

''No thanks are necessary,'' Peter said smoothly. ''I see in you a most promising young man.''

A tinge of pink came to Sergius' plump cheeks. ''Ah. Well, I am glad. I wish to speak of my future.''

Peter waited without replying. His silence seemed to make the other man uncomfortable.

''Well.'' Sergius paused to clear his throat. ''You have heard that my half-brother has reappeared.''

Peter nodded.

''After all these years.'' Sergius laughed nervously. ''One would have thought he could remain safely buried, but as ill luck would have it—''

''You spare no love for the son of Alberic?'' Peter asked wryly.

''None. That is my point exactly. Once, perhaps, we may have—'' Sergius averted his glance, unwilling to finish the thought. ''No,'' he insisted, ''no, I have no reason to bear him any love whatsoever.''

Peter waited while Sergius wrestled with his thoughts. The young man's blush deepened.

''I suspect that my mother favors him,'' he managed at last.

Cardinal Peter's smile grew more pronounced. He cocked his head. ''Your mother's favor should not be a barrier. You have risen on your own, Sergius. I do not see how your mother can affect your position.''

"Ah, but you don't know her." Sergius sounded bitter. "She is very gracious and charming, but when she wants something. . . ."

"What does she want now?" Peter seemed suddenly interested.

Sergius avoided the eyes of his elder. "Vengeance." The word fell like a stone.

"Against whom?"

"Surely you know."

Peter laughed and waved his hands. "That was years ago. True, she seemed quite mad with grief for a time, but she recovered. We all do, Sergius. Our pains are forgotten when we learn to live with the world we are given rather than the one that was promised to us."

Sergius stopped pacing and stood very close to Peter, all his nervousness gone. "I tell you, she has never let go of Alberic and she never will. I sometimes think this semblance of grace is only the height of her madness. Inside she is screaming, Peter. I know she will not rest until the pope's blood has been spilled—and yours as well."

The cardinal took an involuntary step backward, responding to the glittering intensity in the young man's eyes, but in a moment he had regained his composure. The sneering smile returned.

"If that is her intention—"

"You know it is her intention. She lives for nothing else."

"You brought me here to tell me this?"

"No." Sergius shook his head. "No, I merely wish you to know that whatever happens I will not join her in any treachery against the church. As far as I am concerned, Alberic and Theophylact received their just reward."

Peter was incredulous.

"You do not believe me?" Sergius demanded. "You

think I have no reason to renounce my mother's family? Listen then, and I will tell you. One of the servants here—Cleanthus—you know her?"

Peter nodded.

"She once served a nun by the name of Teresa, a friend of my mother's. It was Cleanthus who told me how my father died."

Peter looked up, startled. "He was found murdered in the baptistery. The identity of the murderer was never discovered."

Sergius gave a bitter laugh. "You are mistaken. One person could have named the murderer—that nun, Teresa. But she was silenced by my mother."

Peter drew in a sharp breath. "Then tell me, who murdered Pope Sergius?"

The young man's eyes were blazing. "My mother and Alberic had a tryst in the baptistery. They were discovered by my father. He and Alberic fought to the death."

Cardinal Peter turned away and stared at one of the crucifixes on the wall. Then he crossed himself. "I see."

Sergius grasped him by the shoulder. "I will come and go at my mother's house," he said fiercely. "I will hold Anthony in my arms and welcome him, singing thanks that he is alive. But between you and me, Peter, I have only scorn for those who live in the House of Hadrian. Will you remember that?"

"I will."

Sergius nodded with satisfaction. "No doubt Anthony will gain the support of some Lombards, Spoletans and Beneventans—whatever rabble he can draw down from the hills. But I swear to you, he will be helpless against the church."

Peter smiled. "Nonetheless, it would be good to know his plans in advance of his movements."

"Exactly. So you see, I may prove useful to you and your brother."

"I do see, yes. Quite clearly."

"And I can expect—?"

Peter considered for a moment. "The pope has been unhappy with several bishops in the Romagna. As you know, it is a rich province."

"And close to lovely Venice." Sergius' delight could not be concealed.

"I will speak to him after his return."

The blush in Sergius' cheek was now a warm, steady glow. Impulsively he crossed to the east window and lifted the new crucifix from the wall. The rubies gleamed blood red in the sunlight.

"Even as I made the trade, I thought you might like to have this," he said to Peter. He stroked the gold once with a fleshy finger before handing the crucifix over.

If Peter felt any strong emotion, he gave no sign. "I thank you," he murmured.

"The Romagna must be rich in such things," Sergius added.

Peter gave a slight bow. "Now, if you will excuse me." He turned at the door. "You were wise to make your position known to me," he said, his eyes searching Sergius'. "For some time, I have wondered, and of course I could never be sure. A young man's loyalties can be fickle."

Sergius' smile of triumph vanished. He paled and made a motion to say more, but Peter was already gone.

Chapter 46

Anthony did not rush into the purchase of a horse. He searched carefully, spending many hours in the stalls and markets of Pisa. In the end it was neither the sleekest courser nor the fastest that attracted him, but a plain, sure-footed sable mare. The Arabian blood was clearly outlined in her narrow head and light shoulders, but she was taller than an Arabian and had the graceful power of the Frankish breeds.

Carrying only light provisions, the young man left Pisa on a market day, when the streets were crowded and he could slip unnoticed through the gates. He followed the Arno upriver, where the going was easiest, but at the branching of the Elsa he turned southeast and picked up the Via Cassia at Poggibonsi. Here for a time he moved more speedily as he followed the cobbled road into Siena, and that night he found lodging at the monastery of San Andrea.

At first he hesitated to mention the name of Alberic, not knowing how the holy fathers would regard a man who had been deemed traitor by the pope. Then he discovered that these cloistered Sienese held aloof from the business of Rome. It was all distant scandal to them. Their attitude was much like country people's disregard for the behavior of the rich in a foreign capital.

As for Alberic, he was fondly remembered. No one

here took stock in the trumped-up tribunals and rash executions ordained by their pope. They only prayed that His Holiness' vengeance would not be visited upon themselves.

Alberic had once raced through the streets of Siena, winning the Palio, and many of the Lombards who now lived here had served under him in the campaign against the Saracens. They knew him as a great general, a noble Lombard, and they honored his widow, who had chosen to ally herself with their duke.

Thus reassured, Anthony felt emboldened to proclaim his patronymic. Word of this spread throughout the monastery, then leapt the walls. That night the Sienese crowded to the outer doors to catch a glimpse of him, and within the cloister the friars listened attentively to stories of his childhood, his secret life with Gallimanfry in Pisa and his travels to foreign shores.

When he left the next morning the women by the well stopped their chattering and turned to watch him pass. Children ran after him, dashing perilously close to the horse's hooves, reaching out to touch his spurs for luck.

Anthony could not follow the easy way of the Via Cassia for long. When the spires of Siena were out of sight he turned east, following the hill path that led to the lake called Trasimeno outside Perugia. There, just beyond the third ridge, where the pathway dropped into a sheltered stand of poplar trees, he was set upon by bandits.

They ambushed him from the forest, six men on horseback dressed in ragged leather and carrying light sharp swords. Apparently they expected a lone rider to be easy prey, for they dashed straight for him, waving their swords and howling shrilly.

Anthony did not turn and flee. Instead, when they were several lengths away, he spurred his mount and charged them, pulling his sword. His headlong rush took him into their midst, and his short broadsword flashed left and right.

The first bandit was caught under the chin, his cry cut short as Anthony's sword sliced into his neck. His head fell backward, and blood sprang from his nostrils. By the time he fell, Anthony had turned in his saddle and caught the second bandit in midstroke. The man looked startled as Anthony's sword plunged into his chest. Screaming with pain, he wrenched free of the blade, hurling himself to the ground. He squirmed in the dust, clutching at his tunic, then collapsed and died.

Awestruck, the remaining four bandits backed away and circled, plotting their next move. Anthony did not wait for it. Spurring the mare, he thundered down the mountain path into the poplars and made good his escape.

The bandits halfheartedly pursued him for a time, but it was clear that for them the day's adventure had soured. Their hoofbeats faded in the distance and again Anthony was alone. Only then did he notice the cut on his hand. One of the bandits' swords had sliced through to the bone. Cursing, he tore off a piece of his tunic and wrapped it tightly around his knuckles to stanch the flow of blood.

That night and for several nights thereafter he slept on the ground with a thin cloak pulled up around his shoulders. His wounded hand ached. His only food was dried fish, given to him by the monks in Siena, and whatever berries and green shoots he could find on the hillsides. By day he traveled warily, always on the lookout for bandits. Twice more he was attacked, and each time he saved himself by riding off into the hills, far from the beaten path. The second time he wasted the better part of an afternoon trying to find his way again.

Finally at the lake of Trasimeno he found a hospice of cloistered monks and rested for a day. His hand was healing slowly and his mare needed the day off. The monks were pledged to a vow of silence, so Anthony was left in peace, disturbed only by the eerie questioning of their silent glances. One monk seemed to be practiced in the healing arts, and he applied a balm that smelled of liver oil to Anthony's wound. This he covered with a poultice of ground clay and bread meal spread on grape leaves.

The following morning as the red sun rose over the lake Anthony said his prayers in the stone chapel, made an offering to the religious order and headed his mount toward Tavernelle. Three days later he stood on a hillside overlooking Spoleto.

It was a breathtaking sight, the stark grey town with its massive walls locked in the hold of the mountains. Across the valley on the ilex-covered slopes of Monteluco stood the duomo of San Giuliano and the sacred grove where the hermits from the Near East had built shelters in which to pray.

Dismounting for the steep descent, Anthony felt a great peace creep over him, a feeling of homecoming. This was where his father had made his name. Here lived men who remembered Alberic and honored him. It seemed magnificently still, as if the mountains' sheltering arms kept everyone safe from harm.

Outside the walls at the church of San Alvatore Anthony dismounted and slipped the reins of his horse beneath a stone. The chapel was a simple one with high arches and fluted columns, but the light that poured through the clerestory windows cast a brilliant glow throughout the nave.

Sinking to his knees, Anthony offered up a silent prayer. With God's help the prophecy that had been cast long ago in Tusculum might now be set in motion.

When Anthony emerged from the chapel, the sun's pink glow still lit the snow-capped peaks of the Apennines toward Norcia, but Spoleto was already cloaked in shadows. He entered through the Porta della Fuga in the west wall, joining the tide of Spoletans returning to the city for the night. From their haste he surmised that it was dangerous to stay in the hills after dusk, and as he passed the arch of Drusus to enter the main square, he heard two old peasants muttering curses against the brigands who lurked in the countryside.

When he asked his way to the house of Duke Bardulf, the boy led Anthony to a mansion built in the Roman style, with a broad facade of ornately worked stone. By the fading light the frescoes and carvings seemed to come alive, reminding him of everything that was dear to the Lombards. The peacock plucking fruit, the deer and snake, the lion's struggle, the sly fox, the creature with a lion's tail and a serpent's head—all these brought back stories his father had told him in his childhood.

A servant answered the door, opening it only a crack and peering out suspiciously. The name Anthony son of Alberic seemed to make no impression on him, for he only nodded and slammed the door before retreating to announce the caller. When he returned, however, his demeanor was quite different. Flinging open the door, he stepped back into the foyer, bowed low and reported that the duke would see his visitor at once.

Anthony was led through an atrium with a bronze rain basin in the center, past the sleeping rooms and the dining chamber to an open court lined in mosaics. Torches burned along the walls.

A tall, burly man with a thick mane of dark hair crossed at his approach. Without a word he seized Anthony by the shoulders and embraced him, searching every detail of the young man's face. What he saw seemed to satisfy him, for his gaze softened. Then he broke into a smile.

"So you are the son of Alberic," he remarked.

Anthony fell on one knee and bowed his head. As the duke's hand touched him, he rose again. "My father always spoke fondly of you, my lord. He held you in the greatest respect."

Bardulf's eyes glittered. "I deem it lucky that once in a lifetime I had the privilege of serving such a man. It seems I shall have a second chance."

"No, no," Anthony protested. "I am just a poor knight with no arms and no men. I have been too long a wanderer to claim service from a great lord like you."

Bardulf shook his head. "Nevertheless, the bond between us holds strong."

Anthony regarded the duke with admiration, suddenly grateful for Gallimanfry's guidance. Duke Bardulf was everything he could have hoped for, and more.

"It is true I will need the service of your soldiers," he began. "That is, if you can spare them."

He got no further, for he was interrupted by a young woman who entered the courtyard in a tremendous rush. Long ribbons flying, she burst in upon them. Then, seeing Anthony, she drew up short and stared at him, her eyes widening.

Anthony had a sudden impression of insolent pale blue eyes, a high forehead and a proud chin. One reddish-blond strand had come loose from her hair and fell at her temple. With an unconscious motion like someone swatting at a fly she swept it away. Then with a curious birdlike motion she turned to her father.

"Who is he?" she demanded.

"Francina, respect!" He was angry. "This is Anthony the son of Alberic."

Again there was that swift turning of the head. She studied Anthony with renewed curiosity.

"Where did he come from?" she asked.

Now Bardulf was exasperated beyond all patience. "I

must apologize for my daughter," he said gruffly. "She is spoiled and willful"—he turned on her—"and just leaving. What brings you here anyway, bursting in—"

"A wonderful thing has happened." She seemed completely unaffected by his reprimand.

"Oh, and what is that?"

"A white swan has come down in the garden."

"So what?"

"She won't go away."

He sighed and gave Anthony an apologetic smile. "Well, I can't be bothered with it now."

"Don't you see?"

"See what?"

"She's here to stay."

"Oh, damnation. Now, what is this?"

She lowered her eyes and folded her hands. Then with a thoughtful expression she turned back to Anthony. "Perhaps he will understand," she said, fixing him with her earnest gaze. "The servants tell me it is an omen."

In the days that followed Anthony made rapid preparations for the journey to Rome. Time was of the essence, for he had no idea how long Pope John might remain in Hugo's court at Pisa. No one could tell him of the setbacks and delays those two allies were suffering, and he had every reason to believe they might even now be on their way to Rome.

Duke Bardulf lent him every possible assistance. A call for men went out and hundreds of loyal followers answered. They moved into the fortress and citadel of Totila the Goth just beyond the north gate. At night their songs and laughter filled the air, drifting down to the city.

On the fifth day after his arrival Anthony was ready to march forth. Before he departed he bent his knee to Bardulf.

"You have honored my father's name," he began with barely suppressed emotion, "and you proved a true friend. My gratitude—"

Bardulf would not let him finish. "On your feet," he cried. "What are these, the antics of a Moroccan court?" He laughed as he offered Anthony his hand. "Lead my men honorably," he added, suddenly serious once again. "That is all I ask."

Chapter 47

An earthquake shook Rome. It was not large, hardly more than a tremor, but it brought down the transept of a Lateran chapel and reduced to rubble the diaconia of San Teodoro. In the convent of Saint Petronilla, near Saint Peter's, there was pandemonium. Nuns ran to and fro screaming and crying, and some rushed into the Piazza San Pietro to pray for God's mercy.

It was my duty as abbess to try to restore calm in the convent, but I soon realized that superstitious fear had spread far beyond the Leonine Walls. As the earth quivered underfoot and cracks appeared in the ancient buildings, people began to believe that Rome was being torn asunder. Indeed, ever since Guido and his troops appeared in Rome, her citizens had feared civil war.

Now it seemed there could be no question that bloodshed lay ahead. God had spoken.

For me, however, the earthquake contained a hidden blessing. I suddenly had so many things to do—seeing to the injured, repairing the damage to my convent, comforting the poor orphans and foundlings who had been terrified by the tremors—that I was distracted from the thoughts that had been uppermost in my mind.

Ever since the pilgrim brought news of Anthony, I had expected Gallimanfry to appear. I did not know how I could face him or what I would say. Since his departure there had been times of bitter loneliness, when I had prayed to God to tear the heart out of the man who had possessed me and ruined my virtue. But there had been other voices in me as well, voices that called out to him, longed for him and begged for his return. I could not drive him from my mind, nor could I look with anticipation toward our coming encounter. Nonetheless, I was certain from the moment the pilgrim brought the news that I should see him again. And with that certainty came undeniable joy.

It was four days after the earthquake that he appeared.

I was attending the poorhouse attached to the Convent of Saint Petronilla, where hundreds of homeless citizens had come seeking shelter. For days I had hardly eaten or slept as I went about my rounds.

A nun called me to the courtyard, then took her leave. For a long moment we gazed at each other, astonished by what the years had done. I do not know how he saw me. I know I was plumper than before, and my tightly drawn wimple could not disguise the wrinkles that had crept into my cheeks and brow. But these were matters of vanity.

As for him, I must confess that he looked much the same as I remembered, though his hair was greyer, his ragged beard untrimmed and his shoulders more hunched. Obviously traveling in disguise, he had taken but little care to groom himself. A torn cloak splattered with mud hung from his shoulders, and his clogs and leggings were so filthy I could scarcely see the laces.

"Just as I thought," he muttered, stepping closer, that familiar calculating gleam in his eye. "Ten years with the hogs has made me hoglike. My lady's heart no longer beats faster for me."

"With hogs?" I answered softly. "More like with

mutes, Gallimanfry. In all these years I have heard not a word."

He sighed. "I had a duty to perform."

"How fares Anthony?"

Gallimanfry grinned. "Better than I, for he has had someone to look out for him—which is to say, me—whilst I have had no one to look out for me except me, who am the poorest of the self-soul's lookouts."

I could not help smiling. "I have no doubt that with yourself to talk to you had ample company."

"Ample but not interesting. I began to find the old man tiresome, redundant, speculative in his thoughts and slow in his actions."

"But perhaps not so old after all?"

"Who can say?" He shrugged. After a moment's hesitation he said more gently, "I have missed you, Lena."

"And I have tried to forget you, Gallimanfry."

"And succeeded?"

"No, failed." I paused, wondering whether to tell him. His eyes were searching. "Besides—" I began. "Besides, there was always a reminder."

"Ah." He seemed to find it hard to speak. "Was it—" He could not finish.

"Come with me," I offered at last.

The foundling house at the Convent of St. Petronilla was adjacent to the poorhouse, but a locked door separated the one from the other so that the destitute would not mingle with the innocent. As abbess I carried the keys, and it was a simple matter to unlock the gate and effect an entrance into the schoolyard.

There was only one other in attendance there, Sister Coinreda, a young and serious woman with a good heart. She nodded as I came through the doorway. She knew I loved to come and watch the children at play.

I saw her looking askance at my companion. She shot me a questioning glance, as if to say, Why have you brought a man from the poorhouse here? I had to turn away so she would not see me blush.

"Do you see the little girl by the far wall?" I asked when we were out of Coinreda's hearing. "The one with the flower at her waist who plays at jackstraws."

Gallimanfry searched the crowded courtyard, his face serious. Then his eyes lit up as he spotted her. "Yes, I see her."

For a long while he watched her as if hypnotized, only his eyes moving as he followed her animated play. His gaze was still upon her as he asked, "What is her name?"

"Thessalina."

"Would . . . would you call her?"

I hesitated. "She was born outside Trastevere," I warned him. "No one here knows her parentage. I have told them she was found by the roadside during the last sickness."

"Of course," he replied, and with that I called to the child.

Thessalina looked up at the sound of her name. Smiling, she slipped her wooden ball and jackstraws through the placket of her plain little shift and ran toward us.

"Holy Mother?" She curtseyed swiftly.

I took her hand. "Thessalina, I would like you to meet someone." She looked curiously at the mud-spattered man who stood beside me. "This is Gallimanfry. He has come from very far away."

She stared up at him, her eyes full of wonder. "How do you do, signor?"

"Hello, Thessalina."

There was an awkward silence. Then she turned back to me. "May I go play now?"

"Yes, of course," I replied. "Run along." When she had left, I turned to Gallimanfry. He nodded.

As I opened the gate and we returned the way we had come, I felt the eyes of Coinreda upon us. She was not the type to exercise a wagging tongue, but I wondered what gossip she would have for her cronies that night.

It is the nature of some women, I believe, to assume that erotic love is their natural right. These women are often the most beautiful as well as the most grasping, for they demand nothing less than that a man worship, follow and adore them. Such women when left alone or cast aside soon find another man to feed their appetites, to love and praise them and flatter their beauty. Inevitably the man who has left or scorned them is considered a traitor; he is hated and maligned because he has withdrawn his adulation.

Perhaps it is because I am plain that I did not find it in my soul to hate Gallimanfry in this way, or perhaps it is because I am a nun, to whom erotic love itself is no right, that I cannot hate the man who once left me for a time. Whatever the reason, I could not find it in Gallimanfry, nor could I shun him, least of all when I saw what tenderness he bore for our daughter Thessalina.

At the edge of the Borgo there was a small heated chamber, a *caminata*, with shops in front and a cottage in back. Here by my privilege of rank I could stay many nights when the weather was cold. It was just off the Via del Borgo Nuovo, where a single aqueduct brought water to the houses of Santo Spirito and public baths were provided for all to use.

Considering the condition of Gallimanfry's body, the convenience of the baths was fortunate. The sand glass on my sill had turned over twice and almost run dry again when he finally returned to my chamber.

His face was red as a rooster's plumage, the hair of

his beard fluffed out like a prophet's locks. He walked with a stagger, as if the steam had sapped him dry. He was chagrined at my laughter and I had to cradle him in my arms like a little boy to appease him, but the stillness that came over him portended a manly passion I recalled very well, and a love I had long awaited.

I do not know whether Gallimanfry had deprived his flesh these many years, but the question was of little import, for he did not hesitate or flag in his attentions. That night the little caminata, lit by firelight, was a joyful place indeed.

"And what of Anthony?" I asked at dawn, when Gallimanfry was preparing to leave.

"He will soon be on his way from Spoleto."

I sat up against the bedstead. "Gallimanfry, I beg you, be careful. Marozia has a thirst for vengeance that exceeds all reason."

"I know." He was fastening his leggings with clean laces. He rose and said, "These will be hard times for Rome, but when they are over, Lena, I pray that you and I and Thessalina may find our way together."

Then I knew what other women must feel. I did not want him to go. I wanted him to stay with me forever. There was no charity or understanding in me, but only the deep selfishness that sweet love engenders.

"If God is willing," I said as I turned away, hiding my tears.

He must have understood, for he left the caminata without any further word.

Chapter 48

Tasha was the first to see the young man. Marozia had ordered sandals from a tanner in the scorticlaria. A servant had been sent to fetch them and Tasha was keeping an eye out for him.

Instead of the footman's familiar face she saw the weathered, finely cut features of a tall, bearded Lombard. He wore a grey quilted gambeson covered with a soldier's mail. There was a helmet under his arm.

At first he didn't see her, for his gaze was attracted by the pilum that stood by the front door. Seeming bemused, he touched it. Something in that gesture, that curiosity, was terribly familiar. Then it came back to her—the image of a little boy who had touched the weapon in just the same manner, always wanting to play with it.

She let out a short cry. Anthony turned, smiled, and his nursemaid rushed into his arms. She didn't know what to say to him. His quick embrace was crushing. He had only been a boy when she saw him last, and now he was a man.

She pulled away, ashamed of her spontaneous rush of emotion. "I must tell your mother," she stammered. "At once."

"Tasha?" There was a puzzled look on his face. "Aren't you glad to see me?"

"Oh, signor," she breathed, eyes alight, "this is joy—joy." She rushed off before she could say any more.

*   *   *

It was early morning and Marozia still at her bath. She sat at her ease in the clouds of vapor rising from the heated stones. Sunlight streamed through the high south windows and lit the frescoes near the ceiling. She was musing on the glowing figures when she heard Tasha's cry.

"Mistress, mistress, he is here!"

Springing to her feet, Marozia signaled to a bath attendant for a cotton gown. She lifted her arms as the woman slipped the garment over her head and fastened it at the waist. It all seemed to take an extraordinary amount of time. As she fidgeted her eyes lifted to that sunny band of light near the ceiling and she thought, So this is what happiness is like. She had almost forgotten.

"Signora, come quickly." Tasha burst through the door.

"Yes, yes, I heard." Marozia clasped Tasha's arm as she left the room. "How does he look?"

"Oh, very—" Tasha's eyes shone as she searched for the right word. "Very manly, signora."

"Manly?" Marozia laughed. "Well, he would be, wouldn't he?"

"I mean to say—but signora, your hair." It was dripping wet, streaming down Marozia's shoulders.

"Never mind." She pulled Tasha away to the audience room.

At the door Tasha hesitated, releasing her arm. Her mistress stepped forward a pace, then two. At the same time Anthony fell to one knee and bowed his head.

Marozia flew to him and touched his shoulder. "Rise," she cried, "rise at once."

When he was standing again, she seized his hauberk in both hands and shook him. "See? See? You *are* real, and so like your father." He smiled down at her and she wagged her finger at him.

"Don't judge me, Anthony. I've only just come from my bath. It must be a very important visitor to drag me away looking like this." She touched her hair. "Tasha, summon Elgina. I will dry my hair in the solarium with a young man by my side."

All this time Anthony had done nothing but regard her with a kind of wonder. It prompted Marozia to ask impatiently, "Well, what do you see?"

He struggled for a moment, then said simply, "My mother."

And so it was. Though time and distance and circumstance had separated them, he still could not see her plainly except as a part of himself. Her face, her gestures, her expressions—all were so deeply ingrained in his memory that it seemed as if nothing had changed. If anyone had asked him to describe her now, he could not have done so. She was just as she had always been.

Though it was not yet Lent, the air was warm and springlike. All day those two never stirred from the solarium, though Marozia's chancellor was kept busy all day long explaining to callers that the senatrix was not seeing anyone. She sent to summon Guido from the Castel Sant'Angelo, but his spies had seen Anthony's troops camped near the Bassilla on the Via Flaminia, and the duke was already on his way.

"So this is the long-lost son." His cool appraisal as he entered the solarium brought a tiny light to Anthony's eyes, but Marozia would not let his aloof manner mar her happiness. "*Our* son," she insisted. "You must treat him as yours too."

Nonetheless, it was apparent to all of us at the feast table that night that the duke did not quite trust this new member of his family. His toasts were halfhearted and without imagination, and when Anthony raised his own cup to speak, the Sienese lowered his eyes and listened with a trace of a smirk.

Guido needed allies; even he could see that clearly. The return of Pope John and Duke Hugo was imminent. Rumors were already spreading that the pope and his new general had left Pisa. They were said to be within three days' journey of Rome—and with them were more than a thousand armed men.

With this threat looming before him, Guido agreed that Anthony's Spoletans should be admitted to the Castel Sant'Angelo—provided, of course, they kept separate barracks. However, he would not commit himself to action outside the city walls. He refused to mount raids on the Via Aurelia to harass Hugo's men as they approached, insisting instead that he and Anthony wait and consider. Clearly he hoped that a simple show of force would eat away the last remnants of the pope's declining power, making a clash of arms unnecessary. Anthony knew this was impossible, but his arguments made no impression on the older man.

Despite these differences the feast was a great success. Gallimanfry came at dusk, just as the tapers were being lit, and he roamed the halls and chambers of the old palace before finally settling down to the table. He strutted like a proud sire who had just rested up from some legendary act of begetting, and from the way his eyes shone when he looked at Anthony you would have thought Creation itself was his doing.

When Sergius arrived, he flung his arms around his brother, and it would have required a sharp eye indeed to detect any falseness in his greeting.

There was music and mountains of food. All the noble families of the Via Lata came crowding into the banquet hall, and I was pleased to see that those who had once reviled Alberic now strained to catch a glimpse of his handsome son. Yet as she watched them I could see in Marozia's eye a vengeful, haunted look that came and went like a flickering fire. I knew how she despised them, all those who had turned against her Lombard husband. I was certain she would find a way to use that hatred against the man who had been responsible for Alberic's death.

"What of Grandmother?" Anthony asked me that evening. I knew Marozia had been reluctant to speak of Theodora, and I sighed, not relishing the prospect myself. But the other guests were lost in their festive drunkenness, and Anthony had pinned me with his demanding eyes.

"She remains in the House of Theophylact," I said sadly, "burning with jealousy, envy—I know not what."

"Then the pope shuns her?"

"He has no more use for her. He likes them young these days. She was merely the steppingstone to his power. Once she had served her purpose, she was cast aside."

"And you, Lena? Does she—"

"She refuses to see me," I interjected before he could go on.

When I looked away, he said, "I am sorry if my questions have hurt you. I know so very little of what has happened here."

"No, no, Anthony." I took his hand, ashamed of myself. "You must ask. It's only that I do not know how some of these things have happened. We must learn to endure despite them. And yet these bitter circumstances seem wrong." I paused. "Theodora was never the same after your father and grandfather died. She was blamed, you see. Some say she could have interceded with the pope. Your mother will never forgive her for not trying.''

"And you, Lena, what do you believe?''

Anthony's face was flushed with emotion. I could see that these evil memories had dealt their own blow to this young, ambitious man.

"Do you want the truth?'' I asked; and his eyes shouted for the truth.

"I believe that Theodora was crushed by that man, just as we have all been crushed.'' I crossed myself, knowing that my words contained greater heresy than that for which Alberic had been punished. "I did not witness the execution of my father, but I have heard from nuns in the Lateran that my mother was present.''

"Then that proves it. She wanted to see him die.'' Though Anthony's voice was low, several guests turned at his outburst.

"It proves nothing of the kind,'' I snapped. I lowered my head. "Anthony, her hands were bound. There were knives at her back, held by the cardinals, who were forced to do John's bidding. They say the pope smiled as he watched the execution, but it was not my father who amused him. It was my mother's suffering.''

"You know this to be true?'' he choked.

"It cannot be doubted.''

"Then surely there is no one in heaven or earth so despicable as he.''

I did not reply; I could not.

After a moment's pause Anthony touched me on the shoulder. "Lena, dear aunt, do not fear. Our family will be avenged. I swear it.''

His words were no comfort to me. Indeed, they summoned up all my long-buried fears. "Hush, Anthony. You have been away from Rome too long.'' I looked about the room. "You don't know which of these men are

Pope John's. They will stay loyal as long as he is strongest. There are many here tonight to welcome you who will go straight back and report to him.'' I could not keep my eyes from Sergius, who was chattering nervously with one of the aged senators. He kept glancing at Anthony and me as if we—or they—were plotting some wicked deed.

Anthony followed my glance but said nothing. Soon thereafter he was drawn back among the guests, and he and I spoke no more secrets that night.

Chapter 49

One person absent from the celebration that night was my grandfather Eusebius. In the morning I accompanied Anthony and Marozia to the scriptorium to see him.

Everything was just as before, the scribes bent over their tablets, the manuscripts stacked in the corners. Even the air seemed unchanged, with its smell of dry parchment and faint odor of incense.

Only the master was missing. No longer able to make his way to the scriptorium every day, Eusebius lay in his bedchamber, a silk damask robe pulled high about his chin. His face was wasted now, the plump cheeks withered away to nothing, but his eyes still gleamed as he slowly dictated to the scribe Gregory, who sat by his bedside. Old Tiberon lingered at the doorway as we entered. He had devoted himself to Grandfather ever since we lost Gaius.

Slowly, deliberately Eusebius continued his dictation, struggling on when each breath was painful to him and his words could scarcely be heard. Gregory, a slim, handsome young priest with a tangle of thin brown hair around his tonsure, bent forward to catch the master's words. Then he leaned back with a nod of satisfaction, his stylus scratching the parchment on his knee.

Eusebius hated to be interrupted at his work, and he gave a mutter of disapproval as we came in. Ignoring Anthony, he glared at Marozia as if to say, How dare you?

"Look, Grandfather," I put in before he could object, "see who has come."

At my insistence he squinted at the tall young man who stood smiling by his bedside. Then he looked away, puzzled, glaring at us as if to discover whether this was some plot we had devised to fool him.

He licked his dry lips. "Anthony?"

Anthony's smile broadened. "Yes, Great-grandfather, it is I."

"Come here."

The old man's gaunt hand reached out and touched Anthony's bearded features. Then he looked up at Marozia.

"So this is where the Roman and Lombard are mingled." He smiled, showing the hollow gaps in his line of darkened teeth. "Who has been keeping you, my boy?"

"Gallimanfry."

Again the smile. "That rogue? Then you've learned more foul language and clean thoughts than a sailor turned saint."

Anthony laughed. "Perhaps I have, but I am glad to return to Rome."

"Rome. Stinking pit." Eusebius' voice drifted off and he looked away. Gregory still waited, his stylus poised. "You may go," the old man croaked, "but mind you, be back before midday."

"We won't stay long, Grandfather," I said. "We don't want to tire you."

His laughter was dry. "My *Histories* would not be complete without an interview with Alberic's son." He lowered his voice. "You are destined for great things, Anthony. One day you will rule Rome."

The young man stiffened. "Please, *bisavolo*, you shouldn't joke of such things."

"It's not a joke, young man. Dying men have certain privileges. Vision is one of them." He stirred in his bed and winced as if the movement gave him pain. "Now then, you must tell me where you have been and everything you have done."

And so once again Anthony recounted the tale of his life with Gallimanfry, including his travels and his many adventures. Before he finished, Tiberon entered without warning, skittered to the bedside and murmured something in the old man's ear. "Show her in, show her in," ordered Eusebius.

Tiberon hesitated. "But Master, are you sure?"

Eusebius waved him away. "I do not have much time, Tiberon. If they are to meet in my presence, you must."

Tiberon bowed and retreated. A moment later he reappeared at the door and stepped aside. I finally saw the woman who accompanied him. It was my mother, Theodora.

A palpable tremor shot through Marozia's frame. She drew back. "Why did you allow this?" she protested.

"I wish to see a reconciliation between you," Eusebius said quite clearly.

"Never," Marozia cried.

For a long moment the two women examined each other like hated enemies who have finally met on the field of battle.

I could see that Anthony was shocked by the change that had come over his grandmother. Well, it shocked me. I didn't see much of her, so I wasn't used to it myself, but to him she must have been a strange sight indeed.

Her hair had gone completely white, and the snagged old caul that bound the loose strands was badly fitted and tilted awry. Her magnificent features had turned sharp and hard, and her darting black eyes were full of venom. Still, it was her manner of dress that was strangest of all, for as her power waned she had begun to affect the trappings of various officials of the empire, as if she could conquer them all by mingling their sashes, banners, robes and badges. This time it was a scarlet cassock, a purple-bordered toga, a rather fine gilt laurel wreath and chains and brooches bearing nearly every coat of arms ever seen in Rome.

"I came to see see only you, Father," she said haughtily.

He shook his head. "You cannot see me without my family—*our* family—Theodora."

Ignoring all of us, she rounded the bed and bent to kiss her father's dry hand. He allowed her to do so but then seized her wrist. Her eyes widened with alarm and she looked down at the clenched fingers as if a bird of prey had grasped her in its steely claws.

"What do you want of me?" she demanded.

"I wish to see you reconciled with your daughter."

She did not reply. For a long moment they made a tableau, the old man with his insistent grasp and the once-beautiful woman in her clanking motley grandeur. Finally Eusebius released her, letting his hand fall to the coverlet. The strength he had shown since Anthony entered the room now seemed to leave him.

"Good-bye, Father," said Theodora, rising.

"Good-bye, my daughter," he muttered, not looking at her.

Without a further word, giving no sign that she acknowledged our presence, Theodora turned from the bedside and departed.

That same day Anthony rode out to the Bassilla and gathered his troops. They marched in formation down the Via Flaminia through the north gate to the Via Lata. All along the way, at San Lorenzo in Lucina, San Silvestro in Capite and San Andrea de Columna, the people turned to gape and stare.

It was a silent welcome, and Anthony could sense the wave of unease that swept through the crowd as the soldiers passed. He knew very well what they were asking one another. Were these enemies of Guido or of the pope? Who was the tall, bearded man on a sable mare who led them unchallenged through the streets?

Anthony was wearing his green tabard this day, and the pennant on his carroccio carried the lion rampant and the bear cub, a banner that had not been seen for many years. Recognition held the crowd spellbound. This was Anthony son of Alberic, a man risen from the dead.

Turning west on the Via Recta, his troops marched in close formation through the scorticlaria to the church of Santi Celso e Giuliano. As they wheeled and turned north Anthony could see ahead through the open gate in the Aurelian walls. There, across the Ponte San Angelo, was the great Castel Sant'Angelo, looming at the entrance to Saint Peter's City.

He did not slow the pace of his charger, but his hand trembled on the reins. It seemed only yesterday that he had arrived in Pisa, a footloose sailor returned from his travels. Now he was a general, challenging the very gates of Rome.

This was his right, his destiny. As surely as his father's memory burned brightly before him, he had known this day would come. He wanted to spur his mount, to shout aloud his excitement.

Instead he tightened his hold on the reins. Head high, he led his troops across the bridge and in through the open bronze gates of the fortress.

Castel Sant'Angelo with its star-shaped breastworks dominated the banks of the Tiber on St. Peter's side of the river. Within the massive outer walls, on the open grounds surrounding the mausoleum, Guido's men had made their encampment. Anthony's troops would establish themselves to the west, still within the fortress walls but separate from the Sienese. Like the duke, Anthony would stay in one of the frescoed rooms that overlooked the city.

In the afternoon Anthony and Guido reviewed their forces. They dined together that night with officers of the Spoletan and Sienese armies. Although the two men seemed to be in harmony, Anthony sensed an undercurrent of distrust, which disturbed him greatly. Thus he was glad when the officers' mess finished early and he was able to retire.

Entering the western part of the courtyard, he found a welcome in the glow of braziers and the soldiers' voices. It was reassuring, reminding him of nights on shipboard when sailors' songs and long-winded tales provided an accompaniment to the wind in the rigging and the creaking of the hull.

After checking the provisions and making his round of the guards Anthony stopped by some of the tents to listen to the men's gossip and share a few words. Their voices dropped in respect when they recognized him and he noted that their conversation seemed less natural.

He knew the feeling. He too had lowered his voice and carefully considered his words whenever a galley captain approached. He knew that in time some of the soldiers would hate him, would stare at his back with venom in their eyes, and some would love and respect him.

Oddly, this reminder of who he was and what he had become was the greatest evidence that his course was irrevocable. Whatever happened, he could not be the young, innocent voyager he had been.

Anthony returned to the fortress and mounted the stairs that led to the upper apartments. As he entered the stuccoed splendor of the Sala Paolina, the guard signaled and whispered a name to him. Anthony smiled and quickened his steps.

In this room was a magnificent triptych of the Madonna and the saints, though partially blocked by a statue of Perseus holding the head of Medusa. As Anthony advanced he caught Gallimanfry gazing spellbound at one of Medusa's serpents.

"Dreadful, is it not?" the tutor commented, glancing up as his pupil drew near. "These snakes of hers—" he laid a hand familiarly on the marble—"we must assume she could see through their eyes, think their thoughts, feel their hunger. Is it any wonder her temper was bad?"

"Secretly you love her," Anthony retorted, smiling.

Gallimanfry shrugged. "She intrigues me, yes, but there are other women with fewer snakes and more substance who intrigue me more."

"My mother?" asked Anthony, puzzled.

"Perhaps so." Gallimanfry gestured toward the corridor. "It is stuffy in here." He was looking at the guards at both doorways.

"Very well." Anthony acceded to the unspoken suggestion. They proceeded through the hall and the Garland Room to the Treasury, then mounted a staircase that led to the top of the fortress.

From the terrace above, where the chapel was surmounted by a travertine angel, they could see all of Rome from the glistening Tiber to the heights of the Lateran. There was a full moon, and the buildings and trees seemed covered with a dusting of hoarfrost.

"So now you are a conqueror," remarked Gallimanfry, leaning against the parapet.

"Not yet." Anthony's voice came out of the shadows. "I shall continue to need your help."

"Help." Gallimanfry puffed out his cheeks. "Yes, I can still offer that easily enough. Just don't ask me to lift a sword. I have never enjoyed shaking hands with steel, and as the years grow longer, my grip seems to grow colder."

Anthony laughed. "Never fear. I have all the men I need, thanks to Bardulf."

Gallimanfry nodded. "Your father won men's loyalty and kept it firmly. He would be glad to see his son reaping the benefits."

"Bardulf's soldiers are exceptional," Anthony added. "I have never seen men so well trained, so willing to serve."

"All the better," Gallimanfry said darkly. "You will need them."

Anthony glanced at his tutor, whose face was now hidden. For the first time he felt unsure. "Is it such folly, to go against the pope?"

"Does it matter?" Gallimanfry spoke bitterly. "Think what he has done. Think how your mother longs to repay him."

Anthony did not hear the warning, or if he did he chose not to acknowledge it. "I wonder," he mused, "whether the Synod will rush to John's defense. Surely there must be loyal bishops, cardinals—"

"Listen, Anthony," Gallimanfry cut in, "the cardinals may be deceived by the pope's wealth and generosity, but the duchies have felt the weight of his hand. He has ruled Lombardy, Tuscany and the Papal States just as he ruled Ravenna, ruthlessly and with bloodshed. Not a single duke in this land will come to his defense. Whatever happens in Rome will affect only the Romans. I promise you, the duchies will not intervene."

"What if Siena is pitted against Pisa?"

Gallimanfry shook his head. "That too will be determined here. The battle between the brothers *is* the battle between your mother and the pope. Without the passion of their leaders those two are nothing."

"You think so little of Guido?" Anthony had suspected it, and yet to hear Gallimanfry call his stepfather a weakling was a shock.

"Why do you think he has not yet moved against the Lateran?" Gallimanfry asked. "All of your mother's exhortations have not succeeded in overcoming his fears."

Anthony nodded. "The man is jealous and wary. I can see how it galls him to have me here in the castle. He won't get rid of me, though. He knows he is not strong enough to take the Lateran by himself."

Gallimanfry sighed. "It will be your mother's choice what to do with him when this is all over. At the moment, I fear, her soul is consumed with a single passion—vengeance on the pope."

Again the young man refused the bait. "My thirst is the same."

"You have not nurtured it so diligently." Gallimanfry stared out across the city. "I fear the harm Marozia may do to herself—and others."

"Surely you don't mean me?" There was real pain in Anthony's voice.

"Not by intention"—Gallimanfry chose his words carefully—"but watch her, Anthony, I beg you. There may be devils in her that she cannot constrain. When one has hated for so long, it is not easy to put aside evil. One cannot regain one's innocence."

Tense silence hung on the night air. Then as if to ease the harshness Gallimanfry spoke again. "There is something I must tell you, Anthony."

The young man was startled by the sudden gentleness in Gallimanfry's tone. "What, then?" he demanded.

"You cannot guess?" The tutor seemed cautious, almost tentative.

"No, I can't guess."

Gallimanfry's eyes met his. "It's not the kind of

thing a doddering old fool usually tells his pupil," he began, "but of late I begin to crave a more settled life. You see, today I went to visit my daughter in the found-ling home of Saint Petronilla."

"Your daughter?"

"Yes, you fool, my daughter."

"And the mother?"

"The abbess."

"Aunt Lena? Aunt Lena, really? Gallimanfry!" Delighted laughter rose to the angel above them.

A messenger was waiting in the Garland Room when they returned to the tower. He fell to one knee as Anthony and Gallimanfry entered.

"What is it?" demanded the young general. "Has the pope arrived at the Lateran?"

"No, signor." The messenger lifted his head and Anthony saw that it was Gregory, the slim priest who had sat by Eusebius' bedside. There were tears in his eyes.

"My great-grandfather?"

"Yes, signor. He passed away not an hour ago."

Chapter 50

The funeral for Eusebius was held in Saint Peter's. He was laid to rest in a family crypt beneath the sanctuary. All the noble families of Rome attended, and Cardinal Sergius read the oration.

Gregory had transcribed mountains of dictation during my grandfather's final days. After the funeral work resumed in the scriptorium, where the slow, painstaking copying of the *Modern Histories* continued without cease. My grandfather had little in the way of material offerings, but the gift of his words was legacy enough in itself.

Several days later on a bright, sunlit morning after a night of rain Pope John and Duke Hugo entered the city. Avoiding the Via Triumphalis, which would have brought them before the doors of the Castel Sant'Angelo, they chose to enter through the gates of Trastevere. The pope's blessing was offered at Santa Maria in Trastevere and the troops passed over the Ponte Santa Maria into the abitato.

Chain mail glistened in the sunlight, and steel helmets bobbed like pebbles in a stream as the massed troops surged through the streets. At each church and diaconia in the abitato deacons, abbots and bishops bent their knees to receive the papal blessing.

Pope John wore a scarlet robe worked with Byzantine gold and trimmed with ermine. His magnificent golden tiara was surmounted by a tall cross and studded with precious sapphires and rubies. In his left hand the pope carried the golden orb of office, which also bore a cross.

Duke Hugo rode at the pontiff's side, mounted on a white charger draped with hangings of soft dyed leather. His knees and thighs were capped in Frankish armor fastened with thongs and buckles. His plain iron crown was worked with images of lions, boars and serpents.

In the Piazza del Senatore they were acclaimed by the senators, who made themselves conspicuous on the steps of San Adriano. The senators surged forward to kiss the pope's ring.

Seated on his charger, Hugo watched this display of respect. His eyes raked the crowd, searching for a female face among the senators, but there was none to be found. Both Marozia and Theodora were absent. This was also noted by the pope, who seemed disgruntled.

As the papal forces progressed through the city, Hugo began to detect in the faces of the people the uneasiness, fear and suspicion that lay just beneath the surface. Today the citizens of Rome would welcome the pope; they would even accept the man who rode at his side. However, they would not forget the troops posted in the Castel Sant'Angelo.

Pope John avoided the Via Lata and made no attempt to approach San Silvestro in Capite, for to do so would have meant passing in front of the House of Hadrian. Likewise, a blessing at Saint Peter's was out of the question; to approach the Leonine City he would have been forced to challenge the gates of Sant'Angelo.

This was the deepest humiliation, that Saint Peter's, the most sacred shrine in Christendom, was denied to the pope himself. Without a word to Duke Hugo John spurred his gelding along the Via Tusculana toward the welcoming gates of the Lateran.

*   *   *

The imminence of war hung over Rome like a pall. In the fields to the north of the Borgo and along the Via Triumphalis Anthony and Guido led their troops in exercises and forays. Curious citizens continued to observe them from the city walls, but they turned away and hid their faces whenever the papal guards drew near.

There were ugly scenes in the streets of the city. Hugo's guards set upon and murdered a band of Sienese visiting a brothel in the scorticlaria. Their bloody corpses hung from the windows as a warning.

Two nights later a papal messenger was kidnapped, doused in naphtha and set afire in front of Santa Maria Nova. His dying screams could be heard in the deepest recesses of the Lateran.

At first the Magyars were blamed for this atrocity, but later a coin with Bardulf's insignia was discovered in the street next to the messenger's charred body. In a rage Pope John exhorted the Senate to ban all Spoletans from Rome and the Leonine City. The senators debated for hours, then issued a proclamation, which was duly ignored by Guido and Anthony.

Whenever Marozia ordered her palanquin she was accompanied by a guard of thirty men. Duke Guido himself never went anywhere without an escort. Anthony, fearful of tempting his adversaries, confined his movements to the Castel Sant'Angelo, the Leonine City and the Via Triumphalis.

As for Theodora, she was without fear and without shame. One afternoon she left the House of Theophylact wearing alb, chasuble, wedding crown and the arms of Ravenna. Her hair was heavily daubed with ocher and she had darkened her eyes with kohl in the Muslim manner. In a large palanquin with tattered curtains she rode triumphantly toward the Lateran, followed by a wagon that bore a hundredweight of gold reliquaries and silver chalices. The citizens whispered as she passed and barely hid their laughter behind their hands, but she gazed at them with haughty disdain.

It was her last great assault on the man she loved, but her passionate gesture was in vain.

The guard at the gates of the Lateran challenged her and refused her entry. The pope had sent orders that she was not to be admitted. However, Theodora refused to go away.

After hours of waiting the exhausted slaves lowered her palanquin to the pavement. Night fell and a steady rain commenced. Still she refused to leave.

In the darkness marauders approached her treasure wagon. Like rats filching grain from a cellar they seized the precious objects and scurried away into the night.

When the bells sounded for lauds, a high wailing issued from the palanquin. It continued intermittently until dawn. Then finally, as the sun broke over Santa Croce in Gerusalemme, a single word issued from the carriage: "Home." The drowsy servants stumbled to their feet, lifted the litter poles to their aching shoulders and marched with weary steps back toward the Aventine.

On the night of Theodora's lonely vigil there was only a sliver of moon. Three days after this event Cardinal Sergius was summoned to the House of Hadrian.

These had been difficult times for Sergius. Living in the Lateran, attending the pope's daily councils, privy to all the business of the Synod, he was held in suspicion by those very men who had once appeared to trust him. No one could ignore his family ties to Marozia, who even now was inciting civil war.

Though he went out of his way to demonstrate his loyalty to Pope John and Cardinal Peter, Sergius was acutely aware of the discomfort his presence caused. For this reason if for no other he had grown shrill in his denunciations of Marozia, Anthony and Duke Guido. His speeches were loudly applauded in the Synod, but after he left the room, the cardinals and bishops cast each other sidelong glances as if to say, He protests too much.

To be summoned by Marozia at such a time was more than an embarrassment; it was a disaster. The man who brought her message was hustled into a private chamber, where Sergius berated him roundly. Then he was impelled to depart through the stable door.

After he left, Sergius fretted. What was he to do? If he defied his mother he would bring down her wrath, and yet if he obeyed— He recalled the denunciation and excommunication of a fellow cardinal, Pietro of the Viminal, and shuddered at the thought of such a public disgrace.

In the end Sergius chose to hedge his bets. The young cardinal departed by the same exit as the messenger, through the stable. In place of scarlet robes he wore a peasant's cloak, the hood low over his face.

At the House of Hadrian even Tasha did not recognize him at first, and when she finally saw who it was, she laughed out loud, so wounded pride was added to Sergius' bad temper. He entered Marozia's presence in a foul mood.

"Why, Mother, why have you put me in this position?" He had pushed back his hood and his face was flushed. "You must know I am in great danger. At a time like this! How could you?"

Glancing at his disguise, Marozia dismissed the servants. "You should not have to treat yourself this way," she remarked.

Sergius threw up his hands. "Oh, no? What am I to do? Already I'm suspect. I sleep with a dagger beneath my pillow. They are all wary of me, even Peter."

"Their suspicions will soon come to an end," she said calmly.

"All very well for you to say," he snorted, "but when? How much longer must I go on like this?"

Marozia gave her son a measuring glance, then laid a hand on his shoulder. Her gesture had a calming effect, but as her silence grew protracted, Sergius again seemed ready to burst out in protest.

"I am sorry for what you've had to endure," she said at last, dropping her hand and withdrawing a few paces. "There was a reason for it, you know."

Sergius sniffed. "I hope it was a good one. My patience is at an end."

"Mine too," replied his mother in an undertone. She touched the brooch at her throat. "For over ten years I have endured that man." Her eyes glittered.

"Mother," Sergius said desperately, "this vendetta, this personal war, it is folly. The pope can call on all the legions of the campagna to combat you."

"Can he?" Marozia demanded coldly. "Why does he not, then? Surely this would be the time to do so." She eyed her son with sharp disdain. He shifted nervously but did not reply. "No, Sergius," she went on, "he has summoned all the bishops of the Patrimony of Saint Peter—from the Romagna, Verona, Aquileia and Capula—from all the marches. They have answered in their own way. Oh, yes, they sent their tithes and offerings, and they swore to dispatch their loyal battalions. Tell me, where are those battalions, Sergius? Where are the loyal troops of Christendom that move at John's command?"

Sergius had gone pale. "I tell you, Mother, they will come. I saw the bishops pledge—"

"Pledges mean nothing when fear is the only law," Marozia cut in sharply. She stepped closer. "Listen, my son. You have been deceived. Because you are dear to the

Pope's brother, because you rarely stir from the Lateran, you believe the whole kingdom is a banquet hall. The Papal States are torn by strife, and that deceiver, Pope John, is at the heart of all our woes. He rules by bribery, deceit and intimidation. He cannot summon the battalions from the campagna because they will not follow him. Duke Hugo is his only ally—a fool, dissolute, bribed by the promise of kingship.''

Sergius began to speak, but Marozia raised her hand to silence him.

"I know what Peter tells you," she said bitterly, "and perhaps you have come to believe that John is just and merciful. I knew him when he was Bishop of Ravenna, when he taxed the people and drove them from their land, leaving them in ditches to die like animals. His ways have changed, perhaps, but the man has not. Only now it is all of Italy that sickens under his reign.''

Sergius shook his head. "You speak from bitterness, Mother.''

"Should I not?'' She looked at him with burning eyes. "Have you forgotten that he murdered your grandfather, your stepfather?''

"They were not murders,'' exclaimed Sergius. "Those men were tried in the Synod. Even the Senate voiced its approval. Gaius and Alberic were proven traitors.''

"*Proven!*'' Marozia's voice rose almost to a shriek. "Proved by a man like Petronius, vile, a ferret, a jilted suitor. No, Sergius, I can see I have been mistaken about you. I thought you could learn the ways of the Lateran, that the strength of your natural father would bear you above the waves of this bigotry and favoritism, but I see you have fallen prey to the spell of this evil man and his brother.''

"Do not mock me, Mother,'' Sergius said hoarsely. "I have managed to make my own way and I have accomplishments I can be proud of. Do not forget that you speak to the youngest cardinal of the council.''

She laughed. ''Yes, it is true you have risen quickly, son—but now you can rise no higher.''

Sergius lowered his eyes.

''Yes, I know how you desire to be pope.'' Marozia spoke gently, enticingly. ''There are even times when I see your father's ghost in you. How can you be pope when this man and his brother hold the reins of power?''

Her question met only silence.

''Sergius,'' she whispered, ''the time has come. Look at me.''

Reluctantly he raised his eyes.

''Tonight,'' she said urgently, ''while there is no moon, Duke Hugo and your brother Anthony will storm the Lateran. Do you understand? Tonight, this very night, Pope John will be in my power.''

''Mother,'' he gasped, ''you are mad.''

She smiled. ''No, Sergius. I have planned too well to be mad.''

''But—but this is folly. With Hugo in the Lateran, and the College of Cardinals as well. What do you think they will say if you take such a step?''

Her eyes blazed. ''Why should I care what they say? I despise them as I despise the man who rules them. As for Hugo, he is a coward. If you think loyalty motivates him, you are sadly mistaken. He has come only to plunder the papal treasury, I assure you.''

Sergius gave his mother a sidelong glance. His lip curled in a sneer. ''If you are successful in this mad endeavor, I am sure that Anthony will be crowned in glory.''

''That may be so.'' Marozia's voice had regained its even tone. ''Both he and Guido have much to gain from our success tonight. Still, it is you, Sergius, who will gain the most of all.''

She did not need to explain. At her words his hands trembled and writhed. He took a few limping steps and almost stumbled. But he was suspicious. "How can I be sure?''

"You have my word," Marozia replied softly. "I have never wanted anything else for you.''

The nervous clenching continued. "What must I do?''

At this she returned to his side. "I fear Pope John less than I do his brother. Peter is a snake in the grass. See that he does not live the night.''

A sharp intake of breath met her words. "What else?''

"The Lateran gates are strong. We shall have the greater advantage if we enter by stealth. The Portal of Saint Jerome in the south wall—can you see that it is opened between matins and lauds?''

"There are four guards at the gate.''

Marozia's eyes never left the clenching hands, the limping step. "Very well," he said at last, "I will see that it is done.''

There were dense beads of sweat on Sergius' forehead, but Marozia seemed to relax.

"Only one night," she urged, "and then the kingdom will lie at your feet. You will be pope, my son.''

He nodded vacantly, like a man in a daze. "I—I had better go now. Peter must suspect nothing.''

As he turned, his mother caught at his sleeve.

"Wait," she said. There was a stiletto in her hand. "Take it. You will not have time to prepare a weapon and the blade is keen.''

Like a guilty man accepting a bribe, Sergius received the knife and slipped it through the fitchet in his cloak. Once again he turned to go, then hesitated.

"What is it, Sergius?''

"I have often wondered," he said softly, "whether you loved my father."

"I hated him," she replied without hesitation.

Sergius winced as if she had slapped him, but Marozia did not seem to notice. Her eyes had a faraway look. "He gave me only two things of value, both against his will. The first was you, my son." She paused but did not look at him.

"And the second?"

"The weapons that a woman must possess to rule."

"In Santa Maria in Cosmedin," Sergius said slowly, "there is a stonework mask on the wall of the chapel. You know of it? They say that this is the Mouth of Truth. Pilgrims hear it speak. Yesterday I went there to pray."

"And what did the Mouth say to you, Sergius?"

The young cardinal made a gesture as if to speak, but his brow was furrowed in pain. Without answering he turned and limped away.

Chapter 51

It was the first day of Lent and the pope said mass in the afternoon in the basilica of Saint John's Lateran. As the abbess of Saint Petronilla's I was obliged to attend, but I wished to be as inconspicuous as possible.

I had never made any attempt to sever my ties to my family. Throughout the years I had freely visited Eusebius at the scriptorium, Marozia in the House of Hadrian and our poor mother—when she would have me—on the Aventine. I had even gone to the Lateran chambers of Sergius and admired his collection of jeweled crosses.

Despite my freedom of movement and the office of grace that God in His mercy had granted me, I felt the weight of animosity that lay between the church's highest leader and those who were my kin. My most dreadful nightmare was that I would have to take sides, choose between family loyalty and my devotion to God's work.

That night in the basilica when I spoke my private penance I could not feel any remorse for my long affair with Gallimanfry nor for the beautiful child born to us out of wedlock nor even for my continual flouting of the vows of the convent. No, these sins seemed petty. There was no true regret in me for the sweet pleasures I had tasted or for the dear girl who would run to me in the courtyard of the orphanage.

What weighed on me was the privilege I had taken upon myself, the privilege of hiding from the world and sheltering myself from its troubles. Once I envied my sister, but now I could see what a terrible burden she bore. The ghastly world of torment, heartbreak and violence had forced her to obey its laws. I could retire to my chapel and forgive the man who tortured my father; I could witness vile acts of injustice and still pray for those who committed them. I could retreat.

While I sheltered myself, others were forced to live in my stead. Acts of vengeance, cruelty, war and murder—I was capable of all, and yet I withdrew, leaving others to fight the great battles.

These solemn thoughts pursued me as my litter was borne through the streets toward the Leonine City. The gates of Sant'Angelo were sealed, as always at night, and I had to make my way across the Ponte Santa Maria and out the gates of the Trastevere to reach the Borgo. Vespers was sounding as I drew toward Saint Peter's.

There were few people about. Ordinarily during Lent huge services would be held in the square before the great church, but the local bishop was no substitute for the pope and the mass had drawn only a few parishioners.

Darkness had fallen by the time I approached the caminata near Saint Petronilla's. I was startled when a figure emerged from the shadows.

"Ah, my favorite abbess." I was relieved to hear that it was Gallimanfry.

"So early?" I asked, laughing. Usually he waited for compline before visiting my chambers.

"There are matters afoot," he said abruptly. "May we go inside?"

I dismissed the servants with the litter and unlocked the door. Inside a single taper was burning. I began to light another, but he stopped me.

"No, wait. We cannot stay long. I came to tell you that you are needed in the Castel Sant'Angelo."

In the dim light I searched his face. "Why? What has happened?"

"These superstitious rascals," he growled. "Tonight's the night, while there's no moon—but they haven't said their damned proper penance and the swine won't move unless they're drowned in ashes and muttered over."

"Tonight?"

"Yes, and high time too. Get it over with. Signor Fidgets has been making his way through the ranks, and a bad pest he is." He took my arm. "Now, my sweet abbess, come along. You've a duty to perform."

"I am not suited," I protested. "You could find a priest. Perhaps Father Tomaso of Santo Stefano Miccini . . ."

"Come, Lena," he said urgently, "your sister has waited more than ten years for this night. The men will not march without the Lenten blessing. I would gladly summon a priest in your place, but there are none who can be trusted." When I still did not reply, he added, "Lena, you are a Theophylact."

He knew what he was saying. It was I who would give hope to these men as they marched against the Lateran. I who would give my blessing as the man who held Saint Peter's Chair was brought to ruin.

Was this God's call or only the insistent blind human desire of the man who stood before me, a man I loved?

Regretfully, almost as in a dream, my limbs compelled by other forces than my will, I turned from him and snuffed the taper. I did not wish it to shine on my face when I returned.

Natural suspicion made Cardinal Peter as wary of servants as he was of other men. When he retired to his bedchamber at night, his door was barred to all. Only the

most important visitors on the most urgent business would
be admitted after compline. And so it was that Sergius,
standing before the massive gilt-edged door that led to
Peter's rooms, realized he would excite the cardinal's
suspicions. Few dared disturb Peter at this hour.

He rapped once, then again more forcefully. At last a
square panel in the door was pulled aside and Peter peered
out.

"Cardinal Sergius, what brings you?" The voice was
far from welcoming.

When Sergius leaned closer, a lamp moved behind
the door, shining through the opening to light his features.

"This concerns my family—and that matter we spoke
of. Please, it is most urgent."

The lantern light wavered; then the panel slammed
shut. A moment later the door swung open.

Peter had slipped a loose robe over his shoulders. His
hands were tucked inside for warmth. "What is the news?"
he demanded.

Sergius glanced at Peter's face and almost lost his
resolve. There was no greeting there, no sympathy. Instead he saw only impatience and scorn.

"You . . . you have promised me the Romagna,"
Sergius stammered.

"You will be rewarded." There was indifference in
the other man's voice.

"The Romagna," Sergius repeated.

The contempt in Peter's face was unmistakable. "It is
the intention of my brother and me to reward you. There is
no need to say more."

Resentment rose in Sergius' heart. He had come here
certain of his purpose, firm in his intentions. In the silence
of his own thoughts, thinking over his mother's words,
everything had seemed clear to him.

He would not kill Peter. The cardinal was his friend.

He was close to the pope, a man of power. Everything that Sergius wanted could be gained through him. All Sergius had to do was reveal his mother's plot and the Lateran would be saved. John and Peter would be forever in his debt.

Anthony would be forced to flee for his life. Marozia and Guido would be ruined. What did he owe them, anyway? His life was here in the Lateran, where his father's name was held in honor.

Now Peter too seemed to regard him with scorn. Had he erred in his choice? What if his mother was right? What if this man should . . . Sergius' hand crept toward the fitchet in his cloak. Then he stopped.

The gleaming eyes were upon him, the cardinal's lips curled sarcastically. "What have you come for?" The harsh voice cut through his reflections.

"I was sent—" Sergius paused, almost gasping for breath, then lowered his voice, ashamed. "My mother sent me to kill you."

"Then get on with it." Peter's hands were motionless beneath his robe. It was obvious he had a weapon there. He showed no fear.

Sergius shook his head slowly. "You know I do not wish to harm you. You know you are my friend."

There was no rely.

"I was summoned to the House of Hadrian today," Sergius went on in a rush. "My mother told me that Anthony and Guido plan to attack the Lateran tonight. I was to assassinate you, then open the Gate of Saint Jerome."

There was a moment's silence. In the lamplight the cardinal's features were remote and still. Searching those cold black eyes for some sign of thanks, Sergius saw nothing. Suddenly he felt faint. The pounding of blood in his ears thundered inside his skull.

"Is that all?" Cardinal Peter asked quietly.

"All?" Sergius had begun to tremble. "Don't you

understand? They will attack *tonight*. The Lateran is in danger.''

Peter nodded. ''I will inform my brother and alert the guards.''

''Then . . . what do you wish me to do?'' Sergius' voice was choked.

''Nothing. You have done your duty, and I am grateful for it.'' At last Peter smiled. It was a thin smile, like a hard scratch on the surface of a glass. ''I suggest you retire to your chambers.''

Sergius stared at him. ''But—but I don't think you understand. They are well armed. We may all be in danger.''

''Then God's will be done,'' Peter said dryly. ''Go now.''

Sergius nodded weakly and turned away. At the door he paused. ''I hope you know what this has cost me,'' he whispered. His face twisted with pain. ''I could not let them carry it out. When my mother told me I must murder you—*you*, Peter, my dearest friend, the man who has guided me—I realized the evil. . . .''

Peter inclined his head ever so slightly, a token gesture of gratitude.

Sergius seemed on the verge of saying more, then thought better of it. He turned and for a moment his back was to the cardinal.

He heard the rustle of cloth behind him and realization flashed through his mind: I was wrong. He knew it with the absolute clarity of the condemned.

Panic shot through him. He flung open the door, reaching at the same moment for the stiletto in his waistband. But as he fumbled in the folds of his cape he felt a hand dragging at his arm. The fingers had astonishing strength.

A searing pain shot through his back and he lunged against Peter's iron grip. He could not get away. Again the pain, then again and again—he coughed and choked, spilling blood as he fell, thinking, My friend, my friend. . . .

The citizens saw them first—dark lurking figures moving through the shadows of the abitato. One old pantrywoman, roused from sleep, thought they were youngsters playing in the courtyard. Dragging out her chamber pot, she went to the window to douse their enthusiasm, then saw to her horror that these were not children but men in mail with spears and shields, passing through the alley with furtive steps and fixed purpose. She shivered and crawled back into bed.

In the abandoned monastery of Saint Andrew the soldiers assembled around their leaders, who issued hushed commands. They handed out oil lamps, their vents covered by dark cloths so the flaring lights could not be seen by the Lateran guards. Then as silently as they had come the soldiers streamed back out into the city, to make their way toward the Gate of Saint Jerome.

Matins was long past and still the men lay in the shadows, shivering. Inside a hut near the walls of the Lateran an ironworker's family with two wide-eyed children cowered in a corner, guarded by one of Bardulf's men. The single window was draped in black. As the door opened, a lean bearded figure slipped inside.

"Well?" Impatiently Duke Guido turned to the young man.

Anthony shook his head. "Still no sign. I fear he has failed."

"Damnation." Guido glared fiercely at Anthony. "We cannot wait much longer. Lauds is almost upon us."

"I know." Anthony glanced at the ironmaker's family, then turned away at the sight of their fearful faces. "We will have to storm the palace."

Guido rolled his eyes. "What? Are you mad? We cannot go over the walls. They will slaughter us like sheep."

"We have the element of surprise," Anthony replied calmly. "If we can mount the ladders and breach the gates—"

"*If* we can. Ah yes, if." Guido's voice rose in fury. "No, my fine young man, you're dreaming. You may take your men over the walls if you like, but not I. I have no wish to sacrifice myself for a useless enterprise. I tell you, if the gate is not open at the sounding of lauds my men and I will return to the fortress."

Anthony appeared unmoved. "Very well," he said quietly. "If you refuse, my men will do it alone. I am sure Duke Hugo will be pleased to hear that his brother turned tail at the gates."

Guido flushed. "Do not *speak* of my brother," he snapped.

Anthony gave him a long stare, then gestured to his henchman, who brought him his sword. Before sliding it through the loop at his waist, he paused for a moment to admire the workings on the hilt. "This is my father's sword," he remarked, "given to me by my lady mother, your wife." He looked up. "Do you think I have a choice?"

Guido could not meet the young man's eyes. His hands moved nervously, passing over the links of mail in his long hauberk as if he wished to wipe them clean. "Very well," he said at last, his voice almost inaudible.

"We shall wait until lauds," Anthony replied.

"At the sounding of lauds." Guido agreed with a nod.

Without another word the two men went out the door and into the dense stillness of the night.

Chapter 52

From the Chapel of the Sancta Sanctorum inside the Lateran a single bell rang out, echoing from the basilica walls. A nun in dark weeds painfully lifted herself from the cold stone floor and genuflected. Glancing at her three companions, who had pledged to pray through lauds until morning, she silently turned up the aisle to withdraw. Men's shouts and the clattering of armor fell heavily on her ears.

Inside the massive banquet hall the tables had been pushed aside to make a council chamber for war. At the end of the room stood Pope John, chain mail draped over his Byzantine silks. His face glowered in anger as he barked orders to the bishops and men-at-arms, who scurried about to do his bidding.

Bishop Peter stood at his side—silently, his eyes darting to follow the movement of those who came and went.

Almost the instant the bell sounded for lauds a young messenger rushed into the room.

"Your Holiness," he panted, "it has begun. The attack has begun."

"By the God of mercy," Pope John roared, "Hugo! Where is Hugo?"

"He cannot be roused," stammered the messenger. "He is deep in slumber and his men—"

"Damn the pig and his men! Where are his men?"

"They have been summoned, but they are in confusion."

The pope rounded on his brother.

"Peter, you must go and command them. We can't let that upstart take the walls."

Startled, the cardinal gazed at John as if he had lost his mind. "Your Holiness," he said placatingly, "I would go, but I know full well the gates are sealed. We are secure and—"

"Don't bicker with me," the pontiff shouted. "Would you show yourself a coward too? Go, go!"

Reddening, Cardinal Peter wheeled and left the room.

In the courtyards, alleys and outbuildings of the Lateran all was confusion. Officers driven by fear rather than valor shouted commands and countermands almost in the same breath. Near the palace walls the skies were lit by blazing torches. The roof of a storehouse had caught fire; its flames leapt toward the heavens, smoke roiling into the darkness.

Turning down the alley toward Saint Jerome's Gate, Peter was aghast to see that all the guards had fled. He watched with horrified fascination as the huge doors sagged inward, groaned—and groaned again. From the other side he could hear ax blades biting into wood, steel grating against steel.

Along the balustrades men with bows and arrows lifted their heads to fire down on their attackers, then ducked behind the parapets. Their shooting was sporadic, listless. There was no one in command. Each man cared only for himself, and they all ran for shelter after firing a single shot.

A soldier rushed by. Peter recognized him as one of the papal captains and seized him by the arm.

"Bring up some men to hold the gate," he shouted above the noise of the crackling fire.

The captain swung around in fury, struggling to wrench himself free. "Let go of me. Let go of me or by God's wounds, I'll—"

"Coward!" Peter's swift blow sobered the man. "Bring your guards to the gate or I'll have you flayed."

With bloodshot eyes the soldier gazed at the cardinal, finally recognizing him. "Yes, Your Eminence, at once—at once." He rushed off into the night.

The first withering fire from the parapets took Anthony by surprise. He expected only a few guards to meet his initial rush, but as bowmen appeared all along the ramparts, he realized with sickness in his heart that the pope's men were prepared for the attack. Somehow they had received a warning.

He shuddered as the ghastly truth swept over him. There could be no other explanation than that his brother Sergius had given away their plans, and now—

There was no way to turn back. Already his men were scaling the ladders, howling with pain as the arrows poured down upon them.

Guido rushed past, shouting, "Retreat, retreat!"

Then Anthony noticed that something was wrong up above. The men on the bulwarks were beginning to fail. The return fire from Anthony's bowmen was taking only a few defenders, but still the others seemed to lose hope.

Suddenly Anthony realized what had happened—the men on the parapets were leaderless. They fired randomly, moving about without pattern or plan. Now that Anthony's men had found their range, the papal guards lifted their heads only intermittently; their arrows dropped harmlessly to the stones, shot off hastily and in desperation.

"Goldino, Tarsus, Giorgio," Anthony called to his

captains, "bring up your axmen and pikers. Scale the
walls with the lighted brands."

Briefly there was confusion as Guido's men, rushing
in retreat, collided with Anthony's, thundering toward the
walls. In the melee Guido's call to withdraw was somehow
forgotten, and the stampede of flight turned into attack as
Goldino, Tarsus and Giorgio waved their men onward.

Flaming brands flew over the parapets and axmen
hewed at Saint Jerome's Gate as Anthony's bowmen kept
up a steady rain of arrows, forcing the men on the bulwarks to cower behind the crenelations. Guido had halted
to watch, and now he saw that the tide of battle was
shifting. Turning his remaining men, he urged them back
to the line.

The main storehouse was a blazing ruin, and new
fires had started up in the granaries, stables and outbuildings.
Horses freed from their stalls poured through the courtyards,
eyes wide with terror, whinnying shrilly.

As Saint Jerome's Gate was breached, the regiments
of Spoletans and Sienese poured through the gap. The
papal guards leapt from the parapets, only to be cut down
in their tracks as they fled.

Inside the palace Duke Hugo finally staggered from his
bed. His watery eyes were bloodshot and bleary; his hands
quivered as he raised them to his head. His debaucheries
of the evening before were plainly written on his features,
even in his stance. His lieutenants, although accustomed to
their duke's habits, were aghast at the sight of the man
who emerged from the bedchamber. The soldiers glanced
at each other in terror.

Hugo raised his hand to shield his eyes from the
lamplight. "Damn. So—damn him and damn him." His
muttering was like a litany.

"The pope demands to see you," one lieutenant ventured. Hugo thrust him aside, staggered.

"The walls are breached," the lieutenant added. "Our men—"

"Damn our men. Breached?" Hugo paused, swayed. "My horse. My horse!"

Again his men exchanged sheepish glances, as if ashamed to witness this spectacle.

"I regret, my liege, the stables are burning."

"Burning, you say? Burning?" Hugo lashed out. "You stir-mutton, you vile son of a mother's—" He passed his hand in front of his eyes. For a long moment there was silence.

Hoarse shouts and the crashing of timbers broke the spell. A man rushed into the room, his face bloody and blackened with soot. "The palace," he cried, "they have reached the palace."

With sudden resolve Hugo lowered his hand from his eyes and turned to his nearest lieutenant. "Lothar, come with me. Einhard, Arnolfo, you and you, come along as well. The rest of you, see to the men. Make sure they hold firm. Do you hear me?" His voice had risen. "Do you hear me? See that they hold firm. Go now, go!" He waved his hands as if to clear away a swarm of bees.

Obediently the men hastened from the room while Einhard, Lothar and Arnolfo turned to follow their duke.

Outside the door of the papal palace the guards finally closed ranks. Realizing there was no further retreat, they fought desperately for their lives. Bows were useless at this close range. Here spears, swords and knives were the weapons of combat.

Fire was the enemy of all. The burning granaries threw harsh tongues of light into the air, blinding the men who hacked and thrashed in a surging mass of indistin-

guishable bodies and limbs. Men shielded their eyes from
the blaze, stumbled and reached out. For them, death leapt
from the shadows—a sword, a lance, a piercing stiletto.
Dim creatures battling in the night, they knew only darkness,
screams of pain, the touch of steel.

Cardinal Peter stood just inside the palace doors.
Here, where a second battalion of guards crowded the
hallway, there was eerie calm. Outside could be heard men
fighting, screaming, dying. They hammered at the door,
begging pitifully to be allowed entrance.

Their cries, muffled but still audible, cast a strange
spell over the troops within. They shuffled their feet
nervously, bowing their heads under the flickering torchlight.
No one seemed able to meet the eyes of his companions.

The ranks broke as a soldier made his way through
from the rear.

"Where is Hugo?" demanded Peter of the messenger,
for perhaps the hundredth time that night.

The man looked wild-eyed. "He has fled, Your
Eminence."

"Fled? Damn you, man!" The cardinal seized the messenger and shook him. "He cannot flee. How could he
possibly escape?"

The soldier trembled in his grasp. "I beg you, sire. It
is so. He was seen climbing the walls."

"Coward!" Peter flung the man aside. "You did
nothing to stop him? Coward! I am surrounded by cowards!"

Backing away, the messenger tripped and fell. Maddened by fury, Peter swung out his sword, fully prepared
to end the soldier's life. Then there was a sudden explosion like an enormous wave bursting on shore and the
palace doors flew open.

The thin shield of safety was gone. In an instant
blood-mad warriors filled the hallway, their swords whirling.

The terrified papal guards fell like ninepins, hurled back by the relentless attack.

Peter scarcely had time to think before the enemy was upon him. At the forefront, bearing down like a vengeful god, a tall bearded man with piercing black eyes slashed this way and that, oblivious to danger, his blows falling with deadly sureness. He was a fearful sight. Hair matted with blood and grime, sweat glistening on his bronze features, he mowed down all those who stood in his way, fighting with the demonic fury of a man with no fear of death.

This must be Anthony, thought Peter, the son of Alberic. I shall kill him. I shall put an end to all this.

The thoughts were only dreams. They were still, clear and concise, far from this hallway filled with madness. They were thoughts that seemed detached from Peter's own hands, which lifted his sword to strike the blow.

Suddenly the warrior was upon him. That glittering eye, that sweating face were all too real—and the sword whistling down on him. . . .

Peter met the first sweep. He felt the force of steel striking steel, a blow that seemed to shatter his forearm. He reeled backward, struggling to recover his balance.

Anthony's speed was inhuman. Blood whirled away from the tip of his sword as he swung it round his head, preparing to hurl it downward.

A woodsman, thought Peter, he swings like a peasant woodsman.

Again Anthony was cutting down, striking. His sword was a razor of pain in Peter's side.

"Help me, help me!"

Who was that screaming? Peter wondered, unable to recognize his own voice. Surely Anthony would not strike again. Surely not.

Peter fumbled at his sword. With one stroke he swept

the blade up to Anthony's. For an instant he saw the demonic reddened eyes of his foe, heard the panting wind that hissed through his teeth.

They crossed swords and crossed again. Each clash sent a shiver of pain through Peter's forearm. This nemesis was so young, so strong! If only someone would come to the rescue. "Soldiers, soldiers, help me," he cried out again.

No one could hear him. Each man fought desperately to save his own skin.

Peter's back was to the wall but he was holding his own, somehow raising his sword each time to meet the fierce, hacking blows. Then suddenly there was a break in the surging crowd of attackers and Peter saw a chance to escape—if he could only parry those terrible slashes. He glanced along the wall again. Yes, there was a passage, if he could run.

He looked aside for an instant too long. As he raised his sword again, turning to meet Anthony's furious blows, the rhythm of combat changed. Deftly Anthony shifted his grip on the hilt of his sword. No longer was one hand slashing with it. In the upstroke, as quickly as a falcon snatches a bird from the air, both hands turned, hesitated and spun the sword in flight, then snatched it into a reverse grip.

It was a beautiful, delicate gesture, and Peter admired it, awed by the clarity that came over him as he understood that his next parry would be wrong, that he could never bring his sword around in time to meet the lunging tip that now drove down bearing the full weight of his attacker, aiming steadily, purposefully toward his heart.

It was a blow, as if a sharp stone had been hurled against his chest. Then there was only the spinning darkness, the relief of falling away and his own voice crying, "Dear Jesus!"

*   *   *

The din of fighting men could be clearly heard from the banquet hall at the heart of the papal palace.

"Peter, Hugo! Damn them, where are they?" Pope John's voice rose shrilly.

The bloodied men around him stared as if they could not understand. They edged away from him, crowding fearfully against the walls, trampling on the dead and wounded who had been dragged away from the battle.

"Shut the doors," cried the pope. "Do you not hear me? Shut the doors at once. We will defend the palace."

Did he not know it was futile? The palace was already taken. All around them the remnants of a beaten guard were being driven back toward the banquet hall.

"Shut the doors," he shouted, "shut the doors." At last he was obeyed.

"Form ranks," cried the pope. "We will fight them to the end."

It was hopeless. They could already hear Anthony's men outside in the corridors. Pikes and franciscas hammered at the doors. The papal guards pulled away, their eyes wild, searching for escape.

The door at the lower end of the hall was the first to give way. There was a shattering blow and the crunch of steel; then the hinges yielded. A moment later Anthony's soldiers burst through, the press of men crowding into the breach. They met no resistance.

"Hold, hold," cried a powerful voice behind them. The triumphant soldiers lowered their weapons but remained alert as a single figure strode through their ranks.

Scarcely glancing about him, Anthony made his way down the length of the room. Blood dripped from his bare sword.

"Pope John," he shouted, "by the command of

Senatrix Marozia and the people of Rome I order you to renounce the Holy Chair of Saint Peter.''

The pontiff drew himself up to his full height. "You are a traitor," he cried defiantly, "and the son of a traitor. The church's power is vested in me by God alone. It shall not be taken away by mortal man. I demand your obedience to the Office of Saint Peter and to the Holy Roman Empire."

The two men stared at each other. Then the pope raised his hand, holding out the signet ring.

Anthony strode forward. His soldiers glanced at one another with wondering, fearful eyes. For a moment it seemed the young man would fall to his knees and kiss the ring. Then two paces in front of the pope he leaned over and spat on it.

The pope snatched back his hand as if he had been stung and a groan went up from the men around the room. After that came laughter, at first hesitant, then hearty and joyous.

"Baronio, Flavius," Anthony's voice rang out, "bind his hands. Take him to the Castel Sant'Angelo. My mother awaits us."

Chapter 53

Pope John was placed upon an open palanquin. From the Lateran palace down the Via Papalis, past the Colosseum, the Piazza del Senatore and Santa Maria in Capitolio he rode with downcast eyes, surrounded by Anthony's victorious soldiers. Behind him, stretched on a long shield, lay the body of Duke Guido of Siena.

Guido had fallen inside the Lateran walls in one of those dark alleys where so many skirmishes had taken place. A spear had pierced his chest. Around him were the bodies of three other men he cut down in his final attack.

Dawn was breaking as the entourage turned in to the winding Via Papalia, which led to the Ponte San Angelo. Washerwomen, tradespeople, merchants, pilgrims, Saracen slaves and Roman nobles, all roused by the terrible events of the night, had gathered in mute wonder to watch their pope pass by. Now and then he would raise his head, scanning the faces of the crowd as if to find a sympathetic eye. Then his shoulders slumped, his head fell and the pontiff resumed his dejected pose.

From the upper terrace of the Castel Sant'Angelo I witnessed his approach and sent Tasha to tell Marozia. It was not until the soldiers had stepped onto the bridge that I saw the shield that carried Guido. I chased after Tasha to the rooms below. Along the way I passed the guards and heard them murmuring among themselves. News of the victory, of the pope's imminent arrival and of Guido's death had traveled rapidly.

The sight of Marozia startled me. She appeared wild-eyed and distraught, as if with the realization of victory some dreadful change had come over her. I must have appeared much the same to her, for as I rushed to her side, she asked me, "What is it, Lena? What did you see?"

"Sister," I said hesitantly, "they are carrying a body on a shield. And the Sienese pennant is black."

"Guido," she murmured, but there was no change in her face. She added in an undertone, "All the more reason, then."

I took her by the arm. "Reason for what, Marozia? What is it you plan to do?" When she did not answer, I tightened my grip. "Sister, I beg you, allow him a public trial."

She wrenched herself away. "What trial did he give to Alberic? What trial could he afford our father before he was tortured to death? No, Lena, I have no pity for the man, no more than he took pity on me in the House of Hadrian."

In vain I tried to reason with her. "He is the pope, Marozia. He has many followers. If the cardinals and the Senate turn against you—" I could not finish the thought, and it was obvious that she was not swayed by my words. "Please, sister," I said softly, "I beg you to remember, you are human too. You are only a woman."

"A woman, yes," she replied archly, "but not a slave. I will not be bound to men who trample justice under their feet and treat me with scorn."

She whirled to face the door. Men's voices echoed from the hallway. Then Anthony was in the room. His mail was blood-spattered, his cheeks limned with rivulets of grime where the sweat had dried. Flinging himself at his mother's feet, he laid his sword hilt first on the floor before her.

She smiled and bent to touch his shoulder. "Rise, Anthony. You have served your father's memory well. Now tell me of the battle."

He averted his eyes. "We have suffered losses," he said grimly.

"I know that Duke Guido is dead." Her calmness surprised him and he glanced at me. "Yes," she explained, "Lena saw the banner from the tower." She paused. "Who else has fallen?"

Before Anthony could answer two soldiers entered, carrying between them a body wrapped in a cloak. They gently placed their burden on the floor, then stepped aside.

From under the edge of the fabric a few strands of reddish hair could be seen. At this sudden dread clutched at my heart. Beside me, Tasha's hand flew to her throat, and I heard a small sound almost like a cry of pain.

"Let me see him," said Marozia.

Anthony drew aside the cloak, then turned away.

Sergius' eyes were closed. The youthful charm was back on his face; that last sight of it will remain forever imprinted on my memory. As the cloak was withdrawn, I saw that his fingers were curled as in deep sleep.

I suppose I behaved shamefully then, but I had once greatly loved this child, and I could not bear to see him dead. I rushed to him and seized his cold wrist, trying vainly to shake life into him. But it was futile, and I put my forehead on his chest and wept until Tasha pulled me away.

Behind me, Marozia remained motionless.

"How did this happen?" she asked, her voice cold with anger.

Anthony took a deep breath. "He was found at the door of Cardinal Peter's chambers. There was a knife in his back and . . . and many wounds."

There was no change in Marozia's expression, but I could see tears welling in her eyes.

"Then he never reached the gate?" she asked.

Anthony shook his head. "No, we were forced to breach it and scale the parapets."

"What about Peter?"

"He was slain in the palace. Hugo and many of his men fled over the walls."

Marozia was silent for a time, milling all this over. Then she looked up and fixed her son with a blazing stare. "Bring me your captive," she ordered.

Anthony hesitated. "He has been remanded to the dungeon."

"Bring him before me," Marozia repeated, her voice rising. "I wish to see him."

With a bow Anthony retreated from the room. After a moment of confusion he returned with Pope John, flanked by guards. The pontiff still wore the papal crown.

"Remove the tiara," Marozia cried as soon as he had entered. "Bring it here to me."

One of the guards made a movement to carry out her order, then lost courage. It was Anthony himself who finally removed the crown.

She turned it in her hands, admiring the gold, the inlaid jewels and the etching on the upright cross.

"I promised this to my son," she said to John in a low, shaking voice, "but Sergius lies here, slain by your own brother."

She stared at the tiara, deep in thought, and then as if on a sudden impulse, she raised it high and placed it on her head.

Silence gripped the room.

"The signet," she commanded.

The pope's wrists were bound. Anthony yanked the ring from John's finger. When he carried it to his mother, she placed it on the finger of her own right hand.

"Anthony," she said, looking steadily at him, "I want this man to kiss the signet of the new pope."

Her son hesitated.

"Will you not obey me?" she asked.

For an instant Anthony stood very still. Then he signaled to the guards. Half dragging, half leading their captive, they brought the pope to his knees.

The guards' hands held his shoulders, but in a last act of defiance John flung his head back to wrench himself away. Anthony thrust him forward, forcing him to bow, and Marozia pressed the ring to his unyielding lips.

At this an expression of peace came over her face. She stepped back. "And what shall we call the new pope?" she demanded, laughing as if it were all a joke. She looked at me, but I could not bear to return her gaze. There was madness in those eyes.

She began to pace, musing to herself. "The successor to Pope John," she murmured, "shall we call her Joan? It's a goodly name, I think." She smiled. "Oh, yes. Pope John and Pope Joan. One has been crushed and the other must rule in his stead."

She raised her head and called for the guards. "Bear him to the dungeon," she cried shrilly.

As they pulled the once-great man to his feet, I felt myself moving forward. "In God's name, be gentle," I urged. "Please be gentle with His Holiness. He has fallen low and deserves our pity."

But as I turned back to my sister I saw that there was no gentleness or pity in her eyes.

A full day passed and still I did not see Gallimanfry. By evening I was frantic. No one in the fortress could tell me what had become of him. No one had seen him in battle.

On the pretense of ministering to the wounded I lingered in the courtyard, looking at the haggard, desperate faces of the men who had been brought down from the

Lateran. Beyond them the corpses of the fallen had been laid on their shields. With terror in my heart I passed among them, kneeling now and again to cross myself and touch the dead. Gallimanfry was not among them.

Later I made my way from the fortress through the Borgo to Saint Petronilla's, where I still had many tasks to attend to. Not least of these was quelling the fears of the sisters in my charge. By now truth and rumor were freely mingled. All knew that the Lateran had been stormed and taken by force, that Guido was dead and Hugo on the road back to Pisa.

What of the pope? Did he still live? Would he be called before a tribunal or executed in the dark cells of the Castel Sant'Angelo? What of this rumor, only now being whispered abroad, that Marozia herself had taken the papal tiara, mocking it with the title of Pope Joan? What of that, indeed!

I heard the nuns whispering among themselves. They did not ask me directly about Marozia; they did not dare. How could I have replied? I knew the scene I had witnessed was madness, and I prayed I would awaken the next morning to find that it was a dream.

Vespers came and went, the bells ringing out from Saint Peter's. To me they sounded a dreadful tolling, a death knell for God's kingdom on earth. In the chapel that night I prayed fervently, but there was no respite for my soul. My mind kept wandering back over all that had transpired. I begged God to forgive the vengeance that lay in my sister's heart.

Long after the others had gone to rest, I retired to my caminata. There, waiting for me in the darkness by the door, was Gallimanfry. Somehow my trembling fingers managed to turn the key. Somehow I managed to lift the latch and open the door. By some mysterious power I managed to keep my lips sealed until we were alone.

Then I could restrain myself no longer and I rushed into his arms. He seemed to understand, for he held me a long time before either of us spoke.

"I feared you—I feared you wounded—or dead," I whispered.

He laughed a gentle laugh. "No, no, Lena. Wounds fester and death doesn't suit me. Neither appeals to my taste."

"I am half mad with anxiety and you make jokes," I gasped, for I was not ready to forgive him.

"I'll joke in other ways before the night's finished." He glanced into my eyes and shuddered. "Ah, the horror of a woman's fear—but never mind. Where's the wine? I won't be solemn, I promise. I've had a good day."

I filled a chalice from the amphora. "A good day," I said bitterly. "The Lateran is in ruins. Sergius and Guido are dead. The pope—"

"The pope is where he belongs—in hell or close to it." I had never heard Gallimanfry speak so venomously. Then as if to apologize he added brusquely, "Alberic I loved."

"Do you know what Marozia has done?" I asked. "She is mad, stark mad." I shook my head and tears came to my eyes. "It is for Sergius that I grieve."

He took my chin in his hand and forced me to look at him. "You loved Sergius as a boy," he said. "I am not sure the man deserved that love."

I closed my eyes. "Please, Gallimanfry, I will hear nothing—"

"Very well," he said curtly, "but there are some who ask for their fate. Sergius was to murder Peter and open the gates to our men. Instead he was found in Peter's chamber, knifed in the back. His own weapon had not been drawn."

"You mean he went to him to—" I could not finish.

Gallimanfry nodded. "To warn him, yes, and was murdered for his trouble."

I bowed my head and my love came close, but before he could speak, I burst out, "Gallimanfry, what shall we do? Marozia cannot persist in—"

Again he cut me short. "She *will* persist, Lena. She has touched the ring of power and she will not let it from her grasp."

I knew it was true; I felt coldness come into my heart.

"The cardinals?" They had put up no resistance to the attack on the Lateran.

"They are helpless and confused. None has the power to oppose your sister if she continues on this course."

"Surely the Papal States will rise against her."

Gallimanfry sighed. "In time, perhaps, but do not forget, Lena, Pope John has overseen the slow ruin of his empire. There are many more who hate him than who love him. Even his closest ally, Duke Hugo, failed him in the end. Whoever opposes Marozia will have to put forth his own name for the papacy, and there are few now who would dare such a thing."

"So she is destined to remain this mockery, Pope Joan?" He did not reply. "And John, what will become of him?"

Gallimanfry had finished his wine and now he placed the chalice on the hearth. The bells for compline began to ring.

"It is late," he said. "We must go to bed. Otherwise this hour may slip through our fingers, and heaven knows we will never see it again."

Chapter 54

For three days after the fall of Pope John no one heard from Theodora or saw her stir from the house on the Aventine. On the fourth day, however, Gallimanfry met Tiberon near the church of San Angelo in Pescheria. In a cracked but deferential voice the old servant muttered that Theodora wished to see Gallimanfry immediately.

Gallimanfry was astonished at this information. Even when he was tutor to her grandchildren, Theodora had rarely spoken to him. Now that she lived alone, severed from her past, few were ever called to the once-noble House of Theophylact. He went unwillingly, not knowing what awaited him.

As Tiberon ushered him through the atrium into the council chamber, Gallimanfry noted on every hand the signs of wealthy neglect. Long disuse marred the carved and inlaid furniture from Ravenna, the Venetian tapestries and gaudy Muslim ornaments, spoils from the Saracen campaign. Over all there was a layer of dust, an air of dinginess, as if Theodora could no longer be bothered with the things of this world.

Gallimanfry was forced to wait a few moments in the council chamber before Theodora entered. She nodded to him condescendingly but did not offer her hand when he bowed.

Her eyes were ferverishly bright. On her fingers she wore a great many rings that sparkled when she moved, and around her neck were several sashes of office. Gallimanfry recognized the imprimature of the archduke of Brindisi, but the others were unfamiliar.

"You are Gallimanfry?" Theodora asked. "He who has served Marozia and her family?"

"The same, signora."

"I seem to remember you from times past." Her voice drifted off and she looked away. Then as if called back to the present she added, "You have been faithful in her service?" There was a curl to her lip.

"I have done my best," Gallimanfry acknowledged, "though one man's best may be another's worst."

Theodora let this pass. "What do you think of this folly of hers?"

He took a long breath. "I do not know whether it is folly or not. As you may have heard, she intended to make Sergius her pope."

"I am not privy to her plans," Theodora said sharply.

"Sergius, alas, is dead," Gallimanfry continued. "Marozia had no one else to turn to, and so the crown is hers."

Theodora fixed him with a steady look. "They say she has called herself Pope Joan out of mockery."

Suddenly he felt pinned beneath her gaze. "Whether it is mockery or not I cannot say, but yes, she is called Joan."

"How is Pope John?"

"As far as I know, he is well kept in the dungeon of Sant'Angelo."

"Yes, but what does she intend for him?"

"I cannot say, signora." At last he was beginning to understand why she had called for him. Her next words confirmed his suspicions.

"Gallimanfry, you must use your influence to save him."

He stepped back a pace as if attempting to diminish the force of her appeal. "Beg pardon, signora, but I believe there is little I can do. Your daughter seems bound in a spell of some sort. I cannot say how much is calculation and how much madness, but she does not take kindly to suggestions."

"You shall, Gallimanfry." Theodora's eyes glittered. "She must not murder him. It would be sacrilege. It would be—" She stopped abruptly and a look of bitter sadness swept across her face. "You must not let her," she repeated, this time more feebly.

Gallimanfry knew there was no arguing with her. He bowed from the waist. "I will do what I can."

"Not 'what you can,' " Theodora snapped. "You must do everything—everything, do you hear—to ensure that this man does not die. It would be the ruination of Rome, of the Papal States, of the empire! Do you understand?"

Gallimanfry nodded. He dared not look at Theodora, pleading so piteously for the lover she had lost.

"You must promise me," she urged. "Promise me that you will do everything, that you will use your influence—"

Gallimanfry cut her short. "I have already promised, signora. I do not want to see a man die needlessly."

She glared at him. "This is not 'a man,' this is the pope. Do you understand? Do you know who made him so? Was it not I?" She paused, searching for the right words to convince him.

"Look at me," she begged, her voice falling. "Tell me, you know it is true. Tell how much I gave to make him pope, how I sacrificed for him. Now my own daughter—"

Gallimanfry could not endure any more. "Signora," he said firmly, "you have given me a mission. If I am to carry it out, there is no time to be lost. Even now—"

"Yes, yes, of course," she said quickly, "go at once, and when your mission is done, when you have succeeded—" She hesitated and a wild light came into her eyes. Then suddenly she lifted a sash from her neck. "Brindisi will be yours, and Paestum and Amalfi." She held the sashes out to him.

Coloring, Gallimanfry waved them away. "All in good time, signora. Now, if you will permit me, I must go."

She nodded. "Yes, yes. Tiberon, show him out." As he turned away from her, Theodora's voice came to him again, bitter and rancorous. "See that you do not fail," she called.

The gates of the Castel Sant'Angelo had been left open since the fall of the Lateran. Citizens came and went freely and emissaries from nearby principalities were welcomed in the Hall of Justice. Tentatively at first, then in growing numbers, bishops and cardinals ventured from the Lateran to the castle courtyard, where they mingled, waiting to see the woman who called herself Pope Joan.

When Gallimanfry arrived there, he made his way through the straggling crowd of churchmen, soldiers and street-hawkers and entered the first guard room.

Anthony rose at his tutor's approach and dismissed the man to whom he had been speaking, a captain from Bardulf's reserves.

"Gallimanfry," he cried, "am I glad to see you."

Since the night of the attack on the Lateran they had hardly laid eyes on one other.

"I have just come from your grandmother," Gallimanfry replied without preamble. "She fears for the life of Pope John."

Anthony looked sharply at him. "She has reason to fear."

"Can the execution be halted?"

"For what purpose?" Anthony's face was flushed. "Was there anyone to halt the execution of my father? To speak for him when his name was dragged through the mire?"

"I promised her I would do what I could," replied Gallimanfry evenly.

Anthony shrugged. "I do not know what fate my mother has planned for John, but I suspect, as do you, that he will not live long."

"Then I must see her at once."

Anthony gazed at his tutor in astonishment. "What? You would plead for that man? Ask forgiveness for him? Have you taken leave of your senses?"

Gallimanfry sighed and shook his head. "No, Anthony, but I have seen the look in Theodora's eyes. She loves him still, this John, for whatever reason, even though he has scorned her. The time for mercy is now, or there may never be an end to the killing."

Marozia sat on a throne in the Hall of Justice wearing the papal tiara, a scepter in her hand. When Anthony entered the men around her moved aside and lowered their voices, though they looked curiously at the plainly dressed figure who accompanied the general.

"Gallimanfry has come to make a plea." Anthony bowed to his mother, then stepped aside.

"What is it?" Her voice was cold.

Gallimanfry advanced to the base of the dais. "I have come to ask God's mercy on the man who lies in prison, the man who once was pope."

"God's mercy," Marozia repeated as if the words were strange to her. She thought for a moment, then

looked at Gallimanfry, her eyes wild with triumph. "If
that is what you wish, then come with me. You also,
Anthony, my son. You will both see God's mercy."

Those in the hall bowed and stood aside as she rose
and passed through the room. Gallimanfry and Anthony
followed her along a hallway with a rich coffered ceiling,
then through the Chapel of Leo IV and beyond to one of
the smaller courtyards. From there a flight of steep stairs
led down to the frescoed rooms of the heated baths. Just
beyond them lay the prison cells.

Marozia hesitated at the top of the steps, listening. To
the ears of Gallimanfry and Anthony came a soft, high-
pitched sound like steam escaping through a fissure. They
glanced at each other, not daring to speak. Then Marozia
pressed on, the long scarlet train of her velvet cape just
touching the stairs as she descended.

The dungeon was dank. Droplets of water clung to
the stone walls and the odor of rotten wood permeated the
still air.

The prison door was open. Flaring light from the
burning torches within danced and twisted along the wall.
As Pope Joan entered the main chamber, there was movement in the dimly lit corners. Four guards came to attention,
their spear butts rapping on the floor.

Gallimanfry was scarcely aware of these faceless
guards, for his attention was riveted by the figure in the
center of the room—a man, stripped to the waist, seated on
a high wooden stool with his hands bound behind him and
his head held against an upright post. It was from this
man's throat that the strange, whistling sound proceeded.

Gallimanfry took a step closer, then halted, suddenly
sick with fear. The reason for the man's awkwardly rigid
posture was now apparent. Around his neck, bound to the
pole behind him, was a leather thong.

The horror of the scene seemed to affect everyone in

the room. Every eye was on that petrified figure. His eyes
were wide and bulging. His tongue already protruded from
between his lips.

Gallimanfry knew the torture. The leather thong had
been soaked in water. As it dried—slowly in the dank
atmosphere of the dungeon—the band was shrinking, gradually crushing the doomed man's windpipe.

Gallimanfry glanced at Marozia and saw no gloating
in her eyes, no victory. She might have been standing on
shore, helplessly watching while a drowning man far out
in the water sank from sight.

Was she truly mad?

"Your Holiness," Gallimanfry ventured, "be merciful.
Let him live."

All eyes turned toward Marozia, awaiting her answer.
Even the guards surveyed her with veiled glances, spears
poised nervously at their fingertips as if they might suddenly be called upon to act.

Marozia stared at Gallimanfry, then Anthony. At last
she spoke.

"Anthony, your knife."

He handed his mother the stiletto, and she turned to
the prisoner. His bulging eyes were fixed on her, the hatred
burning even through his agony.

Awkwardly, as if the weapon were unfamiliar to her,
she reached out with the blade. The rest watched breathlessly,
wondering whether she intended to put him out of his
misery or to slash the thin cord that bound him.

They would never know, for as the blade approached
his throat, John suddenly lurched forward. A bellow of
rage burst from the half-naked figure as he kicked out,
tangling his legs in the folds of her robe and hurling her to
the floor. She fell heavily, lurching to one side. The tiara
slid from her brow and went rolling away. For a moment

she was at his feet, the great papal robes spread around her like the wings of a wounded bird.

The guards stepped forward, their spears ready, but there was no need. That effort had been John's last. In his sudden desperate lunge he had toppled the stool on which he sat.

For a moment after Marozia fell he hung on the post, no sound coming from his throat, his face darkening. His feet struggled for purchase on the dank floor. His manacled hands clawed behind him, vainly attempting to break free.

An instant later the gestures turned feeble, then ceased. Only one finger continued to move like a loose, dry leaf blown against a fence post. A spasm wrenched his body. Blood ran from his nostrils and seeped from his ears. His head twisted, quivered and went limp. For a moment longer could be heard the dry scuffling of his limbs twitching against the post. Then all was still.

Whining like a wounded animal, Marozia staggered to her feet. Reaching for the papal tiara, she realized she still held the dagger in her hand. She opened her fingers and watched it fall as if she had never seen it before. The sound of it striking stone seemed to amuse her. She laughed. Then, raising her eyes, she grasped the crown and put it back on her head.

Chapter 55

For two years my sister Marozia reigned as Pope Joan. It was a strange time in Rome, a time of secrecy and confusion, when the faithful did not dare ask too many questions and God-fearing Christians saw portents of disaster on every hand. All this was because a woman reigned.

Among Roman Christians this has been called a dark period. No matter how evil the popes who preceded her—some of whom showed cowardice, betrayed their friends, plundered the empire and disdained their holy offices—these men were forgiven. Their deeds were rewritten in the memory of the people and they were exalted for their accomplishments rather than condemned for their misdeeds. Not so Pope Joan. As abbess of Saint Petronilla's I owed my first duty to God, my second to Jesus Christ His Son and my third to the Church of Rome. I knew that God and church were separate, that neither my sister nor the men who went before her were obedient to God's wishes. I told myself that my sister was no worse than any other.

How will our sins be forgiven? What will be God's judgment on the Day of the Apocalypse? Will He find that Pope Joan should be cast out because she is a woman, while Pope John may enter the gates of heaven with praise?

I do not like to cast such questions into the face of the Almighty. I know the answer though; women are sinful.

Women are unworthy. God has chosen us as servants rather than rulers.

Because of this I too feared God's punishment, but even I could not have foretold that it would be yet another woman—our own mother—who would bring about the downfall of Pope Joan.

During the two years that Marozia held the papacy Anthony's power and influence increased rapidly. With the guidance of Gallimanfry he soon came to understand the intricacies of Roman politics. At first, of course, the city's leading families regarded him with suspicion and hostility, but he knew how to flatter a host as well as carry a spear, and his steady judgment combined with a notable lack of bitterness toward his father's betrayers soon made him a favorite of the families on the Via Lata. They were pleased to see that since the death of Pope John the young man's thirst for vengeance seemed to have disappeared.

In one thing only did Anthony disappoint the Romans. If they hoped to tempt him with their eligible daughters, they were doomed to failure. Anthony was courteous to Helena, the daughter of Junius Bassus, who lived by San Andrea de Columna, but that courtesy never turned to a proposal. Then for a time there were whisperings about Anthony and Berenice, the lively, quick-tempered daughter of Senator Benedictus Carushomo. This also proved to be nothing more than rumor, and the gossips were left wondering who would win the young general's heart.

Their curiosity was finally satisfied when Duke Bardulf of Spoleto came to Rome accompanied by his daughter Francina. Within a fortnight the betrothal was announced, and the banns were posted outside the church of Santi Cosma e Damiano. Anthony and Francina were married within the twelvemonth.

For Anthony the marriage solved the remaining difficulties surrounding his status in the city. Having come to Rome with Bardulf's legions, he had few men he could call his own, and he could not demand an oath of fealty from soldiers who were already pledged to Bardulf. When the marriage vows had been sworn, though, Bardulf readily offered his men to Anthony and granted lands to the newly sworn liege.

While he was setting his domestic life in order Anthony was consolidating his political power. Now that his mother was pope, she could no longer hold secular office, and it was only to be expected that Anthony take her place in the Senate.

Other members of that body were clearly unhappy with this. In the first sittings rival senators did everything they could to cast doubt on the young man's fitness to rule. They reminded him through comment and innuendo that he was not one of them. Despite his mother's lineage they still considered him a Lombard, a foreigner.

Anthony seemed oblivious to every slight, and his steady determination threw them off guard. If he had tried to affect the Roman bearing, to speak, act and dress like one of the nobles who surrounded him, they would have had an easy target for derision. Instead through it all he remained a Lombard. He was plainly dressed; there were no adornments around his neck and wrists. He used none of the affected, polite mannerisms of speech that were fashionable among the other senators.

His rise came gradually, almost despite the looming presence of his mother, and when it was accomplished, the secular realm was fixed under his leadership.

He left the world of the church to the woman who had sought her vengeance there. Marozia no longer seemed the same person who had once been his mother, and yet he knew, despite her obvious madness, that he could never bring himself to act against her. Instead he sought power in other spheres and kept himself apart from her. Much as it pained him to admit it, Gallimanfry's warnings had been justified.

Under Anthony's guidance Rome prospered. The city's gates were thrown open to trade and the roads of the empire, guarded by loyal Lombards, became thoroughfares where merchants and pilgrims traveled freely without fear. The Romans saw their purses filling with gold, their store-houses with grain, and they blessed Anthony for their prosperity.

It was to Anthony, therefore, that every eye turned when tragedy befell Pope Joan. It happened in Saint Peter's shortly after Easter, when the pontiff, in the manner of her predecessors, came to the basilica to say the holy office.

In the apse there was a beautiful mosaic inlaid with colored tesserae showing Christ on a throne flanked by the Apostles. At their feet was a landscape with lions, flowers and lambs on the banks of a flowing river. The inscription read, "This is the See of Saint Peter, this is the temple of the Prince of Apostles, the glory and mother of all churches."

Under this mosaic Pope Joan had chosen to stand for the reading of the benediction. I sensed in the crowd that filled the basilica that peculiar anxiety which seemed to follow her wherever she went. Though she performed the office according to time-honored custom, the people could not forget or forgive her sex, and though her madness was often held in check, they seemed to expect it to spring forth at any moment.

It was as Pope Joan pronounced the end of the benediction and turned away to raise the scepter that I noticed a dark-cloaked figure kneeling on the floor beside the altar. I took it to be a woman and thought idly that her form was vaguely familiar. As she crossed herself her face was concealed, but something in the set of her shoulders made me look at her more closely. Suddenly I realized it was Theodora, so completely concealed under the dark robe and ample hood that even I had been unable to recognize her.

Why had she come here? Why had she tried so hard to keep her identity disguised?

Terrible fear seized my heart. She made a movement. From that time on a terrible force came into play, sweeping us to a dread but inevitable conclusion.

Theodora's forward rush was so swift that no one could stop her. One moment she was kneeling with the rest; the next she had flung herself upon the pope.

My sister was taken by surprise. The scepter flew from her hand and she stumbled.

As she grappled with Marozia a scream burst from my mother's throat, high and piercing, the wail of a victorious animal. Her clawing hands sought her daughter's neck, found their hold, clung. She was like a jackal bringing down her prey, straining to wrench the last breath of life from Marozia's body.

All this happened so rapidly that no one seemed able to move to help the pope. I myself stood shocked, frozen and helpless.

At last I came to my senses. Marozia was gasping, struggling, her hands ripping the air, clawing at my mother's face, but her strength was fading. Theodora's death grip was too strong.

The crowd between me and the altar was dense. All were on their feet now, wide-eyed and silent, like spectators at a play. Rudely I thrust them aside, fighting my way forward.

I caught a glimpse of a woman's pale face, a peasant. She seemed astonished to see me, a devout abbess, roughly pushing and shoving. A deacon who was standing near the front cursed me as I stepped on his long robe and lurched against him. I heeded nothing, only the voice of my mother, screaming, "Harlot, murderess, whore!"

At last I burst from the crowd and staggered toward the two women, reaching out to separate them.

I was too late. With an inhuman cry of fury Marozia freed herself from Theodora's desperate grasp. My sister spun away, but again my mother attacked—and that was when Marozia caught her and hurled her to the floor.

There was a sickening thud as Theodora's skull struck the marble—then silence.

Marozia stood transfixed, her eyes on the unmoving form. As she raised her head her gaze met mine and I saw there all the anguish of a trapped and desperate soul.

In all of Saint Peter's no one stirred save only the doves high in the clerestory as they fluttered to their perches.

With a graceful, gliding movement, as if she were performing a duty of office, Marozia stepped forward and knelt beside our mother. She reached out and touched Theodora's forehead. There was blood on her pale skin, spreading among the strands of grey hair.

"Lena, oh, Lena." Marozia collapsed against me and buried her face in her hands.

Chapter 56

It was Anthony who first recognized the consequences of that disaster. In the Senate, over which he now presided, there was an immediate clamor for a trial of the pope on the charge of matricide. Anthony knew only too well what would happen if his mother appeared before the tribunal. All the antagonism of church and state would be turned against her. The humiliation that these men had borne would finally be given vent under the guise of a legal proceeding.

She would surely be found guilty; she would die under torture. Even if by some miracle she was spared in the Senate, Anthony was certain the jealous cardinals now biding their time in the Lateran would find an opportunity to destroy her.

"There is a convent in Martigny," Anthony said to me. "You must take her with you—you and Gallimanfry. Leave Rome tomorrow. I will speak to her myself, to make certain she understands."

His wife Francina was standing nearby and she listened to all this with widened eyes. I pitied her. She still had much to learn about Roman ways.

I hugged them both warmly as we said good-bye, not knowing if I would ever see them again.

*   *   *

The next morning I called Sister Coinreda to my room and told her I wished to take Thessalina to visit the relics in Trastevere. Though the good sister did not seem to doubt me, she must have suspected Thessalina was going on a longer journey, for when Coinreda packed the girl's belongings, she put in much more than was needed for a day's travel. In the bottom of the bundle were several pairs of warm hose and a wool jerkin the sister had knitted for her charge.

Thessalina, not knowing any better, gave Coinreda only a quick kiss good-bye. I saw the anguish in poor Coinreda's eyes as we turned away.

We hurried out of Saint Petronilla's and as soon as we were out of sight we turned to the north toward the Porta Sancti Petri, away from Trastevere. Only then did Thessalina realize that our journey was not what it seemed. She wept when I told her she would not see Sister Coinreda and the convent children for a very long time.

A peasant cart was waiting for us in the field of the Prati outside the city wall. Thessalina and I tossed our bundles into the back and climbed in among the hay and corncobs. Barely acknowledging our presence, the peasant clucked to his oxen and lashed their broad backs with his whip. Creaking and groaning, the cart started off for Ostia.

The sun was warm. The bees buzzed around us. As the cart rocked and swayed, I told Thessalina the truth about herself and the parents she had never known. When she discovered that I was her mother, she flung her arms around me and hugged me tightly.

It was such a relief for me to be free at last of the burden of secrecy that I could not keep the tears from brimming to my eyes. That upset her. She thought I was crying because she was my daughter and she had done something wrong, so I had to dry my eyes and hasten to reassure her. She seemed to take comfort in this, and at last she nestled in my arms, falling fast asleep.

I shall never lose my belief in the power of prayer, and I shall never cease to praise God, for he gave me that perfect hour when Thessalina's head lay peacefully upon my breast, when we rocked through the fields with the scent of mown hay all around us. In that single hour I felt all the happiness a soul can desire.

Gallimanfry, Tasha and Marozia met us in Ostia. My sister had been carried from Rome in a covered palanquin wearing the plain white garments of a noblewoman so she would not be recognized. None but Anthony knew that she had left the city.

As we boarded the scow that would take us to the waiting merchant ship, Thessalina gripped my hand hard. Looking down, I saw that she was staring at Gallimanfry with awe. I squeezed her hand and was gratified by her answering smile.

There was a mournful silence among us as the oarsmen bent to their work, pulling the scow across the water. I watched as Marozia stared at the shore with a stony face and unseeing eyes. Once she made a gesture as if reaching out to draw us back to the receding shoreline, but then her arm fell and she folded her hands in her lap, regarding them as if those fingers held the last remnants of her earthly possessions.

We sailed that night for France, leaving behind all the troubles and woes of Rome.

Epilogue

Martigny, in the Province of France, A.D. 934

It is now Good Friday. Two years have passed since I began this chronicle. There are many things I might have wished to omit, for there are matters here that may be distasteful to the reader. However, I did not want to hide the truth, so I have striven to record events as they actually took place, be they ever so sinful in the sight of God.

Marozia's condition, I am pleased to say, has been much improved since my chronicle began. The sisters of Martigny are good to us, and our life here is very peaceful.

Thessalina has grown into a comely young woman with long dark hair and lovely brown eyes. On fine days she accompanies Marozia on long walks into the countryside and I am left alone to pursue my studies and my writing.

Gallimanfry grows restless with this womanly life and is often away, traveling to and fro on matters of state. When in Rome he frequently counsels Anthony, who continues to hold his tutor in high esteem. I must bear these separations patiently, for I know that Gallimanfry could not endure being confined to a place like this. Yet I find that I long for his return, and each time we part, I am sorely distressed with doubts and fears.

The steady influence of Anthony has been felt in the city in a marked improvement of secular and religious affairs. Wisely, he did not give up his hold on Castel Sant'Angelo, and the Lombard troops continue to make their garrison in the fortress. Anthony's private home, however, is the House of Hadrian, where his mother lived. Francina has borne him two children, both sons, and Gallimanfry has sworn that he will bring the boys to visit me when they are old enough to travel.

The house on the Aventine where my father and mother lived now belongs to the Cluniacs. Anthony gave it to them. The order has transformed the palace into the monastery of Santa Maria in Aventino.

As always, thousands of pilgrims make their way to Rome to see the sacred relics, to make their offerings and to receive their pardons. Many speak in whispers of the woman who was pope. According to the rumors among them, she will someday return to Rome to take up the papal crown again. I alone know it cannot be so.

She stands near me now, watching as my stylus moves across the page. Tasha, as always, is beside her. Soon she will speak. A bright band of sunlight comes in the clerestory window, lighting up her hair. When she is calm she is still very lovely, as though the blessing of God were on her, but I know there are demons in her soul—demons that cannot be still. In the dark of the night I pray for this woman, my sister, who dared to call herself Pope Joan.

A NOTE ON HISTORICAL SOURCES

While this is clearly a work of fiction, it includes a number of historical figures who dominated political and social life in Rome during the early tenth century. The family Theophylact, including Gaius, Theodora, Marozia and Lena, and the popes Sergius III, Anastasius III, Lando and John X as well as Alberic, Berengar, Guido, Hugo and many other Lombards mentioned by name, are all familiar to historians of the period. While many details of their lives are unclear, we know for certain that two powerful women, Theodora and Marozia, played leading roles in the city's affairs. Both of Marozia's children, the son of Sergius and the son of Alberic, are also based upon actual figures.

The most detailed information about this era of Roman history comes from a single primary source, the chronicler Liutprand, who served in Duke Hugo's court in Cremona. However, since Liutprand was devoted follower of the duke, he is not entirely trustworthy. This whole period of Roman history, for example, he dismisses as a "pornocracy." Nevertheless, he is the best we have.

For a more panoramic view of the events occurring in tenth-century Italy I am particularly indebted to Ferdinand Gregorovius' monumental *History of the City of Rome in the Middle Ages*, Vol. III (A.D. 300–1002), translated from the German by Mrs. Gustavus W. Hamilton and published in London by George Bell & Sons, 1903 (second edition, revised).

Many other sources contributed an understanding of the customs, events and beliefs of the past. Three books proved particularly valuable: *Rome, Profile of a City, 312–1308* by Richard Krautheimer (Princeton: Princeton University Press, 1930); *A History of Christianity* by Paul Johnson (New York: Atheneum, 1976); and *Warfare in Feudal Europe, 730–1200* by John Beeler (Ithaca: Cornell University Press, 1971). Without these sources any reconstruction of this twilit period of Roman history would have been impossible. Needless to say, these authors should not be blamed for any inaccuracies I have ruthlessly introduced to serve the convenience of fiction.